EL LABERIN

KERANA

CAZADORA

ALSO BY ROMINA GARBER

Lobizona

CAZADORA

ROMINA GARBER

WEDNESDAY BOOKS
NEW YORK

First published in the United States by Wednesday Books, an imprint of St. Martin's Publishing Group

CAZADORA. Copyright © 2021 by Romina Garber. All rights reserved. Printed in the United States of America. For information, address St. Martin's Publishing Group, 120 Broadway, New York, NY 10271.

www.wednesdaybooks.com

Endpaper art and interior illustrations by Rhys Davies

Library of Congress Cataloging-in-Publication Data

Names: Garber, Romina, author.
Title: Cazadora : a novel / Romina Garber.
Description: First edition. | New York : Wednesday Books, 2021. |
    Series: Wolves of no world ; 2 | Audience: Ages 12–18.
Identifiers: LCCN 2021008178 | ISBN 9781250239150 (hardcover) |
    ISBN 9781250239167 (ebook)
Subjects: CYAC: Werewolves—Fiction. | Identity—Fiction. | Belonging
    (Social psychology)—Fiction. | Magic—Fiction. | Fantasy.
Classification: LCC PZ7.1.G3675 Caz 2021 | DDC [Fic]—dc23
LC record available at https://lccn.loc.gov/2021008178

Our books may be purchased in bulk for promotional, educational, or business use. Please contact your local bookseller or the Macmillan Corporate and Premium Sales Department at 1-800-221-7945, extension 5442, or by email at MacmillanSpecialMarkets@macmillan.com.

First Edition: 2021

10 9 8 7 6 5 4 3 2 1

For all the separated families that will never be whole again.

Y para Papá, mi inspiración, gracias por enseñarme a soñar.

Tus ojos abiertos son la única luz que conozco
de las constelaciones extintas.

—PABLO NERUDA

Your wide eyes are the only light I know
from extinguished constellations.

—PABLO NERUDA,
TRANSLATED BY STEPHEN TAPSCOTT

PHASE I

1

I inhale hints of Buenos Aires.

We must be by the border. My heart catapults into my throat.

The air has grown so dark that I can't make out the portal's rocky walls. I have no idea what happens when I reach the checkpoint and come face-to-face with a border agent.

All I know is that Tiago, Saysa, and Cata walk beside me. After everything we've been through, the one thing I'm sure of is, I've found where I belong. With my friends.

They're my manada. *My pack*.

Tiago's fingers squeeze mine, like he can read my thoughts. The surrounding blackness has become so opaque that it obscures even the glow of our eyes.

Countless Septimus march with us, our collective footfalls whispering across this passage that bridges two realms of reality. We're returning to Earth from Lunaris, a land of magic and mist and monsters that's the source of our power.

By law—and bio-magical imperative—brujas and lobizones sojourn in that realm every full moon.

We're here, I think as I breathe in notes of coffee, leather, and paper. But when I'm hit with Ma's almond scent, I know I'm not actually smelling my homeland. I'm inhaling Ma's memory of it.

That's how she described Buenos Aires to me a month ago. *A lifetime ago.*

The last day we ever shared together.

I used to think I grew up in hiding in Miami because Ma and I were undocumented and on the run from my father's crime family, who'd killed him for attempting to abscond with her. But the true story isn't even in the same genre.

Turns out, I'm not entirely human. I'm also part Septimus—a cursed species of Argentine witches and werewolves.

And my father is very much alive.

All these years, he's been a teacher at a magical school just a couple of hours away.

Ma's almond scent has been teasing me since we left Lunaris, like she might be around every dark corner. Tiago warned me the portal crossing would jostle my senses, and the most powerful memories from the past moon could break through the surface.

But I know Ma isn't really here.

She's in a detention center in Miami, awaiting deportation.

That's why I'm traveling to Kerana, the Argentine city where most Septimus live. In such a populous place, my friends and I will have a better chance of avoiding discovery by the Cazadores. *Law enforcement.* And once I'm in Argentina, I'll find a way to reunite with Ma.

Light floods the tunnel, and the walls wilt into a massive underground station. I blink as Septimus swarm around us, rushing toward the checkpoints ahead, probably eager to get home and sleep.

But my own legs grow leaden as I see the border agents in the distance, flipping through Huellas—*Septimus documentation*. And the old mantra runs through my mind: *Don't come here, don't come here, don't come here.*

In the human realm, discovery meant deportation.

Here, a hybrid like me is subject to execution.

Tiago's hand squeezes mine, and I realize I've stopped walking. "You all right, Manu?"

His voice is a song.

I look up, and I'm enfolded in a blaze of sapphire. Tiago caresses my cheek with his thumb, and I hear the shakiness of my exhale.

"We have to keep moving," says Cata, her face wan. Beside her, Saysa's blank expression is inscrutable, her presence unusually muted.

I reach into my dress pocket and touch my forged Huella. Saysa's friend Zaybet made the passport-like booklet for me in Lunaris. This will be its first test.

Even though it's a fake, just holding this paperwork makes me feel like less of a forgery myself. Growing up, there were no photographs of Ma and me around the apartment, no documents of any kind proving I exist. And while the details in this Huella may be falsified, at least it's my face inside.

Evidence I'm real.

I exist.

We keep wending through the throng, and it strikes me that no Septimus travels alone. They move around in clusters, and when I glimpse a pack of guys doing a double take of our group, I know I haven't been imagining the looks we're getting.

It must be my eyes.

My sun-like irises stand out in all my worlds. Even Septimus don't have yellow eyes.

I keep my gaze low, and I feel Tiago's tension from the way

he picks up his pace, pulling Cata and Saysa forward. Then he gives my shoulder a quick squeeze before walking away from us.

I stare after him in speechless shock, until it registers that all the wolves are splitting off in the same direction. There are separate checkpoints for brujas and lobizones.

I feel the urge to follow Tiago, but I'm back to pretending I'm a bruja. A lobizona would draw too much attention. And, as Ma likes to say: *Attention breeds scrutiny.*

So I'm a secret again.

"Come on," says Saysa, leading me away from Cata.

There are distinct zones for each of the four elements. The breezy area we're cutting through is where the Invocadoras are—wind witches—and I watch Cata join their queue. The temperature drops a few degrees as we pass the Congeladoras—water witches—then Saysa and I line up in the toastier section designated for Jardineras. Earth witches.

The heat isn't coming from us. To our other side, and at the far end of the space, are the Encendedoras. I don't need to look at the fire witches to feel their presence.

I'm afraid if I turn my head, I'll meet Yamila's bloodred eyes.

Ever since the ambitious Cazadora discovered my existence, she's been intent on hunting me down. My arrest would be career-making. My friends and I just barely got away from her in Lunaris, right before entering the portal. It's only thanks to Saysa we made it out.

But some magic comes at a higher cost.

I clutch the forged Huella in my pocket. I wish Saysa would say something reassuring, but she's haunted by what she did. Her already tiny figure seems even smaller, and her deep brown skin has lost its warmth, shadows encroaching on her face.

As our line moves forward, I begin to feel a familiar alarm.

And I flash back to crawling under Perla's bed, while ICE agents pounded on our neighbor's door.

Perla is my ninety-year-old surrogate grandmother. She took Ma and me in years ago, homeschooling me and letting us live rent-free in exchange for looking after her.

Memories of El Retiro accelerate my panic, and I lock my jaw to keep my teeth from chattering. I can't stray too close to thoughts of everything I've lost, or I'll lose all my resolve.

I have to think more encouraging things.

Like discovering El Laberinto, an ancient city of crumbling stone structures that looks like it was swallowed by the Everglades. That's where I made my first friends. They saw the real me and accepted me. It was also there that, after trying on and discarding too many identities, I found the right one.

Not human.

Not bruja.

But *lobizona*.

As if the word summons the shift, a shiver trails down my belly. There's only one small group in front of us, then it's Saysa's and my turn.

I feel the twist in my uterus, and I bite down to keep from gasping.

I'm going to transform.

Yet the heat of the shift is countered by another sensation, a cold sweat that reminds me of the day the Cazadores popped into Señora Lupe's class for a surprise inspection of our Huellas. I'm having a panic attack.

Only now that I'm a lobizona, my anxiety seems to trigger the transformation.

I want to say something to Saysa, but she's still not looking at me. As the group of Jardineras ahead of us steps forward, I want to beg her to calm me down, distract me, but she might as well not be here.

There's a rush of conversations going on around us, and I'm still getting a lot of stares. I wish I could slip on my sunglasses, like I used to do as a human in Miami, but Septimus must always show their eyes.

Particularly brujas, as each element is associated with a pair of colors: Purples and pinks for Invocadoras, blues and grays for Congeladoras, browns and greens for Jardineras, and reds and blacks for Encendedoras. My only hope is that my yellow eyes pass off as a very light shade of amber.

My fingertips tingle, like my claws are struggling to come out.

I can't stop this from happening.

I need help.

"H-hey," I manage to say to Saysa. It feels hard to use my voice, and the word sounds strangled.

She stares at me, startled. Like I'm already in wolf form. And something seems to dawn on her because her lime-like eyes grow round, and she whispers, "Oh *no*."

I want to ask, but I'm afraid if I open my mouth, my fangs will slide out.

She keeps scanning me, like she's trying to find a solution in my dress. Then she mumbles something too low for any of the brujas to hear. "You bathed in La Fuente de Flores Feroces."

The Fountain of Fierce Flowers, I translate. What the fuck does that mean?

She doesn't repeat herself because the agent calls, "¡Próxima!"

Next!

I'm either going to transform or throw up. If I move, I'll implode.

Sweat pools along my hairline, making my scalp itchy. Saysa steps up, and I know I need to go with her, but I'm primed to shift.

I suck in an inhale, my bones buzzing as I fight to contain them, and I drag my feet forward.

When I've made it over, Saysa has already handed the agent her light green Huella. The Cazadora compares the likeness to Saysa, then she flips through the pages.

"Estás estudiando en El Laberinto," says the agent, studying her. "¿Qué hacés acá?"

You're a student at El Laberinto. What are you doing here?

"Lunación." Saysa summons a carefree demeanor from some other universe and flashes the Jardinera her winningest smile. I've never heard the term, but it sounds like a mix between the Spanish words for *moon* and *vacation.*

The agent returns Saysa's Huella, and at last she looks at me. I'm sure I must be a sweaty, wide-eyed mess.

She doesn't hold out a hand for my Huella.

She just frowns.

My pulse echoes in my head, and I feel the rush of blood as my skeleton begins to crack—

"By law," she says in Spanish, narrowing her gaze, "brujas must match their clothes to their eye color in Kerana. Or have you forgotten?"

I'm not even breathing as she examines my dress.

"Why is your garment gray?"

I blink, unsure how to answer. I'd forgotten I traded dresses with Bibi in Lunaris to get past the Cazadores guarding the Citadel. My golden dress was too conspicuous. This is what Saysa must've noticed.

"I bathed in La Fuente de Flores Feroces," I hear myself say.

The agent surveys me a moment longer, examining my eyes, and I hold my breath, not daring to make a sound.

"Those flowers have a mind of their own," she says at last. "But they usually dye fabrics in brighter shades."

I don't say anything as she holds up her palm, and I hand over my golden Huella. She takes her time examining every page, like she finds my story a little too interesting. Then she looks up, and from the way she's staring at me, I know she has questions.

What if she grills me about La Mancha, the manada I'm claiming to be from? I don't know anything about it—

Shouting breaks out at the other end of the station, where the wolves are. The agent looks over, along with the other officials, to see what's happening. Since brujas don't have heightened senses, none of them can make out what's going on.

I squint in the direction of the wolves, honing my hearing, until I make out that it's more of a howl-cheer. They're celebrating something. Or someone.

"Take it," says the Jardinera, stuffing my Huella back in my hand. Then instead of calling up the next group, she leans back to listen to the update that a Cazador is bringing over to her and the other brujas.

Saysa and I join the crowd headed to the exit, toward the city beyond. As we climb uphill, I inhale a stream of fresh air.

It's still dark out, and tendrils of silver reach down like the moon is guiding us home. I'm aware that Saysa and I are avoiding each other's gazes. It feels like we just pulled off a major heist, and we're waiting to celebrate until we're in the clear.

I'm free.

In my ancestral homeland.

With my pack.

Yet as I bite back a grin, high off my newfound freedom, I know it's only illusory. Even if Yamila rests today, she'll still strike tomorrow.

We both know I can't run for long. In four weeks, on the next full moon, we'll have to take a portal back to Lunaris. She could mobilize the entire force of Cazadores by then, and I won't have anywhere to hide.

It's not a question of *if* the Cazadora will catch up with me . . .

It's a matter of *when*.

2

Kerana is a woman and a land.

The first time I heard her name was in the history of the Guaraní, people indigenous to South America who were massacred when Europeans colonized the continent. In their stories, Kerana is the granddaughter of the first man and woman created.

According to Septimus lore, a demon broke out of Lunaris and impregnated Kerana, forcing her to birth a line of cursed children. From then on, all seventh sons were born lobizones, and all seventh daughters were born brujas.

When the earliest Septimus banded together to form the first manada, they traced their magic to las Cataratas de Iguazú. The largest waterfalls in the world.

Iguazú also comes from the Guaraní. Legend has it a deity wanted to marry a woman named Naipí, and when she fled with her mortal lover in a canoe, the deity sliced the river, creating the waterfalls and separating the lovers for eternity.

Within Iguazú, the Septimus found a hybrid realm that exists between Earth and Lunaris. This border world saved the species from human persecution.

It became their motherland.

So they named it *Kerana*.

We just traded the giant dandelion fields and mountainous rock formations of Aires for a manada named Belgrano, a bustling city built into the leafless trunks of colossal purple tree-buildings. Bald branches break off from every story, operating as landing docks for hot-air balloons, which seem to be this community's preferred mode of transportation.

Lining the streets, and in the crevices between tree-buildings, are clusters of spindly blue-gray organisms that every now and then disappear and reappear.

Don't step on the mushrooms.

It's the number one rule for traveling through the manadas of Kerana—and if Tiago, Cata, or Saysa reminds me one more time, I will strangle them. I already got the message loud and clear when I watched a girl step on a white button-cap and get sucked through the ground.

Gaping at the spot where she vanished, I tugged on Cata's arm to ask where she went, and she just said, "El Hongo."

The Mushroom.

Then she hissed at me to keep my ignorance to myself until we're alone. But privacy is hard to come by these days.

The four of us slow down by an opening in a purple trunk, where an enticing aroma lures us in for closer inspection.

We study the menu posted outside a place called Parrillada Paraíso.

"They have *lomitos*," I say, my voice low with longing.

Tiago's stomach growls his assent. We've run through almost all our semillas—*Septimus currency*—so this could be our last good meal for a while.

Semillas are seeds collected in Lunaris that grow into plants whose leaves produce powerful potions. The rarer the seed, the higher its value.

It's been three days since we crossed the border into Kerana, and I've learned that manadas cover their residents' basic needs—housing, food, clothing, education—and in turn, residents contribute most of the semillas they earn to their manada. Households that earn above their contribution can afford things like vacations, nicer clothes, fancier homes.

Basically, one's manada funds their life, and one's savings funds their lifestyle.

"We'll go in. You two wait here." Saysa's terse tone is indistinguishable from Cata's these days.

Tiago and I only nod. Since there are werewolf ears everywhere, we've adopted a minimal speech regimen.

There's a flash of light on a bough above us, and I watch an Invocadora land a sun-yellow balloon. She springs out from the basket right as a pack of transformed wolves bounds past, scaling the branches to reach higher stories. There are no leaves obscuring the view—just smatterings of colorful balloons—and I can see all the way to where the purple treetops tickle the blue sky.

I don't spot any more business signs that high up on the trunk, and I wonder if those levels are reserved for residences—

There's a tug on my hand, and I look down into an even bluer horizon. Tiago's eyes narrow a fraction, his lids heavy from lack of sleep, and I nod my understanding. We're supposed to be looking out, not *up*.

He's been on edge this whole time, probably because of what happened with the border agents.

Turns out when Tiago told me he's the only Septimus to have encountered one of the six living demons of Lunaris and survived, he forgot to mention he's *world famous* for it. There's even a nickname for him: el lobo invencible.

The invincible wolf.

He was the cause of the commotion at the underground station when we first arrived. As soon as Tiago identified himself with his Huella, the lobizón agent got excited and alerted the others, and soon everyone was calling him by his nickname and congratulating him for taking the Septibol championship.

No doubt Yamila knows by now that we're in Argentina, so we've been moving from place to place to avoid getting caught. I can't help thinking of my parents, and the life on the run they never got to have.

"I staked out the detention center."

I press my nail into the palm of my hand at the memory of the Cazadora's venomous voice.

"I waited and waited and waited, thinking you would come visit your poor, abandoned—"

My hand stings as I slice my skin. And as the fire witch's voice bleeds away, I try to focus on the Septimus around me.

A lobizón lopes past in an electric-blue suit with platinum epaulets on his broad shoulders, then an Encendedora catches my attention in blood-orange boots that rise to her thighs and match the flames of her eyes. My friends and I are dressed way too casual for this manada.

We're wearing blue pants called indigos that are like jeans

but more comfortable, and Cata, Saysa, and I paired ours with shirts that match the shades of our eyes. Mine is more of an amber-brown color, since yellow would give me away.

A wisp of red smoke draws my gaze back to Parrillada Paraíso, and my gut hardens into a wall. I feel Tiago tensing beside me as he senses the shift in my attention.

But the bruja entering the restaurant has darker skin and hair. She's not Yamila.

I blow out my exhale and scan the names of the surrounding businesses. *Vestidos de Victoria, El Lobizón Fino, Pociones Para Pequeños, Locura por los Libros* . . . These shops sell everything from clothing to potions to books. When I spot the public restroom signs, my stomach stiffens again.

BRUJA

LOBIZÓN

There's no accompanying symbols, but there's no need. The gendered language makes it clear which one is for girls and which one is for boys. There's no breaking out of the binary, no room for anything in between. Nor does Septimus vocabulary include *brujo* . . .

Or *lobizona*.

I flash to the moment before the Septibol championship, when I looked between the two locker rooms, unsure which one was mine. And I remember the way Gael's coral gaze fell when I chose *bruja*. He looked as disappointed as I felt.

I still can't believe I found my father.

Even more unbelievable is that he's also secretly *Fierro*—the most celebrated Septimus outlaw. It's hard to process how famous he is when I barely know anything about him.

Fierro used to stage public demonstrations that defied the system's rigid, binary nature, until he vanished eighteen years ago. Only my friends and I know the truth: He was about to run away with Ma, until his sister, Jazmín—Cata's mom and the headmistress of the academy at El Laberinto—learned of his plans and betrayed him.

She didn't give up his identity, but she told the Cazadores that Gael had gone rogue and tried to capture Fierro himself. He and Jazmín were sent away to El Laberinto for interfering with the investigation. As punishment, neither of them can return to Kerana until they capture Fierro.

To keep my parents apart, Jazmín lied to Gael and said the Cazadores knew he'd been meeting with a human. She convinced her brother that Ma would be killed if he ever contacted her again.

"Shit."

The musical lilt of Tiago's voice shocks me anew after so much silence. Then I register what he said.

My gaze locks on a gaggle of girls by the neighboring tree-building. They're huddled together and darting glances at us, like they're deciding something. Then we hear the whispered nickname.

El lobo invencible.

"Let's try that one," says Tiago, in a would-be casual voice, guiding me toward the nearest store. But by our next step, the brujas are rushing toward us.

I blink in confusion as they wave stone-handled mirrors in the air—like the one Zaybet used to capture my likeness for my forged Huella—and Tiago takes my hand as he pulls me into a sprint.

We're faster than the brujas, so in an instant, we've put a dozen trees between us. But they have *magic.*

An ugly gray cloud forms over our heads, like a GPS marker announcing our location. Then bucket-sized drops of rain explode over us.

They probably expect me to shield us with my own magic, only I'm not a bruja. Tiago and I cut in a new direction, trying to outrun the storm as we round our way back, water bombs exploding all over us—

We skid to a stop as a girl with glowing pink eyes steps into our path. Cata's gale blasts the cloud away, taking the rain with it.

As her magic fades, a more dangerous storm brews in her gaze. Saysa comes up beside her, scowling at her brother as she shoves a large sack of steaming food at him. "What did you do?"

"No time," he says, shaking the water from his hair, while I wring out my strands. The four of us hurry back to the arboledo—*tree transport*—that brought us here before rumors of Tiago's sighting reach the wrong ears. Hopefully those girls didn't get the chance to capture any images.

We run past a bruja at the arboledo's opening who's negotiating a fee to escort a large group of lobizones to their destination. Her brown gaze flashes to Saysa, and they trade barely perceptible nods of Jardinera solidarity.

The earth witch's eyes cut to mine next, and she blinks, her kinship wavering as she decides if I'm one of them. We're gone before she makes up her mind.

Inside the trunk is a cavernous station with living brown walls, where new passages are constantly opening and closing as Septimus arrive and depart, each group led by a bruja with eyes glowing in shades of browns or greens. Saysa's lime-like orbs flare bright against the living passage, as she communicates with the root system to deposit us in a new manada.

Only Jardineras can reroute root systems. Invocadoras pilot air balloons. Congeladoras freeze bridges across bodies of water. Encendedoras power engines.

As soon as an opening appears in the brown wall, we pile into the tunnel, and the passage seals itself behind us as the root twists and turns through the earth. Since each path is unique to the witch who paves it, we can speak freely here.

"The fuck happened, Tiago?" demands Cata, rounding on him.

"I was watching for Cazadores, not *schoolgirls*—"

"That's what you get for underestimating us!" snaps Saysa.

"This is the *second* time you've caused a scene," says Cata in a warning tone. "You need to be careful, or *else*."

"Or else *what*?"

"Or else you can't stay with us," finishes his sister.

My pulse gallops into my throat at the thought of us splitting up.

"I'm not leaving any of you," says Tiago with a growl, easing my heart. "We can't do this alone. You need me."

"Not if you're endangering us," declares Cata.

Now that he was spotted, we'll have to travel far. This is going to be a long walk.

Unlike the smooth walls of Flora's tunnels, this arboledo passage is veined with smaller root networks and patched in places with white cottony webbing. The air is dense, and it has a slightly roasted aroma that makes me think of coffee beans. It reminds me of the way Ma described the scent of Buenos Aires.

The first thing I did when we crossed the border into Kerana was ask the others how we can access the human part of Argentina from here. But since we're in the Iguazú Falls, we'd have to swim or sail to the human side, and the barrier is heavily patrolled by Cazadores.

As Fierro, Gael must have managed to visit Ma often because he was a Cazador himself. I need to reach him so I can know if Ma is safe. Cata said communications to El Laberinto are always monitored, but there must be some other option—

Tiago's fingers lock with mine, wrenching me back to the

present. When I meet his gaze, he seems more than just worried.

He's hurt.

"Is it always like this for you in Kerana?" I ask, clearing my throat. I'd rather focus on anything but my own thoughts.

"It's why I haven't been back in five years."

I try to let that sink in. He's been away from home all this time, and now he's returned, because of me. I don't know what to say to that, so I'm glad when he speaks again.

"I was thirteen when I survived the demon's attack, and as soon as we got back from Lunaris, I was being hounded by the press. I couldn't go anywhere. There were books being written about what happened, and Septimus wanting to study me, and invitations from manadas with offers of leadership positions if I moved—"

"The politicians were subtle compared to the parents," says Saysa darkly. "I remember a pair so desperate to breed their daughter with *the invincible wolf* that they wanted Mami y Papi to agree to an underage marriage—"

"I applied to the academy in El Laberinto to get away."

Tiago's tone has the weight of finality, and yet I can't help asking, "What about when you're in Lunaris?"

"I'm usually with the team, so Javier and Pablo make sure I'm left alone. Besides, I'm much less interesting there."

"But wasn't it a big deal at El Laberinto when you showed up?" I prod.

"At first. I guess it's what drew me to Cata. She knows what it's like when others want to be your friend for the wrong reasons. But by now, nobody cares."

That's not exactly true, since Tiago is the most popular werewolf at school. I'm sure being a Septibol star doesn't hurt. Or his movie star looks. Or that sexy ballad of a voice—

My belly flips as Tiago's hand tightens around mine. Sometimes I feel like he reads me as intimately as a favorite book.

"If we could leverage your fame for favors, we'd be staying at the best places," says Cata wistfully. "If only we knew someone trustworthy enough to keep their mouth shut—"

"All it'd take is *one* word—"

"I know, I know," she says to him.

In a pack species, there are no secrets. The warning lingers in my mind, along with Ma's lifelong survival adages. Just one whisper, and Yamila will find us.

"We should split up."

Saysa's suggestion kills the conversation. She said the same thing last night, and it murdered the mood then too.

In the fringe of my gaze, I see Cata bite her lip, and my shoulders tauten in fear that she's about to agree. It's hard enough being far from Ma and Gael without knowing what's going on. I can't handle being apart from my friends too.

Yet before anyone speaks again, light floods the horizon.

And Saysa's warning shot goes unheeded a second time as we step onto a field of wild grass as golden as the ground of Lunaris.

3

I've seen this classic Argentine setting in countless images before. "I know this place—La Pampa!"

"Pampita," Saysa corrects me as we cut across the empty field.

"Let's get a few hours' rest," says Cata, "then head out before morning."

Tiago and I pivot around, surveying our surroundings. Behind us, the arboledo we arrived through is the only disruption to the flat landscape. The sun is setting in the far distance, its final rays blazing against the silhouettes of squat homes, stables, barns, and pens.

"We can sleep under the stars," Tiago murmurs to me, his elbow brushing mine. His stare is steadfast, pinning me in place. We haven't had any alone time since the sand dwellings of Lunaris, and the thought of being in his arms again makes my other worries flit away.

"Food."

Saysa snatches the bag from Tiago's hands and drops onto a tuft of grass. She digs into the sack, pulling out a bamboo box and a stack of napkins.

When she yanks off the lid and we're blasted with the smoky aroma of four fat lomitos, the rest of us join her on the ground. The growl of Tiago's stomach is thunderous as we each reach for a steak sandwich—stuffed with lettuce, tomato, onions, fried egg, and chimichurri—and none of us speaks as we savor it. Afterward, one by one we lie back on the grass, bellies fit to burst, as the stars wink into view.

The air fills with insects' high-pitched songs, but I don't see any bugs near us. In the distance, I can just make out the low drone of animal calls. Night is setting in swiftly, and I find myself missing the golden light of the doraditos from El Laberinto.

"We need a plan," says Cata.

"Say, check if you've heard back from anyone," Tiago tells his sister.

"I already told you Yamila spread rumors I'm her new informant." Saysa sounds like she's rolling her eyes. "No one trusts me now."

By the way Cata and Tiago look at Saysa sometimes, I know none of us has forgotten what she did to Nacho—Yamila's brother—in that Lunaris cave. How she pressed her hands to his chest until his face grew shriveled and gray and skeletal—

"The Coven will find us," Saysa insists, but the Tinkerbell glow that once underscored her passion has been snuffed out.

"Not this again," groans Cata, and before I can ask, she explains, "It's this mythical resistance manada where nobody judges anybody, and everybody can be themselves, and we all live happily ever after."

"Only it's *real*," Saysa cuts in, her voice sharp.

"If it's been around forever, then why is there no *proof*?"

Before this becomes a fight, I say, "I don't think Yamila told the other Cazadores about me yet."

"Me neither," says Cata, sounding relieved for the new subject. "I bet she wants to be the one to bring you in."

I picture the Cazadora in that cave, cradling her near-dead brother in her arms, and I can still hear her throat-scraping sobs. Even through her devastation, there was a fire in her bloodred eyes that turned her tears to steam.

That wasn't anger.

That was *hate*.

"This is why we need a plan."

The fact that Cata's repeating herself, and in a tone more superior than usual, makes me wonder if she already has one.

"What is it?" asks Tiago, like he hears the same thing.

"We can't risk returning to Lunaris next moon. It's too soon. We need another solution."

"Like?" prods Saysa.

"We're too powerful to be sedated by Septis, but we can try to score some Anestesia. Septis just dulls a local pain for us," she goes on for my benefit, "but Anestesia puts us in a kind of magi-medi coma. It's an injection because it needs to be administered into the blood, and it's reserved for stuff like medical procedures and subduing prisoners at the full moon. But there's an underground market—"

"With what semillas?"

Saysa's tone is even, like a heart flatlining. The way it's been every day since Lunaris. She's trying so hard to make what happened with Nacho mean nothing that she's making it mean everything.

"We can catch transportation fares," suggests Cata.

"Transportation is the most underpaid industry because it's

bruja-dominated," says Saysa dismissively. "We'll never make enough in time."

"Well, I don't hear *you* coming up with anything—"

"None of us has slept well in days, so let's get some rest." Tiago's voice is as gentle as a lullaby. "We'll take off in the morning, okay?"

"Again, *we're almost out of semillas*," says Saysa in a deadened monotone. "Where do you expect us to go?"

"Home."

At Tiago's answer, Saysa sits up so fast, I think she must have seen a Cazador. Only she's staring at her brother.

"You want to incriminate our parents?"

"They're probably worried," says Tiago, straightening and wincing at the harshness of her voice. "They would want to help us. And it would be good for us to see them."

What he means is, it'd be good for *Saysa*. He doesn't say it outright, but he doesn't have to.

"Behold el lobo invencible!" she declares dramatically. "At the first sign of trouble, he runs to Mami y Papi!"

"Cata's right!" he snarls. "All you do is kill our ideas without contributing any—"

Cata sits up as soon as she's invoked. "Yamila is definitely watching your manada, so it's the last place we're going near."

"Bathroom?" I ask, getting to my feet.

Cata and Saysa look up at me like they know I'm just trying to put an end to this discussion, but I'm sure they have to go. We haven't been since Aires.

The three of us head into a thicket of wild grass for coverage. Cata erects a force field just in case. Then we join Tiago and wash up at a well that's probably for the animals. As a final step, Saysa boosts our immunity and disinfects us, the way she's done every night.

While Cata and Tiago browse the area for mushrooms, Saysa takes my hands, and green vines grow from her wrists and curl up my arms. I blink, and they're gone. Just like what she did to Perla when we visited her on my birthday. I hope she and Luisita are still taking care of each other.

My skin stings, which means Saysa zapped plenty of germs. It's a pretty cool Jardinera perk. If I could do it, I'd probably start skipping showers.

"I'm worried about my mom," I admit when she drops my hands.

"Gael will protect her." Saysa's tone is still lifeless, like she's not the least concerned.

"But what if Yamila got to her first?"

"Manu, he's *Fierro*. The most famous Septimus in history. He's outsmarted the Cazadores his whole life. She'll be fine."

I can't tell how much of her answer is fueled by her faith in Fierro and how much is her inability to give a fuck. "What's up with you?" I ask. "Why won't you talk about what you did to Nacho?"

Her eyebrows shoot up like the question is a surprise, and her green gaze goes blank. "I'm fine."

I'm not sure she's met my eyes since Lunaris. "Saysa, you're my best friend," I say softly, squeezing her arm. "Nothing could change that. We're beyond judgments."

She blinks, and I think she seems more exhausted than anything else. "I'm fine," she insists.

"Found some llao llao mushrooms," says Cata, and I drop the subject now that she and Tiago are back. "We can check messages in el Hongo when we wake up."

"Your immunity boost cured my headache," says Tiago to his sister in awe.

Saysa's expression loses its sharp edges, like she's flattered by the compliment.

"Your healing abilities are definitely beyond ordinary," affirms Cata. Only unlike Tiago, she sounds like she's leveling a criticism.

"I don't know if I should thank you or apologize," Saysa says to her.

"You should be at a top healer institute, like Los Andes. Not wasting your time at El Laberinto."

"You're my *girlfriend,* Cata. Not my mom."

Tiago's fingers close around mine, and we're off. We take long strides, making sure to put enough space between us and Cata and Saysa, so they don't have to worry about us eavesdropping. Not that there's anything to hear; all they've done is argue our whole time in Kerana.

Tiago spins me around to face him. There's nothing but open space for miles as his arms wrap around my waist, and for a moment, I let myself bask in the inconceivable idea that he chose to run away with me.

Same as Ma would have done with Gael.

"There are so many stars out," I say, too nervous to meet Tiago's simmering gaze. In the absence of doraditos, the night sky is strewn with silver lights, and I trace dozens of new constellations.

He leans in closer, and I inhale his musk of cedarwood and thyme, spiced with that something wild and tantalizing and headrush-y. "*Stars, hide your fires,*" he murmurs into my neck, "*let not light see my black and deep desires.*"

Just when I thought he couldn't get more magical, the beautiful boy quotes Shakespeare to me.

"*Not from the stars do I my judgment pluck,*" I respond in kind.

Tiago stares at me in surprise. "Shakespeare fan?"

"The biggest," I say, remembering days on El Retiro's rooftop when I had all the time in the world to read poetry.

"Is that a challenge?" His soft voice is as dangerous as the devilish look in his eyes.

I frown and survey the field around us.

"*Where?*"

Tiago's face splits into his heartbreaking grin, and I feel a pang in my chest, like I do when I'm close to finishing a favorite book—elated to experience something so exquisite, but devastated that there will never be more than these few moments between us.

As romantic as his sacrifice is, Tiago is bound to realize he's given up too much.

We exist in different realities.

"What if we just stay here, Solazos?" he breathes, brushing a hand up my back and sliding it into my hair. His scent is as intoxicating as the petals of a blancanieves.

"Get jobs as farmhands?" I ask as he kisses my jawline.

"Uh-huh," he hums, his musical mouth by my ear. "And whisper Shakespeare as we fall asleep beneath the stars."

"¿De qué manada sos?"

The lobizón's black eyes drill into mine, mining me for secrets.

I wish I had an answer, but all my anxious brain seems able to produce are English subtitles. What pack are you from?

I chance a look at Tiago, but his sapphire gaze only makes my thoughts less coherent.

"You do realize you sound just like a Cazador," says Saysa between small sips of hot mate.

Pablo's face snaps to hers. Even though he's snarling, he looks less like a werewolf than an angry goth kid.

"La Mancha," I blurt, at last remembering the manada's name from the backstory Cata crafted for me last night.

The information has the quieting effect she anticipated. Apparently, it's one of the more problematic packs in Kerana, rife with corruption, so they'll assume my reluctance has to do with shame.

I pluck a medialuna from the basket of facturas and place it on my plate, just to do something.

"Glad that's settled," says Nico, who seems as relieved as me that this interrogation is over. I'm still not used to the way his silver irises blend with his pupils, giving him a celestial aura.

"Doesn't matter," booms Javier, his boulder-like body at odds with his baby face. "You're a Laberinto bruja now!" He cuffs my shoulder, and I feel more like a lopsided scale.

Even Diego flicks me a quick smile between the pages of his book.

Then at last Pablo speaks: "Manuela de La Mancha."

He sounds like he's testing the name, seeing if it fits. The words sound beyond foreign to me—the title is more befitting an old-timey socialite or the star of a telenovela.

"If you're going to be friends with us," he goes on, "there's something you should know."

His inky gaze is bright, like he's about to transform. I stare apprehensively at his dark brown arms, with their matching leather cuffs, expecting to see fur-like body hair sprouting and lethal claws curving from his fingers—

He leans forward, and in a blink, my medialuna is gone.

"We don't respect boundaries," he says, swallowing the flaky pastry.

My laugh gets caught in my throat.

A shadow falls across the golden morning.

My friends and El Laberinto disappear, and I'm surrounded by rocky walls, enclosed in dimness. Claustrophobia smothers my skin like a shroud, but the fear doesn't set in until I recognize the place.

One of the most lethal locations in Lunaris.

The stone mountain.

I take my first step across the feathery ground, and I search for my wolf-shadow along the wall. But I'm alone.

A small hand squeezes mine, and I look down into Ma's brown

eyes. Panic tastes like blood in my mouth, but the adrenaline focuses me. I bring a finger to my lips so Ma knows not to make a sound—

Screeching stabs the air.

A dozen bird-monsters shriek, forming a V-shape as they prepare to dive. "Run!" I shout, but I'm too late.

They're too fast.

MA—!

My eyes fly open, and I gasp for air. There's a whooshing of wings in my ears as I scan the shadowy space for a sign of metal talons or ivory beaks, my skin slick with sweat.

But I'm in Pampita, lying on the golden grass next to Tiago. And the morning is already yellowing.

"If they catch you, forget me. Rewrite your story."

Ma's last instructions resound in my head, the nightmare making her feel more present. Her words drop like ice cubes down my throat, freezing my veins.

Is that what I did?

Did I forget her?

"I waited and waited and waited, thinking you would come visit your poor, abandoned mother."

It's Yamila who answers my question. Her voice is a weapon that's been unsheathed, only this time, I don't defend myself.

I neglected Ma.

I let her rot in a detention center while I made friends.

"Do you know they barely feed her?"

Yamila's question stabs me like a blade.

"Do you know the way the men look at her?"

Even if the Cazadora only said these things to wound me, it doesn't change the facts. She saw Ma. She knows where she is.

What if Gael didn't make it to the detention center in time?

What if the reason Yamila isn't chasing me is she's too busy torturing Ma?

I choke back a sob.

Mami.

For seventeen years, she protected me, and now I proved I wasn't worth the sacrifice. Shame sears my mind as I recognize this pack *isn't* where I belong.

I should be—

Footsteps race closer, and I tense up, wiping the tears off my face.

Cata's face pops into view, her golden-brown hair frizzy and covered in leaves and twigs. "News!"

Tiago sits upright beside me, and then the four of us are combing our fingers through our hair while we wait for a broadcast to begin on an enormous watery screen that was definitely not here last night. Or if it was, I didn't notice. It looks like a shimmering billboard with the word: ¡NOTICIAS!

We hang back from the crowd, but an elderly couple breaks away to approach us with mate. Every morning, it's been the same in every manada: Mate gets offered, no questions asked. It unites all Septimus, young and old, rich and poor, bruja and lobizón. Mate keeps the magic going past the full moon.

The most commonly traded semillas are the seeds for growing the yerba that gets packed into the gourd for this drink. Without it, wolves couldn't transform at will and brujas would be at the mercy of their magic.

"Están mugrientos," says the elderly bruja, keeping her distance from us. *You're filthy.* She sends the calabaza gourd sailing to Cata on a gust of wind, and her husband approaches to pour hot water.

"¿De dónde vienen?" he asks, sniffing at us. *Where are you coming from?*

"Una fiesta en Tigre y creo que tomamos demasiado," says Saysa, faking a giggling sound that she would never make. "Ya nos vamos." *A party in Tigre, and I think we drank too much. We're on our way out.*

The lobizón nods and frowns, like a disappointed grandfather. When it's my turn to drink, his wife squints her lavender eyes at me, like she can't place my element. I drain the mate, and none of us speaks until they've moved on.

"What if we call Pablo and ask what's happened?" asks Tiago in a low whisper.

"How can we call him?" I ask, shocked no one's brought up this option before.

"We use a public caracola."

"Cara-*what*?"

"They're conch shells from the seas of Lunaris," says Cata in a hurried whisper. "Each one is unique, and their energies are networked. Only we're not allowed to have one at school, so all calls get screened through my mom's office. They'd trace our location instantly."

I thought El Laberinto was technologically primitive because it's swallowed by a swamp, and I just assumed they used magic instead. But now that I think of it—

"So you all don't have technology? Like, if you want to look something up, you can't jump on the internet?"

"We have Flora," says Cata, like that settles the issue. "And can we wait to talk about this in a more *private*—"

"Remember how I told you information travels through the air in Lunaris?" Saysa doesn't bother keeping her voice down, so it's a good thing we're not near the crowd.

"You said that's how I knew terms like the Citadel and the Sombras in my dreams."

"It works that way in Kerana too. Technically, the knowledge is traveling in spores."

"Spores?"

"What did you think el Hongo was?" asks Saysa with an eyeroll.

"It's a fungal network that connects us to Lunaris," says Cata, "to communicate plants' needs and imprint our universal knowledge."

"Yeah, why didn't I think of that?" I ask, rolling my eyes back at Saysa.

"Flora is part of the network, and that's how her library works," Cata goes on in a hurried whisper. "All manadas are linked to it. That's why the mushrooms are everywhere—they're our connectors. It's how we access the data. Just think of our World Wide Web as more literal than the one you're used to."

But a different phrase comes to mind: *Wood* Wide Web. I read about it in the glossy books about trees that I used to love leafing through at the Miami library. Fungi form underground networks through mycelia—thin threads that link the roots of neighboring plants to trade updates. That's how they find out what nutrients are needed. It's also how they gang up to poison an unwanted new plant.

An image flickers onto the watery screen.

Then it crossfades into the face I've been dreading to see.

Yamila's eyes look even more bloodred than they did a few days ago. Or maybe I misremembered them.

She's in a skintight black number with knee-high boots,

auburn hair pulled back in a braid, and scarlet scarf spun around her neck. She would fit in on the stylish streets of Belgrano.

Wherever she is, it looks important because the Septimus symbol is carved into the stone wall behind her, and there are a couple of rows of Cazadores in the background, as if to give the impression that she speaks for the full organization.

"Septimus, I come to you with breaking news of historic proportions," she says in Spanish, her breathy voice adding to the gravity of her declaration.

"Today, we unmask Fierro."

The world tilts upward, and if not for Tiago reaching out to steady me, I would crumple.

"Tenemos un testigo," she goes on. *We have a witness.*

My chest is too tight to breathe. Jazmín must have betrayed us. I shouldn't have left Gael behind, but I needed him to protect Ma—

Ma.

Without him, she's defenseless.

"We'll be at La Rosada in two hours to hear from her."

Their witness is a *her.* Yamila steps back, and the camera lingers, like the broadcaster is expecting someone more senior to step forward. When no one does, I feel a loosening in my chest.

This can't be real. If Yamila really knows Fierro's identity, why not reveal it now? I take deep breaths like Perla taught me. Gael is in Miami with Ma. Saysa's right: He took on the entire system as Fierro, so *of course* he can handle one fiery Cazadora.

I blow out a long exhale, expelling my worries and fears—but when I inhale, I choke on the oxygen.

Embedded among the Cazadores is a pair of coral-colored eyes beneath a head of golden-brown hair, the same shade as his sister's and niece's.

Gael is in Kerana.

4

One look at my friends' faces tells me they saw him too.

Chatter breaks out in the throng, and I'm too numb to feel Tiago's touch as he guides me away. When we're adrift in a sea of golden grass, Cata opens her mouth to speak, and I say, "I'm going."

"Stop. And. Think." Her voice is cold, like she's carved from the same ice as her mother. "If they really have a witness, why are they telling us before they've interrogated her? Why tease the investigation? And why is *Yamila* making this announcement instead of someone more senior?"

"Did you miss the part where *Gael is here*?"

"Yes, and we have no idea why—"

"I don't give a fuck *why*, Catalina!" Spittle flies out of my mouth, and for a beat, I feel insane even to myself. So in a lower voice, at a slower speed, I say, "If he's here, that means my mom is alone, and I need to find her."

"Manu, I'm sure he left her in a safe place—"

"Well, as long as you're sure!" I snap at Saysa.

"If I were Yamila," says Cata, her jaw clenched, "and I had your mom in custody, I'd play that card instead of trying something this desperate. It's *obvious* she wants to bait you because she's come up empty, and the Cazadores are letting her take the fall if this plan fails—"

"*Or* she knows the truth about Gael, and she wants to make sure I see what's coming before it happens! She could be giving me a chance to trade myself in for him—"

"Okay, *Pablo*," says Cata, I guess implying I sound like a conspiracy theorist. "No offense, but Fierro's a slightly bigger prize than you."

"He's also my father and *your uncle*. Don't you care about him at all?"

She winces like I've hurt her, and she doesn't snipe back. We haven't had a chance to discuss our newfound familyhood, but I wonder if learning that Gael is Fierro has affected her feelings for him.

"This is a trap," Tiago says to me, only his tone lacks Cata's judgment.

"I still have to go. I need to know my mom is safe."

"You're not going to like this, but I have to say it." Tiago swallows, and I hear the dryness of his throat. "If Gael is in custody, there's nothing we can do to save him."

I feel the sheen of sweat moistening my forehead, but I try to keep Tiago's words at a distance. "I still have to go."

"Then I'm going with you."

I was expecting this, and I stare at the golden grass, unable to meet his gaze when I say, "I know you want to help, but you'll draw too much attention."

It takes him a moment to react, like the rejection was unexpected. "Manu, there's *no way* I'm letting you go alone—"

My neck snaps up. *"Letting me?"*

"Letting her?" echoes Saysa.

"You know what I mean!" Tiago shakes his head like he's flustered. "La Rosada is the capital of Kerana. It's where the tribunal meets and one of the most dangerous places for you!"

"This is about my *parents,*" I say, my voice trembling on the word. "I know you mean well, but you'll get recognized—"

"No, he won't."

We both look to Saysa as a familiar fervor illuminates her features. "*None* of us will, because we'll be faceless."

"Fierro masks," says Tiago before I can ask.

"Fierro's followers used to show up at his demonstrations wearing these white featureless masks, all claiming to be him," Saysa explains. "The tribunal outlawed the plant used for the masks, but since it's an ingredient in some potions, it's still around, just hard to come by. I think I know where we can find it, but it's a seedy spot."

"Shocker."

Cata says the word under her breath, but we all hear her. She hasn't had much time to process Saysa's involvement in the illegal sale of Septis.

"We'll have to steal it," says Saysa, looking directly at Cata. "And I think we're best off breaking the law in a place that's already breaking it."

Cata doesn't answer, and Saysa crosses her arms in annoyance. "We're out of ideas and semillas, and we need help. Gael must have contacts from his Fierro days. If anyone knows about the Coven, it's him. It's a risk, but we'll wear masks, size things up, and go from there. What's wrong with that?"

"Assuming Tiago isn't spotted on the way, and we don't get arrested for stealing a highly regulated plant," says Cata—and from the tone of her voice, it's clear she's not in support of this plan—"then we'll show up to La Rosada with masks on, and we probably won't be the only ones. Since the Septimus who own these masks are all older by now, Yamila won't look for us among the faceless. It might work."

Speechless, Saysa stares at Cata, as stunned by her twist ending as the rest of us. I breathe a little easier now that our plan has met with Cata's approval, but my stomach still feels knotted.

I can't lose my father.

Not when I only just found him.

Kukú is a shadowy village built of dark cobblestone, with narrow passageways and pointy rooftops. The little hairs on my skin are electrified as soon as we step out from the arboledo, and every part of me wants to turn around. But we have a little over an hour left before my—before Gael—

"There it is."

If Saysa weren't pointing to it, I never would have noticed the store. All I see is a copper doorknob protruding from the cobblestone wall.

"You can't come," she tells her brother. "Brujas only."

"You two are not going in alone," he argues. "They'll have security—"

"They won't be alone," I say, and it's hard to tell if he looks more or less worried now.

"Keep your face down," Saysa tells her brother before we cross the street toward the store. My stomach flips, like I skipped a step, and I want to look back to make sure Tiago is still there, but I know better.

When Saysa twists the knob, a camouflaged door swings inward. I bite back my disbelief as we step indoors, into a forest of black trees that's swathed in a purple night. The full moon shines overhead like a silver sun.

Our eyes are as bright as the glow-in-the-dark plants, making both us and the merchandise easy to spot. I feel like I'm in a game of Pac-Man when the ghosts turn blue. "Is *everything* with your kind an adventure?" I whisper.

"Everything worth pursuing."

The way Cata says it makes Saysa look at her. They hold each other's gaze for long enough that my presence feels intrusive. I push on, threading a path through the inky black trees and scanning for signs of movement. My friends walk in my wake, inspecting the foliage closer to the ground.

The brightest blooms must be the most powerful plants because their glow casts deeper shadows around them. I think back to my first lesson in Señora Lupe's class, when she assigned us to pluck a single petal from a dozen flowers, and I wonder what will happen if we do that now. Will an alarm go off? How exactly is this a *store*? Shouldn't there be a shopkeeper or customers or price tags?

"Go right," says Saysa, her eyes alight with magic, like pools of chlorophyll calling to the plant we need. Cata sticks close to me as we pad across the soft soil, zigzagging through the woods, until at last Saysa stops in front of a desiccated-looking plant.

Before she can say anything, a pair of icy blue eyes materializes from the darkness.

"Hundred semillas," says the Congeladora in accented English. She must have heard us speaking.

"We're just looking around," says Saysa.

"And yet you took a very particular path."

"Well, I hate to be obvious."

"One hundred semillas."

"One hundred don't-give-a-fucks."

"Excuse me—?"

"She doesn't mean it," says Cata, shoving her way in front of Saysa and flashing the bruja an innocent smile. "She's just in a mood, so we thought bringing her into your beautiful shop would soothe her."

Behind Cata's back, Saysa's eyes swirl with lime-green light.

"You can't be in here unless you're buying," says the sales witch, not noticing that the desiccated plant beside her is starting to shed.

"Oh, okay," says Cata, faking disappointment with a shrug. I count four large, billowy petals dropping soundlessly to the dirt. "Anything on sale?"

"Follow me," says the Congeladora, her icy blue gaze jumping to me, pausing like she's placing my element, then searching for Saysa, who just then steps out from behind Cata. Her eyes are no longer illuminated.

"Keep your eyes in view at all times," says the bruja, her own gaze glowing with magic as she freezes a path of roots by our feet. Then she stands guard over the desiccated plant, watching our faces as we walk past her down the crystal carpet she laid out for us. When she blinks, I reach out and swipe the four fallen petals.

Since I don't transform, my eyes don't light up. Still, everything down to my breath freezes with guilt as I'm passing her, and I spy her blue gaze narrowing.

I wasn't fast enough.

She must have spotted me—

"Jardinera, right?"

I jerk a nod, exhaling, and move along at a quicker clip, eager to get out of here. We have what we need. I don't know how long has passed. Gael is going to be unmasked soon, and I need to be there. *Where is the exit?*

The icy path ends in a part of the woods that seems malnourished or poisoned. The trees here aren't black but gray, and they look like ghosts in the purple night. Their branches jut out at odd angles, making them seem broken.

"Everything here is on sale," says the Congeladora, crossing her arms. "Fifteen semillas or less."

"*Fewer*," Cata corrects her, then she bites her lip, catching herself too late.

Now the sales witch looks as annoyed with her as with Saysa, so she turns to me. "You all seem young enough to be in school."

"I—uh—we get that a lot."

Her gaze hardens with suspicion. "Show me your semillas."

"Excuse me?" asks Saysa.

"Prove you can pay."

"Forget it, we don't need this," says Cata with a wave of her hand. "We're not going to buy from a place that treats us this way. We're leaving."

"I don't think so."

The Congeladora tips her head, and three witches come out from the surrounding woods. There's no way they were there a second ago, or I would have seen them.

There must be hidden doorways.

"See, we have a new deal with the Cazadores," says the Congeladora, moving toward us. Saysa and Cata step back, and I pull them closer to me. "They leave us alone most of the time, and we agree to alert them of any shady new characters visiting our manada."

We don't have time for this.

"What do you find so threatening about us?" asks Saysa as the three other witches close ranks, boxing us in. I can tell by their eyes that all four are different elements.

"You *wish* you were a threat," says the Congeladora. "You're merely a curiosity."

Her blue gaze flicks to me.

"And I have a feeling the Cazadores will agree."

It's natural to be drawn to the unnatural.

Attention breeds scrutiny.

Discovery = Death.

Ma's warnings flood my mind. She was right—my eyes were too interesting to ignore in the human world, and now they're too interesting for the Septimus.

The shop brujas' irises light up at the same instant as Cata's and Saysa's, and I shriek as four metaphysical walls manifest, blocking everything from view.

One wall is sizzling red smoke, the second is cool purple clouds, the third is humid gray steam, and the fourth is brown dust.

I extend my arm to reach through the steam, but Saysa yanks it down. "Don't touch it! That's pure power."

"They're *containing* us!" says Cata, her pink eyes lighting up and fizzing out quickly, like a match trying to ignite in a room without oxygen.

"What do you mean?"

"They're canceling our magic," explains Saysa, looking smaller than usual, her eyes also flashing and failing to illuminate. Her short brown strands are damp with sweat from the effort of trying to summon her power. "You need to—"

"*No*," Cata cuts in. "Manu can't. It's too risky. If *she* hears about it, she'll know we were here, and she could figure out our plan."

She being Yamila.

"It's either that, or we get arrested right now!" snaps Saysa.

"How are they doing this?" I ask.

"They're powerful, they outnumber us, and they represent all four elements—so they're *containing* us," says Cata. The word sounds like it means something more. "It's a magical cage that doesn't last long—"

"Just long enough for the Cazadores to arrive," finishes Saysa.

"Fine, I'll trans—"

"You *can't*," says Cata, dropping her voice like she's afraid the brujas can hear us. "You're drawing too much attention as is."

I flash back to the cave in Lunaris when we faced off with Yamila and Nacho, only this time it's not Saysa's power I'm thinking of, but *mine*.

Something else happened in that cave that even my friends don't know about. When Yamila tried to bind my wrists with fiery handcuffs, I shook off her heat before it could burn me. *I stopped her magic.*

Only I don't know how I did it, or even if I really did it, and besides, this time there's *four* brujas, not just one.

But maybe I don't need to fight off their magic. If I could just bring down one of these walls, the cage would break, hopefully killing the spell.

The roots breaching the soil beneath us are still frosted with the Congeladora's ice. I feel around on the ground for a weapon I can use, like I used to do in my lunaritis dreams. My fingers close around a heavy rock about the size of my palm.

I squint at the wall of gray steam, and I'm able to make out the faint outline of the Congeladora's body. Aiming for her torso, I hurl the stone as hard as I can.

"*Ah!*"

She cries out as it knocks into her chest, and the misty wall dissolves as she falls to the ground.

The sudden breaking of the spell causes the other brujas to fall too, and as their walls come down, Saysa's eyes light up and the world starts to quake. I take her and Cata's hands, and I run.

Cata sends a blast of air behind us in case the brujas are following, and we weave between the black trunks. "How do we get out of here?" I ask.

"They have hidden passages . . . but I can't access them," says Saysa, her breaths coming in bursts. "They have some kind of . . . enchanted lock."

I slow down so she and Cata can manage better. "Then what do we—?"

The Congeladora appears in front of me. She has dead leaves in her hair and dirt on her clothes and her expression is deranged with rage.

As her blue eyes fill with light, I feel winter's touch in my chest, like my heart has frostbite. I bend over in pain, and Cata and Saysa do the same. It feels like my lungs are freezing over, and soon I won't be able to catch my next breath—

Cata and Saysa fall to the ground like they're about to pass out. If I drop too, we're done.

I concentrate and try calling up my inner wolf, until I feel the light pooling in my eyes. The start of the transformation generates enough heat in my bones that I break free of my paralysis and I launch myself at the bruja before my body shifts.

She topples to the ground, and, now free of her spell, Saysa and Cata scramble over. Cata pulls me up. The Congeladora tries to rise too, but Saysa's eyes are pure light as she grips her wrist.

"How do we get out?" she demands.

The bruja doesn't answer, and her brown features begin to grow gray. Veins protrude from her face as the skin tightens around her skull.

"Stop," says Cata, keeping a wide berth of Saysa. "I'm serious!"

The bruja looks more corpse than alive, but Saysa doesn't seem to care. "Good night then—"

"*Okay.*"

The word is barely more than a broken breath, but it's enough to make Saysa's eyes dim.

The Congeladora feebly lifts her other hand, and her eyes flicker as a line of ice forms along the dirt, disappearing into the underbrush. I hear the sounds of the other brujas approaching, and Cata dashes to the point where the foliage swallows the ice. She ducks down, and Saysa and I hurry after her.

I close my eyes as prickly plants scratch at my face.

When I open them again, the purple night has dawned into a golden day.

5

We're back on the cobblestone road. Tiago is at our side in an instant, and from the glassiness of his gaze, I can tell he's been worried. "All good?"

"We need to hurry," I say, thinking of Gael. "How long do we—?"

"Ten minutes."

We rush to the arboledo, and as soon as we're ensconced in a private tunnel, Tiago asks, "Did you get it? What took so long? I was about to go in—"

I pull the four petals from my pocket, and Saysa reaches out for them. But Cata moves between us.

She's staring at Saysa like she doesn't know her.

"If you do that again, we're through."

She sounds like she's fighting back tears, but it's hard to tell. Cata's not much of a crier. "If you want to talk to me about what you're going through, I'm here. But if you keep going like this, I won't be."

She doesn't wait for Saysa's response and just starts walking forward. Tiago and I follow her, and he looks at me curiously while Saysa lags behind.

"So, what's the plan?" I ask.

"We embed ourselves with faceless crowds so we'll get lumped in with them, and we try to work our way as close as we can to where Gael is." Tiago sounds like he's on the Septibol field discussing a play. "But, Manu—"

"I know," I say, my heart thumping too loud. "If they have him, there's nothing we can do."

Yet even as I say the words, my thoughts betray them. If I dodged Yamila's fire before, I should be able to do it again.

"We're close," says Saysa. "Let's put on the masks."

She goes up to her brother first, and he bends his knees so she can reach his face. Saysa places the white petal over his features like it's a sheet mask, and the plant begins to meld with Tiago, expanding over his entire head. He opens his mouth, but the mask stretches like latex, and I doubt he can breathe—

Saysa pops the hole, and the exposed edges curl around his lips. The petal has somehow even sucked in his tousled hair, making him look bald. He turns to me and grins. He looks like a creepy mannequin.

"Can you see?" I ask.

"You'll see," he says, as Saysa comes over to me. "Or not."

I roll my eyes as I shut them, and the petal stretches across my face. I feel my hair bunching up closer to my head, as a cool, velvety texture presses into my features, like a new layer of skin. I can breathe through my nose just fine, but I open my mouth so Saysa can puncture the mask, and it wraps around my lips.

When I open my eyes, it's like looking through a veil of white mesh. Everything is slightly muted but still visible.

Saysa steps up to Cata last. Though she doesn't move away, Cata keeps her gaze averted and jaw clenched.

"I don't want to lose you."

Saysa's admission is as fragile as a snowflake.

Cata finally looks at her, and her stoic expression cracks with pain. "That's up to you."

Saysa doesn't say anything else as she tenderly places the petal on Cata. I turn away and meet Tiago's eerie faceless stare. "How bad?" he mouths.

"Bad," I mouth back.

Tiago turns to his sister, who's about to put on her own mask. "Wait," he says, and my foot starts tapping the ground. Yamila's announcement will be any second now.

"Say, we can't keep tiptoeing around you. I attacked Nacho too, remember? I dug my claws through his throat." Tiago's voice fades on the last word. "We've all been pushed beyond our limits. Whatever happened back there, it wasn't us. We have to let it go."

There's something so big brotherly about his voice and the way he's looking at her that it makes me ache for a sibling of my own.

"Good talk, bro," says Saysa in her flatlining tone. "Can we go now?"

Tiago doesn't answer, and his expression is veiled by the mask.

"No speaking when we get outside," warns Cata as Saysa presses the petal to her face. "We stick together and try to blend in. *No heroics.*" She looks in my direction. "We don't act until we've worked out a plan."

I nod, but it's a lie.

The truth is, I don't know what I'll do.

La Rosada lives up to its name.

We step onto a pink sidewalk crowded with Septimus, all going in the same direction. I blow out a long breath when I see that about half the crowd is faceless, and we get nods of welcome as we join. Strange how such a creepy sight can be so comforting.

Even creepier is the contrast our ghastly masks make against the Valentine's Day surrounding us.

The capital of Kerana is what I imagine a Hallmark movie set in the Roman empire would look like. Up and down the street are stately and ornate stone structures with rose-laced columns, arches, and domes. The flowers are everywhere—bordering buildings, bursting from windows, breaking through cracks in the pink gravel.

I look up at a tree-sized red blossom that offers shade to half the block. The trunk-thick stem is armored with deadly thorns, and as I study the crown, I notice that instead of the soft folds of a rose, these petals have pointy ends. They look like a cross between roses and Argentina's national flower.

Thanks to her plant obsession, Perla never missed a chance to tie local flora into our lessons, so she once shared a Guaraní legend about the red ceibo flower. There was a woman named Anahí who fought against the Spanish conquistadores and was burned at the stake. Legend says that by dawn, her body had turned into a ceibo tree, from which clusters of red blooms hung like flames.

Or blood.

Thinking on the history of that flower is like removing a rosy filter from my gaze. The Roman architecture of La Rosada feels less romantic now, considering that it's reminiscent of the Europeans who colonized Argentina.

And still, the ceibo flower grows. Rising through the layers of civilizations that have tried to tame it and claim it, defying our hand-drawn lines. Reminding us that the land doesn't recognize our borders.

Vehicles zoom down pink streets, and balloons dot the sky overhead. Everyone is headed to the same place, a gargantuan construction that makes me think of the Roman Colosseum. There are multiple entrances, and I read words etched over an archway:

CADA FLOR CAE. Every flower falls.

Another sign has been hung beneath it: SOLO LOBIZONES. Werewolves only.

It must be a new rule because an outraged mass is already forming. Some of them have angrily removed their masks and are shouting at the Cazadores. As more and more Septimus join the protestors, it strikes me how many of them have come here as part of a bruja-lobizón couple. Romance must really be in the air at La Rosada.

Tiago nudges me, and I realize Cata and Saysa have crossed the street. We follow them across the pink gravel and slip between marble buildings, down a dark alley lined with wilted flowers. It's musty and stinks of rotting roses.

"This is Yamila's doing," I say as soon as we're huddled together.

"It's definitely a trap for you," agrees a faceless Cata.

"We need to hide your body." Saysa grabs the hem of my shirt with both hands and tugs at the fabric, like she's trying to rip it open. The material expands, stretching before our eyes. When she lets go, the shirt is a few sizes too large, hanging to my knees and concealing my shape.

"There," she says. "No more curves."

"I guess," says Cata, cocking her head as she examines me. "What about her arms? They're not as big and hairy as the others'."

Saysa yanks on my short sleeves until they stretch all the way to my wrists, and Cata nods her approval.

"I look ridiculous."

"Boys do stupid shit like this all the time," Saysa points out.

Tiago doesn't confirm or deny her report. Instead, he asks, "What will you do?"

"We'll earn semillas offering transportation," answers Cata.

"Be careful."

"You too. After you find out what's going on with Gael, we'll meet here to work out a plan." Cata turns to me. "Keep near the exit. Don't draw attention. There's power in numbers."

I'm too nervous to speak, so I just nod. Then the four of us part ways, and Tiago and I join the queue of guys filing into the Colosseum.

Crammed amid so many tall bodies, I can't see ahead until it's our turn to go under the arch. The instant I walk through, I feel the twist in my gut—

And the transformation sets in.

I want to scream as my skeleton elongates, my skin ripping as my muscles expand. I feel my body hair thicken against the fabric of my clothes, and my gums and fingers tingle as fangs and claws slide out. I look up at Tiago in terror that our masks will tear, but even though his body has grown beastly, his head remains wrapped in the white petal.

Are you okay? he asks me telepathically.

Yeah, I say, looking down to make sure my shirt is still hanging loosely off my frame. My chest juts out more now, but it's fine when I hunch my shoulders. If my arm muscles were bigger, I could at least look like a bodybuilder.

Why did we transform?

When these many wolves come together, if enough of us shift, it pulls on the rest of us, he says as I follow him into the arena, the ground cushioned with rose petals.

We orbit the space in search of a good place to stand, sticking to the outskirts so we have access to the exits. *Yamila must have wanted it this way,* I say into his mind. *But how did she convince the Cazadores to keep the brujas out?*

It wouldn't take much. She probably played on the lobizones' fears of the brujas using magic to interfere.

Disgusted as I am by how she betrayed the other witches to feed her ambition, Yamila did us a favor, since now we can communicate. Tiago and I join a cluster of guys in masks, and a couple of them nod at us in solidarity. I hope we look like part of their group.

The place keeps filling up, everyone crowding the elevated dais where a legion of werewolves awaits. I scan their faces, and my gaze snags on *hers.*

The only bruja in the whole Colosseum.

Yamila's scarlet scarf flaps in the breeze as her fiery eyes survey the crowd, no doubt searching for mine. But I keep sorting through the faces until I spot Gael's golden head.

My father is standing in the far back, like he's trying to avoid being seen. He doesn't seem to be in shackles or anything, and I exhale in relief.

By now, I can sense my telepathic channel to Tiago easily, since we're so close, but Gael and I have only spoken this way once. Concentrating on his face, I focus on transmitting my thoughts to him.

Gael?

His coral eyes go wide as they sweep the crowd, and he strides across the stage. *Manu?*

I'm near the back, with Tiago. We're masked—

Leave! Right now! He's practically shouting. Even from this far I can see the splotches of red on his face. *Hurry!*

But Yamila said—

She's baiting you!

What about Ma? Where is she?

She's safe. I've got her.

My whole system stalls. It feels like every muscle just relaxed at once, and it takes me a moment to make sure I'm still breathing. Ma is free at last.

Where is she?

I'll explain everything, but not now. Trust me.

Why are you here?

There's no time! You need to go—

WHERE?

The question is a shout even inside my head. My spine stiffens, and I feel Tiago's gaze on me, like he senses my conversation.

W-we don't know what we're doing, I admit to Gael, my inner voice softening. *We haven't found any allies, we're out of semillas, and it's only a matter of time before—*

The Coven, he says matter-of-factly. *I thought Saysa would have made contact by now.*

My eyes widen beneath the mask.

It's real?

"Bienvenidos, lobos." *Welcome, wolves.*

Yamila cuts into our conversation, her sultry voice amplified into every corner of the Colosseum.

She looks at Gael questioningly, and he retreats, blending into the row of Cazadores behind her.

"A single name has summoned you here," she goes on in Spanish. "Even decades later, he haunts us."

I look up at Tiago. *I just talked to Gael. He says—*

"Fierro."

From the way Yamila scans the crowd, I know she's still searching for me. "Like so many Septimus, you haven't forgotten him. You want answers. You want closure. And right now, you can have it."

We need to go, I say to Tiago.

"One of these wolves is not like the others." Yamila's tone is taunting.

Come on. Tiago turns toward the exits.

"Step forward and reveal yourself, or we will be forced to come find you."

The two of us freeze. To move now would be to give ourselves away. *We shouldn't leave together,* says Tiago. *You go first—*

"The exits have been barricaded."

My breath hitches in my throat, and a rumble of reactions rolls through the gathering. *She's bluffing,* says Tiago. *She wants to provoke us. Don't react.*

Gael's urgency wrings my chest, but Tiago is right—everyone is looking around, scrutinizing their neighbors. Those of us in masks are getting the most stares.

Cazadores are walking through the crowd looking for you! Gael's voice breaks through my mind. He sounds desperate enough to do something stupid.

This was a mistake.

Gael says they're in the crowd looking for us! I tell Tiago.

There's jostling in the throng, ripples from the Cazadores searching for the only girl here. *Let's go,* says Tiago, gripping my arm. *I'll fight anyone stationed at the exit, then we run—*

But as soon as I take a step, I feel a tingling in my skull.

Tiago drops my arm and brushes his fingertips across his face like he feels it too. Then I exhale, and my mask curls off, joining the wilted petals on the ground.

All at once, my heavy hair tumbles loose, and my clothing cinches to frame my curves. I stare at Tiago's hairy face in horror, and the words over the Colosseum's entrance come flying back to me.

Every flower falls.

The group of wolves has been unmasked too, and one by one their eyes lock onto me in surprise.

I'm the only one without a bushy beard.

The only one whose body hair hasn't darkened.

The only one—as far as I can see—with breasts.

Tiago's voice tears through my numb mind: GO!

I want to run, but there's a tug on my insides, and I gasp for air. My bones sear in agony as my skeleton caves in, my claws and fangs retracting, skin tightening, until even my veins feel squeezed. Once it's over, the other wolves have also transformed back, and they're all gawking at me.

"¿Qué es eso?"

"¡Es una niña!"

"No puede ser."

"Tiene que ser brujería."

"Una bruja no puede transformarse."

"Ella no es bruja."

Half the crowd thinks I'm a witch, the other half doesn't know what to make of me. Their words funnel together into an unintelligible jumble of sounds, until at last, I hear it:

"Es lobizona."

6

Yamila's bloodred eyes lock onto mine from the dais, and I'm overcome with the real reason I've been terrified to see her again.

"What. Are. You?" she asked me in that Lunaris cave.

The question is a curse that's followed me across borders and worlds. It's my fear of the answer that's kept me from confiding in my friends about how I evaded Yamila's magic.

But *she* knows. Yamila knows all my secrets. Except one.

Fierro.

"STOP HER!"

At Yamila's shout, Tiago breaks into a sprint, pulling me with him to the exit. Since we stayed near the back, we don't have far to go—but Cazadores are already blocking our path.

There's at least five of them crowding the nearest archway like goalies, waiting to catch us. Until a thunderous explosion rocks the dais, and the ground shudders as a curtain of black smoke spreads swiftly through the air, enshrouding everything.

"Gael!" I cry out, but Tiago clings to my hand, not letting me go back.

He pulls me forward with him slowly now, since we can't see. His grip tightens, and I hear the cracking of bone as Tiago uses his free arm to punch a Cazador. Then he shoves me away as something huge collides with him.

I bend my knees and raise my arms, ready to defend myself if a Cazador breaks through the smoke, but someone squeezes my shoulder and leads me out of the Colosseum, onto the rose-laced streets of La Rosada.

I spin around, relieved to see it's Tiago and not an officer who's got me. But the feeling only lasts a beat.

The crowd outside is as big as the one inside, and they all rush forward as soon as they see me. Tiago and I are swarmed by Septimus shouting questions at us. Mirrors are held up to our faces, and my petrified reflection stares back at me everywhere I look. In Spanish, they ask:

"What's your name?"

"Where are you from?"

"Who are your parents?"

"How did you keep this secret so long?"

"Can we see you transform?"

"Aren't you el lobo invencible?"

They don't sound like Cazadores. They sound like—

"Press," growls Tiago.

The pink streets of La Rosada are infested with reporters. They jab at me with their mirrors as Tiago parts a path for us, but at least their presence creates a buffer between us and the Cazadores. Yet they're also making it impossible for us to escape.

As more and more Septimus are drawn to the commotion, I hear different types of footsteps—the fast, hard, chasing kind.

We start shoving our way through the mass, but even if we make it out, how will we find Cata and Saysa in this madness?

"¿Son novios?"

"¿Por qué te buscan los Cazadores?"

"¿Es verdad que tenés información sobre Fierro?"

Are Tiago and I dating, why are the Cazadores after me, is it true I have information about Fierro—?

An icy wisp of wind curls around my ear and curves under my skull. It feels more like a whisper than weather, and Tiago cuts in a new direction. The curious crowd follows us like a current, and we push our way toward the largest tree in sight, with flakey bark and feathery leaves. Its limbs are waving in the wind, even though there's no breeze.

"¡Ahí están!" shouts Yamila.

I feel her approach like a heat wave, and when I spin around, I spot Gael first.

I exhale in relief that he wasn't hurt in the explosion, then the Cazadores elbow in, and Tiago and I are pressed against a wall of Septimus. There's too many bodies between us and the arboledo, and we have no room to maneuver. We're never going to make it.

"I can't breathe," I say, getting an idea. Then I pretend to faint into Tiago's arms.

"Manu?" he asks in a panic. "*Stand back!*" he roars at the crowd, and my heart stalls at the feeling in his voice.

The crowd backs away just the tiniest amount, but it's enough. "Get them!" shouts Yamila in Spanish.

With a burst of speed, Tiago knocks over a few bodies as we dive into an opening in the arboledo's trunk. As soon as he sets me down, a small hand closes around mine, tugging me into a tunnel.

Once we're sealed inside our own passage, I bend over to catch my breath, nearly collapsing from my nerves.

"What happened?" Saysa and Cata ask almost in unison.

"I was exposed."

"Yamila had a backup plan," says Tiago, hugging his arms across his chest. "She tipped off the press. She left us nowhere to hide."

He looks a little peaked, and I wonder if that crowd just triggered memories from five years ago, when he became el lobo invencible.

"What about Gael?" asks Saysa.

Shaking his head, Tiago says, "They don't know who he is."

"Then why is he here?" demands Cata. "What happened with your mom? And where are your masks—"

"Gael didn't explain," I say. "He just said my mom is safe, then he warned us to run, and before we could go, our masks fell—*everyone's* did—"

Saysa smacks herself on the forehead and looks at Cata. "*La Rosada!* The rules for roses are different there! How did we miss that?"

Cata frowns. "But the mascarete flower isn't a rose—"

"Not *now*, but originally it evolved from the rose family. I should have known!"

Cata looks paler than usual, but she doesn't say anything. Being wrong isn't something she excels at.

"How'd you escape?" Saysa asks us.

"Some sort of explosion," says Tiago. "I still can't believe we got away."

"I can," says Saysa. "If the Cazadores had brought their bruja agents, you'd be in custody by now."

None of us disagrees.

Tiago blows out a hard breath. "We're going to have a much harder time keeping a low profile now that everyone knows Manu and I are together."

Cata's shoulders cave in, and she looks like she's seconds from dropping to the ground. I'm not used to seeing her so defeated. Saysa stares at the patterns of smaller roots and the patches of cottony cobwebs, and even Tiago leans against the wall, seemingly out of ideas.

"Gael said to find the Coven."

All three faces snap to mine.

"What?" asks Tiago.

"He said that?" asks Cata.

"Did he say *how*?" asks Saysa.

I shake my head at the last question. "He seemed to think you'd find a way."

Saysa's eyes glow bright green, and without another word, she marches down the tunnel, leaving us no choice but to follow.

By the time light fills the horizon, my legs are aching and I'm breathing in salty air.

I hug my arms around my torso as we pop out on a small wintry island in the midst of a vast ocean, where Septimus are walking on water. I blink a few times.

Staring at their feet in amazement, I squint until I spot the glint of frozen walkways along the sea's surface. The paths connect a smattering of tiny islands.

"Marina," says Tiago as he scans the view. "We used to love it here as kids."

"It's a manada made up of one hundred and twenty-seven islands, including the most dangerous place on Earth, La Isla Malvada." Cata is quick to spout her knowledge of each place we visit, but she never shares anything personal, like a memory. She always sounds like she's reciting from a textbook.

"Do you and your mom visit your dad in Kerana often?" I ask her.

"No."

There's an awkward silence, which Saysa fills. "This is where Zaybet's family lives."

"Is she why we're here?" asks Cata. "I thought you reached out to her a bunch of times already."

"It's different now."

We follow Saysa around the arboledo's upraised roots, to the other side of the tiny island, where a new vista is revealed: a large landmass with colorful buildings and icy streets. "We could be recognized," warns Tiago.

"We need to change," notes Cata, and she reaches into the back of her shirt, like she's digging for its tag. "These fabrics have a winter setting," she tells me. "Just crack the tab."

"I'll help you," says Tiago, and when I look at him, his white shirt is already a turtleneck and his sneaker-like shoes have become boots.

His breath is on my neck as his fingers slip into the waistline of my indigos, feeling along the seam until they snag on something. He places my fingers where his are, and when I snap the tab, my legs grow warmer as the fabric of my pants thickens. His hands find the neckline of my shirt next, and it grows into a sweater.

Breathing in Tiago's heady scent, I think of how he fought our way out of the Colosseum, and I feel a rush of feeling that goes beyond appreciation or admiration or adoration. It doesn't make me want to kiss him or cling to him—it makes me want to get stronger, so I can protect him too.

Tiago drops to the icy ground and presses the tongues of my Septimus sneakers. They lengthen into boots, the soles toughening and the inseams growing plusher.

He looks up at me, his hands grazing the sides of my body as he rises to his full height. His lips hover by mine, and I feel a tingling in my tongue, a craving—

"Let's go," huffs Cata, pushing between us. Despite the warm clothes, she and Saysa look cold and miserable.

Tiago takes my hand as we step onto a frozen pathway on the ocean's surface, where we're surrounded by nothing but blue sea. A chill nips at the exposed skin of my face, and in the nearing distance, I trace the outlines of colorful constructions cut from crystal or frosted glass.

Water slops over the edges of the ice, and I'm relieved for the boots' protection. The sensation of crossing an ocean on foot is so surreal that it's hard to walk while taking it all in, so it's a good thing Tiago is pulling me along.

Sand covers the ground when we reach the mainland, and my stomach knots at the sight of dozens of Septimus going about their afternoons. Crystal buildings sandwich a large icy avenue flanked by sandy sidewalks. All manner of sleds whoosh down the ice, in every size and variety, and I'm itching to admire everything, but Tiago and I have to keep our heads down to avoid being recognized.

Most Septimus here are dressed in glistening cloaks that shimmer like liquid, similar to the silver one Zaybet wore in Lunaris. We are clearly not excelling at blending in. We've barely made it past a blue building, when a mega-sized watery screen materializes over the street.

¡NOTICIAS!

The word keeps flashing, and the four of us exchange panicked looks. The other Septimus have also stopped moving—even those in sleds stall their vehicles—as footage begins to play. It's of me running out of the Colosseum with Tiago.

A reporter's voice narrates the montage of shots in Spanish. "Have you seen this Septimus? Her name is Manuela, and she's on the run with Santiago Rívoli, also known as the invincible wolf and star of El Laberinto's championship-winning Junior Septibol team. If you spot them, contact your local Cazadores immediately."

Tiago's fingers close on my arm, and the four of us slip into the sandy alleyway between the blue building and a squatter green structure.

"Should she cross your path"—the reporter's voice goes on behind us—"beware the girl's misleading eyes. Despite what you think, she's not a Jardinera. In fact, multiple witnesses claim she's not a bruja at all."

I'm dragging my feet, so Saysa and Cata have sprinted ahead of us. When I realize where they're about to step, I open my mouth to warn them—but I'm too late.

Their feet go right through the fuzzy mushrooms poking out from the sand, and they're sucked belowground.

"If reports are to be believed, she would be the only one of her kind."

As Tiago tugs me toward el Hongo, I glance back at the watery screen one last time. My eyes are glassy, my hair is matted, and my expression is blank. I look less like a lobizona and more like a lost little girl.

"She's a biological and historical anomaly."

The newscaster's voice reverberates in my ears.

"The first—"

7

My belly tickles as I drop.

Then I'm standing upright with my friends in a cobweb-infested cavern.

The air is warm and toasty, like we're *very* deep underground. If this is el Hongo, then the webbing wrapped around the walls must be mycelium. I move closer and spy small sparks lighting up the white bands, like the firing of synapses in a neuron network.

Cata and Saysa dig their fingers into the webbing until their whole hands are buried in the mushroom's root system. Then they close their eyes in concentration, and the veins of their arms begin to glow white.

"What's happening?" My voice comes out a murmur, and I have goose bumps.

"They're plugging into el Hongo," Tiago murmurs back. "It's how we sync with Lunaris if we want information, or to send a message, or even just to commune with the land."

Ma never took me to any places of worship, nor do we observe any religion. I've never set foot on any ground I've personally considered sacred or hallowed. Yet as more and more lights spark in the mycelium's brain-like network, I feel a keen sense of cosmic smallness.

I'm inside Lunaris's mind. Maybe even the universe's.

"This feels like discovering el Aleph."

I doubt I'd drop a Borges reference in any other company, but I already know Tiago's a fan. *El Aleph* is about a guy who finds a window into the universe through which he can see all of existence exactly as it is, without distortion. A point in space that contains all others.

"That's one of my favorite stories," says Tiago, his voice not just lower, but deeper. Like the words are coming from a profound place. "That's how I feel when I'm with you."

His slight accent resurfaces, and as I feel the intensity of his blue gaze, my winter clothes grow stifling. El Hongo starts to shrink so much that we could be back in Tiago's secret bookish cave in the Everglades.

"All set," says Saysa, and the tension disbands as she disconnects from el Hongo. "Sent a meeting place to Zaybet. Now let's go and hope she shows."

"You've been trying her for days," says Tiago. "Why do you think she'll listen now?"

"She's the one who forged Manu's Huella. If she sees her on the news, she'll put it together that we're on the run and Yamila must be trying to cut me off from my allies."

I wonder if the class where Saysa met Zaybet was Criminology 101.

"Anything useful?" Saysa asks Cata as she joins us.

"Never found anything useful about the Coven before, so why should that change now?" She shrugs and crosses her arms.

"There was one thing, though. It's not *useful*, but it's interesting. There's a theory that if the Coven exists, the only way it's possible that no one in history has been able to expose it is that Lunaris must be complicit."

"What does that mean?" I ask.

Saysa's eyes flash with something like pride. "It means we're her children too."

Saysa and Cata leave el Hongo first to buy us the cloaks everyone in Marina wears. Tiago and I wait until we think they've had enough time, then we follow them through the exit within the webbed wall.

Just as I watched Cata and Saysa do, I insert my fingers into the mycelium. It feels both intrusive and insubstantial, and as I step forward, it's like I'm walking through a curtain of thick cobwebs that smother my face until I almost can't breathe—then we're back in the alley between the blue and green buildings.

Out on the street, I see Septimus congregating in groups, no doubt discussing what they just watched.

Cata and Saysa are now cloaked in pink and green fabrics that match their eyes. Tiago accepts a sheet of sapphire. My cloak is a light shade of brown, more amber than gold.

"We used all the semillas we had left," says Cata. "We were a bit short, so we donated some blood."

Tiago's dark skin seems to pale, but he clenches his jaw and nods.

"I don't understand," I say.

"The most powerful potions need a particular blood type, depending on what the spell is and the element and the method of disbursement—"

"Not now," says Cata, cutting off Saysa's lesson.

A group of cloaked brujas has turned the corner, and they're headed toward the mushroom patch beside us. They're so busy tittering about me that they don't immediately notice we're here.

"¿Vos te creés lo de esta chica?"

"Para nada."

"¿Por qué nos van a mentir así?"

"Capaz los Cazadores se la creen."

While they debate whether I'm real or a hoax, Tiago and I twist away to pull on our cloaks. They're windbreakers that guard against the chill here, and they can be sealed all the way up, until they cover one's whole face—minus their eyes.

Most Septimus leave their hoods off, but Tiago and I raise ours. The brujas are closer now, and they're still debating the footage of me. Falling back on my old anxious habit, rather than focusing on the meaning of their words, I translate them.

"Para mí que es una bruja." *I think she's a witch.*

"Pero dicen que la vieron transformarse—" *But they say they saw her transform.*

"Debe haber mezclado demasiadas pociones de potencia física y algo le falló." *She must have mixed one too many performance enhancers and something went wrong.*

"Que algo le falló es obvio." *That something went wrong is obvious.*

In my periphery, I see Cata and Saysa nod to the brujas in greeting. All this time, the two of them saw me as potentially being some kind of revolutionary symbol, but the Septimus are no different from humans in their ability to see what they want. This entire mission is starting to feel not just hopeless, but pointless.

As we're leaving the alley, the massive screen has vanished, and the scene has changed. Most sleds have been parked to the side of the icy street and abandoned, and the crowd is thinning out as fast as it formed.

When only a few clusters of Septimus remain, I realize they're all making for the nearest mushroom patches. Many of them are running around and searching the ground, even though the streets were lined with mushrooms moments ago.

"Too many of us accessing el Hongo at once," explains Tiago.

"The mass exodus could start any moment, so hurry," says Cata.

Since we have the street nearly to ourselves, I venture to ask, "What are these huge screens that keep appearing from out of nowhere?"

"They're called pantaguas, and they're created from water droplets that get magically charged," says Saysa. "The water stays dormant until it's activated. We have handheld versions too."

"Why don't wolves have to show their eyes?" I might as well get all my questions out while I can.

"Right?" says Saysa, as though I'd made a declaration and not posed a question. "They're so afraid of our magic that they're desperate to control it."

"That's not it," says Cata. "We're a *pack* species, and eye color reveals a bruja's brand of magic. It's how element sisters can identify one another."

"That's about as naïve as I've heard you get," says Saysa, earning herself one of Cata's patented scowls. "You think a bunch of brujas woke up one morning and decided it would be a fun challenge to force a dress code on themselves forever?"

"That's reductive, and you're missing the point. Sometimes you take your argument so far that it infantilizes us. You make it seem like brujas don't have any agency of our own."

"What agency? Look at the gender imbalance in the tribunal and the Cazadores! Or the fact we're not allowed to explore Lunaris without a wolf escort—"

"Calm down," says Tiago, but Saysa is a few orbits past calm.

"If we're so weak and wolves are so almighty, then why is our scariest storybook monster a *girl,* la ladrona?"

"*La ladrona?*" I echo. The word means *thief.* "What's that?"

"A bedtime story," says Saysa with an eyeroll. "She's this demon who will supposedly be born if—"

"Where did you say you first met Zaybet?" Tiago sounds like he's run out of patience. I get the impression he doesn't care for this story.

Saysa takes a long moment to answer, and then she mumbles something even Tiago and I can't make out.

"What?"

"La Isla Malvada."

"You're joking."

Tiago practically stops moving, and I have to nudge him. We're approaching a coastline with a boat harbor, so we won't have privacy for much longer.

"That place is supposed to be swarming with Cazadores!" says an outraged Cata.

Saysa looks straight ahead, keeping her voice even. "It was the most secure message I could think to send, in case the Cazadores intercepted it. *Meet me where we met.*"

"I thought you said she was an old classmate?" I ask.

"Obviously you don't use someone's real identity for illegal stuff. You call them an *old classmate* or a *cousin.*"

Sometimes Saysa acts like the rest of us graduated crime school with her.

"This is going to be impossible," huffs Cata under her breath. "Especially now that everyone's looking for the two of you! We should split up—"

"We can't," says Tiago, blowing off her suggestion. "Brujas can't enter the island without a wolf escort."

"But this isn't Lunaris," I argue. "I thought that rule only applied there."

"It applies wherever the tribunal sees fit," Saysa corrects me, with the air of one who's just proven her point.

We stop talking as we approach the harbor, where there are no signs of any mushrooms left. There's still a handful of Septimus aboveground, but thankfully they're gathered around a screen. I don't breathe easy until we step off the sand and onto the sea's surface.

This frozen pathway is wider than the one we took earlier, so we walk side by side, forming a wall against the bitter gales. Our hoods are up, covering everything but our eyes.

There are Septimus in the distance ahead of us, and squinting, I make out a sky-high glacier pressing into the horizon, armed with hundreds of thousands of long, thin blades of ice, all leaning in the same direction. The sight looks almost extraterrestrial.

"They're called penitentes," says Tiago, his voice muffled by his cloak. "They're formed by the high altitude and strong winds, and they always point to the sun."

They form in the human world too. I recognize them from images I've seen of the Argentine side of the Andes mountains.

The Septimus ahead of us have vanished, and as the mist clears, I spot a dark mouth in the ice. I raise my voice over the wind and ask, "Are we going *inside* the glacier?"

"It's not a glacier," answers Tiago. "Whatever Lunaris force forged this island, its magic is beyond even the brujas' abilities."

"Some think it's a stepping stone to Lunaris," chimes in Saysa. "Since creatures sometimes get through, we know there's a portal on this island that's active all month, but no one's found it."

"That's why you need lobizón escorts?" I ask.

"Some of those creatures are immune to magic," says Cata. She's the only one of us who keeps her hood off. Her hair blows behind her, pink eyes glowing gently, like she's embracing the wind as an old friend.

"That's why Cazadores are always on patrol for protection," says Tiago, and now I'm beginning to see why this is such a bad idea.

A chill that has nothing to do with the ice ripples down my spine as we step inside. I tilt my neck back to take in the frosty construction, and I feel like I'm in Superman's Fortress of Solitude.

A gust of wintry air blasts from the island's depths as we arrive at a hollow and high-arched main hall.

There are a couple dozen Septimus here, and the Cazadores are easy to spot—they're the wolves who walk with a predatory gait. Their eyes seem to move in more directions than the typical Septimus, and I watch as one of them approaches a group of teens. "You'll need a second wolf escort for so many brujas," he says in Spanish.

Tiago scowls at Saysa, like the guard's words are her fault. Then he makes a sound at the back of his throat that sounds like a grunt.

"You can't still be upset," whispers Saysa as we take a sharp turn down an empty passage. "That was five years ago."

"Betrayal doesn't expire."

"*Betrayal?*" she balks.

"Both of you really need to get over this," snaps Cata, who appears familiar with this argument. "Tiago, you came back from your first trip to Lunaris a folk hero, while your sister still had another year to go to inherit her magic. She was clearly jealous and—"

"I wasn't jealous," Saysa cuts in. "I just wanted to do my own thing."

"You could have told me that instead of selling me out!" he growls.

"I didn't sell you out—"

The wall to our right evaporates into mist, and Saysa's voice drops out.

We're now part of a chamber that's populated with Septimus. There are gasps as we're revealed, and some of them march toward us.

I think I'm going to have a heart attack, but they walk right past us to investigate the passage.

Tiago and I keep our gazes lowered, while Cata and Saysa scan for Zaybet. When Saysa grazes my arm, we keep moving.

The four of us file through an archway into a round chamber where a group of Cazadores are chatting in a corner. The high ceiling makes it harder for sound to travel, but I feel a punch to my gut when I catch the word *lobizona*.

Only they're not talking to me. They're talking about me.

Faint screams ring out in the distance, the echo reverberating off the walls, making it impossible to pinpoint where it came from. A few Septimus hurry out of the room like they're eager to queue up for whatever fun ride that was.

There are three tunnels leading out of this chamber, and Saysa is guiding us toward the narrowest one when something furry and ferocious comes flying out.

She screams and ducks, just as a grizzly bear–like creature with red eyes and a long tail leaps out with claws extended.

Tiago grabs Saysa and Cata, his body a blur as he yanks them to the wall for safety. The other wolves pull their bruja companions away, while the Cazadores transform.

"Manu!" shouts Tiago.

When I hear my name, I realize I haven't moved.

The beast is charging at me.

Only instead of running away, I roll my shoulders and bend my knees. And as the creature closes the distance between us, I let out a monstrous, guttural growl.

The beast's jaws are inches from my face, but it stops.

Tiago is already at my side, transformed beneath his blue cloak, and towering over both the creature and me.

In the tense silence, a girl's voice whispers, "Ma, ¡es la lobizona!"

The Cazadores stiffen, heads tilting like a pack of wolves catching their prey's scent.

The Lunaris beast turns toward the girl and licks its lips, and the officers rush forward to engage it—but a handful of agents stalk toward me.

They move in unison, like this is a dance they've done a million times before.

Tiago pulls me into a sprint, and Cata and Saysa hurry behind us as we vault down the same passage the creature came through.

"¡Paren!"

The Cazador shouting for us to stop sounds unnervingly close. Cata screams, and Tiago and I whirl around—

An agent has a fistful of her hair, and another one is reaching for Saysa. Tiago breaks the Cazador's hold on Cata, and I yank Saysa behind me as the tunnel starts shaking.

"Saysa—"

"It's not me!"

Cata's pink eyes flare, and she sends a blast of air at the Cazadores, shoving them back half a step. And that's all it takes.

A wall hardens in the spot where the officers had just been, barely missing Tiago as it barricades us in. Then the shaking stops.

"They're gone—"

Cata's sentence shreds into a scream as the ground tips down and the tunnel turns into a slide.

I shriek too as we twist through the glacier, the cold infecting me even through the cloak and winter clothes. The drop goes on for long enough that I start to feel dizzy, until finally, we're spit out.

Tiago and I scramble to our feet and survey our surroundings. We're in an icebox. It looks like a basement of sorts—the room is void of Septimus or splendor, but stuffed with random odds and ends, like a storage space.

The silence in here is deep, and the high ceiling makes the room feel especially buried in the ice.

"I think we're alone," I say.

Even though the ground is freezing, Cata and Saysa don't get up. They stay down, limbs limp like they're done.

"This was a bad idea," says Tiago. His hood has fallen back, and he rakes a hand through his hair, melting the dusting of sparkles frosting his roots. "The entire force of the Cazadores is going to bear down on us here. We're trapped."

"We can't leave anyway," says Saysa from the floor. "Zaybet is our best chance at finding the Coven."

"Forget that fairy tale!" snaps Cata.

"*Why* would Gael have brought it up if it's not real?"

"You both seem to have recovered your breath," says Tiago. "Let's keep moving. We need to find a way out."

He offers his sister a hand, and as he pulls her up, he asks, "When exactly did you say you met Zaybet?"

The expression on Saysa's face makes her look like a mischievous little sister. "The day I *betrayed* you."

Tiago rolls his eyes.

Just then, I notice small shadows flitting in and out of my peripheral vision. I stare hard at the ground—*they're fish.*

"There's only ocean beneath us," I say, breathless. "If the ground melts . . ."

"There's got to be a way out," says Tiago with renewed vigor. We investigate every corner of this basement, passing a crystal chair with serrated armrests, a stash of spiky icicles that look like penitentes, a nest of dark metal chains . . . "A dungeon?" Tiago looks at me for confirmation.

"It's definitely some kind of torture chamber."

There's a soft, rhythmic trickling coming from the far end of the space, and Tiago and I stare into the depths of a circular tub of dark water. The liquid hardens into ice, then melts, then it evaporates into mist, then pools into liquid again, then it hardens, and so on, over and over and over again.

"Not clear on what type of torture this is," muses Tiago.

"I'd classify it as *Sisyphean*."

He cracks his roguish grin, and knowing my nerdiness produced that megawatt smile fills my belly with doraditos.

"Those agents could have led us here," says Cata as we approach her. "We have to find a way out, *now*—"

"Zaybet's coming," insists Saysa, joining us. *"Trust me."*

Cata rolls her eyes, but Tiago narrows his. "What exactly happened the day you met her?"

"You mean the day I *betrayed* you?"

"Yes." The word is almost a growl. "I mean the day we came here for a brother-sister adventure, until you yelled out, '¡Es el lobo invencible!' and fed me to the crowd."

Saysa looks like she's stifling a grin. "Every older sibling gets owned by the younger one eventually—"

"Saysa, you were *eleven*—"

"And a *half*—"

"You hadn't inherited your magic yet, and you were alone in the most dangerous place in the world! You could have *died*—"

"I almost did!"

She sucks in a breath, and from the way Cata's staring at her, I gather even she doesn't know this part.

"After I left you," says Saysa, no smile on her face, "I met

Zaybet and a bunch of brujas. Only she was acting just like you, overprotective about me being on my own, so I tried to get away—but the floor melted. If not for Zaybet—"

Saysa pauses a moment, like she's not sure where that sentence is going. "She manifested ice under my feet, and I made it back to solid ground. She saved me."

"How could you not tell me any of this?" asks Tiago, the anger gone from his voice.

"I was embarrassed," Saysa admits. "But trust me. *Zaybet is coming*—"

"Shhh!"

I hold up a hand to Saysa. Something is different about the sounds in the room. It's quieter than before.

The Sisyphean pool has gone still. And the hairs on my neck stiffen as I hear it.

A footstep.

Tiago wrenches Saysa and Cata behind him as a black-clad figure steps out of the tub.

Their wet suit extends around their head and mouth, and they have no scuba mask or oxygen tank. They look like a shadow.

More figures step out of the pool of water, and Tiago reaches into the pile of penitentes and hands one to each of us. The icy weapon is heavy, and I hold it like a baseball bat.

This must be some elite team of Cazadores. Yamila isn't taking any chances.

There are six shadows in total, and when they step forward, the four of us raise our weapons in anticipation of an attack.

The first figure reaches for their neck and yanks off their mask. The girl has wild black strands with frosted white tips that fall across her shoulders, and a pair of sharp metallic eyes.

She flashes me a feral grin.

"I knew you weren't a Jardinera!"

8

"Zaybet!"

Saysa's penitente clatters to the ground, and she leaps forward to hug her friend. "How did you find us?" she asks, as the rest of us let our weapons fall.

"This is pretty much the dumbest place you could come if you're on the run, so I knew the Cazadores would catch up with you. I just hoped you'd make it to this room first."

She greets each of us with a hug, and Cata says, "We need to hurry—they chased us down here."

"Don't worry," says Zaybet. "The Cazadores can't get in."

"What do you mean?"

Zaybet admires the room like it's cozy and familiar. "Ages ago, this dungeon was used to torture Septimus who strayed from the norm."

A chill ripples down my spine. Saysa's and Cata's eyes grow bright, and they scan the space like they can see its ghosts.

"Then one day, this chamber sealed itself off." Zaybet shrugs. "No one knows why, but only Septimus in need of a safe space can find it now. Some of us think the generations of blood spilled here left an invisible map that only a chosen few can follow. I had a feeling you'd find it."

"Who are your bodyguards?" asks Cata, staring at the still-masked Septimus.

One of them steps forward with a stack of black cards. "Put these on," says Zaybet, ignoring Cata's question as she hands one to each of us. When I unfold the square, the fabric is so compressed that the wet suit looks toddler-sized.

A neighbor in El Retiro had a pet python she let me hold once, and that's what this reminds me of—snakeskin. The material is strong and smooth and textured. There are two pieces: bodysuit and mask. I see Saysa widening the neck hole until she can fit her leg through. She doesn't remove her boots.

I pull off my cloak, then I stretch out the suit material. It expands easily, and I'm able to fit my entire body inside. Once it's on, the fabric adjusts to my shape, sealing me in completely. Like the others, I tie the sleeves of my cloak around my arm so I don't lose it.

"Follow us," says Zaybet, and we march into the Sisyphean pool. I pull on my mask, and it's similar to the mascarete petal, only this one doesn't have a mouth hole. My breathing is fine, and I can still see, but my view is dimmer.

There's no oxygen tank attachment, and we're going underwater. Yet no one else says anything, so I keep quiet. Maybe the ship is close.

I don't feel the water's frigid chill. The only other difference is that now I'm weightless. The ocean is dark, but I make out colorful fish and algae—what I don't see is a vessel.

We swim in a school together, and soon my head starts buzzing from holding my breath. I let the air out slowly, trying to resist the urge to breathe in. I just need to hold on a little longer . . .

But my muscles grow leaden, my movements losing steam, until I can't take it—

I inhale.

The mask presses into my nose and shoots up a burst of fresh air. The fuzziness in my brain fades, and I press onward with renewed energy. I catch up to the others and continue breathing normally, or as normally as it gets with my wet suit blowing oxygen up my nostrils.

I feel a heave on my limbs as the current starts to pull away, tugging on my muscles with its force. And a shadow the size of a whale looms over the horizon.

The others swim toward the creature, only it's not an animal at all.

It's a giant, spiral-shaped seashell that's gray and half-fossilized and could be from prehistoric times. Except it's spinning through the water with purpose—and coming directly for us.

When the shell slows down, one of our group approaches its underbelly, and the rest of us follow behind. A part of the crusty shell cracks open, and we pull ourselves inside.

As I cross the threshold, I feel a tingling sensation, like I'm passing an energy barrier, the way I did when I first entered El Laberinto. I'd assumed it was some kind of magical membrane meant to keep humans out—and I wonder if here it's to keep the sea from flooding in.

We all remove our masks, and I register that everyone on Zaybet's team is a bruja—with the exception of a dark-skinned wolf with broad shoulders and a head of bouncy curls.

"Welcome to *La Espiral*," he says in perfect English. His voice has a raspy edge that masks any hint of an accent, if there is one.

The shell is pristine on the inside, its halls bathed in a warm glow. The curving walls are pearlescent, and the floor is spongy and pink, like a tongue. We keep twisting around the space until at last we arrive at what must be the shell's core: a room with a round recessed floor that's smothered in puffy pillows of every size and style. Ringing the area are a dozen reclining seats with backrests at varying angles.

A panoramic window is the only disruption to the shell-ship's exterior. Beyond the glass are dark waters, and standing in front of the view is a bruja with ebony skin and tightly coiled curls.

"Welcome to my ship," she says with a very slight accent as she approaches us in a flowy spring dress. She has firestorm eyes. "I'm Laura."

Her voice has a pleasant lilt to it, and I can't help thinking she'd make a great audiobook narrator. Up close, her irises are black with flecks of red bleeding through, like fiery lightning in outer space. They remind me of black opal.

Encendedora.

"I'm Enzo," says the only guy on the crew. He's stripped his wet suit halfway off, baring his cut upper chest.

"And that's Rox, Ana, Nati, and Uma," says Zaybet, gesturing to the four brujas who are now losing their suits and dropping onto chairs or pillows. They nod or wave in greeting. None of them are wearing outfits that match their eyes.

After we've introduced ourselves, my friends take off their suits and I do the same, folding it over my arm along with my cloak.

"Okay, Captain, take us out of here," says Zaybet, joining Laura at the helm.

"Why do I still have to explain that the captain gives the orders?"

"Got it," says Zaybet. "Won't happen again."

"That's what you said when your tango instructor told you to let the lobizón lead," says Enzo in his raspy voice. "You quit the class instead."

"What are you saying?"

"You're a sucky number two."

"Hate to admit it, but the wolf's got a point," says Laura. There are ashy handprints on the wall beneath the window that look like they were burned in, and as she lines her palms with the prints, the red streaks in her eyes light up like flames.

The ship jerks forward, and I reach out to steady Cata as we hurtle into the watery depths. We soar across colorful beds of coral, outstripping every fish in sight, and soon we enter open waters where the sea floor is too deep to make out.

"Where are we going?" asks Tiago.

Zaybet and Laura frown, and I'm not sure what he said wrong. Is it possible they don't hear the music in Tiago's voice?

"A safe space," says Zaybet in a tentative tone.

"Those two don't take too kindly to wolves," says Enzo to Tiago and me, and I'm strangely gratified that he counts me in the wolves' club.

"*This* wolf is an exception," says Zaybet, beaming at me. "I knew you couldn't be a bruja. Your eye color doesn't grow in any of the known fields of Lunaris. I had to mix pigments from dozens of flowers to get something similar for your Huella. I don't even know if I managed it."

She holds out a hand, and I pull out my Huella from a pocket. Zaybet holds it up to my face. "Not quite," she says, returning it in disappointment.

"Where is this safe space located?" asks Cata.

"El Mar Oscuro," says Laura, who doesn't seem to mind answering questions if it's a bruja asking.

I thumb through my Huella before putting it away, so it takes me a moment to register the silence.

"You're not serious," says Cata.

"Yes, she is, because captains never lie about a destination!" Zaybet looks eagerly at Laura. "Right? I remembered!"

"But it—it's impossible to access," sputters Cata. "And it's dangerous—there's pirates and storms and the underground market—"

"And the *Coven*."

We fall silent when Zaybet utters that word.

"Let's offer our friends food first, and terrify them later," says Laura in her honeyed voice, coming over from the helm. Her eyes are still glowing, and the ship seems to be on autopilot. "Take a seat, relax."

We settle into chairs, and one of the brujas hands us a tray of sandwiches de miga. We each take a stack and pass it down. I don't look back up until I've devoured them. Was our last meal the lomitos last night? I don't remember eating since then.

I lean back in my chair, and I notice that Saysa is the only one of us who's barely touched her food. She's shaking her foot, and her eyes have a far-off look. After believing in the Coven despite everyone's doubts and taunts, I'm sure she's eager to see it for herself.

When I glance away from her, I meet seven sets of eyes watching me. Nerves jostle the food in my stomach.

"How'd you stay hidden all these years?" asks Zaybet.

I meet her metallic stare and try not to blink. "Same way as the Coven, I guess."

She regards me a moment, then turns to Saysa like she'll find more answers there. "You met at school?"

"Manu ran away from home last moon and tried to hide in El Laberinto," says Saysa, and while it sounds like she's filling her in, she's keeping the details deliberately vague. "The school was going to let her stay, but when the Cazadores came after her in Lunaris just for being different, we ran."

"Good for you," says Enzo, nodding at me.

"What's the plan?" asks Zaybet. From her tone, she's already onboard.

"A revolution, Z," says Saysa, sounding like her familiar insurgent self. "You in?"

Zaybet's grin is wild. "Naturally."

The water beyond the window darkens to pure black, and I'm drawn to the view. It looks less like an ocean and more like outer space.

My friends join me by the glass. "El Mar Oscuro," says Saysa softly. "How did we get here?"

"There are access points in the depths of the sea," says Laura. "You just have to know what you're looking for."

Objects float in the darkness, some suspended, others in motion. We sail past interconnected rings that make me think of the Olympics, then we weave through coral clusters that move like asteroid fields. I ogle a swarm of glowing, lightbulb-like insects, until a stream of bubbles the size of small islands jets out, scattering them in every direction.

"I didn't know it was like this." Tiago looks as entranced as his sister.

"No one does until they see it," says Zaybet. "Images of this place don't imprint. The tribunal has been trying to find a way to control it, but el Mar Oscuro is untamable."

We pass a variety of prehistoric shells just like this ship, and I wonder how many of them are what they seem. "What is this place, exactly?" I chance.

"Nobody knows," says Zaybet.

"The space between worlds," says Laura with a mysterious smile.

"Some think it's the buffer that keeps Lunaris and our reality from collapsing into each other." Enzo's rasp makes the words weightier, and for a moment, the whole universe feels fragile.

"Whatever it is," says Zaybet, "surviving out here requires a ship and a crew for fending off storms and piratas."

This is the second time someone's said *pirates,* and I'm starting to think they mean it.

A spherical rock grows larger on the horizon, bruised and cratered, with debris crusting its surface. The moon-like body looks like a magnet for space trash. The kind of thing you want to steer clear of.

"If we don't change course, we're going to crash into that shit pile," warns Cata, and I worry that the rock really does have a magnetic pull.

"That shit pile," says a grinning Zaybet, "is the Coven."

9

"Our base has to look like something you'd want to avoid," Zay-bet explains as we follow her down a dim rocky tunnel. "That way we won't draw attention."

"How long has this place been around?" asks Cata.

"There are no records. We know nothing except that it always has been, and it always must be. Protecting the Coven matters more than the life of any individual member. That's why every new generation makes improvements. They say Fierro stole blueprints from the Cazadores—"

"*Fierro?*" I blurt.

"The one and only." In her gleaming gaze, I see a wisp of Pablo's fanaticism. "They say he liked to even the playing field. He wouldn't smuggle weapons because he didn't want to incite violence. He only wanted to empower the disenfranchised."

I think of the black smoke that helped us escape at the Colosseum, and I wonder if that was Gael's doing. I turn to

Tiago, and he's looking at me like he's just made the same connection.

"But then," says Cata in a would-be casual voice, "you guys must know who he was?"

"I wish," says Zaybet. "He delivered his secrets anonymously. Even if he was the alter ego of a member, there are no records, so we'll never know." She looks at me like she wants to say more, but moonlight pools on the ground ahead, and the tunnel spills into a cavernous space.

It's like a courtyard boxed inside an apartment building. If that building was carved inside a rock.

The air is silvery white, and I look up to see a star-studded ceiling projecting a waning gibbous moon.

Septimus are spread out beneath the enchanted sky. They're gathered at wooden communal tables, lying on mismatched couches, meditating on yoga mats, or pulling books off shelves. The balconies of five stories that span all four walls look down on the common area, adorned with stringy black curtains that are unevenly and unnecessarily draped across the banisters. They look out of place, and sometimes, like they're moving . . .

"Ah, that," says Zaybet. "It's the only plantlike life that grows in this realm, and we need them for oxygen."

My vision adjusts, and I identify the curtains as vines planted on the fifth story's rooftop. The smaller ones only reach that top balcony, while the longest ones can almost touch the ground.

They look like burnt versions of the green ivy guarding the Citadel, except these aren't shielded with spiky thorns. They have *jaws*.

Mouthlike slits open in the black vines, and the plants bare their sharp teeth. After grinding them together, the maws seal shut.

"We call them vampiros," says Laura, her pleasant voice at

odds with the unpleasant-looking plant. "Don't worry—their bite's not venomous."

When at last I drop my gaze, I'm face-to-face with a few dozen Septimus.

They've stopped what they were doing and gathered in front of us.

In front of *me*.

"Es un honor conocerte—"

"*English*," says Zaybet, correcting the bruja who spoke.

"It's an honor to meet you. Are you hungry?" Her peachy pink eyes light up, like she's summoning food.

"We ate on the ship, thank you." I look to Zaybet. "Why English?"

"It's always been that way at the Coven. Changing languages when we come here helps us keep our worlds separate, so we don't slip up when we're home."

"Are you in charge here?" Saysa asks Zaybet, and I detect a note of something sour in her tone. Jealousy?

"No, no one is. Everything is done by consensus, but each of us is responsible for any new members we bring in. So you're my charges."

"Let's see the lobizona transform," says a guy in a striped Septibol jersey.

"Her name is *Manu*." Tiago has some kind of stare-down with the wolf.

To deflate the tension, I say, "Thank you for letting us come here." My gaze drifts to the upper stories, and for a moment all I can think about is slipping into one of those rooms, bathing for the first time in days, and sleeping in a real bed. "We've been on the run since Lunaris, so if it's okay, I think we could use some sleep."

"And showers," says one of the guys. When everyone else laughs, I'm mortified.

"Reasonable demands," says Zaybet. "We can talk in the morning."

"I'll take them up," says Enzo in his smoker's voice. He's still shirtless, and in pants that look like cotton sweats.

We follow him to an alcove where there are stairs. "Meet me on the fourth floor," he says as he steps onto a stone platform. Then he pushes a lever, and the platform shoots up.

He's waiting for us when we finish climbing, and he leads us down a balcony draped with vampiros. Up close, they're grotesque.

They look like hoses made of scratched-up black leather, and when they part their lips, their pointy teeth are stained red. The grinding of their steely jaws is like the gnashing of blades.

I focus instead on the shifting lines of Enzo's back muscles as we stride past crimson door knobs. He moves with his own unique swagger. "We might only have three empty rooms on this floor, so if you want to be near one another, two of you will have to double up. We've got more space on the fifth floor."

"Cata and I can share," offers Saysa.

"Um," says Cata, stiffening like she's been called on to give an answer in class. "Sure. I mean, we're best friends, so why not?"

Saysa casts her a nasty glare and walks faster, catching up to Tiago and me, leaving Cata to trail behind.

As we turn the corner into the next corridor, a vampiro swings forward from the ceiling, flashing its fangs in my face—

I shriek and duck my head, heart shooting into my throat.

"You get used to them," says Enzo, his green eyes crinkling, and Saysa rests a consoling hand on my back.

"Here you are."

Enzo stops in front of the first doorknob that's not crimson but bronze. "There are no locks here, but no one will invade your privacy." He turns the knob a tick, and as it clicks, the bronze darkens to deep crimson. "Now this room is officially occupied." He swings the door open for whoever wants it, and I spy a strange black band around his wrist that almost seems to be digging into his skin.

"Thanks," says Saysa, swooping inside without waiting for Cata.

"See you in the morning," says Cata to the rest of us, exhaling as she shuts the door.

We pass a handful of crimson knobs, until we come across a pair of bronze ones adjacent to each other. "Thanks," I say as Enzo opens the doors for us. Tiago winks at me as he slips into his room, and then I step into mine.

The lights go on. I'm in a small cave where the walls, floor, and ceiling are made of sparkly bands of white, silver, and black agate. There's only enough space for a bed, a dresser, and a bathroom. Even though it's tiny and temporary, it's the first room I've ever had to myself.

I look in the drawers and find neatly folded stacks of fabric—wet suits, indigos, shorts, shirts in various colors. There are no size designations because all Septimus materials mold to the wearer's shape.

I pull out a pair of foam-soft pants that look like the comfy ones Enzo had on, along with underwear and a white tee, and I lay everything out. I also find two strips of cottony fabric that look like socks, which I assume to be bedroom slippers.

Then I perch at the edge of the bed, and when the plushy mattress cradles my weight, I let out a moan of delight. It's so soft, and I'm so tired—but I really need to bathe.

My mind feels both fried and frazzled, like I'm deliriously drained but too amped up to rest. Today has been as long and overwhelming as the day ICE took Ma away and I discovered the academy.

ROMINA GARBER

I strip off every item of clothing, then I step inside the narrow shower. The water is cool and refreshing, and I think of where Ma might be and how she feels about everything Gael has told her. Will she believe I'm a werewolf? Is she disappointed?

Can she love a monster?

I wrap myself in a towel, and as I brush out the knots in my hair, I wonder if Ma is okay with Gael, or if she's feeling alone and scared. Why wouldn't he give me more details? What if he's just telling me what I want to hear so I won't do anything dangerous?

Can I trust him?

I need to talk to Gael again. I have to find out where Ma is, and why he's here with the Cazadores. There must be a way to reach him. Maybe through el Hongo? I'll ask the others tomorrow.

I pull on the clothes I laid out on the bed, and just as I'm wondering how to turn off the lights, I hear a knock on my door.

"Come in."

Tiago steps inside, and a wave of self-consciousness crashes over me as he surveys my wet hair and clean face and bedclothes. "The rooms are soundproof, so we can talk freely," he says, shutting the door. "Can I kiss you?"

I nod, and he closes the distance between us in a blink. His arms circle my waist as we make out, and by the time we pull apart, my lips are numb and our breaths are shallow.

"You okay?" he murmurs into my mouth.

"I guess. I don't know. I just need sleep."

"Rest, then. I'm going to check on the girls, and I'll see you in the morning." He presses his lips to mine for a long moment and turns to go.

When he reaches the door, I say, "Tiago?"

"Solazos."

He marches back and sweeps me in his arms, capturing my

mouth with his. This final kiss saps whatever energy remained, and my knees give out. He carries me onto the bed and pulls the covers up to my shoulders. "Tiago," I murmur again.

He leans down by my face. "Solazos."

"How . . . do I turn the lights off?"

The last thing I hear is his soft chuckle before darkness overtakes me.

I wake up feeling as rested as I do after lunaritis. This must have been my first night of real sleep since El Laberinto. I'm vaguely aware of a noise, or a shaking, that roused me, but as I sit up, everything is calm and quiet.

The room's lights glow on as soon as I set my feet on the agate floor. After using the bathroom, I pull on a pair of indigos and a black shirt, then I step out, eager to see my friends.

A rush of noise rises up to greet me from the courtyard. It sounds like I'm the last one to awaken.

The enchanted sky is bright and diffused, like a sunny day filtered through stringy clouds. I knock on Tiago's door. No answer.

There are no vampiros clogging the view this morning, and I wonder if they're as nocturnal as their namesake. I stick to the inner side of the balcony as I approach the stairs, not wanting anyone in the common area to spot me before I'm ready to be seen. In fact, I'd really like to find a familiar face before coming across any new ones.

Yet when I've climbed down to the ground, that becomes a more daunting prospect.

The air leaves my lungs as I scan the area. There must be a couple hundred Septimus here. Whether standing or sitting, most are talking over mate and facturas, a nervous energy zapping the air, like spectators waiting for a show to begin.

Calabaza gourds zoom through the Coven, and water kettles boil in Encendedoras' hands, while lobizones lug up additional couches and tables from what must be a basement storage space. A star-studded gourd flies to me on a gentle breeze, and when I catch it, I see that the yerba is already brimming with hot water.

The Invocadora with the peachy pink eyes who spoke to me in Spanish yesterday waves from a distance. Then a head of white-tipped black hair snags my attention.

"Morning!"

I accept the elbow Zaybet offers me, and she pulls me in her stride. As I sip the mate, I notice she's wearing the same crushingly tight wristband as Enzo. From up close, it looks rubbery and veiny and—

"After that news report, Septimus from all over have come to meet you!"

I'm glad for the mate's distraction so I don't have to respond. Even though this is what my friends and I wanted—to find supporters, a place to land, a new pack—I'm no Fierro. I'm just trying to survive.

Zaybet steers me to the stairs. "Where are we going?" I ask as we climb up a level, and then I spot Tiago, Saysa, and Cata, along with Laura and Enzo.

"Finished?" asks Cata, holding out her hand for the calabaza gourd. I suck the rest of it down, then her eyes glow with magic as she sends it sailing to a table below.

"Every time one of us recruits a new member," says Zaybet, "we're in charge of introducing them to the Coven. So you know, most of us don't get this level of turnout."

Her metallic gaze flashes as she twists to face the crowd. A sprinkle of rain falls over the space, so light that it evaporates on touching our heads—yet strong enough to get everyone's attention.

"Welcome to the Coven!"

Zaybet waves a hand over the courtyard, and everyone breaks into cheers and applause.

"Given the importance of secrecy, ours has always been and must always remain an oral tradition. Admittance to this manada is by Lunaris's invitation only."

I flash to the Lagoon of the Lost, when Lunaris revealed my father's identity. She also told me I no longer have a home . . . I have *two*.

It's surprisingly not hard to believe she led us here.

"The Coven was originally a brujas-only manada," Zaybet goes on, "but over time, Lunaris extended her invitation to lone wolves. Brujas still outnumber wolves three to one. There are secret spaces all over Kerana like the dungeon where we found you, and they only appear to select Septimus. We've been able to identify forty-nine of these locations, and we patrol them regularly. They separate the *commoners* from the *Coveners*."

Amid renewed cheers, she says, "Welcome to our resistencia."

Once the noise tamps down and quietness spreads, the nervous energy from earlier intensifies. Then Saysa steps forward, like she instinctively knows what to do.

"We're proud to join you. I'm Saysa Rívoli."

"Hi, Saysa!" the crowd chants, including Zaybet, Laura, and Enzo.

She's beaming as she steps back, and panic strikes me as I realize I'm going to have to introduce myself too.

Cata steps up next, face drawn and fingers fidgety at her sides. "I'm Catalina—*Cata*—del Laberinto."

"Hi, Cata!" everyone chants.

My gut churns as Tiago steps forward.

I don't know my name. Not really.

"I'm Tiago Rívoli."

"Hi, Tiago," says most of the room. But some of the wolves, including Enzo, greet him as "Tiago el invencible."

Zaybet frowns at Enzo, but now it's my turn, and I don't know what to say.

Manuela Azul is from my human life, and the name isn't even real because my mom's true identity was *Liliana Rayuela*. The name on my Huella, *Manuela de la Mancha*, is also fabricated. I don't have a home in the Septimus world. No manada to claim.

"Hi." I feel a magical charge, like the nervous energy has reached its pitch. "I'm Manu . . ."

I let my first name linger, intending to fill in the rest, but I don't know how.

"Hi, Manu!" the crowd chants back.

Then Zaybet says, "Manu la lobizona."

I think she added the epithet to equal Enzo's introduction of Tiago, but regardless, the weight of her words settles on the brujas. Magic sweeps through the Coven—the ground shakes, the temperature rises and falls, everything from the couches to the calabaza gourds clatters and trembles, like the place is destabilizing, becoming too big to be contained.

I feel hundreds of eyes on me, and my heart is pounding so hard that the room might actually be pulsing.

"So, that's it?"

The magic zaps out. Tiago and Saysa scowl at Cata, and I hear brujas at the far end of the hall asking what she said.

"What do you mean?" asks Zaybet.

"Don't you want to question us?"

I want to slap her. What is she doing? Saysa seems to be thinking along the same lines because she murmurs, *"Chill."*

"That kind of persecution goes on *out there*," says Zaybet as the wolves' whispers carry the words to the brujas. "In here, you share your story if and when you want to."

Cata crosses her arms like this too-good-to-be-true answer only heightens her suspicions. She reminds me of Pablo. "How do you know you can trust us?"

"That's enough," growls Tiago, staring Cata down the way he did the wolf last night.

"She's allowed to challenge the world all she wants," snaps Zaybet, glaring at Tiago, unfazed by his sense of authority. "The reason we've remained a secret forever is we trust Lunaris," she says to Cata. "If you didn't belong here, you wouldn't have made it to that dungeon. As for whether or not to join us, that's your choice."

Cata looks like she's considering this answer, and I wonder if she's also thinking about what she read in el Hongo. *If the Coven is real, Lunaris must be complicit.*

"Where do your manadas think you are?" asks Cata, landing on a new challenge.

"Visiting a friend, working on a project, going on an adventure, any excuse we can think of. At most, we're able to spend a few days here each moon, so crews are constantly rotating."

Sounds a bit Lunaris-ish.

"Manu," says Zaybet, and my throat parches as the room refocuses on me. "We won't ask you to tell us anything about your past until you're ready. But there's one thing we have to know—"

"Who's Fierro?" shouts someone from the crowd, beating her to it.

I almost forgot that Yamila's way of baiting me was using my father's identity.

"It's a lie," says Saysa, jumping in before I can speak. "Same as they lied about me." She looks at Zaybet, and from the way her friend nods, it's clear Saysa was right about Yamila spreading rumors. "They're coming after Manu because she dares to be different. And she's stopped being afraid. *We all have.*"

There are cheers from the Coveners, and Zaybet is clapping as hard as the others. "We can protect you," she says to me. "We know how to open our own portal to Lunaris, and we have the numbers to do it. You're safe here."

I can hardly process how quickly our situation has shifted. My friends look back at me with the same blank amazement.

"You all are making me sad," says Laura, her sweet cadence cutting through the heaviness. "Respiren. *Everything is going to be fine.*"

So I do as she says. I breathe.

I inhale enough oxygen to illuminate every cell in my body, even the ones that thrive in darkness, so they don't forget how warmth feels. Then I blow out the light.

That's how Perla taught me the breathing exercises when I couldn't sleep the first night Ma and I moved into her apartment. I was eight. I haven't thought of those words in so long, yet now I find myself in a new home, with what could be a new family. If they truly accept me.

The real me.

Not Manu la lobizona.

Manu la ilegal.

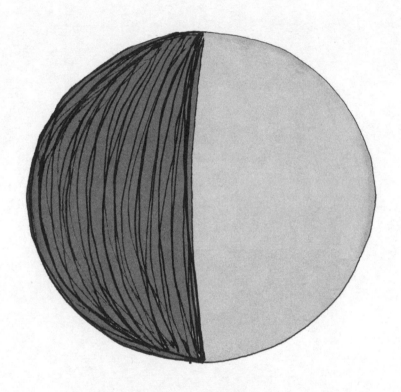

PHASE II

10

The next few days at the Coven are a spectacle of magic and music and parrilladas and infinite introductions.

Just like Zaybet said, Coveners constantly cycle in and out, dropping by as their schedule allows. Only not enough of them seem to be leaving. Each new crew is bigger than the last, and soon we're testing the place's capacity.

The best part about new arrivals is they bring stores of food and supplies. The perishables get delivered to the kitchen, where Encendedoras sear a sampling of the meats and veggies on the spot, and Congeladoras freeze the rest for storage. Once the Encendedoras prepare the trays, Invocadoras fly the food around for a tasting.

During the day, Jardineras climb up to the crawl spaces beneath the Coven's ceiling, where nests of vampiros hibernate while the fake sun shines overhead, and tend to them. Wolves take advantage of the vampiros' retreat to stretch their muscles by leaping up and down the balconies.

As more and more Septimus flood the Coven, our energy thrums through the rock, vibrating within us, seeking an outlet.

"This is Oscar," says Zaybet, introducing me to a lobizón who towers over us in six-inch heels. "She's our only royalty," Zaybet goes on, and at my expression, she clarifies, "Self-anointed."

I blink as Oscar gives me a low bow, and not knowing what else to do, I return the gesture. "I would kiss you," she says, "but I don't want to smudge my lipstick."

Zaybet and I crack matching smirks, and I look to my other side to see that Cata and Tiago are smiling too. My friends have faithfully stuck by my side through an avalanche of these greetings, and the only one who seems to be losing patience is Saysa. She's nearly gnawed off her bottom lip. She looks beyond ready to socialize on her own.

"Your makeup is perfection," I say, admiring the detail that went into Oscar's shadowy eye.

"Thanks, cariño. One day, I'll walk the streets of Kerana with my true face."

I remember the way I felt hiding behind my sunglasses in Miami, how I dreamt of one day stepping out as myself, without worrying about stares or strangers asking me what I am, and I say, "I'll walk beside you."

No sooner are the words out than I feel a hard kiss on my cheek. I couldn't move that fast even without the heels.

"I always identified as a lobizona on the inside," says Oscar softly, her vivid makeup growing heavy on her features. "I just didn't dare say the word out loud . . . until now."

Like all the other Septimus I've met, Oscar doesn't ask about my past. Not a single Covener has made me feel like I owe them any answers.

"This is Paloma," says Zaybet, and I meet a bruja in a shirt that says *Septima ≠ Bruja*.

I offer her my left cheek for a kiss while I rub off Oscar's hot pink lips from my right one. "*Septima* does not equal bruja," I read out loud. "I never heard that term before," I add, tossing Cata back the towel she blew my way, my cheek raw.

"Obvio," says Zaybet, short for *obviously*. "That's why you're so important."

"Regardless of our powers, not all of us identify as *brujas*," Paloma explains.

"I know I don't," I say with a grin, making Tiago and Zaybet chuckle.

As someone who's been raised to keep hidden, the most startling part of these introductions is how easily everyone hands over their secrets to me. Secrets that could harm them beyond the Coven's walls. I wonder if that's because in this manada, what makes you different is what makes you fit in . . . Or maybe this is the only place where Coveners can take pride in who they are.

From what I've seen, they're strong-minded, nonconforming individuals with every variety of worldview. The only thing that seems to unite them is they all seek the freedom to choose their own lifestyle.

Most want to unlink power and gender. The brujas—*Septimas*—want equal representation in government and higher pay for their magic and more priority given to curing the debilitating postpartum depression that plagues every new mother. Yet I wasn't expecting some of the other reasons why Septimus feel ostracized.

Some of them long to be free to see the planet beyond Lunaris's manadas. They don't think it's fair that humans get to run the world, while Septimus stick to just a few settlements. They want to come out of hiding.

It's hard to imagine what that universe would look like: Humans living side by side with witches and werewolves who drink mate every morning and get grouchy if there's not enough dulce de leche.

Yet there are some parts I can predict.

Humans have a hard enough time sharing the planet among themselves, so I don't see them being gracious about sharing land with the Septimus. If people discovered magic is real, and that potions and pills capable of all sorts of enchantments exist, they would want in on that.

Even still, I can't help wondering—if humans and Septimus were to share the same borders, would there be a place for me?

It's our fourth night here, and by now my throat is sore from so much talking. I've never been this social in my life. The last quarter moon glows overhead, and the vampiros are out, putting an end to the lobizones' balcony workouts.

"¡La loba!" calls out a jovial wolf named Ezequiel who's been calling me that since we met a couple of days ago. *The she-wolf.*

I wave back to him and watch longingly as he sits down to dinner, while I'm stuck standing here, with my friends as some kind of royal guard, as Zaybet calls the next Septimus forward to meet me. "This is—"

"I'm done!" Saysa grabs Cata's hand and declares, "We're going to eat."

To my surprise, Cata's fingers don't unlace from Saysa's as the latter leads her through the throng. It's the first time I've seen them show any kind of public display of affection. They join a group of brujas who've been waving Saysa over all night.

"I'm amazed she lasted as long as she did," says Zaybet.

"Me too," adds Tiago, stuffing his hands in his indigo pockets.

Since we're too large a group to eat meals together, we have to rotate. A smoky aroma teases me, and I sneak glances at the plates of entrañas and mollejas and alas de pollo and papas a la provenzal and palmitos con salsa golf. My stomach grumbles.

"Are you kidding me?" roars a lobizón, slamming his plate with a clatter, the food spilling over. "They'd wipe us off the planet, like they've done nearly every species! Have you forgotten our beginnings?"

"We're past that," says another wolf. "We're powerful now."

"You're foolish and dangerous if you really believe that!"

I frown. "What's that about?"

"That's Joaquín, remember him?" asks Zaybet, and I nod, recognizing the wolf who slammed his plate. He wants the Septimus to come out of hiding. "Sergio—the guy with the buzz cut—gets under his skin because he wants us to take over as the planet's apex predators. You'll meet him at some point."

Suddenly I'm not hungry. I'm nauseous.

"Anyway, like I've said three times now, *this is Nuni*."

"Oh—yeah. Hi," I say, kissing the cheek of a young, gray-haired bruja, while stealing glances at the back of Sergio's head to try to glimpse his face.

"As you probably know, Nuni is one of—if not *the*—top potion makers of our times," says Zaybet, and I swing my gaze back to the small girl who's about Saysa's size. There's a heaviness in her caramel-colored eyes that, coupled with her gray hair, makes her seem older than she is.

"It's nice to meet you," I say. It's clear from her skin and features that she can't be more than twenty, but her hair is dry and brittle and her eyes are sunken in—like some parts of her have aged more than others.

"I brought you something." Instead of opening up about herself, she hands me a glass vial. "Invisibility spell. My own recipe."

The irony that I now need magical aids to become invisible isn't lost on me.

Zaybet's eyes are wide on the vial, and Tiago peeks over my shoulder for a closer look.

"That's one of the most powerful Jardineras in the world," says Zaybet as Nuni marches away; I get the sense she isn't big on crowds. "Her potions are among the priciest and top ranked, and they always have her signature aftertaste. A plant no one else has been able to find or replicate."

I wrap my fingers around my new treasure and slip it into my pocket.

"So, you're the first lobizona."

The voice prickles the back of my neck, and I look up at Sergio. A wiry werewolf with burgundy eyes and a buzz cut who would assert the Septimus' dominance over humans—even though Septimus don't make up even one tenth of one percent of the human population.

He's younger than he seemed from the back. Early twenties at most.

"Manu, this is Sergio," says Zaybet.

He starts to lean in for a kiss, but I stay stiff, so he plays it off like he's greeting Zaybet. Then he says to me, "Let's see you transform."

More like *demands*.

"Another time," I say, as I've repeated countless times to other Coveners.

"Why?"

I feel Tiago tensing beside me, so I speak first. "Because I'm not comfortable shifting right now."

"It's our natural form," says Sergio, and from his locked-in stance, it's clear he's not budging. "So what's the problem?"

"The *problem* is I don't do tricks on command."

His burgundy eyes widen like he wasn't expecting this much resistance, and then Enzo appears and says to Sergio, "Come talk to me a moment."

I didn't realize he was keeping such a close watch on things.

"Where do you stand on the issue of Septimus coming out of hiding?" Sergio continues interrogating me.

"I don't like borders," I say, and in my peripheral vision I notice Tiago's chin tilt toward me in surprise. "But I don't like bullies either."

Sergio's smirk freezes on his face.

As I'm being introduced to a bruja, I make sure to keep Sergio and Enzo in my view. The two of them disappear by the stairs, then they pop up on the fifth-floor balcony.

"You must be famished," Zaybet tells me, and I realize I haven't registered the faces of the last few Coveners I've met.

"Yeah, actually."

"Let's eat."

"Why don't you sit down, and I'll fill your plates?" offers Tiago.

"How many bites will that cost me?" I ask, alluding to the time at the academy when he offered me room on his plate for the price of a bite.

Tiago grins, but Zaybet looks confused. I can tell she's torn between accepting his chivalry and asserting her independence, so I answer for both of us. "That would be great, thanks!"

She and I sit at the end of a packed table, and the others look at us. I'm relieved when they don't try to rope us into conversation.

"Don't worry," says Zaybet. "No one expects you to remember their names."

"I'm a bit confused by this place. Is it a safe house or a rebel base?"

"Can't it be both?"

"I'm not sure," I say, considering it. "There are just so many of you with competing agendas that you could never move in one direction."

"You're confusing progress with politics," she says, leaning into the table. "We have no platform because we're not trying to build a new system. We're trying to tear down the existing one."

She reaches for a tray of clean silverware and pulls it closer to us. Then she takes out a handful of knives and begins to fuse them together with ice, like she's making popsicle-stick art. Once she's finished, the Septimus Z symbol is standing upright on the table, the metal gleaming like her eyes.

"To build something, you have to puzzle pieces together. That means knowing where everything goes, and what the design should look like when it's done."

She snaps off the middle knife—the bar between the inverse 7s—and without the support, the top 7 clatters to the table too. All that remains is a solitary, upside-down 7.

"But dismantling something doesn't require a consolidated vision. We just need to prove the current system is flawed. There are too many leftover pieces for this to be the right design."

I think of the spare ace the last time Ma and I played chinchón. Zaybet is telling me there's a spare in every match, but if all of us leftovers band together, we can create our own winning hand.

She sees the enlightenment dawning on my features and says, "We're going to force them to draw a more inclusive picture."

"So you're like a catalyst, a force for change—"

"No, *you* are." Her eyes fill with energy. "Your existence *is* change. You're a wrench in the machine, Manu. That's why you have the power to bring hope to so many—because the system can't ignore you, and that means it can't ignore *us*."

Tiago sets a pair of plates down, like punctuation to Zaybet's declaration. While he goes to fill his own, I scan the room for Saysa and Cata. I spot them on a couch, surrounded by the group of brujas from earlier.

"Not surprised they found Saysa so soon."

I look at Zaybet, who's just shoved five fries into her mouth. I wait for her to chew, then I ask, "What do you mean?"

"She emanates power. You've been here just a few days, but ever since Saysa started tending to the vampiros, they're producing forty percent more oxygen."

"Oh" is all I can say.

"It's a good thing she has all of you. I don't know if it's like this in your manada too, but in Marina, some Jardineras are revered as goddesses because their touch can bring someone back from the brink of death. But there's a cost for so much power. If their emotions destabilize, their magic can turn deadly. It's rare, but some can twist their ability so far, they'll drain a Septimus of their life force."

I blink back images of Nacho and the sales witch in Kukú, both of their faces graying as Saysa sucked their energy. "So, um, who are the Septimas she's talking to?" I ask to change the subject.

"They're part of a *choice to be child-free* movement. They're among the most powerful Coveners, and they're very selective about who qualifies into their clique." Something about Zaybet's tone tells me she didn't make the mark.

By the time I've devoured every last bite of meat and vegetables, I'm so full of food and so drained of energy that I'm not sure I can trust my feet to hold me up. "I think I'm going to sleep," I say as an Invocadora sends our empty plates zooming to the kitchen.

Cata and Saysa are still sitting with those brujas, only now the group has grown. I'd like to go over to say good night, but their couch feels too far away, and I have to reserve my energy for the stairs.

"I'm going too," says Tiago, and as we both stand, Zaybet climbs onto the tabletop.

Lightning flashes in her eyes, and a light mist kisses our heads. The place quiets down as the Septimus take note of her.

"I've been informed we are officially over capacity. So if you don't have a roommate, get one—we're doubling up!"

I'm suddenly aware that Tiago is right next to me.

"We need to bring up more blankets and pillows. Who's helping me?" a wolf calls out. A handful of lobizones—including Enzo—and a few brujas follow the guy to a basement storage space.

Meanwhile, Tiago and I head up the stairs. Neither of us says anything as we walk down the vampiro-laced balcony, and when we reach our adjacent doors, I blurt, "We slept next to each other in Pampita."

"That's right."

"I'm sure we can share a bed."

"'Course." He grips his crimson doorknob and looks at me. "You sure you're sure?"

I nod because the doraditos in my belly won't let me speak. Then he twists it a tick, so it turns bronze.

He goes inside to gather a couple of things before following me to my room. *Our* room.

Okay, that does sound weird.

"I can sleep on a couch downstairs," he says, lingering in the doorway. "I don't mind—"

"Don't be stupid," I say, spinning away so he'll quit reading me, and my eyes land on the bed. It's probably full-size. We're going to be pretty close.

I grab the oversized green tee I've started sleeping in and go into the bathroom to change and wash up. When I come out, the room's lighting is dimmer, and Tiago is in cotton-like shorts and a white tee, sitting on the bed, reading a wrinkled paperback.

I perch beside him and peek at the book. "What's that?"

"The Chocolate War."

"Sounds delicious." My shoulder bumps his arm as I try to get a closer look at the forlorn football player mired in mist on the cover.

"It came out in the 1970s," says Tiago, twisting toward me so our arms are touching and our faces are inches apart. "I found it downstairs. Just finished, if you want to check it out."

His velvety voice makes my skin extra sensitive, and I lock my gaze on the paperback to keep my thoughts from straying. "What's it about?"

"An all-boys high school ruled by a secret society of pranksters. Basically, one kid refuses to do their bidding, and he's bullied by his classmates for trying to change things."

"Why'd he refuse?"

"He read a T. S. Eliot quote." Tiago's arm presses into mine, and I look up into his oceanic eyes. *"Do I dare disturb the universe?"*

I lower my gaze to the shadows that cling to his cheekbones. "Sounds instructive." Then something clicks. "Wait, is this a human book like the ones in your cave, or a remastered edition where the humans have been replaced with Septimus?"

"All the books here are human originals. There's more of them boxed up in the basement than what's out on the shelves, in every language and genre, even religious texts." He presses the paperback into my hands.

While Tiago goes to the bathroom, I climb under the covers and thumb through the book's first few pages. But I set it down the instant he walks out.

Tiago strokes the agate wall with his fingertips, until the dimness fades to darkness. Then he lies beside me.

The space is so tight that I can feel the heat of his body.

I stare at the black ceiling. I'm used to sleeping on my side, but there's barely any room to move. Besides, the adrenaline of lying in bed with Tiago is burning off my drowsiness.

My pulse grows louder in the lengthening silence.

Tiago's fingers fold around mine, his warmth relaxing my breathing. Then I roll onto my side, and he turns to face me too. We're close enough that I inhale his minty breath.

His nose brushes mine, and our mouths are at once drawn together. When I part my lips and our tongues touch, it's like I drank a bouquet of Lunaris flowers and every color is rushing to my head.

I dig my fingers in Tiago's tangle of hair and barely contain a moan when he presses against me. He cradles my neck with his fingers, his other hand sliding under the covers, until it slips beneath the hemline of my oversized tee.

I feel something blossoming inside me, the way I did when Tiago touched me in Lunaris. Like my body is ready to be closer to him.

Even if I'm not.

"Solazos," he murmurs. "We don't have to do anything." His fingers rest on my hipbone. "Just kissing you transports me."

"It's just . . ." I clear the roughness from my voice. "You have so much more experience than I do."

I can't believe I said that.

"This is new to me too," he says, and I frown in protest. Does he think I don't know he's dated all the girls of El Laberinto?

"I've never been in a relationship."

Now he's the one who looks like he wasn't expecting the words that came out of his mouth. Or *word*.

"I'm sorry," he hastens to add. "I shouldn't have said that."

"Oh." Pain cleaves my chest. "No worries."

"What I mean is," he says, pulling me closer, "I haven't asked you." He looks into my eyes, as serious as a proposal, and I think I'm having a stroke.

"Manu . . . would you be my girlfriend?"

The question sounds so innocent after all he's given up to be with me. Looking into his sapphire orbs, I can still hardly believe this isn't Other Manu's life, but mine.

And I say, "Obvio."

11

Tiago and I make out all night long, until we pass out, limbs entangled. I feel like I've been asleep only minutes when the walls start rumbling around me, and from behind my closed eyelids, I sense the room's lights flickering on and off.

It's the Coven's wake-up system. The alarm goes off at three intervals of the morning. This was a short tremor, so it must be the first alarm.

I blink my eyes open to find I'm nestled into the crook of Tiago's shoulder, gazing at his scar. Pablo's ink tattoo doesn't come close to capturing the real thing. The thick, dark gashes stick out, like scales or dragon hide.

My bare chest is pressed against his, and I suddenly remember my shirt coming off too.

"Morning, girlfriend."

Tiago's sleepy mouth meets mine before I can check my breath. "Sleep okay?" he asks, his fingers combing back my mane of hair.

I nod into his chest, too embarrassed to speak because his hand just got stuck in a thicket of my hair.

"Hold on," he says, freeing his other arm. I keep glued to his chest as he detangles the knot, my eyes rolled up to watch him work.

"I know you don't like all the attention," he says, brow knit with concentration, "so we can go down separately."

"Yes, please," I say, eager to avoid gossip. And I'm going to need a while with my hair.

When he's freed himself, Tiago reaches for the sheets and pulls them up to my shoulders. "I'll be quick."

He kisses my forehead and heads to the bathroom. I admire his cut upper body until he disappears.

That's my boyfriend.

The thought is almost as unbelievable as *I'm a lobizona.* And I'm overcome with the urge to gush to Ma about Tiago.

I want to know what she thinks of him—and Saysa and Cata and the Septimus and Gael and the fact that I'm a *werewolf.* I asked Cata about sending Gael a message here in Kerana, and she said it's not safe because it could be intercepted. She thinks that since he used to be one of the Cazadores' best trackers, they must have tasked him with finding me.

She also said that since I'm his blood, we might be able to establish a connection if we plug into el Hongo at the same time.

I hear the shower running. I feel around for my shirt, then I fix the bed, and when I look up, Tiago is in front of me. He's in indigos and a hooded sweater, his hair windswept and dry. He looks like he's headed for a photo shoot.

"That wasn't quick. It was hypersonic."

He flashes that roguish smirk from the night we met, and I know I'm in trouble. "I've been thinking about something. You were raised as a human for so long that whenever you're not in lobizona form, your wolf stays dormant."

He lopes toward me, and my body grows alert. "I feel it's my duty to help you find your inner wolf . . . even if it's difficult for you."

"Why difficult?" I ask, twisting my neck to follow him as he walks around me.

His mouth brushes my ear. "You have to know when to quit thinking and let your body lead."

I lean back, until I feel him against me, and my breathing shallows. "Don't think," he murmurs, and I shut my eyes, waiting for his hands to touch me. "Just *know*. What do you hear?" *Tiago's song of a voice.* "What do you smell?" *Tiago's intoxicating scent.* "What do you feel?" *Tiago's hard body against mine.*

A shiver runs through me, and I spin around to reach for him—but he's already out the door.

I wait until the second alarm to head down, and as I walk toward the stairs, something about this morning starts to feel different.

It's quiet, and there are no lobizones leaping from balcony to balcony.

When I get to the ground floor, it looks like the place emptied out overnight. All I see are a couple dozen Septimus, most of them meditating on mats.

The bruja with the peachy eyes brings me the star-studded mate, like she has every morning.

"Gracias, Rocío," I say, accepting the calabaza gourd. We were introduced a few nights ago, and she told me she's infertile. Apparently, it's a rare condition among Septimus, and many manadas are superstitious about it, so she's ostracized back home. She tries to spend as much time at the Coven as she can.

I'm infuriated for her, but I'm glad she has this place.

I spot my friends at one end of a long, empty table, and as I walk over, I think of what Tiago said. And instead of listening with my human ears, I hone my hearing until I feel a veil of silence extend to the sounds nearest me, attuning me to farther frequencies.

"Just let *me* tell her—"

"Shhh."

Saysa's voice cuts out, and they don't say another word until I'm at the table.

Enzo and Laura slide apart, patting the space between them on the bench. I sit down across from Zaybet, who's yet to take her eyes off me.

"Morning, Manu."

"Hi."

Tiago sits to her right, and from his alarmed expression, he looks blindsided. On Zaybet's other side, Cata's wrapped in her usual air of disapproval, but Saysa's lime-green eyes are so bright that she looks like the girl I first met. I'd almost forgotten she had dimples.

At the center of the table are a stack of plates and a brown pouch that's tied off with a rope. A beaming Saysa slides me a clean plate, and Enzo passes me the basket of facturas. I get the feeling no one's going to speak until I've finished my mate, so I drain it quickly.

Today's silence is such a stark contrast to the past few days that I feel like the world is on mute. As I suck on the metal bombilla, I think about how Perla taught me that energy can't be created or destroyed. There's no way all that excitement just disappeared. The buzz is still here, but different. Focused.

Like it's been channeled into something.

"We've been concerned about your legal predicament," says

Zaybet once I set down the drained calabaza gourd. Cata blows it away. "The past few days, we consulted with all the Coveners who came through, and we agree the best way to protect you is with a preemptive strike. If we wait in fear of the Cazadores, we're wasting time we could be using to win over the public."

"Widespread support will be your weapon," says Saysa, leaning into the table, like a match catching flame. "We need to make you too much trouble to have as an enemy." While she's entitled to her opinions, I wish she would wait to find out how I feel before endorsing whatever this plan is.

The facturas sit untouched on my plate. "And how do we do that?"

"By doing what Fierro did best," says Zaybet, and my heart skips a beat at the name. *"Public demonstrations."*

"We have to take a stand so the tribunal can't brush you under the rug," insists Saysa. "And *fast.*"

I know she's not just talking about my being a lobizona anymore. She means my other, heavier secret.

"What do you mean by *public demonstrations*?" asks Tiago.

"All of us have heard you're a lobizona, but few have actually seen you in your transformed state," says Zaybet, answering me as if I'd asked the question. "So what if we visit one of the busiest places in Kerana—el Centro Comercial in el Bosque Blanco—and you transform in front of a large crowd? We'll have Coveners planted among the commoners, so we can control things."

"Sounds dangerous," says Tiago.

"Sounds like Manu's choice." Laura's voice verges on unpleasant.

While I'm moved to know they've been strategizing ways to protect me, I can't help feeling I've just become a pawn in someone else's game again.

"So I visit this manada, transform in front of a crowd, then I run to safety?"

"It's not as simple as you make it sound," says Zaybet, her expression more serious than I've seen it. "This is about sending a message that you're up to meeting the Cazadores' challenge. That you're not ashamed of your identity because you've done nothing wrong. You're showing those Septimus who think the status quo is their only choice that they have another."

When she puts it like that, it's hard to turn her down. If I'm going to be a Septimus, I need to learn how to start thinking as an *us*. I've been taken in by the Coven, and now I have to play my part.

A dark liquid leaks through the bottom of the brown sack, onto the table. It looks like blood.

"Of course, we'll have to find a way to magnify your identity," says Zaybet, steepling her hands together. "A rallying cry for your followers. Something to make this moment bigger, so it lingers."

"She could carve Fierro's *F*," suggests Enzo.

"Manu needs her *own* symbol."

"I have one," I hear myself say, and they all turn to me. "An *M* that's two sevens that don't meet. I carved it into Lunaris before taking the portal to Kerana."

There's silence at the table again, only this time it's more of the speechless variety. Tiago's gaze is bright with awe, and I remember him telling me Lunaris hadn't invited a Septimus to do that in a while.

If the way Tiago's looking at me makes my stomach flutter, Zaybet's stare is a cold shower. I feel like she's Morpheus from *The Matrix,* and she's convinced I'm the One.

"When you transform, claw your *M* into the wall." Her metallic eyes glint with whatever vision she's seeing. "That's how you go from maverick to movement."

Her words bring to mind everything Saysa said to me before the Septibol championship. Of course she would support this plan. It's everything she believes in. And I already know Tiago will back me on whatever I choose. "What do *you* think?" I ask Cata.

"I think it's risky and reckless," she says with a sigh. "And it's not just a bad option, it's your *only* option. I can't come up with anything better."

Apparently, Tiago and I can't either.

"We have a couple of days, so we'll set up a course here and do some practice runs," says Laura, her dulcet tone lightening the mood. "As soon as those guys come back from el Hongo, we'll start."

I look at the wolves and witches she's pointing to and ask, "Aren't they meditating?"

"No," says Zaybet. "They're plugged into el Hongo."

"How?" asks Tiago. Judging by Cata and Saysa's nonplussed reactions, I assume they've already investigated this.

"We can't open an access point into the web from el Mar Oscuro," explains Enzo. "So we have to ingest it."

It sounds like he just said they eat mushrooms.

"Just shavings," says Laura, waving her hand like it's nothing. "It's illegal to eat them in Kerana because the network can overwhelm our mind, since we're tethered to the soil there. But that can't happen here, so it's less dangerous."

"I want to try it," I say, thinking of the possibility of connecting with Gael.

"Sure," says Zaybet as she reaches for the brown pouch. "One last thing."

She lifts the sack, and it drips blood onto the table.

"You may have noticed that everyone at the Coven has one

of these." She holds up her wrist, showing off the black band. "They're called horarios. It's a living creature that grows here, in el Mar Oscuro, just like the vampiros. It's part plant, part parasite. It feeds off our blood and forms a symbiotic attachment with its host."

I try not to let my revulsion show, but Cata doesn't bother. "*Gross,*" she says. Saysa rolls her eyes.

"The horario only sucks a tiny bit of blood, so it doesn't hurt," explains Zaybet. "But we can use it to communicate with one another and transmit our locations—or warn one another of danger. It's also the only way to locate the Coven. We'd like to offer you each your own, if you want it."

Now Cata looks at the horario like it's a bracelet cut of the finest diamonds. I'm still less than eager to attach a parasite to my body, but I recognize a lifeline when I see one.

Zaybet hands the bag to Saysa first.

We all watch as Saysa pulls out a wriggling, leathery band that looks like a flat shoelace, then gently lays it on her wrist. The horario starts crawling up her arm, like a worm, and Cata leans away from her. Then the plant-parasite returns to Saysa's wrist, where it loops in a circle and tightens.

"Does it hurt?" asks Cata.

Saysa shakes her head slightly, like she's attuned to a different conversation. Her eyes have a soft glow, and she seems to be bonding with the horario because the band starts to lighten from black to deep brown, matching the exact shade of her skin.

"It will camouflage whenever you're not in el Mar Oscuro," says Zaybet, "so it will only surface here."

I go last.

The horario feels somewhat thin and rubbery. It wriggles between my fingers, and I hold my breath as I lay it on my arm. Unlike the others—whose horarios crawled all over before settling down—mine goes straight to my wrist and clamps down. Like it's been waiting its whole life to bond.

I feel a tightening of my skin, and a slight sting as it sucks my blood, but that's nothing to the sudden rush of breath in my lungs. As though the horario just released oxygen right into my veins. I don't sense a second consciousness or anything like that—but I feel connected to something larger.

Maybe I'm the one who's been waiting to bond.

"This is the *only* way to locate the Coven," emphasizes Laura. "Without it, you couldn't hope to return on your own."

Tiago's horario settles into a brown a few shades deeper than mine, and Cata's pales to match her lighter complexion. Then they turn into black bands again, since we're all in the safety of el Mar Oscuro.

"The horario stays with us forever?" asks Saysa, sounding delighted.

"Unless you're exiled from the Coven. Doesn't happen often, but when it does, it's always a heavy sentence," says Zaybet somberly.

"Why?" I ask.

Zaybet and Laura don't answer immediately, so Enzo steps in. "Once the horario bonds, it can't live without you," he says in his hoarse voice. "If removed, your horario dies."

It's not until everyone's gone to bed that the four of us finally get a chance to talk alone. We meet in Cata and Saysa's room.

I spent all day shifting back and forth, and then we did drills climbing balconies. Zaybet says that for the demonstration to be impactful, the footage must be both dramatic and cinematic. I'm going to be transforming at a high peak, over a crowd, which means I need to get in shape fast.

Cata and Saysa are sitting up in bed, backs propped on pillows. Cata's hair is twisted into a messy bun, and she's wearing reading glasses while perusing a secure Coven text. She takes them off and sets the book atop the pile beside her. "You're *sure* the rooms are soundproof?" she asks Tiago, as I collapse from exhaustion at the end of the mattress.

"For the millionth time, *yes*."

Saysa is folding a collection of shirts, and I spy the pink *Septima ≠ Bruja* tee in her stack. When I look at Cata again, she's staring at me like she's awaiting confirmation. "I haven't heard anything," I say, scanning the rest of the room.

"Will you relax now?" asks Saysa. "Because you're dangerously close to becoming Pablo."

"Pablo," says Tiago with a dreamy sigh. "I miss that paranoid lobizón."

We've only been here a handful of days, and yet Cata and Saysa have already made this space their own. There are candles and coffee mugs on the dresser, books on both nightstands, and notes of lavender-scented products in the air. It never occurred to me to go through the Coven's supplies in search of comforts like candles or moisturizer or books.

It was the same at El Laberinto. The whole month I lived there, I didn't unpack my duffel bag.

"Yamila has just one move left," I say to escape my mind's introspection. "Exposing me as a hybrid. Which is why I need to come clean to the Coven."

"*No*."

"No way."

Cata and Tiago's reactions are instant. I look to Saysa for support, but she's staring at me just as gravely. "I don't think we should do anything to threaten the momentum you're already generating."

"But Yamila is going to out me anyway—"

"Maybe," says Cata. "But she's also desperate to arrest the first hybrid, and if others find out about you, all she'll ever be is the Cazadora who let you get away. She *needs* you to stay secret as much as you do."

"Even if you're right, the truth will still come out!" I turn away from Cata because she's missing the point, and I look to Saysa instead. "When it does, what will the Coven do?"

She finishes folding a shirt before saying, "You're part of the pack. They'll have your back."

Was she hesitating? Am I imagining it?

"What if they didn't have to know?"

I stare hard at Cata. "What are you talking about?"

"If Yamila makes the accusation, you could deny it."

"She knows who my parents are—"

"Can she produce your mom? Or Fierro? Where's her *evidence*?"

"She's not the only one who knows the truth. There's Jazmín—"

Cata's features pull together, like the air has soured. "My mom won't tell anyone because she can't risk going down for keeping Fierro's secret all this time. And our teammates won't betray you. No one else knows."

Tiago comes over to the bed and stands behind me, gripping my shoulders. "What happens when the tribunal asks to see Manu's Huella? One call to La Mancha, and they'll know her paperwork is forged. The Cazadores will say if she's lying about her past, she could be lying about her legal status too."

His point is so obvious that I'm annoyed with Cata for not anticipating it. Only she doesn't look discouraged. "Olvido."

I frown. *"Forget?"*

Saysa stares at Cata in awe, and Tiago doesn't say anything, so Cata explains. "It's a forbidden plant that's among the most dangerous in Lunaris. The leaves can be milked to make a forgetting spell, and anyone who drinks it loses their memories. It's only administered in extreme circumstances because the effects are irreversible. We can say you were drugged with it, so you don't remember your past."

Tiago's fingers slip off my arms, and he sits beside me. Since we're still quiet, Cata presses her advantage. "Think about it. The first lobizona appears, with no memory and a forged Huella, and nobody reports having seen her before, not in the Septimus or human worlds. What does that sound like?"

"Like I've been held hostage."

"And like someone is covering their tracks," she finishes. "We create a bad guy to take all the blame, and you become an innocent victim whose youth was stolen and whose existence was withheld from the authorities."

"It's a pretty wild tale," says Tiago.

"It's going to have to be if we want to beat the truth," says Cata, looking to me. "That's why the Coven's demonstrations are important. If the public likes you, they'll want to believe you. Zaybet is right—the court of public opinion is just as important as the legal one."

It sounds like a huge gamble, but if Cata is reaching this far to avoid telling the truth, then coming clean is not an option.

"What do *you* think?" I ask Saysa. After all, she was the one who urged me to play in the Septibol match. She supplied Septis to humans. She's been a revolutionary long before the rest of us signed up. If any of us knows what it is to place cause above caution, it's Saysa.

"In the words of the wisest witch I know," she says, taking Cata's hand, "*it's not just a bad option, it's your only option.*"

And even though I smile along with the others, something about her answer feels like confirmation.

Saysa hesitated.

12

Two days later, my friends and I are boarding *La Espiral* with Zaybet, Laura, and Enzo.

Cata and Saysa sit back in reclining chairs, but I hang up front by the helm with Tiago, fascinated by the view. As we soar through el Mar Oscuro, I imagine we're traveling along the bolded black borders that outline countries in maps.

We pass a bouncing pink ball, a shower of spinning starfish, a flock of flapping flower petals, a giant worm eating itself, a school of tiny crescent moons—until blackness bleeds from the atmosphere, and we're sailing through a blue sea riddled with chunks of ice.

La Espiral surfaces in an inlet that's nearly frozen over. Whorls of mist curl along the water, and Zaybet's eyes flare as she ices a solid pathway to the shore. Laura stays with the ship while the rest of us enter the white woods on the horizon. Clearly, el Bosque Blanco gets its name from all the snow blanketing it.

"See you soon," says Zaybet, and I hug her and the others before we part. Tiago is the only one who stays with me. Since he and I are too recognizable, we're going to hide in the forest until it's time.

The others are on their way to el Centro Comercial to make sure everyone else is in place, then our horarios will let us know when to move.

I feel like I did when I jumped into Leather Jacket's truck. Once more, I've hitched a ride without knowing the destination.

"We can turn back." Tiago's sapphire eyes are wintry worlds. "Just say the word."

An icy white powder begins to fall from the sky, catching on his dark hair and lashes. I open my hand to cup the flakes. "I've never seen snow before."

I don't know why I say it, since it sounds so stupid in light of where I'm standing. I'd never seen lobizones and brujas and magic before either. So why is the sight of something as normal as snow this moving?

I turn to watch it fall over the inlet. I always expected snow would look like white rain, but that's not right. The flight pattern is different. Rain is more uniform and falls in one direction, but the snow swirls, like it's dancing. Even though it's daytime, it feels like stardust sprinkling over us, and as I breathe in the cool air, my chest fills with excitement, and I spin to look at Tiago—

Something hard and freezing smashes into my face.

I wipe my eyes, and I see Tiago by the tree line, palming a second ball.

"Don't even—"

He lobs it so suddenly that I dodge at the last instant. When he sees me digging furiously into the ice, Tiago vanishes into the woods.

I pack the ball as tightly as I can make it, a missile strong enough to leave an impact on even his hard head. My hands are numb as I rush into the forest to begin my hunt.

I scan the footprints in the snow, but Tiago anticipated my tactic because he's left prints going in every direction. He must have doubled back a few times. Remembering what he said to me about being too human, I close my eyes and try tapping into my lobizona senses.

I feel my ears stiffening as I hone in on the whistling of wind, the rustling of feathers, the faint footfalls of a werewolf. I listen to Tiago's movements until I can pick up his location, then I open my eyes and set off in pursuit.

My scope of vision is wider than usual, and after a moment, I catch Tiago's tantalizing scent. This time when I run, I'm not moving as a human.

My feet are barely grazing the ground. The woods are a blur as my muscles shift into a new gear, my limbs leaning on instinct. I'm detecting bushes and branches faster than I can even consciously process them. And as I pick up more speed, I realize I've lost his scent.

Only I'm not sure how to slow down.

I don't even know that I can.

What if I run into someone, or I arrive at the plaza, or—

There's a cracking sound, and I cry out as pain shoots up my arm from knocking my elbow into a tree.

"Manu!"

Tiago's at my side in a flash to steady me, like he's been trailing me this whole time. "Are you okay?"

"Yeah," I grunt, hinging my tender elbow.

"Does it hurt?"

I bend it and wince. "A little."

"I'm sorry for messing with you, it was stupid—"

Swinging my hidden hand from behind my back, I smash my snowball into his face.

Tiago barks out a laugh, and a flock of birds soars into the air from the surrounding branches. He dries his face on the sleeve of his sweater, but the front of his hair is soaked. He rakes back the wet strands, and his heady musk wraps around me as he reaches out and pulls me closer.

"I really like you, Solazos."

Warmth spreads through me, and I whisper, "I really like you too."

"But I really, *really* like you."

I frown. "You think you like me more than I like you?"

"No, what I mean is—"

There's a tightness in my wrist where my horario is, like a friend getting my attention. Since Tiago falls silent, he must feel it too.

It's time.

An energy like what I felt when Tiago and I outran the lunarcán pumps through my veins. Blue flames spark to life in his eyes, and they glow with the signs of the transformation.

I feel my vision brighten as the shift takes hold.

Pain scorches my insides, my mouth forming a soundless scream as every inch of my body—from my skin to my bones—cracks and curves and grows. My skin tingles as my hair thickens and lengthens, and my ears sharpen and elongate. When it's over, I gasp to catch my breath.

You still have a choice, Tiago sings into my mind, and I look at the hairy, muscular beast before me as I consider my choices.

I'm about to do the opposite of what I was raised to do—draw attention to myself. Once I claim the label *lobizona,* I won't be invisible anymore. I might never be safe again.

But look at what staying safe and invisible did for Gael. It meant giving up Ma and Fierro and the personal peace he needed to build a life. He never recovered. And that's what it would have been like for me, had I stayed with Perla and Luisita when Saysa gave me the chance. I'd be alive, but not awake.

And I've already slept through enough days.

I want to do this.

We follow the scent of fried finger foods, the snow muffling our steps as the trees thin out. El Centro Comercial flickers into view, a seven-story shopping center that towers over an outdoor courtyard marketplace. The plaza is packed with Septimus, but my eyes are immediately drawn to the massive stone sculpture that sits atop the mall.

It's called *Las cuatro brujas,* and it's like a Mount Rushmore of witches. The four faces are carved from brown sandstone, and their eyes are gemstones, every iris a different hue. The Encendedora's eyes are black opal and ruby. The Invocadora has amethyst and rose quartz. The Jardinera has tigereye and emerald. The Congeladora's eyes are silver and blue sapphire. Snow blankets their heads, making them look white-haired.

I scour the throng of Septimus crowding the plaza until I spot Cata and Saysa by a busy empanada stand manned by a harried Encendedora who uses one hand to accept semillas and the other to heat empanadas. I keep scanning, and I see Zaybet at a tent advertising skincare tonics.

Ready? asks Tiago.

Almost. I shed my coat and hand it to him.

He chuckles when he takes in my outfit. *You look perfect.*

I borrowed Saysa's *Septima ≠ Bruja* shirt.

Okay, I say, excitement fraying the edges of my fear. *Let's go.*

We break into a sprint through the marketplace. No one else is in werewolf form, so Septimus stare as we fly past.

It isn't long before they begin to point and shout, recognizing us.

We race around the side of the shopping center, to where the maintenance stairs are supposed to be—metal bars bolted along the stone. Tiago boosts me up to give me a quick start. I shuffle my hands and feet the way we practiced at the Coven, climbing as quickly as I can, not daring to look down.

Heart pounding in my head, my foot slips on an icy rung, and I gasp. *Easy,* says Tiago in my head. *Don't rush.*

I pull myself up when I reach the roof, and then I finally look down. I've never been this far off the ground.

More and more Septimus look up, and the large waterscreens—*pantaguas*—that were airing advertisements are now broadcasting live footage of me as a lobizona in my pink shirt that says *Septima ≠ Bruja.*

I turn around and face the artwork. It's so large that it's hard to make sense of from this close. I look up at the brilliant gemstones, until I'm standing between the Invocadora and Jardinera—pink quartz and tigereye—then I raise a clawed hand.

My finger tenses as I press my nail into the rock, and I carve my *M* onto the monument.

When I'm finished, I look at the screen, and I see not four girls, but five—each of us representing a different power. My presence breaks the paradigm.

Zaybet was right.

The symbolism matters.

"¡Manu la lobizona!"

"¡Manu la lobizona!"

"¡Manu la lobizona!"

The Coveners start the chant, and just as Zaybet instructed, I wait for other Septimus to join in. The call grows louder and louder, and when it hits a crescendo, my eyes begin to glow like suns.

There's a pull in my bones, and my body is afire as my skeleton shrinks, organs shifting, skin tightening, until I'm human-sized again. Zaybet said this was equally important: Let them see me transform before their eyes, so they'll know it's real and not a magic trick.

The whole crowd seems paralyzed, even the Coveners, as they watch a girl shift for the first time. I scan their faces, and I see lots of kids here with their parents. This is a family outing for most Septimus.

When they start pointing at the sky, I look up and spot the hot-air balloons zooming over. I also notice Cazadores crawling into the crowd. Before they get any closer, I jump off the ledge of the building.

There are screams, but just as planned, seven Invocadoras led by Cata spell the air around me to slow my fall. Tiago doesn't flinch when I land in his waiting arms. Then we run for our lives.

Zaybet and six other Congeladoras are stationed by the closest pantaguas, and as their eyes begin to ripple like liquid, the air over our heads grows thick with vapor, obscuring us from the view of the cameras—and the descending hot-air balloons.

The tree line is within reach, but Cazadores are going to intersect us. The invisibility potion is in my pocket, only as a final option. Zaybet told me it comes from a plant that's very hard to find and distill, and takes many moons to brew, so we can't easily get more.

The ground quakes beneath our feet, and I see Saysa and six Jardineras by the tree line, their eyes aglow. The crowd jostles together, slowing down the Cazadores, and Tiago and I try to keep our balance as we race ahead.

Send Laura our location, I tell my horario as we weave through the woods. I have no idea if it worked until I feel a tightness in my wrist, like my message was received.

Tiago tugs me toward a frozen river. "A shortcut—"

"It might not hold—"

We've only taken a few steps when the ice starts to crack, and Tiago and I scramble back to shore. Just then, seven Cazadores spill out from the trees.

Six hulking werewolves and one Jardinera.

"Stand still, or else," she says, holding a white-bark bow in her hands. Her arrows look like they're filled with liquid. She's going to inject us with something.

Tiago takes a step back, pulling me with him, and I hear the creaking of the ice beneath our feet.

"I'm only going to put you to sleep," says the Jardinera, nocking an arrow and raising the bow to her shoulder. "Or would you rather freeze to death?"

I gasp as the fissure lines expand, and Tiago says, "I'd rather have friends."

The arrow flies just as the ground breaks beneath us—

And we sink to our icy deaths.

13

My lungs seize up, and everything goes dark. This time there's no wet suit to blow air up my nose, or to protect me from the chill. I feel like I'm being stabbed with hundreds of icy blades all over my body. Tiago pulls on my hand, and I spin around.

La Espiral is floating behind us.

Once we're inside, I'm too frozen to speak. Our clothing is dry, the fabric waterproof, but the bite on my hair, face, and hands is enough to make me worry about hypothermia.

I blame Miami winters for making me this weak.

"At least one of you had the good sense to send your location," says Saysa, shaking her head at her brother as she pulls him in for a relieved hug.

I frown. Tiago didn't check in on his horario? Does he not realize how? I try to meet his gaze, but he's embracing Cata now, so I can't see him.

"Thanks for standing on ice," says Zaybet as she hugs me. "You made it easy for me to save the day."

"That was all Tiago," I say into her black strands. "He had faith you'd come. Thanks for saving us."

"Of course. We're a pack."

I think of Saysa's hesitation again, and I wonder if Zaybet and the others would really take it so hard to discover I'm a hybrid. Then I picture Sergio, and I wonder what someone like him would make of my being half human.

We step out of the tongue-like passage into the shell-ship's core, where Laura is at the helm and Enzo is scrutinizing the view. As soon as she sees us, she pulls her palms off the charred handprints. "You must be freezing!"

She rushes over, her black opal eyes still aglow.

"That was masterful!" Enzo calls out to me in his rasp, and I try to speak but my teeth are chattering.

The instant Laura grips Tiago and me by the arm, I feel the sun in every pore of my body, like I'm lying on El Retiro's rooftop baking in the Miami heat. It feels so good that I close my eyes with glee, and when I open them, Tiago and I are dry.

"You were perfect!" says Zaybet, her voice exuberant. "The Coven is going to be packed tonight. Everyone will want to be part of this! You're going to be all over the news for—*forever*!"

"I wish I could have been there!" says Laura, returning to the helm.

"Nice shirt," says Saysa, grinning at me. She and Cata are holding hands, their faces shiny and clothing disheveled. They look happy and exhausted, and it strikes me how much good the Coven has done their relationship.

"It was more amazing than I could have imagined," says a breathless and pink-cheeked Cata.

"You're going to be an *icon*," adds Saysa.

"No one at that plaza will ever forget this day," declares a zealous Zaybet. "I bet this is how it felt to be at a Fierro rally."

Their words warm me as effectively as Laura's magic.

Tiago presses a kiss to my cheek and whispers, "Sos una maravilla." *You're a wonder.*

But when he pulls me into a hug, I can't help feeling there's something in his expression he doesn't want me to read.

When we get to the Coven, there are Coveners I haven't met before, and crews who left days ago return to be part of the celebration. Everyone congratulates each other, like we just won a battle.

But all we did was declare war.

The largest pantaguas plays back footage of me on the sculpture from every angle. It's an out-of-body experience because I don't associate myself with the revolutionary girl on the screen. I feel like a spectator, and I can't deny the image's allure: five Brown brujas defying the traditional Septima depiction of power.

Late into the night, Tiago and I are lying on a couch, watching the news beneath the waning crescent moon. There are Septimus passed out all around us, and Tiago's eyes are so heavy that I can't tell if he's up—but I keep switching from channel to channel, too amped to sleep.

I'm watching a medium-sized screen that's across from the couch, and I keep the volume low. Tomorrow I'll visit el Hongo to see if I can find a way to reach Gael.

"La respuesta es la obra nueva de Esteban Escolar—"

"El tiempo está tranquilo, pero mañana se viene una tormenta—"

"Sin saber que me engañabas con esa bruja—"

Everything from the gameshow to the weather update to the telenovela is in Spanish. Yet not the neutral Spanish I'm used to hearing on Miami television, but rather a range of Argentinian accents. Being here is the first time I'm attuned to some of its nuances, and I wonder if it's spoken differently in every manada.

I stop changing channels when I recognize one of the faces at a roundtable discussion.

"If a lobizona exists, what does that say about the link between power and gender?" asks a guy with bushy white hair. "Should we even be using the terms brujas and lobizones anymore, or is it now more appropriate to say Septimas and Septimos?"

"I think we should use sex distinctions. Male or female," says a Septimo in a bow tie.

The Jardinera I recognized leans into the table. I met her here a few nights ago.

"We're only addressing the limitations of language now that we're faced with a biological paradox, but the issue is much bigger than this." Her name is Graciela. "Until now, our system has assumed female sex assignment equals Septima which equals bruja—and so the terms have been used interchangeably in our governance. Laws must be rewritten. Our entire binary way of thinking must be overhauled—"

"Seems like a lot of work for what's ultimately a bad mutation," says a wolf with long sideburns and a low drawl.

He pauses, and from the way they wait for him to continue, I gather he holds most of the power at the table.

"She's a deformity. An anomaly. Possibly a danger to us all."

My pulse flutters in my throat like a bird.

"I think that conclusion is grossly premature," says Bow Tie.

"And extreme," agrees Graciela.

"She's an enchantress, like la ladrona, and it's her intention to manipulate you," says Sideburns, "through sympathy, science, or simple curiosity. But we cannot waver from what is right."

Ladrona. That's the storybook character Saysa mentioned. I need to look it up in el Hongo.

"Little girls grow into brujas, and little boys grow into lobizones," Sideburns goes on. "We don't need someone setting the wrong example or getting our children confused. We must cut her from our genetic pool before she taints it."

If this is their reaction to discovering a lobizona, they're never going to accept a hybrid.

My heart is hammering too loud in my head, and it's not because of what he's saying. It's because the others have stopped contradicting him.

"Today's stunt only proves my point that she is a threat. If she would have quietly come forth and asked for help, perhaps she could have been saved. But mark my words—she's a demonio from Lunaris come to stir up divisions."

"This not the Septimus way."

Graciela rises from her seat at the table. After a moment, Bow Tie joins her.

"We believe in the sanctity of nature as the source of our magic and power," says Graciela. "If Lunaris saw fit to give a Septima the soul of a wolf, then we must accept her as she is."

Sideburns looks at her almost pityingly. "I see that she's already infected you. If you were thinking clearly, you would agree with me. You are a Jardinera, after all."

"What does that mean?"

"You should know that to keep a garden healthy, one must snip a few weeds."

The next morning, Rocío lingers after handing me the star-studded calabaza gourd, her peachy eyes wider than usual. "Thank you," I say as I accept the drink.

I think she's going to say something, but then she shuffles off, like she's changed her mind. So I say, "Hey, Rocío?"

She turns to me.

"I was hoping to visit el Hongo later."

Her eyes light up with her wind magic, and a small vial comes zooming at her so fast that it bounces off her hand and falls to the ground. I reach out and catch it before the glass shatters.

Her mouth is as round as her eyes. "Gracias," I say with a wink, pocketing the mushroom shavings for later.

I meet the others for another breakfast strategy meeting, only this time there are new faces crowded around the table. One particular pair of brothers does most of the talking.

"Our next demonstración should be explosive," says the one with all the tattoos.

"Not *literally*," qualifies his long-limbed brother. "He just means something as over-the-top as he's being."

"You need to do more than just *look* the part."

"Prove you have more than just the power of a wolf. Show us your *heart*."

"Be loud and provocative, but keep it playful," says the one with all the ink. "*Never* be a threat."

"He means go ahead and break the law, but without *actually* breaking it."

These inscrutably synced brothers go by their nicknames, which makes them sound like a musical duo—Tinta y Fideo. Tinta is younger, and the nickname is because his arms and neck are covered in ink. Fideo just really looks like a long spaghetti noodle.

According to Zaybet, they're sought-after strategists, famous for their 100 percent success rate getting politicians elected. Secretly, they're also Coveners.

"That's pretty much what we did with our first demonstration," Laura points out.

"But let's avoid vandalism this time," says Tinta, looking at Zaybet. "I'm guessing that was your contribution."

Her arms are already crossed. She's been on the defensive since we sat down. "We're making sure the artwork stays relevant. You just don't understand how art works."

Tinta looks like he's battling a smile, and the wolf inked on his neck tightens. "Apparently I don't understand how a great many things work. But I still fail to see how vandalizing one of our greatest and most ancient sculptures—"

"Again, *not vandalizing*. We were making the point that our attachment to the past shouldn't come at the cost of our future. And anyway, that artwork isn't about you. It's about Septimas, and we wanted it to reflect reality—"

"What would you know about reality?"

"We shouldn't wait too long, that way we won't lose momentum," jumps in Fideo, cutting off the squabbling between his brother and Zaybet. "Maybe we could try something from Fierro's playbook?"

"Manu will blaze her own trail," says Zaybet, still staring at Tinta.

"Since you brujas have it covered," he growls back, "you don't need anything from us wolves."

Zaybet uncrosses her arms. "I honestly couldn't have put it better myself."

I tune them out as I think about what it would take to prove I'm a wolf. I've already transformed. I could howl, but I have a feeling that's not what they're after. Fideo wants *heart*.

I don't want to have to talk about myself, or share anything personal, so I need to find another way. What does the average lo-bizón like? Running, roughhousing, hunting, exploring, playing—

"Septibol," I say, the idea striking me like a lightning bolt.

I've no idea if anyone was speaking before I opened my mouth, but at my utterance, the table is silent.

"Manu is a great arquera," says Saysa, her eyes lighting up. "Like, *Tiago-level* good."

Everyone looks impressed by this bit of info, and I stare at Saysa in surprise. I didn't realize she felt that way. She's probably just saying it because she's excited about another demonstration.

But instead of tamping down Saysa's praise, Cata nods like she agrees. "Best goalie I've played with."

A pride like I've never felt before fills my chest, and I'm both surprised and embarrassed by my reaction to their praise. It shouldn't matter, and I shouldn't need the validation, and yet I can't deny it feels good to be admired for something I have some semblance of control over.

"That's *perfect*," says Fideo, his excited expression the twin of his brother's. He looks at Tiago. "If you play too, it would raise Manu's credibility."

"Of course," says Tiago, and from the musicality in his voice, I can tell he likes this plan.

"We'll need access to a stadium," says Fideo, his long limbs leaning in. "And players."

"Leave it to me," says Tiago, sounding every bit like our team captain. "I know what to do."

My mind rockets away from my body.

As soon as I sit down on the yoga mat and chew some mushroom shavings, *everything* melts away. I'm not conscious of physical sensations. It's like all of existence has receded into my brain, and I've become el Aleph from Borges's story.

Like I'm plugged into something infinite, a universal computer that allows me to think beyond my usual reach.

Who is Manu la lobizona? I ask myself.

Rather than my own memories, I see myself from the Septimus' perspective. There's footage of Tiago and me leaving the Colosseum in La Rosada, then I'm in front of *Las cuatro brujas* in el Centro Comercial. I start hearing various news broadcasts, channel surfing among an array of voices, most of it stuff I've already heard.

About how I might be the next rung of evolution—or a genetic mutation that never should have been.

A word keeps popping up that I thought was lobizona, but it's not.

What is la ladrona? I query.

Images of grotesque-looking women fill my mind, like half-forgotten childhood nightmares. And a strange lullaby begins to play in the dark depths of my brain, the lyrics in a variety of languages. I only understand two, but it's enough for me to realize there's only one line in the song that's been translated over and over again:

Si la sangre se abandona,
se despierta la ladrona.

If the bloodline should break,
la ladrona will wake.

Apparently, the Septimus have their own superstitions. They believe if one of their kind ever reproduces with a human, the child will be an abomination known as la ladrona. She will look the part of a Septimus, but in her womb she'll carry a curse—a demonio that will wipe out all life on the planet.

No wonder my friends are so scared. Their whole species has been raised to regard human hybrids as a gateway to hell.

But Septimus can't actually believe this story is real, can they? It'd be like believing in Big Foot or Bloody Mary in the human world . . .

Or witches and werewolves.

I set aside that investigation because it's not why I'm here. I came for Ma, to make sure she's okay. I need to talk to Gael.

Cata said I just have to meditate on everything I know about my father in order to summon his presence, and if he happens to be plugged into el Hongo and within reach, I'll feel him. Tiago said it feels like searching for the telepathic channel that activates when I'm a wolf.

I concentrate, calling up Gael's coral eyes, golden-brown hair, sarcastic smirk—trying to paint a picture in the darkness. But his physical attributes are the least of what connects me to my father. I don't see much of myself in him at all.

Who is Fierro? I ask el Hongo instead.

A montage of moments twists together, the memories spiraling back in time to Fierro's earliest demonstrations.

I watch a masked lobizón in a floral dress run across a Septibol field, painting pink footsteps in the grass as he goes. Next I see a crowd of Septimus staring at Fierro's symbol carved into a monument of a wolf and a witch that looks even more ancient than *Las cuatro brujas* and bears the inscription:

El Lobizón y La Bruja

The words have been crossed out, and new terms have been carved in:

Septimo y Septima

As more of Fierro's public appearances are revealed, there's a deterioration in the quality of the images, like they're photocopies of photocopies. Knowledge seeps into my mind by osmosis, and I fill in the blanks. Even after Gael was punished by the Cazadores for failing to capture Fierro and exiled to El Laberinto, the demonstrations didn't stop.

Since no one knew the real Fierro had disappeared, they took a long time to realize that many Fierro-inspired uprisings were led by copycats. I watch as these disruptions intensify, with Septimus openly defying Cazadores and defacing public property and crashing events in faceless masks.

I wonder how much of this was spearheaded by the Coven.

The demonstrations didn't end because the Septimus realized the real Fierro had vanished. They ended because somebody died.

A Cazador with auburn curls, married, father of two. I watch as he's attacked by a couple of werewolves who are so amped up from a riot held dangerously close to the full moon that a life-or-death animal instinct takes them over completely.

I want to look away from the violence, but I don't know how, when it's happening in my head. Then a new scene begins to form.

There are headlines about Cazadores clamping down on every manada, the tribunal enacting a curfew, hundreds of Septimus charged with disorderly behavior. The two murderers have their day in court and are found guilty and sentenced to a fate reserved only for extreme cases—*Olvido*.

Since population numbers are so precious to the Septimus, executions are rare. The tribunal decides to erase their memories, essentially killing who they were and letting them start over.

I can't imagine the guilt Gael must have felt to know a Cazador died in his name.

I concentrate on my father now, meditating on his face and his voice and these new parts of his story. The more I focus, the more connected to him I feel, until I can almost kid myself he's right beside me—but I don't sense our telepathic connection lighting up.

I try again in the evening.

And the next day.

And the next.

Then on the cusp of the new moon, we set out on *La Espiral* for my second demonstration.

14

For the first time in too long, the nerves in my stomach aren't from dread but anticipation.

I'd never considered how it's possible for El Laberinto's Septibol team to play against schools in Argentina during the regular season. It's not like they're flying back and forth between countries using human airports. Turns out all Septibol matches take place in a manada called La Cancha.

It's a magical soft spot that's riddled with mundos de bolsillo, or *pocket worlds*. Cata describes them as rooms with multiple doors.

She said I've visited a pocket world before—the grove of purple trees within Flora where the brujas sometimes have classes. When the Septibol team plays other schools, they access a mundo de bolsillo within Flora that connects to a stadium in La Cancha.

Since there's no official match scheduled, we're about to break into El Laberinto's teaching tree.

Tiago sent Pablo a coded missive that we hope he'll be able to decipher. If all goes well, we'll be reunited with our friends today.

The prospect is almost too uplifting to contemplate, so I've been trying not to think about it for fear of being disappointed. I'll believe it's real when I see them.

I'm anxious about Ma again. We're midway through the moon cycle, and I haven't been able to connect with Gael in el Hongo. Yamila hasn't been on the news either, so I've had no sightings of him at all.

I can't stand not knowing if he and Ma are safe.

La Espiral surfaces in a sea that borders autumnal woods, on the outskirts of La Cancha. After dropping us off, Laura submerges her ship back into the water, where she'll patrol for signs of Cazadores until we signal her with our horarios.

The parasitic plant blends with my skin now that we've left el Mar Oscuro, and I feel its grip tightening. Not in that way where it's getting my attention, but more like it's tensing in anticipation of our excursion. Either that, or it's feeding on me.

We step into a grove of majestic trunks with gold and brown and red leaves that form a canopy overhead. Yet what's most striking is the way neighboring trees don't touch.

Slivers of sky outline each crown, like blue rivulets, giving the foliage a cracked, stained glass look. "La timidez de la corona," says Saysa, tipping her head back. "Sometimes trees avoid touching one another. We don't know why." Her hand twitches. "We can only guess."

I've read about *crown shyness* before, but I'm more interested in how Saysa's doing. She still hasn't opened up about what happened with Nacho or that shop bruja in Kukú. I keep thinking of what Zaybet said about Jardineras who go dark, and I know we need to talk to Saysa—except it feels impossible since she's always surrounded by her admirers.

I guess I must look the same way to her.

The trees end in a sports town built around a towering Septibol stadium. La Cancha is *literally* a stadium: a black-and-white checkered wall encloses the field, with entryways evenly spaced out. There's a smoky aroma and a slight haze in the air from the fried foods, and as Zaybet leads the way, Tiago and I keep our heads down, as instructed.

But in the fringe of my vision, I take in all the activity. There are tents up and down the street with bruja-operated food stands that offer everything from frosty drinks to complete meals, bookies taking wagers on upcoming matches, and Septimus hawking merchandise for players and teams. Overhead are pantaguas of every size broadcasting Septibol matches, though a few are still playing footage of me transforming.

Zaybet stops at an entrance point into the stadium and deposits semillas into a slot in the door. It pops open, and we step onto a crisp grassy field with tiered seating. About a hundred Coveners are already in the stands.

Off to the side is a group of twenty-eight brujas—seven of each element. They're all holding hands, their eyes bright with light. They're opening a doorway into Flora; when their spell ends, the bridge crumbles, and our friends will stay in El Laberinto, and we'll be back here.

There are twenty-eight wolves standing astride the brujas to serve as power packs, in case the witches need to channel their energy.

Tinta y Fideo are already on the field. "Just waiting on your teammates," says Tinta, the younger, inked brother.

"They'll be here," Tiago assures him.

The Septimus in the stands hold up mirrors to us. "What will they do with the footage they record?" I ask.

"If a tree falls in the forest and no one's there to see it, does it make a sound?"

"They'll anonymously release it to the press once you're back at the Coven," Fideo translates for his brother.

"Is that *the* lobizona?" calls a familiar voice, and before I've even seen him, I'm racing toward Pablo.

A grin overtakes his face, his black eyes inky bright as he opens his arms for me to crash into his chest, and he presses a huge kiss to my cheek. Baby-faced Javier lifts Saysa off her feet, and silver-eyed Nico reels Cata in for a hug.

Yet nothing compares to Tiago's reunion with his boys. His embrace with each guy lasts at least twenty seconds, but the real bromance is with Pablo, whom Tiago approaches last.

"I can't believe you used my made-up language," I hear Pablo say to Tiago as they clasp each other in their arms. "You all laughed when I created it, but I *told* you it would come in handy!"

I'm weirdly envious. Even weirder, I'm not sure if it's because of how much Tiago cares for Pablo or how much Pablo prefers Tiago to the rest of us.

A boulder knocks into me, and Javier spins me around, taking my breath away. "Look at our famous friend," he says, beaming. "Not so invisible after all."

I can't help grinning back.

"Los extrañamos," says Nico as he greets me. *We miss you all.*

I didn't realize how close Diego and Cata are, but they hug almost as long as Tiago and Pablo. "How are you?" Diego asks me after he and I have embraced.

"Better with you guys here."

His periwinkle eyes grow bright. "I think what you're doing is inspired. Winning over public sentiment is a good strategy."

"It was Zaybet's idea," I say, introducing her to Diego and the others.

Gus greets me last. He comes over with his head bowed, somewhat dispirited as he kisses my cheek.

"Where's Bibi?" I ask.

Pablo shakes his head like I should shut up.

"What happened?" asks Saysa when Gus doesn't answer and none of the guys say anything.

"She needs some space," says Gus. "That's all." Behind the bouncy curls, his eyes look rather puffy.

"Okay," says Tiago, corralling us together. "We're doing two teams of four, no magic, just goals. The point is to show Manu can hold her own, so it's not about the rest of us."

"Who are the Septimus in the stands?" asks Pablo, his voice laden with suspicion.

"Press," says Tinta, since we can't exactly discuss the Coven.

"And who are you?" Pablo demands.

"Fierro."

Before Pablo can argue with Tinta, Fideo blows a whistle, and we all scatter to take position on the field. The brothers stay on the sidelines with Cata, Saysa, and Zaybet. It's important the cameras only capture the field, without revealing any Coveners' identities. Enzo is the only one who doesn't seem to care about being seen. He's playing on my team.

Tiago, Gus, Nico, and Diego came dressed in white shirts with black shorts, while Pablo, Javier, Enzo, and I are in all black. We shake hands for a good game, and our team takes possession first.

Javier passes the ball to Pablo, who gets it to Enzo, the only player wearing pants instead of shorts. He manages to evade Gus and kicks in an attempt to score our first goal—

But Diego catches it. Cata cheers.

He kicks the ball to Gus, who outruns Enzo and passes it to Nico. Pablo races to intercept him, but Nico slams the ball in the air to Tiago, who leaps up and brings it down with his chest. Javier veers for him, but Tiago outstrips them all, and now it's just us.

My gaze locks on his feet as they weave around the checkered ball, which could rocket at any moment—

The ball flies like an arrow, straight for the net, and I spring forward and catch it. There's cheering in the stands and among my teammates, but the save feels a bit anticlimactic. This wasn't one of Tiago's better kicks.

I throw the ball to Javier, who brings it down and barely has a chance to step forward before Tiago sweeps in and steals it. He races for the goal, and now my pulse pounds with excitement, as I try to anticipate which way the trajectory will break—

The ball flies into my hands, and I barely need to move. Another arrow-like kick. Again, everyone cheers.

"I need a moment," I call out to Tinta y Fideo on the sidelines. I don't raise my voice because I know they can hear me. Tinta's hands shoot to his hips in annoyance, but Saysa and Cata nod like they're calling the same foul.

"Can you come here?" I ask Tiago.

The wolves on the field will be able to hear me no matter how low I speak, but I at least have a chance to keep those in the stands out of it.

"What's wrong?" he murmurs, at my side in an eyeblink.

"You're going easy on me."

"I'm not—"

"Are too!"

"You are," says Pablo from down the field.

"I'm warming up," says Tiago with a defensive shrug.

"Bullshit. Either play, or *don't*."

The clapping I hear must be Pablo.

"That wasn't your approach at tryouts," Tiago murmurs back.

I feel my face go slack. When I tried out for the Septibol team, I saved two goals, but I let Tiago score. Only Cata and Saysa know I took a dive, and I doubt they told him. He must have noticed and never mentioned it.

Since I don't defend myself, Tiago presses, "You let me win. I don't see what the difference is now."

I'm stunned he doesn't see the difference, and I hear Saysa shout "*Seriously?*" from the sidelines. Tinta y Fideo must be relaying our conversation.

"The difference is *I* was doing it to preserve your fragile male ego," I growl, "whereas *you're* doing it because you don't think I can take you!"

This time, Saysa is the one clapping. Yet I bite my lip as I realize Diego must have heard me. The truth is, he was so gracious about sharing his goalie position that it didn't feel right to best him at tryouts. It seemed ungrateful.

To change the subject, I say, "You went easy on me in class when we had to wrestle each other."

Tiago frowns, but he can't deny it's true. I've seen him fight for real since then, and I know he could have taken me in half a breath.

"Fine," he says, his brow a straight line. "I'll go hard."

He walks back to his place on the field, and something shifts about the energy of the match. I thought it was about endearing myself to the Septimus, so I didn't really think of myself as having to prove anything beyond having a good game and showing my passion for the sport. How naïve the *me* from a few moments ago sounds now.

Tiago's team takes possession.

Gus runs with the ball toward Nico, but Pablo swerves in and steals it. He passes the ball to Enzo, who shoots at the goal. Diego knocks it out with his hands, but he doesn't catch it. Enzo dives for it on the rebound, and he kicks it over Diego's head, hitting the net.

I break into cheers along with the rest of our team. Zaybet screeches from the sidelines.

The ball spends so much time on the other side of the field that it feels like everyone is making an effort to keep it from Tiago and put off our showdown. But I know from experience that the ball can't stay away from him for long.

Javier aims a kick to Pablo, and Nico sweeps in and steals the ball.

As soon as Tiago's team has possession, my legs grow jittery, and the game feels like it's building to a moment. Nico makes a pass to Tiago before Pablo can intercede, and I feel the entire stadium's focus pressing in on us.

Without warning, Tiago blasts the ball in the air with such power that its arc is a blur, impossible to make out. I see it spin in and out of view, like there's signal interference, and it crashes toward the net before I can blink.

All I have time to glimpse is a shadow, and I spring up to the left corner of the box, fingers outstretched—

Until I clutch the ball in my hands.

I hit the ground from the impact, and cheering breaks out in the stands. It takes me a moment to get up, and my gaze goes straight to Tiago.

He's grinning from ear to ear, his face wearing that wild look I'm really starting to love. He seems thrilled for the challenge. And without raising his voice, he says, "You're on, Solazos."

After that, the whole match is a showdown for Tiago and me. He sends powerful kicks that start to reach such high speeds that I can hear the ball slicing through the air. But the harder he kicks, the louder the sound, which makes the trajectory easier to track—though it gives me less and less time to make the catch.

I can tell Tiago's not holding back. Because I'm not either.

I don't miss a single ball.

We're locked into our contest with an intensity I've never experienced, and something inside me urges perfection, warning me I can't afford mistakes. Even if Tiago attempts a hundred goals and only makes one, my ninety-nine saves won't matter. The score would only reflect my loss.

One.

Just as Javier's attempting to steal the ball from Tiago, the ground begins to shake. We stop playing and look at the brujas powering our presence here. Their eyes are flickering. Like there's a magical malfunction.

"What's going on?" Fideo calls out to them, but the brujas don't answer.

The lobizones guarding them touch their arms to shake them awake, but they seem to be in a trance. The Coveners in the stands stow their mirrors and get to their feet, just as a familiar bruja storms onto the field in a purple dress that matches her glowing eyes.

"Did you really think you could magic yourselves into my school without my knowing?" demands Jazmín, angry gusts of air swirling around her. "Get back *at once*," she says to my classmates. "Wait in my office."

They don't immediately react, and I know from Pablo's glower that he's going to be defiant, so I say, "Go. Please."

His gaze lingers on mine, and I can see how much he'd like to defy Jazmín and stay here with us. But it doesn't work that way. As soon as the brujas cut off their magic, Pablo and the others will be back in El Laberinto.

"I'm rooting for you kids," he says with a wink, then he walks off with Gus and Nico. Javier's boyish face never looked so burdened as he turns away from us, and the same heaviness weighs down Diego's expression. His light eyes flare bright against his black skin, and though he doesn't speak, the concern in his gaze feels like a warning.

Or an omen.

The temperature in the air seems to drop about ten degrees, and I'm sure Jazmín is not happy to see her students obeying her only at my urging. "I've let the Cazadores know what's going on," she announces to the field, glaring at the wolves who are still trying to shake the brujas awake.

Their magic is keeping our essences trapped here. Until they cut off the spell, we can't leave.

"They should be tracking you down at La Cancha any moment." Cold dislike lines Jazmín's face as she glares at me. It's hard to stomach that my own aunt could despise me this much.

Cata and Saysa flank my sides, and the wintry gale in Jazmín's eyes falters at the sight of her daughter.

"Drop the force field," demands Cata.

"Why?" asks Jazmín. Blood starts to trickle from her nose, and I realize she's the reason the brujas are in a trance. She's choking their magic.

"Because I'll tell them *everything*."

Jazmín's expression is pure ice, a mask protecting any evidence of her heart, if she has one. She doesn't bother wiping away the line of blood trailing down her lips.

"Enjoy your support, Manu," she says, her amethyst eyes dimming at last. "It won't survive the next news cycle."

"We have to hurry, before the Cazadores arrive," urges Zaybet.

The brujas are awake, and our connection to Flora has severed. A door has manifested, an exit back to La Cancha.

"There's too many of us," says Tinta. "We'll draw them right to Manu."

"We should leave in pairs," says Zaybet. "Enzo and I will go first and scope it out. We'll let you know if it's safe with our horarios."

They open the door and slip out. A moment later, I feel a squeeze in my wrist. "We're good."

"Cata and I will go next," says Tiago. Once they've gone, I wait until my horario squeezes again. Then I glance back at Tinta y Fideo—and the hundred-ish Coveners behind them—and say, "See you tonight!"

The others are waiting for us outside the checkered stadium. Clustered in pairs, we cross the street and make for the tree line.

This manada is mostly lobizones, and it seems rather small. Everyone has their gaze glued to a screen, and I don't spy any signs of a search mobilizing for us.

Maybe Jazmín was bluffing. After all, she wouldn't risk her daughter getting in trouble with the law, would she?

"Laura's in place," says Zaybet.

"Take a left!"

Tiago's command comes right as I spot the Cazadores stepping out from the woods. Jazmín didn't alert just any law enforcement: Yamila leads the troop, with her brother at her side.

Nacho looks fully recovered from his encounter with Saysa. As he surveys the crowd, his sister's same hatred hardens his face. They're not here for justice. They're out for revenge.

I only register they're heading our direction when Tiago pulls Cata into a tent-shop. The rest of us follow his lead, and we blend into the quilt of customers sifting through the Septibol merchandise.

I pretend to be browsing the signed posters while I watch Yamila and her brother instruct the Cazadores.

"As soon as they move, we'll make for the trees," murmurs Tiago as he and Cata stroll past, his voice barely audible.

I lead Saysa by the elbow toward the front of the tent, where the players' jerseys are, so we can get a better vantage of the street. The other Cazadores have split off and begun their search, but Yamila and Nacho are still in this area, scanning the surrounding faces and tents.

They're moving toward this shop.

I busy myself with the racks of shirts behind me, and I blink as I recognize El Laberinto's baby blue Septibol uniform.

A familiar name is stamped on the back.

TIAGO

I realize Saysa isn't moving when her arm slips out of my hold. Sweat laminates her face, and her eyes are wide and glassy. She reminds me of *me* when I had to face the border agent at the crossing into Kerana. She's paralyzed with fear.

I follow her gaze to Nacho, whose broad frame, buzz cut, and ripped arms make him look like a super soldier straight out of a science fiction film. He towers over most lobizones.

"He's healthier than ever," I whisper to Saysa. "No harm done."

Yet she doesn't seem to be listening. I shake her, but she doesn't pull her gaze away from him. So I dig my nails into the back of her hand, just enough to get her attention, and I accidently cut her skin.

Saysa jumps at the sudden pain, and her eyes blaze as she

squeezes my fingers, like a magical fight-or-flight instinct kicked in. There's a tugging inside me, only it's not the transformation—it's the opposite.

Rather than the heat of energy, I feel cold, like I'm losing my strength.

I stare at Saysa in shock. Her eyes are glazed, not like she's emotional, but *emotionless*.

I suck in a panicked gasp as my skin tightens, my skull searing in pain—

Saysa drops my hand, her eyes flickering off. As warmth returns to my body, her own face blanches.

Then I notice Yamila and Nacho have entered the tent. There's no time. I grit my jaw and reach for Saysa again—

She steps away like I'm going to burn her, so I yank her by the arm and drag her toward the back exit. Thankfully, her magic doesn't bite again.

I don't dare look back as Saysa and I cross the street. I try not to walk too quickly, and these feel like the longest steps I've ever taken.

At last we reach the shade of the trees that are too shy to touch, and I pull Saysa into a run. I don't slow until we're deep inside the woods, and she jerks away from me. Without a word, she hurries ahead, after the others.

But I chance a look back, and my heart stalls.

Gael is standing by the tree line, a small figure in the far distance. I know he sees me because his coral gaze never wavers.

I lift a hand in greeting.

And my father turns away, like he never saw me at all.

15

Tonight is the new moon, so our only illumination comes from millions of sparkling stars strewn across the ceiling.

A celebration is getting underway at the Coven as footage of our match plays on the news. Talking heads are debating the legal ramifications of my actions, while sports journalists analyze my moves.

"¡La loba!" calls out Ezequiel. "Great game! Some of us at the Coven like to play. Want to join my team?"

"I'd love to," I say, grinning.

"Where's Tiago?" asks a Septimo named Horacio.

Since he was heading into the shower when I left the room, I just say, "He's coming."

"Probably ashamed to show his face after the beating he took," says Ximena, Horacio's wife on paper. "Looks like he's met his match in more ways than one."

I don't bother biting back my smile.

"I didn't even miss the brujas' magic," says Angelina, her arms around Ximena's waist. "The game was intense enough without it."

"What a showdown!" agrees her husband, Yónatan, who's holding hands with Horacio. The four of them are best friends and neighbors, even though the real relationships are not what the public sees.

Zaybet told me she suspects one of them to be a Cazador because they tend to warn individual Coveners when one of them comes under surveillance. Since everyone appreciates the protection, nobody presses them to explain themselves. They're informally known as los cuatro jinetes—*the four horsemen*—because their approach is a sign of doom.

Zaybet seems especially tickled to have a Covener on the inside of the Cazadores. "I wonder how the Cazadores will react now that Manu escaped their clutches again," she says, her sharp gaze jumping among the four of them like a multiple choice question on an exam.

"That went perfect!" Fideo comes over with his brother, and we all trade hugs. Except for Tinta and Zaybet, who make it a point to avoid each other.

"That's what you should've done the first time around," says Tinta, his copper-brown eyes flashing.

"Are you for real?" snaps Zaybet. Despite her words, there are no hard lines on her face, and she doesn't seem put out.

"I'm getting a drink," says Fideo, while Zaybet and Tinta narrow in on a new argument.

I pull Laura away. "What's with those two?"

She winkles her nose. "Z and Tinta used to date. It was pretty serious."

"Ah."

"Here you go." Enzo comes over with three glasses, and Laura and I each take ours. It looks like red wine.

"Is this malbec?" I ask, recalling the smell of Ma's favorite wine.

"What?" asks Enzo. "That human drink? These are Lunaris grapes, the *real* thing."

I'm mortified by my mistake, but before I can say anything, a new song starts, and Laura squeals with delight. She takes our untouched glasses, sets them down on a table, and holds my hand as she swings her hips.

Enzo sets down his glass to join us. He's in his sweatpants and a *Septima ≠ Bruja* shirt. They've become pretty popular at the Coven since my demonstration. I've heard the slogan is even taking off in a growing number of manadas.

Enzo's pant leg hitches on his calf, and a flash of green catches my eye. When I squint to look closer, he's already fixed it.

Since the whole place has been taken over as a dance floor, portions of the crowd have spread to the upper balconies. Laura and Enzo are so lost in the music that they don't notice when I slip away, toward the stairs.

I climb to the second story, where it's less loud, and I spot Cata and Saysa holding court over a couple dozen brujas. I move closer, but I stop a good measure away so they won't notice me.

Saysa is sitting on the railing, and Cata leans between her knees, arms resting on Saysa's thighs.

The vampiros are out in full force, our bodies a bloody feast for them. While the other brujas sit on the floor or lean against the wall to avoid them, Saysa lets the plants curl around her arms like fanged snakes, and she strokes them.

She looks like Cleopatra.

"I thought they were just prickly by nature, but they love you," says a Septima with the green eyes of a Jardinera.

"Must be your gentle touch," says another bruja, smiling shyly at Saysa.

"Or how you're able to really understand them," says a third, and Saysa tries not to look too pleased with herself, but her dimples are on full display.

She seems completely recovered from what happened in La Cancha, which is more concerning than comforting.

She's not dealing with her emotions at all.

"It's her power," says a witch with hair as red as strawberries who was at the Coven the first night we arrived. "I could feel it emanating from her when she set foot in this place. It announces her."

Cata seems to like this answer best because her chin tips up, like she approves. But Saysa's smile fades.

"How did the two of you meet?" asks the bruja with the shy smile, looking between my friends.

Saysa's eyes light up the way I imagine mine do when I think of the night I met Tiago. "If you ask Cata, she'll tell you we met my first day at the academy."

Saysa leans over Cata's shoulder to look at her for confirmation, and Cata plants a surprise kiss on her lips. The brujas whistle, and Saysa snaps upright, a smitten smile on her face.

I don't know the exact moment Cata dropped her guard and became this openly affectionate with Saysa. I'm just glad she's letting herself be happy after what went down in Lunaris. Cata came out to her mom, only to learn that Jazmín already knew and *actively* disapproved.

It was my aunt who sent Yamila to Ma's clinic, thinking she would arrest Saysa for illegally trafficking Septis. That was her plan to break them up. Yet Yamila found Ma and me instead.

Watching Cata discover her mother's betrayal felt intimately familiar. I know what it meant for my cousin to take her first major stand and disobey her mom.

"But the truth is, we met in Lunaris, one and a half years earlier." Saysa runs her fingers through Cata's golden-brown strands while she talks, and Cata closes her eyes. "My brother used to talk my ear off about his best friend Cata at the academy. *Cata this, Cata that.* I was dying to meet her, only I wasn't thirteen yet. For more than a year, I kept waiting for him to tell me they were dating, or that he was in love with her, but since his feelings never went beyond friendly, I figured she must not be all that special."

A few brujas chuckle, and Cata's lips spread into a grin.

"Tiago hadn't visited Kerana since he started school, so when I turned thirteen, I was too excited about seeing my brother and visiting Lunaris to remember Cata. I broke into a sprint as soon as I spotted him. Then I noticed the goddess walking beside him—and I face-planted in the grass."

"No!" says a bruja, and a few of them clasp their hands to their mouths to cover their giggles.

"I was so mortified that I hid until Cata went to see her family. When we got back to Kerana, I'd already forgotten everything else about my first moon as a witch. The only marvel I'd laid eyes on in Lunaris was Catalina."

Saysa's voice has grown solemn. "She's still the most beautiful sight I've ever seen."

The whole group *awws*, and Cata spins around and melts into Saysa's arms. I feel a small sting on my shoulder, and I swat at a vampiro that just bit me. It snaps its bloodied jaws in my face before slithering away.

All I want to do now is climb into bed and wait for Tiago to join me. But when I get to our room, the lights are already on.

"Oh, hey," I say, on seeing Tiago in bed, shirtless, reading. This image should be printed on a calendar somewhere.

A lock of dark hair falls into his eye as he looks up. The nice thing about the walls being soundproof is the music shuts off with the door.

"Welcome home," he says in his velvety voice, setting the book on the nightstand. Even though we've been roommates and boyfriend-and-girlfriend for over a week, this whole thing still feels surreal.

I perch on the bed to pull off my shoes, and I glance at the cover. "Is that—?"

"*House of Mirth*," he says, leaning forward and planting a kiss on my shoulder, where the vampiro just bit me. "You said it was one of your favorites."

"So you're reading it?"

He shrugs. "I liked *Age of Innocence*."

I'm so moved by the gesture that I don't point out that both book titles start with *The*. Even though it kills me a little.

"What do you think so far?" I ask as I grab my bedclothes and step into the bathroom to change. I leave the door the tiniest bit ajar so I can hear his answer.

"I think it's easy to fall in love with Lily Bart," he says, his voice so soft that it's almost like he's making a point of not raising it. He's forcing me to listen like a lobizona.

"She's a rarity. An individual in a society that prizes conformity, so she's torn between who she is and who she thinks she should be—which is why this Selden guy is pissing me off."

"What do you mean?" I ask.

"He's not helping," he says as I step out and put my clothes away. "She's drowning, and all he has to offer is some lame line— 'The only way I can help you is by loving you.'"

"Ooh, you got to the party with the tableaus! That's my favorite scene." I stroke the wall to dim the lighting. "Okay, so what would *you* have said if you were Selden?"

I climb into bed, and Tiago's gaze locks onto mine in a way that feels like more than just a literary exercise. The scar on his chest expands as he inhales deeply.

"I would have asked Lily to run away with me."

"That wasn't realistic in their time," I say, growing defensive over Lawrence Selden all of a sudden, even though, deep down, I've always felt he should have done more. "Where would they have gone? How would they have gotten by?"

"They're smart, they would have figured something out." He sounds a little too frustrated about this. "Or he should just ask her to marry him and damn the consequences! Who cares if they become outcasts? Why does Lily even want to fit into a society like that anyway?"

Something about his indignation doesn't sit well with me. And I realize I may have just gotten a glimpse of what Zaybet and Laura see when they look at Tiago. His support comes from a place of empathy, not personal experience.

He's an *ally*. But his point of view remains privileged.

"That's kind of a privileged perspective, though." Tiago flinches, and I try to pick the rest of my words carefully. "You're shaming Lily for wanting to fit into the society around her, which might be a natural impulse if you're someone who has the *choice* to belong. But *fitting in* looks different when you're left out by default."

Tiago's shoulders fall, and his gaze grows distant. I don't know if he's unsettled about himself or the book or us. This feels like the indecisive wolf in him—he seems inwardly torn about something, only he's not coming out with it.

"Why didn't you use your horario to send Laura our location in el Bosque Blanco?"

I know I've hit on the right thing when his focus returns to me and his expression slackens, like he's been discovered. "I can't tell if we're doing the right thing."

"For whom?"

"*Us.*"

His eyes brighten and his skin grows warmer, like the blood

is rushing to his face. Saysa's priority is to change the system, and Cata's main concern has always been our safety—but Tiago is thinking about our future together. I guess that's a luxury I haven't dared indulge in.

Same reason I haven't bothered creating a comfortable space for myself here or in El Laberinto.

Ever since ICE took Ma, I haven't been able to see a future past the present.

"Going off on our own isn't the answer," I say, thinking of the memories I experienced in the Lagoon of the Lost. "Trust me. I'm the product of a failed elopement."

"Brujas can't live without Lunaris because their magic is so great on the full moon that it could consume them," says Tiago, "but it's different for wolves. Without the mate, we just wouldn't have heightened senses the rest of the month. Then on the full moon, we could try chaining ourselves up."

"As in, *stay awake through the period pain*?"

He frowns at the force of my answer. "I—I don't know about the period pain."

Of course he doesn't. I can't hold that against him, so I just breathe and explain. "I've had severe menstrual cramps since my first period, the day my lobizona powers should have manifested. I think it must be a combination of my cycle and the pain of the transformation. Tiago, I can't stay conscious for it. I would lose my mind."

I take his hand to show him I'm not upset. "If you think we'd be safer hiding among people, I don't have that choice. Unlike the rest of you, my eyes don't change in the human realm."

He opens his mouth like he's got more proposals, and I press my finger to his bottom lip. "Let's not talk about this right now. Today was a good day. Can't we just enjoy it?"

He takes my hand and kisses each finger. Then he says, "It's just that . . ." From the way he's staring at me, he seems like he wants to confide something serious, and my stomach clenches in anticipation. "I really, *really* like you—"

"Ha-ha," I say, my face relaxing into a grin. "If you keep insisting, I'm going to start thinking this lobizón *doth protest too much.*"

He frowns like it's taking him a moment to get the *Hamlet* reference, which is odd. Then his expression clears, and the heaviness fades from his features. "So what you're telling me," he says, his voice becoming more musical, "is actions speak louder than words."

My pulse spikes as he slides closer, one hand rising up my thigh. "Is this better?" he murmurs. I shiver as he presses soft kisses on my collarbone, throat, jaw . . .

"Uh-huh," I say as his tongue trails down to the neckline of my shirt. Then he lifts his face to mine, lips hovering close but without touching me.

I lean into him, and he pulls back a bit. I reach for Tiago again, and he draws back farther. "What's wrong?"

"I'm not convinced you want me enough."

I stifle my laugh. "Are you serious?"

"I am."

His unrepentant face is a challenge.

One he knows I'm going to answer.

I sense a wildness rear up in me, an untamed impulse that comes from my lobizona side. Digging my fingers into his biceps, I pin him down.

Tiago wrests an arm free and cradles my head, pulling my face toward him. His intoxicating scent makes it hard to think, but before our mouths meet, I make my neck go limp and slide out of his hold.

Tiago's blue eyes are ablaze—a lightning flash of lobizón—and he reaches for my waist, rolling on top of me. He uses his weight to trap me under him, our bodies pressed together so tight that I feel every part of him.

His scent is all over me now, his dark hair grazing my face, his sapphire eyes more animal than man—and I lift my chin, capturing his mouth with mine.

Tiago's tongue is transformative. As we battle for control, I've never felt this untethered before. When at last I moan my surrender, his hands find their way up my shirt.

His fingers ignite my skin, and I feel him everywhere. His touch is like his kiss—confident, insistent, exhilarating—

Tiago's spine suddenly stiffens, like his joints have locked up. And he rolls onto his back.

I blink a few times, unsure what just happened. My body reinflates now that his weight isn't pressing me down, and it takes a moment for my mental haze to clear.

"What's going on?" I whisper, turning to watch Tiago's scar rise and fall in quick succession.

"Don't want," he says between breaths, "to lose control."

"Why not?" My pulse is still pounding.

Tiago is staring at the ceiling, and I hone my hearing until I pick up on the galloping of his heart. It's going so fast that I wonder if he's going to rip out of his skin—but he holds himself together.

When he finally meets my gaze, the werewolf is still in his eyes. "You'll see."

My *M* symbol spreads everywhere.

There are protests all across Kerana calling for the Cazadores to end their persecution so I can come forward without fear.

The atmosphere at the Coven has grown hopeful and energized, but I feel apart from the excitement. I still haven't managed to send a message to Gael. I have no news about Ma. And every day, I feel a little worse for lying to the Coveners.

They welcomed me to their pack and bared their souls—how are they going to handle it when they learn what I've been holding back?

I surf through news outlets on a pantaguas while I wait for today's meeting to start, flipping through stories of schoolgirls refusing to wear dresses, Septimas charging Septibol fields, brujas protesting at La Rosada and demanding higher pay for their magic . . .

But no Yamila.

It's been a week since the Septibol match, and I keep expecting her to expose my secret. What's she waiting for?

The longer her silence stretches, the more I think Cata's theory is right—Yamila isn't in a hurry to share her hunt with the other Cazadores. Once they learn I'm not just a lobizona but a *hybrid,* she'll be competing with the entire force to catch me. Maybe the entire species.

But her silence is troubling in other ways. I've been visiting el Hongo every day, and I've yet to reach Gael. I can't shake the way he looked past me at La Cancha. What is he doing here with Yamila and Nacho? *And where is Ma?*

A pair of bloodred eyes flashes on the waterscreen.

I stop changing channels, my insides tightening as I sit up.

Yamila is giving a rare interview to a reporter. My pulse races in my ears, and I look around to see if other Septimus are watching this screen. I seem to be the only one. Just in case, I drop the volume as low as it goes.

"We are not persecuting anyone," says Yamila in Spanish. "This is an issue of an undocumented Septimus. We want to question her and review her Huella to understand how she could be missing from our records."

"We're hearing that she's had to run away from a traumatic home life," says the reporter. "Can you see how this kind of language may scare her off from coming forward?"

"Who's feeding you this?"

"Anonymous sources."

Or, as Zaybet calls them, *Coveners fanning the flames of my fame.*

"If that's really the case, then let me take this opportunity to speak directly to the lobizona." Yamila switches to English, and her face stares into the camera, right at me.

"We would love to hear more about your *traumatic home life* so that we might offer you help." She takes her time forming every word, like she's savoring each delivery. "If we can't get answers from you, maybe your parents can shed some light."

"Have you identified them?" cuts in the reporter, salivating.

"We're close."

I can barely breathe.

Yamila faces the camera. "I promise if you turn yourself in to *me*—before the full moon—I will make sure you get a fair hearing."

The pretend part of her performance over, her throaty voice deepens. "If we don't hear from you by the full moon, we will be forced to focus our efforts on prosecuting those who have been aiding and abetting you, including their families. And speaking of families . . . next moon, I will no longer be searching for you."

I frown just as the reporter asks, "What?"

"I will redirect the full force of our investigation toward locating your mother."

16

I can hardly sit still through the meeting. Yamila's words chase themselves in a loop through my mind. If she's threatening to go after Ma, that means she hasn't found her yet. Right?

I need to talk to Gael.

"You okay?" asks Zaybet, and I realize I've carved a line down the wooden tabletop with my nail.

"Yeah." I cross my arms over my chest, pinning my hands under my elbows.

"Any last agenda items before we break?" she asks the others. Since everyone's been spending so much time here this moon, the Coven is clearing out so that Septimus can put in face time at their manadas before Lunaris. With me all over the news, no one can take any chances of raising suspicions.

"Just one," says Tinta, and I grow alert as his gaze slides to me. "We need one more demonstración before the full moon."

"Bad idea," says his brother, and I exhale in relief.

"We shouldn't slow down now—"

"We're not. We're still getting a ton of traction."

"All the more reason to ramp up—"

"*After* the full moon," insists Fideo, his foot knocking into the leg of the chair Zaybet set for me at the head of the table. She's sitting to my left, along with Laura, Enzo, and Tiago, while in a row to my right are Fideo, Tinta, Saysa, and Cata.

"Sorry, Manu," mumbles Fideo, straightening up to rein in his long limbs. "The Cazadores are desperate right now. It's too dangerous."

"What if we do something in Lunaris?" suggests Tinta.

"Too risky. Even Fierro never tried it."

"Fierro was *alone*," says his younger brother, tapping the tabletop, bouncing the Septibol ball tattooed on the back of his hand. "Manu has *us*."

"What exactly do you have in mind?" asks Zaybet.

Tinta's coppery brown eyes meet mine, twins of his brother's because lobizones inherit their mother's eyes. "Your story."

His words chill me, and I look to Tiago, whose expression is a mask of inscrutability. I wish I could conceal my own alarm that easily.

"The fuck?" Zaybet snaps at Tinta.

"Absolutely not," Cata answers for me.

"It's up to Manu when she chooses to share," says Saysa, walking a more diplomatic line.

"I'm sorry, Manu, but actually, my brother's right," says Fideo with a resigned sigh. "You're novel and exciting now, but hype fades. What lasts is a powerful *story*."

"It must be so easy to be this cool and aloof when nothing's at stake for you personally," says Zaybet, staring at Tinta, not Fideo. "You strut in here, ask Manu to take on the brunt of changing the system, then head home to your fancy manada where politicians shower you with semillas to help get them elected—"

"¡Andate a la mierda!" snaps Tinta, spiking his fist on the table as he sends Zaybet to hell. "I'm fighting for change by helping *good* politicians get elected, while you're here avoiding the real world—so which of us is really the *cool and aloof* one?"

"You! Circling the rooms at those fundraisers, making me hang off your arm like some pretty doll who can't think for herself—"

"It was all part of a strategy, Bet! But you never could see the forest for the trees—"

As they argue, I realize there is no choice for me to make. Yamila made that clear in her broadcast. Until I raise my voice, I'll still be that passenger in the back of Leather Jacket's truck, without a clue who's driving me or where I'm going.

Yamila knows who Ma is, and she's coming after her no matter what. Alone I can't protect her. Not yet, and not without Gael's help.

What I can do is stop waiting around for Yamila to make her next move and take control of my own narrative.

"I'll do it."

My volume isn't loud, but it silences Zaybet and Tinta, who are on their feet, leaning into the table, inches away from either kissing or punching each other. They sit down.

"Good," says Fideo, not sounding surprised that I've agreed. "Let's plan for the next moon phase. That's in three days, right before Lunaris."

"Excellent," says Tinta. Even though she fought hard for my freedom, Zaybet smiles too. She'll defend my right to choose until she's hoarse, but there's no denying she was hoping for this outcome.

Cata, Tiago, and Saysa—on the other hand—look *livid*.

———

By dinnertime, the Coven is down to just the seven of us.

I feel the force of my friends' glares on me as we eat. I'm sure they're just waiting for the chance to corner me in private. Until then, my plan is simple: Avoid them.

"My water's gone warm," Enzo says to Zaybet, holding out his glass to her.

"I froze plenty of ice."

"Come on, just touch my drink."

"I'll touch your drink," offers Laura, making her finger smoke, and Enzo rolls his eyes.

"How come you three have been able to stay at the Coven this whole time?" I ask as we devour the thin steaks Laura seared to pink perfection.

"My family thinks I'm teaching at our Mexican manada, Cabrera, so we only see one another in Lunaris," says Zaybet.

"I'm a ship captain, so it makes sense for me to be away at sea," says Laura. "As long as each of us contributes our required earnings to our manada, no one has any reason to suspect anything."

"How do you earn semillas while you're here?"

"Transporting Septimus and shipments that are trying to avoid the law. So they pay well."

"You hired me for your Huella, didn't you?" says Zaybet as an example. "We get by."

Enzo is the only one who hasn't answered my questions. When he sees me looking at him, he says in his raspy voice, "No one asks where I am."

Zaybet and Laura look down at their plates, and when Enzo gets up to bring over more steaks, I spy the glint of metal in Zaybet's eyes as her finger grazes his drink. A cold frostiness chills his glass.

It's not until everyone's gone to bed that my friends and I finally get a chance to talk, once again in Saysa and Cata's room. Before Cata can lay into me, I fill them in on what Yamila said on the news. "If she beats us to revealing my secret, we'll lose the Coven's trust."

"I was right then!" says Cata. "She wants to bring you in herself, which means she's not going to say anything because it's her only leverage."

"She said I have seven days—"

"She's still just making threats," says Cata, like I'm missing the point. "If she was going to use this information, she'd have used it. She's probably hoping to catch you in Lunaris—"

"You have no idea what she'll do! These are all just guesses!" Sometimes I think Cata forgets she's not the omniscient narrator of our story.

"What we do know," says Tiago, "is the way you're acting is exactly what Yamila wants. She sent you that message so you'd panic like this."

In other words, he's taking Cata's side.

"I think Manu's right. She can't keep silent for much longer."

I look to Saysa in surprise. The past week since La Cancha, she's been avoiding me. If I'm being honest, I haven't been in a hurry to talk to her either.

I've debated confiding in Tiago or Cata about how she started to drain my life force, but they already know Saysa's not coping well. I've seen Tiago attempt to get some brother-sister time with her, and she's always got an excuse. At least it feels promising that the two of us are on the same side now.

"How do you think everyone here will react?" I ask, remembering her hesitation last time.

"They'll believe it if you do," she says with an encouraging nod, and I'm not sure what she means.

"If we do this," says Cata, who sounds like she's reconsidering, "we need to practice your story until it's perfect."

"My story?"

"We've been over this, Manu," she says with a deep breath. "You're not a good liar, and this time it's not the head of the school you need to convince, but the entire *species*."

"You mean the Olvido story?"

"Unless you've come up with a better one?"

"I just wonder if—"

"You can't announce you're a hybrid," says Tiago bluntly. "They're not ready."

"Well, you can thank Yamila for the ticking clock!" I snap at him.

"That's why you're going to memorize a new story," says Cata in an annoyingly superior tone. "It'll come down to your word against hers."

"And what if the Coven believes Yamila? Then I'll be a hybrid *and* a fraud." I look to Saysa for support again. "They won't forgive us if we betray them."

This fear, at least, Saysa understands. She looks stricken. Of the four of us, she and I have the most to lose if the Coven turns on us.

"You're right," she says, her eyes intent on mine. "That's why it's important you let Cata coach you. This story needs to *stick*."

I awaken to the walls shaking, but it's not the morning alarm.

"Something's wrong," says Tiago, sitting bolt upright. He climbs out of bed, pulls on a shirt, and heads out barefoot.

I yank on shorts and dash after him, my oversized green tee still on because we didn't hook up last night. The conversation in Cata and Saysa's room followed us back to bed and wedged itself between us on the mattress.

The balcony shakes as the walls quake again, and the vampiros slither around unhappily. It's still nighttime.

Saysa and Cata burst out of their room, and we all rush downstairs. Zaybet, Laura, and Enzo are already there. They're in the couch area, staring at the waterscreens, which are projecting a 360-degree view of el Mar Oscuro around us.

Every angle looks fuzzy, like a dirty camera lens. There's a cloud of debris smothering us.

"What's going on?" asks Tiago.

The Coven shakes again, only this time I hear something else. It sounds like thunder. "What is that?"

"A tormenta," says Enzo. Pounding echoes through the rock again, like a monster's at the door.

That's a *storm?*

"What do we do?" asks Saysa.

"Let's try a shield," suggests Zaybet, and the brujas form a square, facing each other.

Their eyes light up with their elements—metallic for water, pink quartz for air, lime green for earth, and black opal for fire.

As soon as the spell starts, the smothering cloud pulls back on every pantaguas, like it can't get any closer. But it doesn't dissipate. It just hovers around, waiting.

"Of course this happens right when everyone leaves," rasps Enzo. "If we had more brujas, the barrier would be stronger."

"What's happening?" asks Tiago as the walls tremble.

"On land, weather exists outside, but in this dimension, storms want to break in. They're violent abstract beings that feed off the vampiros' oxygen. So if it breaks in, it's either the tormenta or us."

"What's the shield supposed to do?" I ask.

"If it holds for long enough, the storm will lose interest or strength and drift on. It usually works, but the lunar cycle has an effect on el Mar Oscuro's currents. And quarter-moon storms are more volatile. We'd have a better chance if we had more than one bruja for each element."

"What happens if their magic gives out?" asks Tiago as the quaking intensifies, and the Coven starts to rock from side to side.

"We'll have to fight."

The brujas' eyes continue to burn, their brows furrowed with focus. Saysa is the first to drop to her knees. She tended to the vampiros today, so she's probably weaker from the blood loss. Enzo vaults into the square and offers her his hand as a power source.

Saysa doesn't touch him.

Laura falls next, and she takes the hand Enzo offers her. After a moment, she stands, new energy coursing through her body. A vein pops in Enzo's temple, but he doesn't give any sign he's in pain. Instead, he reaches for Saysa—

She leaps back, severing the spell.

"Saysa!" shouts Zaybet, her metallic eyes flickering as she falls. Saysa realizes her mistake and rushes forward, but it's too late.

Cata and Laura crumble, like flower petals wilting, the glow of their eyes snuffing out.

On the screens, the cloud still surrounds us, but it doesn't move any closer.

"We have to risk a tunnel," says Laura as Enzo pulls her to her feet. "It's our only choice. We don't have a big enough pack to fight."

"We have no idea where it will lead us," argues Zaybet. "It could put us smack in front of a patrol of Cazadores!"

"That's only a *possibility*," says Laura. "If we stay here, it's a *certainty* we'll lose all our air!"

Zaybet closes her eyes like she doesn't want a vote.

"Fine" is all she says.

The Coven bounces the brujas around as the tormenta grows more powerful. Laura hits a few keystrokes on a small screen, but we're still getting battered. "I think it's too late!" she says. "I can't—"

The Coven jerks forward, and every pantaguas around us goes black.

"What happened?" asks Cata.

"We're taking a tunnel," says Zaybet. "There are wormholes all over el Mar Oscuro—but there's no telling where it will lead. Our orbit will now shift, which could bring new risks."

While we wait to reappear somewhere, bands of tension enclose my chest. Once the screens flicker back on, we're sailing right into a school of rainbow starfish.

They scatter in our wake, and I hold my breath as we scan every screen, searching for other signs of movement.

Nothing shows up visually, and Laura opens some sort of radar grid with red lines. There doesn't seem to be any activity around us. After a few long breaths, Enzo says, "That was close—"

His words are drowned by a high-pitched alarm squealing across the Coven.

"¡Carajo!" curses Zaybet, as a red dot pops up on the radar. Laura switches to camera mode, and we see a spiky red-and-black ball approaching us at record speed.

"It's a small ship," reports Laura. "Must be a base nearby."

"Let's just hope it keeps going," says Enzo.

"Who do you think it is?" whispers Cata as the ship grows larger.

The ball is black and the spikes are red, and it has a pair of metal arms capped with massive claws.

"Piratas."

17

Even Laura's warmth can't make the word sound less ominous.

"*¿Piratas?*" Cata sounds aghast.

"They're slowing down," says Zaybet. None of us speaks as the clawed arms clamp onto our surface and the ship docks, the terror so tangible it tinges the air with a metallic tang. By Zaybet, Laura, and Enzo's frozen expressions, I doubt they've had to defend the Coven from foes before.

"Isn't there a protocol or some kind of defense system?" asks Tiago as a big, burly Septimus in a wet suit files out from one of the red spikes. "It can't be the first time someone's gotten this close."

"It's rarer than you think," says Zaybet.

More burly piratas file out. I count eight in total, but there could be others on the ship. They wade through the black space like it's water, and I wonder about the consistency of el Mar Oscuro.

I don't see any bubbles, and the Septimus seem to be able to float in place without encountering much air resistance. Yet their feet plant onto the surface, as if the Coven exerts some gravity.

"The radar system feeds into the Coven's navigational controls," says Laura. "It reroutes our orbit to avoid run-ins. Most rocks that look like this one have a magnetic pull that will crush ships that sail too close, so Septimus usually keep their distance—"

"Unless they're desperate," says Enzo, his rasp sharpening on that last word. "But to answer your question," he says to Tiago, "we do have security measures. We could set off a bomb of black smoke—"

"No," says Tiago. "That will confuse us as much as them."

"We could fire ammunition to scare them off," says Laura.

"They could call for reinforcements," says Zaybet. "Or come back for us later. It doesn't look like they have brujas with them. We can wait to see what they do, and if they find a way in, we use la dormilona."

"The *sleepyhead*?" I translate.

"An airborne sedative we can disburse through the Coven that they won't be able to detect."

"An airborne potion?" asks Cata, awe in her voice. "That takes a *very* skilled Invocadora."

"The bruja who brewed it died a few decades ago," says Zaybet. "The last time piratas got this close was well before my time. The sleeping agent is mixed in with a hint of Olvido—just enough to make them forget the past few days and disorient them. But we'll need them to take off their masks."

Just then, a pirata's silhouette comes up against the screen, like he's looking right at the camera. He touches something, and I watch in horror as he locates the hidden entrance. It's like he's picked all kinds of locks and knows exactly where to look and what to do.

Enzo shoves something into my hands, and I realize it's a wet suit mask. Everyone else is pulling one over their heads. We can't risk speaking anymore, in case the wolves hear us.

Laura takes a handheld pantaguas, and we hurry up the stairs to the first-floor balcony, where we slip behind the door of the first room. There we gather round Laura as she hits a few keys to shut off the feeds downstairs, and she pulls up visuals of what's happening.

Eight lobizones march into the space where we were moments ago. One is shorter than the others, but his muscles are no less bulky. He must be the youngest.

They keep their movements muted as they survey the area, inspecting our food, books, furniture. I wonder if they're communicating telepathically.

A couple of them point to the vampiros in excitement, and one goes to remove his mask but another reaches for his arm and shakes his head. They're not sure they can trust the air.

There goes our plan.

Before we can stop him, Enzo pulls off his mask. The room's door opens and closes with the barest sigh. Laura makes to go after him, but Zaybet holds her back.

We can't do anything now but watch what he does on the screen.

Enzo leaps off the vampiro-strewn balcony to the floor. Then he knocks his elbow back and pops the guy closest to him—the one who attempted to take his mask off—in the chin.

The lobizón roars and rips off his mask. He's already in his transformed state.

He leaps at Enzo, who doesn't transform for some reason, so he's crushed by the pirata's weight. The others rush forward to back up their friend, and Tiago begins to shift.

His body lengthens and expands, hair sprouting across his

skin and claws curving from his fingers. I feel the pull deep inside me too, and I'm right behind him when he reaches the door, but Tiago doesn't open it.

You're not coming.

I cross my arms. *I'm a wolf just like you.*

His face is concealed by the mask, so I can't see his expression. *If you think you're ready to fight werewolf pirates, follow me.*

He opens and closes the door with a whisper, and he's gone. I reach for the knob to go after him, but I hesitate.

I don't know how to fight yet. And if I get hurt, I'll just distract him. I transform back to human-sized in defeat and join the brujas gathered wide-eyed around the screen.

Tiago is a monster.

Three lobizones jump him, and he fights them off alone, clawing and kicking and slicing like he's performing a martial arts dance. Enzo isn't managing as well because he's been pinned down, but the lobizón springs off him, like he's been burned by Enzo's skin.

I have a feeling if Laura wasn't masked, I would be seeing the dying embers of red in her eyes.

The lobizón charges forward again, but this time his feet freeze to the ground, and he can't move. Beneath the black fabric, Zaybet's eyes must be gleaming like blades.

At this point, only two piratas still have their masks on—the one Tiago is fighting, and the youngest. Tiago ducks to avoid a punch, then he rams his head into the wolf's belly, knocking him to the floor and ripping off his mask.

Then Tiago looks up at the last masked intruder, who seems to be shrinking against the wall.

When he takes a step closer, the young pirate rips off his mask.

Long black hair tumbles out, paired with glowing fuschia eyes.

The Invocadora's suit deflates to hug her real figure as she traps a masked Tiago and unmasked Enzo in force fields. At least I think she does because their bodies are completely still.

I twist to Cata so she'll help them, but she shakes her head. She can't risk tipping off the Invocadora to her presence.

"¿Quién más está acá?" demands the bruja. *Who else is here?*

The piratas start to stand, all of them now reverted to human form. As they shake off their injuries, the guy Zaybet iced to the floor says, "Hay brujas acá."

There are witches here.

"Do it," says Zaybet to Laura, her voice muffled by the mask.

"But Enzo—"

"¿Escuchan algo?" asks one of the lobizones. *Do you hear something?*

"Shhh," I say to Zaybet and Laura.

"He's inside the force field, the spell won't affect him," Zaybet says despite my protest.

"I hear someone!" shouts the lobizón, switching to English, just as Laura taps a button. "Come out, come out, or we'll come for—"

One by one, the piratas fall to the floor.

Yet the Invocadora must have picked up on the potion's presence and dropped Tiago's and Enzo's energy fields to protect herself because she doesn't fall.

Enzo does.

Laura and Zaybet gasp as he crumples to the floor alongside the other lobizones. Only a masked Tiago and the bruja remain standing.

"Do something," I urge Cata and Saysa.

"She's shielded herself," says Cata from behind her mask. "Our magic won't penetrate."

A blast of air punches Tiago's gut, and he flies across the room, crashing into the wall. Tiny rocks cascade down on him as he tries to get up, but he seems disoriented. He hit his head.

Before I know what I'm doing, I run out and leap to the ground from the balcony, landing silently behind the bruja's back.

Like she senses the shift in the air, the Invocadora spins around, fuschia eyes lit up in anticipation of an attack. But they dim down to a softer glow when she sees me.

"¿No me vas a mostrar tus ojos, hermana?" *You're not going to show me your eyes, sister?*

A fog forms around us, over us, until it's blocking us from view of even the cameras. She must be afraid there are more brujas here and doesn't want us ganging up on her. So much for *sisterhood.*

"It seems I'll have to figure out your element for myself," she goes on in Spanish.

I feel the tension in the atmosphere as she balls up a gale of air and lobs it at my gut, same as she did to Tiago.

And just like I would on the Septibol field, I dodge it.

The bruja's jaw drops, and beneath the mask, so does mine.

I flash back to the cave in Lunaris with Yamila, how I evaded her magical strikes. I didn't imagine it. *I can dodge magic.*

The Invocadora's hot pink eyes flash as she sends another volley of air at my chest, and I drop and roll to avoid it.

Tiago breaks through the haze, and he pulls me upright. Just then, I feel the air around us harden, like we've been sealed in an invisible coffin.

The pirata has caged us in a force field.

"See you soon," she says before pulling on her mask, probably so she can drop the protective field around herself. If she makes it back to her ship and calls for backup, we're screwed.

Her magical coffin locks me in tight. Concentrating as hard

as I can, I meditate on the layers that make up my body, attuning myself to the topmost lining, *my skin*. I focus hard on the most minute sensations, until I can feel where the hardened air meets my body hair.

It feels like it's been numbed.

I remember how Zaybet said dismantling something is easier than putting it together, and I hone in on a single spot: my right thumb. I channel all my energy into that digit, trying to will the finger to bend, calling on my power of transformation, on my will to survive, on whatever strength I have in me to—

make—

it—

MOVE.

My thumb bends, and the force field holding me shatters.

Since Tiago is masked, I can't see his reaction, which is probably a good thing. Then I run, until I catch up to the Invocadora in the tongue-like tunnel.

She's a few feet from the exit when she hears my steps and chances a glance back. She almost trips on seeing me. I can feel her summoning a new gale, one harsher than her earlier ones—

I knock my fist into her face. Then I catch the bruja as she falls and rip off her mask.

I carry her back to the others. The fog fades now that the Invocadora is out, which also frees Tiago. He's running to me right as I show up, and he takes the pirata off my hands, resting her with the rest of her pack.

My friends come rushing down the stairs, all of us with our masks on since the dormilona potion might still be in the air. Laura hits a few buttons on the handheld pantaguas. There's a feeling like we've just crossed one of those magical barriers, then she and Zaybet take off their masks and run to Enzo.

"Can we wake him?" asks Tiago, after ripping off his own mask. Zaybet shakes her head. "We need to wait until it wears off."

"He'll be fine, right?" asks Laura, but nobody answers her.

Tiago carries Enzo to his room, then he, Laura, and I leave the Coven in our wet suits to transport the piratas back to their ship.

As soon as we disembark, I grow light as a feather. The blackness around us is so thick that it feels like it's an actual substance.

The mask blows oxygen into my lungs on every inhale, and my steps are impossibly light on the rocky ground. I'm not floating or swimming or walking—it's a new sensation altogether. It's like the atmosphere isn't defined by gravity or its absence, but an as-yet unidentified quality.

We approach the spiky ship carefully, in case there are piratas onboard. Laura is still, and even though I can't see her eyes, I know she's using her magic to scan for heat signatures. When she nods at us, Tiago steps forward and wrenches one of the red spikes open.

Inside, there's a vast panoramic window, just like on *La Espiral,* and seats are bolted to the floor. I go to take off my mask, but Laura grabs my arm to stop me. "There's no oxygen here," she says, her voice muffled.

"So how do they breathe?" The fabric tickles my lips when I speak.

"They fly with their masks on."

No wonder the piratas got excited about the vampiros.

The walls are riddled with cabinets, and Laura starts opening them. In addition to food and clothing, she finds precious stones and sacks of every variety of semillas, like the piratas have been plundering. While she searches their stores, Tiago and I return to *La Espiral* to collect the unconscious crew.

El Mar Oscuro's atmosphere makes it easy to lug the bodies over. Once the piratas are packed inside their own ship, Laura hands me our loot—a few sacks of yerba for mate—and she pockets a small silver wolf with a chipped-off snout. When we disembark, she presses her hands to the ship's exterior, and the spiky ball rockets into the blackness beyond.

We keep watching until the invisible current carries it from view.

Morning is just a couple of hours away by the time we head back to our rooms to get some sleep. Zaybet said the Olvido in the dormilona potion erases the past couple of days to disorient its target, and now all I can think about is how many memories tonight cost Enzo.

How long until he wakes up? Will he be okay? Will he forgive us?

Adrenaline is still coursing through me when Tiago shuts the door to our room. We watch each other, and I expect him to say something about what I did. How I broke out of the pirata's force field.

I wait for him to ask me the same question as Yamila and Ariana's mom.

What. Are. You?

We're not in our transformed state, yet a wolfish energy remains between us. I'm irritated with him, but I don't remember why.

He pulls off his shirt, the look in his eyes far from rational.

I don't know which of us shoves the other onto the bed.

Our mouths are fused, and our limbs are as tangled as our tongues. Tiago's hands dig into my spine, massaging lower and lower, pressing deeper and deeper into my skin, until my muscles are rubbery and loose. I run my fingers through his thicket of hair, while my nails scrape down his rippled back.

He sucks in a sharp breath, and his tongue travels down my neck while his hand slides up my inner thigh.

Desire rushes to my brain like a drug, softening the edges of my vision, burning my skin from the inside. Every part of me tingles, down to my fingertips. My hands curl on Tiago's shoulder, and as I shiver, I slice open his skin.

I gasp and pull my hand back.

My claws are out, and Tiago's blood is trickling down my finger. There's a twist in my uterus, like the transformation is about to set in—

I draw away from him and lie on my back, gasping for air, pushing down the impulse. When Tiago comes closer, I flinch away, afraid I'll shift on contact.

"It's okay," he says gently. "You're not going to change."

He lies beside me for a long time, while I rake in deep breaths. Finally, I ask, "Did I hurt you?"

"Not at all. Are you okay?"

"I don't understand what happened."

"It's why I was trying to slow us down." He goes quiet like he's nervous, and I can't imagine what he's got to feel awkward about. "I've only ever been with brujas before. I-I don't know what sex with another werewolf is like."

I blink.

Somehow, I didn't see that coming.

"But from what I hear," he goes on, tentatively, "it's primal enough to trigger the transformation."

"Oh." After a beat, I'm too curious not to ask, "How does it work with brujas?"

"Brujas can handle themselves because they have magic. Sometimes they like to use it during sex. And for wolves who can't control their shifts, there's potions that help. That's a big part of why everyone looks forward to Lunaris so much."

"What do you mean?"

Now he looks like he's biting back a grin. "Well . . . we can let go completely, without fear of getting hurt."

"Meaning?"

"Put it this way," he says, his crooked smirk breaking through. "Most of us were conceived under a full moon."

18

Tomorrow is my broadcast. It's happening in Juramento, a place that is supposed to be a sacred confessional for Septimus.

These past two days, Cata has been drafting speeches and making me rehearse them on a continuous loop, interrupting with notes like: *Look more contrite! Chin up for this part! You sound rehearsed!*

No shit.

Today we finally settled on the wording. After trashing dozens of drafts, we decided I should say as little as possible in this first address, which is fine by me. I manage to escape her room by pretending I'm running down to get a snack, and the first thing I do is knock on Enzo's door.

"Come in." His voice is raspier than usual.

I find him sitting up in bed, watching Zaybet's and his favorite telenovela on a handheld pantaguas.

"How you feeling?" I accidentally lean into his leg as I perch on the mattress, and I shift quickly when I hear his low gasp of pain.

"Achiness is gone." He adjusts his back on the pillows. "Headbuzz too. Only reason I'm still lying here is you're all hysterical."

He was unconscious for a day and lost much more time than we anticipated. Laura told us the last thing he remembers is my demonstration at el Centro Comercial. He forgot about playing Septibol with us and scoring the only goal of the match.

"We're just making sure you're healthy enough to risk your life for us again."

"I don't know what you're talking about." He digs a spoon into the jar of dulce de leche Laura must have brought him. "I'm only humoring you because I'm outnumbered."

Yet he doesn't actually seem put out; he looks well-tended. I survey the books and snacks on his bedside that Zaybet and Laura probably placed there. They're not usually this open about their affection for him, and I wonder when was the last time anybody took care of Enzo, or made him feel loved.

"Listen," I say, getting to my feet. "I'm sorry we risked your memories like that. It was wrong."

"All good," he says, and he mumbles something else that's too jumbled to make out. He sets down the jar on the nightstand and raises the volume of his pantaguas, like my visit is over. And a flash of silver by the dulce de leche catches my eye.

Enzo notices, and he picks up the chipped wolf Laura plundered from the piratas. "Lau knows I like broken toys," he says with a half shrug.

It's only after I've shut the door to his room that my brain deciphers his mumble.

"If only you'd taken them all."

Before going anywhere else, I close my eyes and concentrate on Cata's lavender aroma, until I sniff her out downstairs. Probably searching for me.

I head upstairs instead, all the way to the top, which leads into the dark enclosure where the vampiros sleep during the day. Their stems are planted here, so the ground is covered in dirt. Saysa is buried in a nest of vines, just as she was in my mate-induced hallucination on the morning of my first transformation.

Only unlike the Citadel's green ivy, the black vampiros don't hurt her. They let Saysa clean their teeth, and they even chew the mint leaves she prods into their mouths.

This alcove is just about Saysa's size, so I have to hunch down to get in. "Hey," I say, inhaling the space's earthy musk. I sit a few feet away to keep some distance between me and the sharp maws.

"Hey, Cata was looking for you."

"Yeah, I'm meeting her in a moment." I hug my knees to my chest as a few vampiros slither closer. "How's it, uh, going here?"

"Good," she says, feeding mint leaves into the mouths of the black vines in her hands. "Almost finished."

"You fit well here." She looks at me quizzically, and I clarify, "Not this enclosure—I mean the *Coven*."

She releases the squirmy plants, shrugging as they twist away. "I've been dreaming of this place since I was a little kid. I've always known it was real and I'd find it one day."

"That's amazing." There's a slight edge to my words, and I

realize I'm a little jealous. I can read all over Saysa that she's found the true home she's been chasing her whole life. Her place in the world.

That's all I've ever wanted.

And at this rate, it's something I'll never have.

"I hate that we haven't talked much lately," I say, clearing my throat. "It feels like since Lunaris, you've been avoiding—"

"We've been running—"

"I think my situation is pulling focus from what you're going through," I force myself to say in one quick clip. "You won't talk about what happened with Nacho. Or the Congeladora in Kukú."

I don't add what happened with me in La Cancha, but it feels like we're both thinking it.

Saysa reaches for a black vine. This one has a few thorns, and she grabs a small blade to clip them. The vampiro lies docile in her hands.

"You don't have to talk about it with me if you don't want, but at least give me a chance to say thank you. For protecting us."

Saysa looks at me sharply. *"How can you say that?* You saw what I did to you—what I almost—"

"That's my point," I say gently. "You're going through something. We *all* are."

She looks down and concentrates on pruning the vine.

"But have you asked yourself what would have happened to us—to *me*—if not for you?"

She still doesn't meet my gaze.

"My first day of class, Señora Lupe assigned us to collect a dozen petals using magic, but you couldn't harm the flowers," I say, keeping an eye on the vampiros so they don't get too close. "It was hard for most brujas to pull off that level of control, but that was the point of practicing. Have you ever tried studying the darker side to your healing magic?"

Saysa finally sets down the blade and looks up. Her eyes are shiny as she shakes her head *no*. "Everyone wants to think of Jardineras as fairy tale princesses who talk to plants and sing to woodland creatures. They don't want to acknowledge the other side to our power."

I scoot closer despite the vampiros and take her hand in mine. "Maybe there's someone you could talk to—"

Saysa wrests her fingers free and clasps a vampiro that's coiled around her neck. She unspools it and picks up the blade to prune it.

"When a Jardinera . . . hurts another Septimus," she mutters, "she has to be reported."

The vampiros are now slithering onto my lap, and I slide back a bit. "But it doesn't seem like Yamila reported—"

"That's not her doing," says Saysa, a hollow look on her face, like a ghost's just walked through her. "Most wolves wouldn't want to admit a bruja got the best of them. Especially not a Cazador like Nacho. I bet he told her not to report me because . . ."

"He wants to handle things himself," I finish for her, and she nods.

"Everyone fears a powerful Jardinera. Even other brujas."

"But repressing your fear isn't a solution," I say, plucking a vine off my knee. "I get panic attacks too. I think that's what happened to you when you saw Nacho again, and the other night when the tormenta struck—"

"I can handle my own shit, Manu!"

Saysa's voice and hand shake, and she snips too deep when cutting a thorn, making the vampiro bleed red. "Fuck!"

The vine shoots away from her, coiling into itself like a snake.

"I'm sorry," she says, but the plant refuses to let her get close again. It bares its jaws at her.

"*See?*" Saysa rounds on me. "I already know I have the same darkness that destroys some Jardineras—but I can't talk about it, because if I do, it'll surface. It's like this volcanic mass of rage in the pit of my stomach that's always on the brink of erupting. I know you think deep down I'm a good bruja, but I'm not!"

Her eyes flicker with power, like neon signs, and the enclosure starts to quiver in warning. The vampiros hunch low to the ground, like they're afraid.

"The Coven is the only world I've visited that makes any sense to me," she says as the shaking stops. "Out there, I'll burst."

From the way she's talking, it doesn't sound like she has any plans of finishing her schooling. "Have you talked to Cata about what she wants yet?"

"The only thing that matters right now is your broadcast." So that's a *no.* "We all need you to take this seriously."

Now she sounds just like Cata and Tiago.

Some of the vines have draped over my arms, and I begin the dreaded process of detangling myself. Irritable jaws snap in my face, and I can feel a few stings on my wrist and shoulder. I slide back until I'm close to the stairs, too near the daylight for them to follow, relieved to be free of the plants' coarse caresses.

"You *are* a good bruja," I say as I'm leaving. "Even before I knew you, the Septis you smuggled out saved my life. And once you learned what I am, you were the first to accept me. I don't know about these Coveners—all I know is *you* didn't hesitate. Just like I know the real Saysa would never compromise her values to fit in *anywhere.*"

I don't linger to see her reaction to my words, and I feel sadness welling in my chest as I trade the dim enclosure for the brightness of the artificial sun. Between Cata's overprotectiveness, Tiago's tunnel vision, and Saysa's dual allegiances, I can't trust any of my friends to guide me through this decision.

They're not objective enough to consider things from my perspective.

They don't realize they're not just asking me to lie . . . They're asking me to become a lie.

I leap down the balconies instead of taking the stairs, and when I get to the ground level, I knock Zaybet off her feet.

"Oh—sorry!"

I reach out and catch her with both arms, right before her head hits the ground. Our chests bump, and her metallic eyes are round with shock as I pull her up.

I feel a sheepish grin burn my face. "Still working on my lobizona skills."

"It's . . . okay," she says, breathing between words.

I inhale a lavender bomb's approach. "Hey, I was hoping to visit el Hongo, but I ran out of—"

"Sure," says Zaybet, walking me to the mats and handing me a shot glass full of dried mushroom shavings.

She looks slightly alarmed by the speed with which I knock it back. As usual, el Hongo tastes dry and chewy. I shut my eyes right as I hear Cata rushing over and calling out, "Tell me she didn't—"

Oh, but she did.

As I launch into the deep end of my mind, at last I'm free to indulge in my thoughts. This is the only alone time I can get lately. Like I do every day, I try sending Gael a message.

Are you there?

I don't feel any kind of connection. It's like picking up the phone and not hearing a dial tone.

I'm the ultimate hypocrite for encouraging Saysa to open up when I'm keeping secrets again. I still haven't told my friends about my ability to deflect magic. Not because I don't trust them, but because I want to figure out what it means before anyone else decides for me.

I'm done being the oddity in the room.

I'm afraid if I keep metamorphosing, I'll pull a Gregor Samsa and wake up a bug. I'll shift one phase too far and become unrecognizable to myself.

It's the same fear I have about tomorrow. The thought of telling my truth terrifies me, but lying frightens me more. No matter what I say, my identity will change—and I'm not sure which direction it should go.

And then there's Yamila's threat of going after Ma. Once I make this declaration, she's going to be eager to tear it apart.

If she hasn't already caught up to Ma, she'll double her efforts. I need to know that she's safe with Gael. That they're *both* safe.

Can you hear me? I try again.

Still no connection.

I distract myself by scanning the latest headlines. The word *ladrona* has been coming up more and more frequently in my searches, and since I'm not in any rush to get back to Cata, I look into the lore again.

The haunting lullaby starts to play in my mind, and I learn that the whole thing is a scare tactic. La ladrona is a cautionary tale made up to reinforce the border between Septimus and humans. A way of discouraging the birth of hybrids like me.

As I go deeper into the mythology, I come across the five tenets that apply to la ladrona:

She will sneak into Lunaris.
She will steal the lobizones' power.

She will match the brujas' magic.
She will be the world's undoing.
She will only be known by her treacherous eyes.

My heart pounds in my chest. Any of these traits could be twisted to sound like they're about me. Especially that last line. It wouldn't be my life if it didn't center around my eyes.

She will match the brujas' magic.

Now I know why Tiago didn't say anything when I broke out of the Invocadora's force field. He probably realizes if anyone learns I can dodge magic, I'll be even more fucked than I already am.

Yamila knows. Just like she knows about Ma. Yamila knows all my secrets, and the only way to protect myself is with a preemptive strike.

I need to take control of my narrative before she does.

Are you there? I snap at Gael. *I really need to talk to you!*

I still don't feel his presence, and at this point, I doubt I'll get the chance to talk to him before my broadcast. But I'm at least going to say what I need to say, even if only the universe is listening.

You'll probably never hear this, but we did what you said. We connected with the Coven. I guess you probably realize that by now. You probably also noticed I've been using your playbook. Sort of.

Tomorrow morning is my final demonstration. I'm going to give a broadcast to the Septimus. Cata baked up some story for me to recite about how I was force-fed Olvido and don't know my own past.

Is that what you and Ma want? Once I own this story, I'll be a secret forever. And our family knows better than most that secrets are defined by their proximity to exposure. I'll always be one step away from losing it all.

I guess I'm just cursed to carry out the cycle I was born into: Hide like Ma, or become a lie like you.

The anger spiking my voice surprises me, but I keep going, needing to pull on this thread until I've undone the knot in my chest.

In Lunaris, you told us to plant a new garden. I even saw your disappointment when I chose the brujas' locker room instead of the lobizones' before the championship. You must want me to speak my truth, no matter the consequences. Right? Even if it kills me?

You sent us on a suicide mission! *Didn't you realize the odds? Why didn't you help us?*

Why didn't you protect me?

Why haven't you ever *protected me?*

I suddenly feel claustrophobic in this realm, and I need to return to my body.

I open my eyes so abruptly that the Coven spins around as I yank myself back to reality. I suck in shallow breaths until the world stabilizes, relieved I only spoke those words in my head.

No one else ever needs to hear them.

"One more time."

"Cata, the speech is short," says Saysa. "Manu's got it down."

"It's seriously so ingrained in my brain that I think it's what really happened."

"Good, then maybe you'll have a shot at pulling it off," says Cata. It's late, and the four of us are gathered once more in her and Saysa's room.

"Is this about me being a bad liar?" I ask.

"This is about your *survival*," says Tiago, and I close my eyes, breathing out my frustration that he's always on Team Cata.

Then I stand straight, stare at the wall in front of me, and say, "Hi, my name is Manu, and I'm a lobizona. Until last moon, I was in hiding because I'm different. My powers were repressed, and I couldn't reach you."

Be contrite but tough, I hear Cata directing me in my head.

"I don't want to be on the run like this, but it's hard to know who I can trust, aside from the friends protecting me. They're my manada."

Now is when I let my feelings show. Since lobizones think brujas are too emotional to lead, Cata thinks the more vulnerable I seem, the less of a threat they'll find me.

But not too vulnerable, Saysa likes to remind me. Or I'll risk looking weak to my new followers.

"Last moon was the first time I remember visiting Lunaris." I'm supposed to pause a beat because this revelation is what Cata calls a *Very Big Deal* and Septimus hearing it may need a moment.

"The first time I dared to exist. I couldn't show myself to you before now because . . ."

I swallow.

"I don't know my past. I was drugged with Olvido."

19

In the morning, new crews rotate into the Coven, and when the star-studded calabaza gourd comes sailing at me on a gentle breeze, I smile because it means Rocío is back.

"¿Cómo estás?" I ask, trying to engage her. I know she has a rough time at home.

"Mejor," she says with a rare and radiant smile. "Desde que apareciste, me siento más aceptada en mi manada. Tu presencia lo cambió todo." *Ever since you showed up, I've felt more accepted in my pack. Your presence has changed everything.*

"English!" snaps Zaybet, coming up behind us right as I'm opening my mouth to speak. "Time to go," she says, pulling me along.

"I'm happy for you, Rocío!" I call back. I slurp down the mate, and I rest the starry gourd on a table on our way out.

Once the seven of us are on *La Espiral*, tension tautens my vocal cords. Juramento is a mountain that can be accessed by land, air, or sea, where anyone can make any kind of confession. It's up to the individual whether they want their admission to be made public or to remain private among the affected parties.

According to Cata, in a pack species, secrets are poison. Juramento is so sacred to Septimus that on-duty Cazadores aren't allowed on the premises because Septimus have to feel safe enough to open up.

Cata, Saysa, and I agonized over whether or not I should match my clothes to my eyes for this broadcast. Saysa felt I shouldn't because I'm not a bruja, but Cata insisted the gesture would go a long way for the tribunal. In the end, I decided on a gold sweater.

"Not to fit in, but to prove that even when I play by the rules, I still stand out in the current system," I explained. This satisfied both of them.

"The press scours public confessions for story ideas," says Enzo while he, Tiago, and I scan the view through *La Espiral*'s window. "Yours will be breaking news."

"Can someone come with me?" I ask, not for the first time.

"*No,*" says Enzo. "Only direct bloodline can access the same confessional."

I work hard not to look at Cata. "You mean like a cousin?"

"Too far removed," says Enzo, his gaze still locked on the view. "But say you and Tiago had a child, the three of you would be able to enter together."

"Thank you for that awkward example," says Laura, her hands pressed to the ship. I look over her head at Tiago to exchange glances, but his attention is rapt on the view—or his thoughts.

Blackness bleeds from the atmosphere until we're navigating through the clear ocean. "Cata and Saysa will escort you to the entrance," says Zaybet. She insisted I pull on her silver Marina cloak so I'm not recognized. "When you're finished, use your horario to let us know."

I nod, my mouth too dry to form words.

A massive wall of earth rises up from the seafloor. The base of the mountain extends as far as I can see, and as we get closer, I spy pore-like openings in the dirt. The shell-ship suctions onto one of them.

"I'll walk you out," says Tiago, taking my hand.

Zaybet, Laura, and Enzo stay behind, while my friends and I pad down the tongue-like hall to the exit. Cata and Saysa disembark first to give Tiago and me a minute.

"You sure about this?" he asks.

I nod since my jaw is locked.

A softness comes over his gaze, and he says, "Manu, I . . . *adore* you."

The word strikes my heart like an arrow. Yet before I can say it back, a frown of dissatisfaction comes over Tiago's features. Like saying it out loud felt wrong.

But *adore* barely scrapes the surface of what I feel for him.

Cata knocks on the ship wall, and Tiago presses his lips to mine before nudging me out.

I join Cata and Saysa in a dirt passage that spills into a cavernous underground where a long line of Septimus are spaced out along a curving and unending rocky wall. We walk around the line in silence, and I notice that some Septimus have come alone, while others seem to need the support of family and friends.

The atmosphere is tense enough that no one gives us a second look. We're not the only ones worried about being identified—everyone here is wearing some kind of hood or veil or hat. I guess shame is a great equalizer.

The ground trembles, and I flash to my nightmares of the

stone mountain as a fissure cracks down the wall, right in front of a group of teens.

Rather than look alarmed, they all take turns hugging one of the guys. As the fissure in the mountain expands into a gap just large enough for one person, the guy's chest heaves a few times, then he steps inside.

The rockface seals behind him.

From the ticked-off expressions and loud complaints of some of the other groups gathered here, individual wait times seem to vary.

"Tiago looked upset," murmurs Cata while we walk in search of a large enough open stretch of wall. Argentines have no sense of personal space aboveground, but down here, each group is very socially distanced.

"Everything okay?" she prods.

"I have no clue," I admit, relieved to have something else to think about. "A week ago, he kept insisting how he really, *really* likes me, and just now he said he *adores* me—but right after, his face changed. Like he didn't feel it."

Like he's trying to convince himself, I don't say out loud. Maybe he's finally realized he's given up too much for me.

"You know what he's trying to say, don't you?" asks Cata.

"No."

Saysa chuckles. "No te hagas la boluda."

Did she just tell me to stop playing dumb? "If Tiago said anything to you—"

Cata tugs on my arm, and for a moment I think she's seen a Cazador. But she just stares into me with her unflappable pink gaze.

"You're serious," she mutters, shaking her head. "You two really are made for each other."

Saysa snorts. "Smart with books, dumb with life."

I spot an empty swath of wall and dart over before anyone else takes it. Clearly Cata and Saysa aren't in the mood to be helpful—

The rockface trembles.

My friends have barely caught up to me when a fissure cracks down the stone. Everyone turns to stare, but it's not the same mild interest the teen guy got. The crowd watching me looks indignant.

"¿Qué sucede?"

"¡Recién llegó!"

They don't think it's fair that I barely had to wait. "Go," urges Saysa, wrenching me into a quick hug. "You got this."

Her warmth makes me hope she's not altogether indifferent to our conversation from yesterday. Cata whispers her own encouragement next, as she shoves me into the mountain.

"Don't fuck it up."

As soon as I step into the dim passage, the exit behind me seals off.

Again, I'm reminded of the stone mountain in Lunaris, and a chill ripples down my spine. I stare at the walls hoping my wolf-shadow will appear, and when nothing happens, I feel more alone than before.

There's a tightening around my wrist, and I remember my horario. It's camouflaged, but I can still feel its presence. Like a friend's grip on my arm.

I don't know if this does anything, but I cup my hand around it, hoping it's like a hug.

The air down here isn't earthy and musty, but crisp and cool, like air conditioning. The passage ahead seems to be unending, and after a while, I get bored of walking, so I break into a run. The speed is exhilarating, and I let myself go until I start to transform.

A silent scream parts my lips as my bones elongate, my hair thickens, my edges sharpen—and when I shift into a lobizona, a light materializes ahead, and I leap into a bright, open space.

I land on my feet, knees bent, claws at the ready, as I behold . . . *a recording studio.*

There's a couch facing a large mirror, which by now I know to be a camera. Yet the mirror is completely dark. There's a red button beside it that I assume I must hit to begin.

Off to the side, there's a smaller area with a bathroom and a large vanity full of products and accessories, plus a rack of fresh clothes. I pull off Zaybet's cloak and set it on the couch. Then I feel a tug in my uterus.

Pain rips through my body as my bones shrink, my fangs and claws recede, my hair thins out, until at last, I'm human-sized again.

Only I'm no longer alone. Someone else arrived while I was transforming.

Someone with an unmistakable almond scent.

"*¿Mami?*"

20

She doesn't answer. Tears flood my eyes as a sob bubbles up my throat, and a single syllable gurgles out of me. *"¿Ma?"*

I can't believe it. She's here and she's safe and she's in front of me.

I know Gael is behind her, but I can't pull away from my mother's brown eyes. They're glazed like she's in deep shock. She hasn't even blinked.

Because she just saw me as a *lobizona*.

The realization paralyzes me as much as it does her. I keep still so I won't frighten her any more than I already have. What if she runs? What if she's disgusted? What if she—?

Ma rushes forward and pulls me into her now-bony arms. Cries erupt from both of us as we clutch each other close. I press my nose to her neck, breathing her in, and she holds me there the way she used to, until I'm safe again.

"Te quiero tanto, Mami," I say into her ear, her shoulders shaking from the force of her sobs. *I love you so much.*

"Mi nena, mi nena hermosa," she moans, rocking me back and forth. *My girl, my beautiful girl.*

"Did he—tell you—?"

"Everything," she says, reaching up and taking my face in her hands, her puffy, watery eyes studying me. "Now I want to hear it from you."

I lead Ma to the couch, and we sit so close, we're sharing a cushion. Then I tell her all about taking the trip to El Laberinto in the bed of Nacho's truck, discovering the Septimus, making friends. Throughout the whole thing, she keeps her expression neutral, like a seasoned card player.

It's strangely easier telling Ma about discovering I'm a lobizona than describing my relationship with Tiago. It's at this point in the story that her poker face cracks. "I thought you'd told me everything," she says, grilling Gael with her stare. "Did you know about this Tiago character?"

"He has a good heart. You don't have to worry about him."

I still haven't taken my eyes off Ma, not because I'm avoiding Gael, but because I'm afraid if I look away, she'll disappear. But I've noticed my father has yet to step in from the doorway.

Once I've finished my story, my shoulders sink in relief that it's over. And yet, the way Ma's looking at me, it's as if she's seeing a stranger. It's the same way she seemed to me when I saw her in those blue nurse's scrubs at Doña Rosa a million moons ago.

"I thought I told you to listen to Perla."

The emotion dries from her voice as a more familiar Ma comes out. Even though she just saw me transform from a were-wolf, her main gripe is I disobeyed her order.

"What were you thinking following some stranger into the Everglades? What if he killed you, and people thought I didn't teach you better?"

I blink.

Then Ma and I burst into our cackling laughs. The ones reserved for late-night shit-talking and old episodes of *El Chavo del Ocho*. Even Gael chuckles, and I look at him for the first time. He seems a bit diminished in our presence.

"I'm so proud of you, Manu," says Ma, making me want to cry again.

"How have *you* been?" I ask, eager to hear her tale. I hold Ma's hands in front of me as I examine her. Other than having dropped at least ten pounds, she looks whole. I don't see any visible injuries or scars.

"What happened at the detention center after ICE took you?"

"Gael rescued me."

There's an undeniable warmth that bathes her voice when she says his name, like she's sharing a secret. She looks past me to him, and he takes a moment to join us, moving rather timidly. He's more subdued than I've seen him. No snarky smirk, no challenge, no words.

He sits on the other cushion, sandwiching me. "The hardest part was locating where they were holding *Soledad Azul*." He says Ma's name like it's an inside joke too, and neither of them suppresses their smiles.

It suddenly occurs to me that they knew each other under different names. He knew Ma by her *real* name.

"Then he broke me out."

"How?" I ask.

"I snuck into the detention center the same night I returned from Lunaris," says Gael, looking past me to Ma. "Your face when you woke up and saw me in your room . . . I was sure you were about to punch me."

His gaze cuts to mine. "And that's exactly what she did."

Ma laughs, and I stare at her with wide eyes. "You hit him?"

"He got off easy."

He bows his head. "Fair enough. Then we went to see Perla at Luisita's, and I left your mom there while I checked in at El Laberinto. The Cazadores offered me a chance to clear my record if I located you—tracking is what I did best when I worked for them."

"But how did you and Ma get to Argentina? I saw you at La Rosada like a day or two later."

"The Cazadores have a fleet of private planes for urgent situations. They're co-piloted by an Encendedora and an Invocadora, so we're not detected by human radar. I had to stow your mom with the luggage."

"Were you okay?" I ask, squeezing her hands.

"What he's not telling you is we made the trip in just a couple of hours. I barely had time for a nap."

"Were you able to visit your parents when you got here?"

She looks at Gael. "We decided it could be dangerous to involve them, with the Septimus so focused on our family at the moment."

"How's Perla?" I ask, twisting my back to Gael, a wall keeping him out.

"She's better—and her eyesight improved! None of her doctors could believe it. She'll probably make it into medical textbooks," adds Ma with a laugh.

I smile, but I'm thinking of the immunity booster Saysa gave Perla when they met. Do brujas use their magic on humans often? Are the effects documented? I want to consult Gael, but now isn't the time.

"She's still too frail to live alone, so she moved in with Lu-isita," Ma goes on. "Every time I call, they both want to be on the line, and all they do is talk over each other, so we never say anything!"

I grin, mostly at Ma's smile, which is incandescent.

"What about Julieta from the clinic? And the woman with the baby?"

"We were all using the same public defender. She seemed good, like she knew what she was doing." Ma's smile grows strained. "It just happened so fast, and I was only thinking of getting to you, I didn't—"

"We'll help them," I say quickly. "How did you find me here?"

I turn to Gael as he says, "When you mentioned a broadcast, I know you were coming to Juramento. Since we're the same bloodline, it was also my best chance to bring you two together."

It takes me a moment to register the meaning of his words.

"You—you heard what I said in el Hongo?"

He nods, once, and awkwardness sweeps through me.

"Manu," he says in a foreign, fatherly tone I'm not familiar with, "I swear I believed I was protecting your mom by staying away. I thought disappearing was the only thing I could do for her."

"Same as you're doing for me?"

I can't hold back the accusation, and I'm reassured when Ma's hands tighten their grip, lending me her strength.

"You have no idea how much I wish I could keep you safe from the world," he says in a choked breath, and Ma drops one of my hands to take his.

"I would give anything to go back and give you a happy home," says Gael, scooping my free hand in his, so that the three of us are completely connected. "Both of you. I wish I knew what I was doing, but I'm just as fucked up as anyone, probably *more*—"

"Language."

Ma gives Gael her no-nonsense stare, and he looks at me to see if she's serious.

"The truth is," says Ma, "none of us had any good choices. Maybe I was selfish to keep you." Her gaze grows heavy as she looks at me, and something squirmy twists in my gut. "The moment I saw your eyes, I knew you didn't belong in my world. But I didn't want to give you up."

"Ma, don't," I say, horrified at the thought of her abandoning me as a baby, and us not having each other.

"Let's just try to make up for the time we lost," says Gael, and something in his tone is very reminiscent of his niece when she has a plan. "The Cazadores offered to reinstate me. I'm going to request to be stationed in our Madrid manada, where I can hide you both better. What do you think? Can we give it a shot, the three of us?"

I feel the muscles of my face loosening, and my shoulders drop as my spine curves into a C. It's like a full-body exhale, expelling air that went stale long ago.

I look at Ma, and her brown eyes are overly bright. "I'm in an apartment in Buenos Aires. We can stay there until the search for you dies down and the transfer is approved. First thing we'll do is call Perla—she'll be so happy to talk to you!"

The smile on my face is so outsized that it feels like it's digging into my ears. This is all so surreal, and I'm slightly drunk on the euphoria.

A couple of months ago, I thought what I wanted most in the world was a green card. I didn't dream of asking for more. I had no idea I could have my family restored.

"What will I do on the full moon?" I ask Gael.

"There's an injection that will put you in a magical coma for a few nights. *Anestesia.* It's not easy to get, but I have access to it through the Cazadores." Hope seems to beam from his every pore. "You don't need to worry anymore. Let me step up and take care of you."

As I'm watching him, I realize we share the same nose. Straight and not large, but still prominent.

"Buenos Aires has changed so much, Manu," says Ma, and I twist toward her again. "I can't wait to show it to you. The apartment has this great little balcony that overlooks a busy intersection, and you'll love the people-watching. It's better than anything you could've seen from El Retiro."

Ma and Gael are still smiling wide, like we're all breathing in the same euphoric air, only its effects are starting to dissipate, like Lunaris mist.

And the new vista being revealed looks all too familiar.

Miami, Buenos Aires, Madrid—it's all the same because I'll be confined indoors. No friends, no school, no photos, no social life. Just watching telenovelas with Ma, waiting for Gael to come home with news, and hiding behind my sunglasses.

Turns out the stone mountain wasn't the scariest thing I'd ever dreamt as a human.

The true nightmare was waking up.

"I've lived that life."

When I realize I said the words out loud, I think I might throw up. "I mean, I didn't—"

I clear my throat and try again. "I don't mean—"

But no matter how hard I try, I can't take the words back. I can't lie to Ma. So instead, I squeeze her hand and stare into her frozen face in a desperate hope she understands. "I outgrew it."

She blinks a few times, and tears spray the air. "W-what are you saying?"

"I'm alive, Ma." I bite my inner lip to keep my chin from trembling. "Thanks to *you*." Tears spill down my face. "You got me here. You kept me safe from werewolves and witches and ICE. In the story of my life, you're the superhero."

Ma's soft sobs fill the room, and I would give anything to stop here. To be the obedient girl Ma used to know, who always did as she was told. But when I try to summon that Manu, I don't know her anymore.

"You sacrificed everything so I would have a chance to make my own choices one day, and that's what I'm doing now."

"I can't protect you in Kerana." Gael's voice is thick, and when I look at him, I'm taken aback by the emotion in his coral eyes. "You can't make it on your own—"

"I'm not. I have the Coven." I try to sound more confident than I feel. "I have my *friends*." Strength courses through me with that word, and I know I'm not alone. "I'm going to change things, like you said."

"You're leaving this place with us, Manuela." Ma manages to call up her old authoritative tone, the one that always made my spine stiffen and my gaze drop with guilt, even when I'd done nothing wrong. She grips my fingers so tight, hers are turning red and purple.

I carefully unclasp her hand, then I rub it to get the circulation back to normal. "When you asked me to leave you at Doña Rosa, I did. Against everything I wanted to do in that moment. So I need you to do the same for me. I promise I'll find you when it's safe."

She stares pointedly at Gael, like he might talk some sense into me. "You can't protect us both," I say as I look at his defeated expression. "I get that now."

"No, no, no, no," says Ma, shaking her head adamantly, and I pull her into a hug, holding her to my chest, resisting her protests. After a long while, she relaxes in my arms, and I caress her hair while she rests her face in the crook of my shoulder.

"Do you know what you'll say in your broadcast?" asks Gael softly.

Instead of Cata's speech, I think back to the party at the Coven after the Septibol match, when I accidentally called the Septimus' wine *malbec*. I'll always make mistakes like these because I was raised human. As much as I might try repressing that part of me, adopting a new culture doesn't magically erase the old one. They get braided together.

Ma sits up and looks at me, her face red and splotchy and wet. "I'm sorry. I'm so sorry, Manu, I've failed you—"

"You didn't—"

"I've always known I couldn't give you what you needed," she says through her cries.

"You're wrong." I take her face in my hands and look into her liquid brown eyes. "Mami, you've given me *everything*."

It feels like hours have passed by the time I'm standing in front of the dark mirror, taking steadying breaths, ready to begin my broadcast.

Parting with Ma was unbearable. Gael had to practically carry her out of this room, and even as they were leaving, I debated going after them.

I don't know the next time we'll be together again.

After falling apart on the couch, I dragged myself to the vanity, where I pulled myself back together. I have no idea if I made the right decision. All I know is I can't go back into hiding. Even if that means risking it all.

I inhale as I hit the red button.

PÚBLICO
PRIVADO

The two words appear on the dark glass, and I touch *public*.
Then the mirror turns clear.

"Hi, um, everyone." *What did I just say?* "M-my name is Manu,
and I'm a lobizona."

I clear my throat of its dryness. I should have brought a bottle of water.

"Until last moon, I was in hiding because I'm different. My
powers were repressed, and I couldn't reach you."

Is this the contrite or the vulnerable part? *Shit shit shit.* This is
probably why I'm such a bad liar. I blink at myself in the mirror,
and I look as if I'm paused.

"I-I don't want to be on the run like this, but it's hard to know
who I can trust, aside from the friends protecting me. They're
my manada."

The truth of these words settles on me. The biggest change in
my life since stumbling upon the Septimus hasn't been having
superpowers. It's having a *pack*.

They're my hope at the end of it all. And they're depending
on me to sell this.

"Last moon was the first time I remember visiting Lunaris." I rest for a beat like Cata instructed me. "The first
time I dared to exist. I couldn't show myself to you before now
because . . ."

Olvido is at the tip of my tongue.

One word, and it's done.

Only . . . only lying right now would be the same as accepting my parents' offer. It may feel different because this cage is
emotional instead of physical, but I would still be crammed into
a space not large enough to fit the full me.

Cata and Tiago are so afraid that they want me to lock myself into a cage for the rest of my life. Same as Ma and Gael. So I think of Saysa, because I know deep down she doesn't agree.

She's just so tired of being excluded that she doesn't want to lose this place. She's so desperate for the Coven to live up to all her expectations that she's refusing to ask the important questions. But we won't know if it's the true manada for us until we do. If Saysa's not thinking clearly right now, I need to be strong for the both of us.

"I'm not like you," I watch my reflection say.

Then for better or worse, I set myself free.

"I'm a human hybrid."

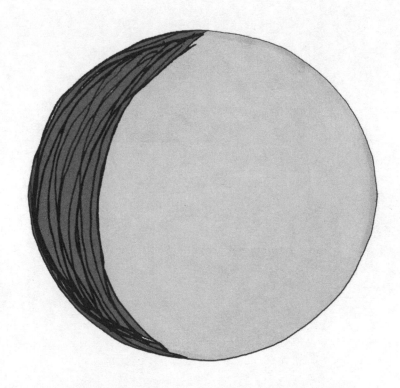

PHASE III

21

The return trip on *La Espiral* is tense. I've been quiet since I boarded, but nobody presses me. They all act like there's an aura around me that they don't dare penetrate, even Tiago.

I'm relieved for the space because I can hardly breathe, much less form sentences.

I focus on Ma to escape the way Cata's stare drills into my brain. I still can't believe I was just with her. I already miss her so much.

Her tears no longer dampen my sweater, and I press my hand to the fabric, wishing I could still smell a whiff of almonds. I wonder what it was like for my parents to see each other again after nearly eighteen years apart. It's hard to tell how they feel from that one interaction. There was definitely a connection . . . I just don't know if it's romantic or nostalgic. Or simply strategic.

A spike of excitement tells me when we're getting close to the Coven. Once we enter its rocky walls, a sense of safety floods my veins, and I wonder if the place is starting to feel like a real home.

There are more ships docked on the surface than when we took off, and by the time we walk into the common area, my legs have grown leaden. Almost a hundred rapt Coveners are staring at the largest pantaguas.

I'm jolted to see myself standing in the office space, midway through my script. My confession must have gone online the moment I finished speaking. News stations wasted no time.

"I don't want to be on the run like this, but it's hard to know who I can trust, aside from the friends protecting me. They're my manada. Last moon was the first time I remember visiting Lunaris."

I swallow in sync with the me on screen, and just as Cata predicted, there are gasps at my admission.

"The first time I dared to exist. I couldn't show myself to you before now because . . ."

I suck in a deep breath.

"I'm not like you."

On my exhale, everything changes.

"I'm a human hybrid."

Every face at the Coven turns to mine in such a synchronous movement that I can't help but admire it. Cata's eyes are bulging in utter bewilderment, and Saysa looks equal parts outraged and terrified. I feel Tiago's fingers close around mine.

The screen cuts to a newscaster who looks at a loss for words. "You are hearing this just moments after us, so we share your shock," she assures viewers in Spanish. "Any moment now, we're expecting word from the tribunal—"

The reporter's face flickers, and a different one appears on the waterscreen.

Cata inhales sharply, and tonight's twists feel never-ending.

It's her father, Bernardo.

Hovering beneath him is his official position: *Fiscal Alfa*. Alpha Prosecutor. He's wearing dark robes, only he's pinned something to the neckline that looks a bit like a flag . . . It's the Z emblem.

"Buenas noches, *Septimus*," he says, and I'm not sure if he emphasizes the word, or if I'm imagining it. "We just received a startling confession. In accordance with our laws, the tribunal is issuing an arrest warrant for the hybrid. We deputize all of you to help us capture her. Should she cross your path, all we ask is that you detain her and contact your local Cazadores. Thank you."

I think I'm going to be sick.

The newscaster comes back on, but her face flickers again, and the screen goes dark as the water melts into a pool. Somebody shut it off.

The Coveners come over, but they don't seem to be looking for an explanation. Judging by their expressions, they've already made up their minds.

The reactions range from stunned to fearful to revolted. Zaybet, Laura, and Enzo stand apart from the crowd, but also away from my friends and me. Like undecided voters.

Zaybet stares as hard as everyone else. "You were raised . . . *human?*"

The shock in her tone is softened by sympathy.

"Yes, but I've been in hiding most of my life." My voice carries, thanks to the wolves' whispers. "I was never really part of that world. It's only since discovering you all that my powers manifested. I transformed for the first time last moon."

There are gasps and hisses and more questions as my words travel, and Laura blurts, "How is this possible?"

"How is *any* of this possible?" is all I can think to respond. "You told me you believe el Mar Oscuro is literally the space between worlds—is one truth any wilder than the other?"

Zaybet's metallic eyes glint with amusement. "What a strange world this must seem to you," she muses. Then she turns to face the mass of Coveners, arms crossed in defiance; and when Enzo copies her posture, I realize what they're doing.

They're supporting me.

Laura joins them after a moment's hesitation. There's a break in the wall of Septimus, and Tinta y Fideo step forward through the crowd. Their coppery brown eyes reflect twin indignation.

"You should have told us!" Tinta snaps at me. "You've just set us back centuries!"

Zaybet jumps in to defend me. "You don't know that—"

"I know she just gave credibility to the conservative party!" he roars over her objections. "Septimus are going to start listening to those nutjobs that have been railing on about la ladrona. She just cost all three of our candidates their fucking elections!"

"We need to do damage control," says Fideo, his long fingers closing around his brother's shoulder. "If it comes to a vote, reach us on our horarios," he tells Zaybet, his mournful eyes sliding to me. "I'm sorry, Manu. Good luck."

They're not the only ones who leave.

About a third of the Septimus march out in protest. Most won't meet my gaze as they pass, except for one pair of peachy pink eyes.

Rocío looks at me like I could attack her at any moment. As though I grew horns between this morning and now.

She hastens to get away, and I can't fathom how she went from admiring to despising me, all over the circumstances of my birth. It's so outrageous that I'm not sure which of us is more affronted.

"Manu has done nothing wrong."

Cata steps forward like she's found her voice. "None of us can control who our parents are. She's only trying to find where she belongs. Until now, you were admiring her for helping defend the Coven against pirates while you were away. You should be thanking her instead of worrying about some old, sexist prejudice!"

"Cata's right," says Zaybet as my cousin joins her ranks, crossing her arms over her ribcage. "I can't believe anyone here could possibly think it's okay to punish someone for being born a certain way."

There's a rumbling in the throng, and some voices shout back.

"She's not a Septimus!"

"The Coven isn't for humans!"

"We don't know *what* she is!"

I try to tune out the barrage of retorts, but my body curves inward, devastated to learn the friendships I made weren't real. This isn't my pack after all.

A Septima crosses the divide and stands next to Zaybet. Her name is Ana, and she was one of Zaybet's crew who rescued us from La Isla Malvada. "If Manu was led to us, Lunaris must want us to help her."

Her friends Rox and Uma also come over. So does Ezequiel. He's soon joined by Horacio, Ximena, Angelina, Yónatan, and Oscar.

When Saysa steps up to join them, it feels like the room quiets down for her.

"I always believed the Coven was real. That's why the world out there has never had the power to hurt me—because I knew I belonged here. But if you don't accept Manu, then there is no true Coven. If we don't stand for everyone's rights, we don't stand for any."

The brujas who've been following Saysa around make their way to the front of the throng. The redhead squeezes into the first row of Coveners, as does the green-eyed Jardinera and the bruja with the shy smile. She's not smiling now.

"We care for *brujas'* rights," says the redhead. "Period."

"I thought we were *Septimas*," says Saysa.

"*We* are." Her narrowed eyes flash to mine. "*That* isn't."

"It's la ladrona!" says the Jardinera. "Pretending to be one of us is part of her plan."

"She probably wants to make an army of others just like her!" shouts someone else.

"How can we trust her?" asks the redhead, staring at Saysa in open defiance.

Saysa looks crestfallen. She doesn't bother answering because there's no point; she's already over this clique. I know it's not losing them that devastates her—it's losing her faith in the Coven.

I feel the same way.

As more crews arrive, everyone demands answers, and soon we're in the middle of what feels like a mob. I surf through the muddle of voices, and I hear labels lobbed at me from every direction, pelting me like rotted food.

Ladrona.

Unnatural.

Abomination.

Mutation.

Freak.

"I bet she's a spy for the humans!"

Sergio's voice thunders through the space, drowning many others. "They fucking know about us, don't they?" he demands, fighting his way toward me.

Tiago positions himself in front of me, while Zaybet and the others close ranks, forming a buffer.

"She's not a *spy*!" Zaybet shouts to match his volume. "She's a misfit, just like the rest of us. She's has nowhere to go. She's not dangerous, she's *in* danger—"

"We don't know she's not dangerous!" someone calls out.

"She could have powers we don't know about!"

"We have to turn her in!"

"No!" growls Sergio. "We're not snitches. And besides, she knows too much. We can deal with her ourselves."

The way he's looking at me sends a shiver of fear down my neck.

"Look, we're not getting anywhere," announces Zaybet. "Manu told us her situation, now we need to deliberate, and obviously her presence here isn't helping." Turning to me and my friends, she says in a lower register, "Grab some food and rest. There's nothing you can say tonight that they'll hear."

We skip the kitchen—for my part, I've never been less hungry—and the four of us retreat upstairs. Cata follows Tiago and me to our room, but Saysa won't even look my way. She goes straight to her room and slams the door.

Once we're inside, Cata leans against the dresser, head slung down and hair draped over her face. I expected her to be upset with me, but it's worse than that. She looks defeated.

Tiago paces, and since the room is tiny, he seems to be spinning.

"What happened in Juramento?" asks Cata in a deadened voice.

"I saw my mom."

She looks up, and Tiago stops pacing. So I describe everything that happened, from the moment I entered the mountain up until my confession. "I'm sorry. I fucked up." I feel tears burning the corners of my eyes, so I dig my fingers into my palms until red crescents mark my skin.

For one ridiculous moment, I thought I was doing the right thing.

I should have known beliefs are harder to change than laws.

After Cata leaves, I climb under the covers fully clothed and roll onto my side, staring at the agate wall. The lights dim, and I feel Tiago's weight settle on the mattress. His arms wrap around my waist, and I let silent tears drip down my cheeks.

The last thing I hear is his whisper. It sounds like a song lyric, but I'm too tired to make out the words.

I showed my true face to everyone tonight.

And they rejected me.

Just like everyone who's ever seen me expected.

"Let's go."

I open my eyes as I feel Tiago's arms pull away. "What is it?" I mumble, shielding my face from the room's brightness.

"Get your things," whispers Zaybet. "We're leaving. *Now.*"

Tiago is already on his feet and stuffing all the clothes from the drawers into a satchel. He dashes into the bathroom for the toiletries, then we soundlessly follow Zaybet down the dark, vampiro-laced balcony.

Enzo marches out of Cata and Saysa's room, lugging a satchel brimming with clothes and candles and other supplies. I smell lavender lotion.

Cata comes out a moment later, hair messy and eyes mere slits. We all stand around for a few moments, like we're waiting for someone to lead the way, and I get the sinking suspicion Saysa's not coming with us.

Then she shuffles out of the room, marching past us toward the stairs, like we're not even there. I exhale in relief to see her, and we follow her to *La Espiral.* Laura must already be waiting on the ship.

The door is open, so we file inside and stride down the tongue-like path to the shell-ship's core. Laura is by the helm, but there's a strange black collar around her neck that looks like a bicycle lock. And she's not alone.

A familiar lobizón is standing next to her, clutching the Encendedora uncomfortably close, and I don't understand why she doesn't scorch him with her magic.

"Going somewhere?" asks Sergio.

There's a scuffle behind us, and Tiago, Enzo, and I spin around just as three transformed wolves snap similar collars around Zaybet, Cata, and Saysa's necks. They brace the brujas' arms, fangs dangerously close to their throats.

Tiago growls, his eyes aglow, and pain explodes inside me as I rip out of my skin. My spine stretches, my hair thickens, my fangs descend—Sergio looks suspended in disbelief as he watches me transform from up close, his mouth hanging open.

What's going on? I ask Tiago. There's a low frequency ringing in my ears, but it's too faint to make out where it's coming from.

The collars cancel their magic, he says as he steps toward the three lobizones holding our friends. They raise their claws threateningly so he won't attempt a rescue.

"There's a human expression," says Sergio, and I turn to face him. His eyes are still wide as they take in my lobizona form. *"The tiger and the lion may be more powerful, but the wolf does not perform in the circus.* These brujas are under the delusion that we actually listen to them . . . but this is *wolf* business."

Humans, brujas, me—sounds like he's an equal opportunity hater.

"We would rather not fight you, Tiago," Sergio goes on, though from the way his burgundy eyes are flashing, I can tell his wolf is eager to throw down. "Since these are your friends, we're willing to pretend this never happened. We won't even tell the others what the traitor Zaybet was planning to do. *But la ladrona stays with us.*"

Tiago steps up to Sergio, towering over him as a werewolf,

but Sergio looks more excited than scared. His inner monster could burst out any moment.

"Fuck off before you get hurt." Enzo hasn't transformed, and he sounds like he's translating Tiago's body language for Sergio.

The low frequency sound is getting louder, and my ears feel clogged. I swallow a few times to try to clear them.

"So, Tiago is going to fight off four lobizones at once, with the pair of you for sidekicks?" says Sergio, digging a finger into his ear like he hears the disturbing tone too. "You think a couple of half wolves add up to a whole?"

"You're forgetting someone," says Enzo.

"Four impotent witches?" asks Sergio, facial hair sprouting across his face and fangs sliding down his lips.

As his body shifts, Laura frees herself from his hold and says, "*My ship.*"

The ringing grows sharper, until it's all I can hear, and I feel myself reverting to human form as I fall to the ground, my head in my hands. My eyes are bleary from the roaring pain in my mind, and I can't tell if I'm screaming, can't hear anything, can't see what's happening—

The sound and pain vanish as Zaybet places a helmet over my head. I watch Saysa help Tiago, while Laura takes care of Enzo.

We let Sergio and the others writhe in agony while Tiago cracks open the collar around his sister's neck, and Enzo does the same for Zaybet and Laura. I grip Cata's collar, and I muster all my wolf strength to crack it open.

"Thanks," she mumbles once she's free, rubbing her skin.

Zaybet gestures for us to remove our helmets, and when I do, the sound is gone. Sergio's cronies have all passed out from the pain, but he's blinking on the ground like a roach on its back that isn't dead.

Saysa crosses over and wraps her small hand around his neck. Then her eyes light up like radioactive limes.

The color drains from Sergio's features, and his gaze widens in horror.

"Saysa, don't—"

"How does it feel to be weak?" she asks, ignoring Cata's plea. Veins bulge in Sergio's neck and face, and his skin takes on a corpselike grayish tinge. "Not much of an apex predator now, are you?"

"You're better than this, Say," says Tiago. "Let him go."

"No," says Saysa, without looking away from Sergio's fading gaze. "This is what I am. Because of wolves like him. Closed-minded, arrogant, selfish, fearful little fucks that make the world what it is. He doesn't belong at the Coven—"

"Is that what you think of me too?" asks Tiago. "That I don't belong at the Coven?"

"Don't try your big brother psychological crap. Every chance you get, you make our lives better—but don't tell me the world wouldn't be better off without Sergio."

"There are Septimus who will say that about me too," I murmur.

The light in Saysa's gaze flickers, just for a blink. Sergio's eyes roll into the back of his head, and he looks like he's got one last breath left.

"*Stop!*" shrieks Cata.

But Saysa is so far gone that she doesn't listen to Cata's pleas. Nor Tiago's. Nor mine.

She's about to cross a line she won't be able to come back from, and none of us can do anything—

"Did I save your life just so you could take another?"

Zaybet's voice is low, but her words are heavy enough that Saysa looks away from Sergio. When she meets her friend's alarmed gaze, recognition crosses through Saysa's numb expression, and she lifts her hand off Sergio at last.

Enzo springs over and places his fingers to Sergio's neck to check for a pulse. "He's alive. Barely."

"Heal him!" Laura charges Saysa. Her eyes are glassy and she looks beyond horrified.

"He's a wolf." Saysa's voice is thin, her face dull and bloodless. "He can heal himself."

"Let's get them off the ship," instructs Zaybet, and Tiago, Enzo, and I carry Sergio and his friends out. When we return, all four black collars are stacked, and the brujas—sans Saysa, who's slumped on a chair—look like they're debating what to do with them.

Tiago sits next to his sister, and I stare closer at the collars. "What are they?" I ask.

"Maldición," says Zaybet. "A stone that cancels our magic. Before the bruja liberation movement, some manadas allowed lobizones to construct houses with maldición so their wives couldn't use magic at home. Others would just fasten these collars around them. Now it's only used in prisons, but obviously wolves can still find it."

"Better that they remain in your custody then," I say, and she and Cata nod in agreement.

"How did your ship know to play that high frequency sound?" Tiago asks Laura.

"I have a maldición detector. It sounds a high frequency alarm that paralyzes wolves with pain, in case piratas try to board."

"Shouldn't we get out of here before anyone else comes calling?" asks Enzo.

"We can't yet," says Zaybet, and she unfolds a small pouch from her indigo pocket. "Before we go, there's something we need to do. It's the only way we can leave without fear of reprisal from the Coven."

"No," says Laura. If she looked horrified before, that's nothing compared to her expression now.

It's as if Zaybet just asked her to sacrifice her puppy.

"This is the rule," says Zaybet, but the look doesn't leave Laura's eyes, and she cradles her wrist lovingly.

"I can't."

Our horarios, I realize. We have to leave them behind.

"You said they'll die without us," says Cata. My gut twists in protest as I look down at the black band binding my wrist. We're in el Mar Oscuro, so the horario is on the surface of my skin, where it's supposed to be safe.

"Isn't there any other—"

"No," Zaybet snaps at me. "There isn't. As long as we're connected to the Coven's network of horarios, our location is exposed. And they're exposed too. They won't let it stand."

"But it's not like they would come after us," says Laura, still cupping her wrist protectively.

"How can you say that after what Sergio just did?" demands Zaybet. "They could tip off the Cazadores anonymously. In fact, when they see we've gone, some might try."

I know this is a stupid question, but I'm desperate. "Can't we just shut it off for a bit or something—"

Enzo reaches for his horario and yanks the plant off his wrist. It starts to wriggle and writhe like it wants to hug Enzo's skin again, but he drops it into Zaybet's outheld pouch. Tiago goes next, so quickly that it's just a flicker of movement. Then Zaybet removes her own, and she walks over to Saysa, who's watching us like she's in some sort of trance.

When Saysa doesn't react to her presence, Zaybet yanks off her horario for her. Saysa doesn't even flinch. But when Zaybet walks away, I spot the glint of moisture in the corners of Saysa's eyes.

When the pouch is held out to me, I think to my horario, *I'm sorry. I'm so sorry.* Then I clasp my fingers around it.

Fighting back the urge to cry, I tug the band off, and my skin itches and stings as my horario peels away. After the massacre is over, Tiago leaves the pouch by the lobizones' bodies for the Coveners to find. Then we detach from the Coven and spiral into el Mar Oscuro.

Already, the homing instinct that alerted me when we were close to the base is receding. And I realize the feeling of excitement and safety and home that I felt when we approached this rock was never mine.

It belonged to the horario.

It *felt*.

22

Long after the blackness has drained from the atmosphere, everyone is still in a sour mood. Saysa and Cata are asleep in their reclined chairs, blankets up to their shoulders, while Enzo and Tiago stand to either side of Laura at the helm and survey the view ahead.

We sail through an ocean's watery depths, past schools of fish and beds of coral. Laura's hands have been burning into the ship since we left the Coven, hours ago.

"You need a break," says Zaybet yet again. She's sitting in the chair adjacent to mine.

"We don't even know where we're going," Laura snaps.

"All the more reason to get some sleep and float. No one has any idea where we are, and we can't be tracked."

"I'm fine." Laura's curls lie limp on her head, and her ebony features lack their usual glow. But it's nothing compared to the shadows in her voice.

I miss her sunlight.

"You can channel me if you want," I offer, sitting up in my chair.

She pulls away from the wall. *La Espiral* starts to slow as the firestorm in her eyes dims, and she stalks toward us.

She sways a little but steadies herself on the back of Zaybet's chair, then she drops into the empty one next to her.

"This ship has a symbiotic link with Laura's fire magic, so energy cycles between them," Zaybet explains to me as Laura pulls the blanket over herself. "It's the same with Invocadoras, since air balloons are sewn from a floating fabric that wants to be in the air. Transportation doesn't drain us as much as you might think—unless you overexert yourself." She casts a pointed look at Laura, who scowls at her.

Now that Zaybet knows I wasn't raised among them, she's taken to explaining things like a teacher—which works out great for me.

"Different spells require different degrees of energy," she goes on, continuing the lesson. "For instance, it's easy for me to modify water from liquid to solid to gas, but it takes more energy to summon water if it's not nearby. That's why spells are more effective when performed in a group."

"We don't have enough oxygen to keep going like this," Laura interjects from under her blanket. "We're going to have to surface soon. Not to mention the full moon is in four nights—"

"I know," says Zaybet, reaching out and resting a hand on her friend's shoulder. "I'll find us a safe space. Once we're settled, I'll reach out to the Coveners who stood up for Manu so they can join us. We can still open our own path to Lunaris." She looks at me. "All isn't lost, because you're not alone."

Her undaunted spirit loosens the knot in my chest. Tiago and Enzo peel their gazes from the window to look at her. Tiago's eyes are bright with Enzo's same admiration.

"We should get some sleep," says Enzo. "I'll take first watch." He dims the ship's lights, and Tiago takes the chair to my other side.

After everyone's eyes go dark, I'm still wide awake. The harder I try to force myself to sleep, the more alert I feel.

"I can take over."

Enzo jerks around, like I snuck up on him. "Can't sleep?"

"Nope, so one of us might as well." I stand beside him, and he nods in agreement, but he doesn't leave.

"That was brave," he says. "The way you stood up for yourself."

"Thanks, but I feel really stupid right now."

"Don't. If they don't accept you as you are, they're the stupid ones."

I think of how he wished the dormilona potion had taken all his memories, and in a softer tone, I say, "Thanks for not being one of the stupid ones."

He grins at me, and I muster the courage to ask, "How come I've never seen you transform?"

"I can't."

I frown. "What do you—"

He swings his leg up against the window and raises the hem of his sweatpants to his knee. The bone has been amputated and replaced by a braid of green foliage; the implant is shaped to look like muscle and sinew, with thin ropes webbing across it like dark veins.

"What happened?" I whisper.

"It was bitten off."

"*Bitten*—?"

"By a Lunaris creature. Jardineras couldn't get to me in time, and I lost part of my leg. A healer was able to create a Lunaris limb so I can still move like a wolf . . . but I can't transform."

"Oh," I say, the word falling from my lips. I want to say something comforting, but I can't think of anything. "Why, though?"

He shrugs. "Some healers think it's a side effect of the poison from the creature's bite. Others think it's all in my head. So am I still a wolf?" he asks, his voice scratchy. "My family doesn't think so."

"I'm sorry, Enzo." My chest twinges with pain for him. It's awful enough when the world doesn't want you, but to feel that rejection from family would be indescribably worse. "You're one of the bravest wolves I've ever met. I'm sorry your family doesn't see that."

His green eyes are bright as he shakes his head, his curls bouncing. "Don't waste your pity on me. I'm not complaining." He gestures with his chin to Zaybet and Laura. "I found my real family."

"They really care about you," I say, in case he doesn't realize. "When you were knocked out with the dormilona potion, they were so worried."

"I know." He cracks a small grin. "I guess our friendship must seem weird, huh? But I like that they treat me like any other wolf."

He nods in the direction of my friends.

"Just like to them, you're no different from any other Septimus."

What can I say?

The wolf's got a point.

By the time I wake up, *La Espiral* is surfacing.

The afternoon sun casts an orange glow across the ocean, the horizon flat on all sides except one. La Boca lies ahead, a forested island built on the back of an active volcano.

"Tell me again why this is a good idea," says Cata as we stare through the window.

"They won't come looking for us here. La Boca has been abandoned for decades, since its last eruption, and it's so far out to sea that most Septimus barely remember it exists," says Zaybet. "Think about it—had *you* heard of this island?"

Cata scowls, probably annoyed to have her ignorance pointed out to her.

"It sounds a little familiar." Saysa's voice is small, as if she's testing it out. She's been rather subdued and has barely addressed us. "I heard it mentioned once."

She squints like she's trying to sharpen a blurry memory. "At school, maybe?"

"No, because then I would know it," says Cata, now doubly annoyed.

"If we can bring together a large enough pack," says Zaybet, "then in three nights, we can open our own portal to Lunaris."

My ears perk up at the news. "How many Septimus do we need?"

"The strongest number is seven by seven, so forty-nine at least. We want seven brujas of each element, which means we need twenty-four more brujas, plus one wolf per witch. But we'll need to recruit carefully," she warns, her gaze sweeping to Laura and Enzo, like she's doling out assignments.

We grab the satchels with our belongings, and Laura anchors the ship offshore. Zaybet freezes a path along the water's surface, and we cut across to the coastline.

Tiago and I make it to land first, and we help the others up the dirt-caked rockface, until we reach the mouth of the forest. "You don't have a hot-air balloon on your ship for emergencies?" asks Cata, huffing as we trek through the trees.

"Sky travel would draw too much attention," says Zaybet. But

I wonder if she's thinking of our last experience with Cata's flying in Lunaris.

The volcano's incline isn't steep, but the foliage we're wading through is wild. Tiago is at the front of the pack, thwacking through it with a wooden staff he found on the ground, paving a path for the rest of us. Branches snake through the air, tangling with the limbs of other trees like latticework, and spiky underbrush scratches at our feet. When we make it to the edge of the tree line, we all stand side by side and stare.

The village is gray and ashen. It looks like a movie set in the aftermath of a bombing. A real-life ghost town.

There are fissures in the soil, like gashes, and slabs of melted-down metal. If there were once any tall buildings, they've been leveled. There's just one construction left standing, a single-story stone structure.

Everything else is smothered in soot and half-buried in the lumpy ground.

"It's perfect!" announces Zaybet, like she sees a thriving garden instead of a dead one.

She turns to face us, the desolate view backlighting her like a bad joke. "The Coveners were in shock, but they'll calm down and welcome us back. Until then, we'll be safe here—as long as Saysa doesn't accidentally set off an earthquake with her magic, so nobody piss her off."

It's the first time Zaybet has addressed Saysa since what happened with Sergio, and the latter looks at her hopefully. When Zaybet doesn't break their gaze, Saysa seems eased somehow.

Even though Cata wasn't exactly warm toward Saysa on the way here, she's also not being cold the way she was after Saysa attacked the witch in Kukú. In fact, no one seems to be holding Saysa's actions against her. It feels like what Sergio did crossed our communal line of mercy.

"Let's see what we have to work with so we can make this place habitable by nighttime," says Zaybet. We follow her lead as we spread out to investigate the remains of this manada. While the brujas scope out the lone remaining structure, Tiago, Enzo, and I sprint to see what lies farther down.

We race past the debris, cutting across a dried dirt crater and more melded metal, and as the release of using my muscles pumps new energy through me, I feel a lightness invade my chest—but my body grows heavy when I see that Tiago's stopped ahead.

Whatever existed beyond this point, we'll never know. The entire landscape is smothered in a stony sea of lava rock that dried in swirling patterns. The volcano swallowed this manada whole.

"I hope everyone made it out," I whisper as we survey the remains.

"They did," says Enzo, coming up beside me, his breathing shallow.

"What'd you find?" Zaybet asks us when we regroup with the brujas.

"Just a crater in the ground," reports Tiago, "and the rest of the place is covered in dried lava. This is all that's left standing."

His musical voice newly startles me, and I realize this is the first time I've heard him speak since leaving the Coven.

"Some fresh air ought to start us off right," says Zaybet to Cata.

My cousin nods in assent, and her pink gaze lights up. "Close your eyes," she warns us, "and hold on." We take one another's hands and shut our eyes right as a massive wind picks up, flapping our clothing against our skin like whips. It blows away from us, toward the crater, and I open my eyes a slit.

Dirt and ash and other dust flies up and funnels in the air, like a trashy twister, and soars away from us. By the time Cata's eyes dim, the view is considerably less gray.

"Now for a little wash," says Zaybet. We're still holding hands, and I feel a slight pull on my energy as her eyes light up and a chill infects the air. The stone structure grows an icy sheen, like it's been crystalized. The frost lasts an instant, then it melts away, the water sloshing down the sides.

As more grime comes off, etchings are revealed in the rock. It says *patio de comidas*. This was once a food hall.

"I'll disinfect," says Laura. A blast of warmth hits us all, and we drop one another's hands to shield our faces.

"Sorry," she says, her eyes aflame. "Guess the lava is a little strong."

Once the temperature drops again, Zaybet looks to Saysa. "We may need some inoculations while we're here."

Saysa looks at her fingers like they're contaminated.

"Whenever you're feeling up to it," Zaybet adds, and Saysa nods grimly.

"Okay, listen up," says Zaybet to the rest of us. "We're going to need to haul over blankets and pillows and supplies from the ship. We also need to clean the patio de comidas from the inside."

Tiago and I get to work lugging supplies over, while Enzo acts as a power source for the brujas so they can cleanse the inside of the stone structure. I want to say something to Tiago, but it's exhausting trudging back and forth through the trees, and I don't think I can handle the emotional workout of a conversation too.

By the time the sun is setting, Zaybet, Laura, and Enzo are in el Hongo. They spotted some chanterelle mushrooms growing under an umbrella-like tree. The patio de comidas is a wide space littered with overturned wooden tables and mangled benches. There's also a kitchen and bathroom signs—*lobizón* or *bruja*.

Saysa and Zaybet reactivated the island's plumbing system with their magic. Cata and Saysa are now sitting at a table, using a fine, flexible rope to thread together a curtain made of leaves and flowers that we're going to hang to separate the dining half from the sleeping part of the space.

Tiago and I are tossing out any furniture we couldn't salvage into a heap outside. When we're finished, the space looks hollow but habitable. Tiago hands me a bottle of water, then he has some himself.

Cata and Saysa don't look up from their threading, and Tiago sits at the end of their bench, gaze adrift. The silence feels too pointed not to ask anymore, so I do.

"What do you guys think of all this?"

Saysa shrugs.

"Of what?" asks Cata, without looking up.

"This whole . . . situation." I look at Tiago, but he just stares at his drink. "You know, Zaybet's plan to recruit enough Septimus here to open a portal to Lunaris? Her thinking that the Coven will change its mind?"

"Does it matter what we think?" asks Cata, her voice so calm, she almost sounds bored.

"Of course it does. I mean, if you have concerns, you should share them—"

"Why? You're going to do whatever you want anyway." Her pink eyes snap to my face.

"Cata—"

She slaps down her threading work on the table. "You think I enjoyed spending all that time thinking of the right combination of words you could say that might keep you safe? I did it because I thought I was saving your life!"

"Well, sometimes it doesn't feel like *my* life," I say softly.

"Then you should have said something."

This time it's not Cata.

It's Saysa.

"I tried to speak up," I say. "You all shot me down so fast—"

"That should have been your first clue it was a bad idea!" exclaims Cata.

"Yamila was going to tell them the truth anyway—"

"Yes, and that's why we had a plan. It might not have been perfect, but it was a start. And more importantly, *it's what we agreed on together.*"

At that last part, Tiago finally looks at me.

"Do you have something to add?" I ask when he doesn't say anything.

"Doesn't sound like you want to hear it."

So they're all against me.

"At least you found something you can all agree on," I say, charging past Zaybet, who's framed in the doorway. I don't know how much she heard, and I don't care.

I venture into the woods. Even though it's dark out, Tiago and I made this trip enough times that a path is beginning to take form. When I've climbed down to the edge of the rockface, I stare at *La Espiral*'s ghostly reflection.

Laura said she'll sink it to the seafloor so no one spots it. The ocean laps against the ancient seashell, and overhead the waxing gibbous moon is just a couple of slivers shy of being full.

I hear soft footsteps and inhale a cool, briny scent coming from the wrong direction. When she gets close enough, I say, "Hi, Zaybet."

She settles beside me on the rocks, resting an empty sack on her lap. After a long moment of comfortable silence, she says, "You, Cata, and I have something pretty big in common."

When I don't respond, she adds, "Comes in a package that's about a meter and a half tall."

Still, I don't speak, so she comes out with it. "Saysa changed all our lives."

Curiosity gets the best of me. "She said you saved her life in La Isla Malvada."

Zaybet nods. "When I met her, she was this little shit who'd just manipulated her brother into bringing her to the island, then schemed to get away from him so she could explore one of the most treacherous landscapes in the world all by herself, without any powers, just because she fucking dared."

Zaybet's gaze glistens with starlight. "She was small for her age, but too large for her size. And there I was, fifteen years old and on a group date where we'd all just run away from our wolf escorts because it was fun to make the boys chase us. In Saysa's presence, I'd never felt more childish.

"After that, she became a kind of talisman for me. When I was too afraid to go against my parents, I'd picture her. She was who I wanted to become when I grew the ovaries. Sometimes I wonder if I ever would have discovered the Coven—or *myself*—without her example."

Ocean spray dapples the stone we're sitting on, and Zaybet circles her finger through the drops. Her eyes glow, and the drops begin to dance around on the rock, like tiny diamonds. I watch their entrancing patterns while I consider what she said.

What led me to the Septimus? Was it ICE arresting Ma? Was it discovering Ma's betrayal? Was it seeing the Z symbol and the red smoke? If not for Yamila, would I never have found this world?

It's impossible to know.

There's only one action I can say for sure led me here, and that was my choice to climb into Leather Jacket's truck.

"I don't know that there's any plan for our lives," I say as the thought occurs to me. "I think we just get confronted with choices, and the more honest we are when making them, the more our life begins to reflect us."

"Hm," says Zaybet, like she's considering my perspective. "You should speak from the heart more. Maybe don't let Cata script all your speeches."

Hearing Zaybet's story about meeting Saysa makes me want to know more about how Zaybet became Zaybet. "How did you end up at the Coven?"

She hands me the sack on her lap, then she gets up and starts climbing down the rocks to the sea. Unsure what else to do, I follow.

"Stay there," she tells me when we've almost reached the water's edge. We're just a few feet apart, but the ocean's roar is loud enough to fill the air.

She perches on a stone that crests the water's surface, and I cradle into a damp crevice between stones in the rockface.

"Laura recruited me into the Coven after graduation," says Zaybet without raising her voice, since she knows I can hear her. "At the academy in Marina, I'd organized a bruja strike. I wanted us all to refuse to use our magic to prove that the world runs on our labor. The Coven got wind of it, so . . . Laura found me."

I get the sense there's more to that story, but she's never pressed me, so I don't press her. Zaybet dips her fingertips into the ocean and swirls them like she did with the drops on the stone. Her eyes are alight with magic as she swims her hands around.

"What about Enzo?" I ask.

"He's been at the Coven for longer than any of us in the younger guard. Sometimes we joke around that he was born there." At last she pulls her hands out of the water. *"Catch!"*

A massive wave suddenly crests, so tall I think it's going to swallow us—then I see the fish, and I understand.

I snap to my feet and open the sack as the water crashes over me, but Zaybet evaporates the liquid, so that just a dozen silver fish rain into the bag. I catch them all.

"Dinner!" she announces.

As we're threading back through the woods, I can't help asking, "What happened with you and Tinta? If you don't mind sharing?"

"I met him soon after I got to the Coven. It was love at first fight. The instant we argued, I knew I was crazy about him. He was as ambitious and radical and impatient as me. When we started dating, we made up a cover story to tell our friends and family, about how we met on a judge's campaign trail—but the truth is Tinta got me that job so we could sell the story.

"To the outside world, we looked like this ambitious power couple that was rising up the system's ranks, and everyone was thrilled for us. But in secret, we were part of the resistance, planning disruptions and plotting a new world order. I loved our double life. It felt like a real revolt, you know? An actual defiance. Until the day he ruined it."

"How?"

"He asked me to marry him." She shakes her head. "I thought we were partners in the same fight, but he thought we could start a family and resist in our free time. That was the problem. To him, our outside life was the real one and the Coven was the fantasy. For me, it was the other way around."

"I'm sorry," I say. "How long ago did you break it off?"

"A few moons," she says, and given how recent it is, I understand the level of passion between them. "My family is devastated, so I don't like going home. They just expect me to start dating again. A Septima's life is a countdown to reproduction. We're not allowed to want anything else."

She reminds me of the protagonists I like to read about in

adventure stories who are independent and free in a way that makes them untouchable. I used to think I was like that because I wanted to be an astronaut and travel the stars. But part of the appeal of outer space was the hope of finding a world where I belong.

"Is it like this for women too?" asks Zaybet. "In the human world?"

"It varies by culture. But overall, most women have to navigate patriarchies, and for many there's a societal expectation to have children."

"At least humans have words like *divorce* and *abortion*. We don't have those in our vocabulary. Or gay or lesbian or bisexual or queer or asexual—"

"I know something about lacking the language to describe yourself," I say, and she gives me a wry smile.

We're almost back to the group, and I can see the patio de comidas through the thinning trees. But before we go any farther, Zaybet's fingers close around my arm.

"Seeing you with Tiago kind of helps," she says as we face each other, her voice low. "The way you look at each other, I mean. Tinta and I didn't have that."

Yet her expression reminds me of Diego's after the Septibol match. Like they see more than we do.

"Manu, you can't depend on him," she says, and I shift the sack of fish from one hand to the other. "However much you love each other, it doesn't change the facts. *You* will be judged. And *he* will get a pass."

"It feels like Laura is one of the Septimus judging me," I can't help saying. "I don't think she wants to be here."

"She was raised in a much more traditional manada where they believe la ladrona is a real demon that will destroy all life on the planet," says Zaybet. "But Laura has never followed her manada's faith, so she knows better. She's ashamed her cultural prejudices are showing. Give her a minute."

"What about you? What do you think?"

I've been afraid to ask because I don't want to discover she's only here out of a misplaced sense of obligation for having brought us into the Coven, or that she's just looking for a good adventure to be part of—because I care what Zaybet thinks. *A lot.*

"All I know is they've been making up stories about independent girls in every tradition since forever," she says, her gaze steadfast. "And I think it's time we take back our narratives."

23

By the time I wake up, a crew of Coveners has joined us, and they've brought more yerba for mate and fresh facturas for breakfast.

I greet the newly arrived Septimas, counting a total of eight new brujas, two of each element. I catch Zaybet, Laura, and Enzo staring wistfully at the witches' wrists, where their horarios must be. No wolves yet, aside from Tiago, Enzo, and me.

Some of the brujas spend most of the day in el Hongo, recruiting others, while the rest of us keep trying to make this manada habitable. We've brought all the tables outside so the patio de comidas can just be for sleeping, and now we're building beds under Enzo's tutelage. I've never met anyone more self-sufficient.

The mood grows more hopeful throughout the day as Coveners continue to arrive—including a few lobizones—with food, bedding, and other supplies. It's startling how quickly we settle into a rhythm, same as the Coven. It makes me think about how much sentimentality we attach to plots of land, when it's actually the seeds we plant there that give it meaning.

When we break for lunch, Zaybet waves me over to sit with her. Tiago and Enzo are at a table of wolves—there's only nine of us so far—and Saysa and Cata are across from Zaybet and me.

Last night, when Zaybet and I returned to the patio de comidas, my friends and I didn't talk to one another. I helped Tiago put up the thatchwork curtain Cata and Saysa threaded together, while Enzo prepared the fish and Laura seared it. After the meal, we were so exhausted that we each grabbed a pillow and blanket and crashed. The brujas and I slept in the area we curtained off, but Tiago and Enzo opted to sleep outside. He and I still haven't spoken.

I guess if he was looking for a way out of this relationship, he found it.

I avoid looking in Cata or Saysa's direction so our gazes won't cross. It's easier if I just focus on physical tasks, so I don't have to think about the future I don't have.

"We've got eighteen brujas and nine lobizones," says Zaybet after doing a headcount to confirm her numbers are right. "We need another six witches—three need to be Jardineras—and fifteen, sixteen wolves. How are we coming on that?"

"Sara's crew is coming in tomorrow," reports Laura. "Natalio isn't coming. No word from Antonio."

"We're only two nights away from the full moon. If we need to cast a wider net, we need to know."

"You mean *non-Coveners*?" asks Laura, dark eyes narrowed in disapproval.

"Manu has lots of supporters. Not all of them have turned on her since the broadcast. They should be easy to track because they tend to be vocal."

Laura sets down her half-eaten empanada. "There's a difference between taking up a cause ideologically and actually volunteering to put your life on the line."

"We don't have a choice," says Zaybet, and now there's a hard edge to her voice. "If we can't open our own portal here, Manu will be arrested."

"How can you even be sure we'll be able to open one?"

"Why do you think I chose this place? All the elements meet here—magma, ocean, forest, sea breeze. It's a powerful magical soft spot. We just need enough Septimus to channel it."

"I knew it!" says Saysa, slamming her hand down. "I *knew* I'd heard of this place before because I remember reading or hearing that fact, but *where*—?"

I spring up to standing, same as Tiago and Enzo and the other wolves.

Footsteps.

The air tingles with magic, and the ground grows warm beneath my feet, as the brujas' anticipation triggers the elements.

We're not expecting anyone else today.

"Standing ovation, huh?"

Tinta arrives with his noodle-like brother, Fideo—and ten more wolves. The air relaxes as everyone gets up to greet them.

"You didn't say!" says Zaybet, and I wonder if the delight in her voice is just relief or something more.

"No paper trail, remember?"

"We have to take extra precautions now," explains Fideo. "Cazadores are looking into everyone. We can't raise suspicions." He turns to me, his coppery-brown gaze soft. "I'm sorry we were harsh with you."

"Yeah," says Tinta, his eyes as gentle as his brother's for a change. "We get so passionate about politics that it turns us into asses."

"Todo bien," I say, and each of them pulls me in for a hug. *All good.*

"¡La loba!" says Ezequiel, who came with them. He pulls me into a hug too, and I don't think I've ever been happier to be called the she-wolf. He and the brothers join us at our table and dig into the empanadas.

"The tribunal deputized the entire species, which of course backfired, because now everyone has been using the excuse of chasing down leads to get out of their usual obligations," says Tinta with a wicked grin that's the twin of Zaybet's. "There's always the usual restlessness before the full moon, but compounded with this news, everyone's excited and things are messy. Which means we get to be more than just *cool and aloof.*"

He looks at her with a challenge in his eyes, and in Zaybet's gaze, I see reflected back what she doesn't think is there. She's wrong about her feelings. She loves him. I think she's just afraid of where that leads—because as long as neither of them is willing to cede ground, they're not going anywhere.

We move a lot faster with the influx of lobizones, and the sky is the deep orange hue of late afternoon by the time we finish building enough beds. At least we won't have to sleep on the floor.

The temperature dropped today, so for merienda we pass the mate and gather round a fire that Laura and the other Encendedoras are constantly controlling so we don't disturb the magma below.

We had another surprise arrival: Nuni, the witch who gave me the invisibility potion. She's sitting next to me. "Use my gift?" she asks, the red flames reflected in her caramel-colored eyes.

"Not yet."

Cata, Saysa, and Tiago are sitting next to one another, across from us, and I feel their collective gaze.

Ezequiel sets a tub of batter beside a heating stone that's illuminated like an ember. "Loba, this is going to be the best panqueque you've ever had," he says, spooning batter onto the stone. He turns it over an instant later, and when it's ready, he tosses it into the fire.

"First one's always bad," he explains, then he spoons a second panqueque. This one he serves on a plate and hands to me.

I've seen Ma do this dozens of times, but for some reason, the way he tossed out the first panqueque bothered me. He barely looked at it. Maybe it would've tasted fine.

Argentinian pancakes are crepe-thin, so he gets through them quickly, and it's not long before everyone is devouring their own. I lather on a liberal amount of dulce de leche, then I fold it up the way everyone else does.

Warmth spreads through me as I bite into the soft, sweet dessert, and every single one of us goes for thirds. I'm warmed by more than just the meal. As I look around, it's the first time I'm sitting with friends who know the real me. The half human me. And they accept me.

I'm out of secrets. The masks are off, and I'm not wearing any lies.

The twitch in my eye is subtle, but I feel it. A tiny stab of doubt. There's *one* thing I haven't brought up. But my ability to deflect magic pales in comparison to my hybrid heritage.

"Still waiting on fourths," says Tinta, holding up his plate to Ezequiel.

"You'll spoil your dinner," says Zaybet, swiping it. Fideo snorts. "We should get back to recruiting. We're still a few Septimus short, and we're low on Jardineras."

As the fire dies down and Septimus scatter to their various tasks, Tiago and I lock eyes. His sapphire orbs send a thrill down my belly.

He stands and gestures to the woods with his head, jostling his overgrown dark strands. I guess he's finally ready to have it out.

"So what was it like growing up among humans?"

Nuni is still sitting next to me, making no indication of leaving. "Um, it was—I didn't have a typical upbringing." I glance at Tiago, but he's gone.

As my chest deflates, I turn to face Nuni more fully. "My mom was afraid of you all finding out about me, so she kept me hidden."

"What about your dad?" she prods.

This time, I don't even consider telling the truth. "Don't know him."

"I'm sorry."

Her heavy gaze is so full of sympathy that I find myself wanting to open up more. "We didn't have papers where we lived. My mom got arrested, and she wanted me to keep hiding. But I guess I just couldn't. I needed to learn the truth about who I am."

"And who are you?" asks Nuni, only the way she says it doesn't sound sarcastic or sappy. She seems sincere.

"Pick your label," I say with a hard exhale. "Lobizona, ladrona, hybrid, freak—whatever it is, I'm always wrong."

The self-pity that's crept into my voice makes me cringe, and I ask, "What about you? What brought you to the Coven?"

The frozen look on her face makes me hurry to say, "I'm sorry—that was rude. You don't have to tell me if you don't feel comfortable—"

But her lips curve into a sad smile. "It's not that. It's just strange, coming across someone who doesn't know my story."

Nuni looks down at her small hands, which are cupped together on her lap. "I got pregnant when I was thirteen."

I wince, both at the words and their delivery. She sounds

detached from their meaning. Like slicing open the same cut again and again, until you're numb to the pain.

"Brujas aren't known to be fertile until closer to fifteen, and pregnancy before twenty is rare. Our magic isn't strong enough yet. I was the first case of my kind, the riskiest delivery on record. I'd only just inherited my magic on the same moon that—that it happened."

The way she stumbles, this other wound isn't as numb, and I know not to press on it.

"My mother caught me trying to mix a potion to end the pregnancy, and she turned me in to the Cazadores. I went before the tribunal and begged for mercy, but they forced me to carry to term."

Zaybet's words come back to me: *Septimus don't have divorce or abortion.*

"I barely survived childbirth," she goes on, resuming her disaffected tone. "My baby was stillborn." Nuni's prematurely gray hair and ancient eyes make much more sense now.

"Then there was the postpartum depression."

I blink as I realize her torment didn't end at childbirth.

"For more than a year, I was powerless, stuck in a home I hated, both pitied and scorned by my pack. All while the lobizón who did this to me was quietly shuffled off to a different manada. He was engaged to be married before my magic came back."

I have never in my life been more speechless. I don't know what to say to someone who's endured so much. "I'm sorry, Nuni." The words ring empty against her horrors.

"Me too. But like you, I learned the truth about who I am." Her eyes spark, as though from the ashes of her childhood, a new Nuni was born. "All that time without magic, I could still mix potions. So I studied the craft, and I practiced, until I brewed the cure that freed me."

"Can your brew cure other brujas' postpartum too?"

"It's . . . complicated. No bruja has ever been able to conjure a one-size-fits-all formula. Part of the problem is that for the mix to be most effective, it requires blood from the father, which means drawing a few drops every moon to test new batches. Not all wolves are willing."

"Why not?" Anger sears my skin. "*We* bleed once a month!"

The way she looks at me makes me feel eons younger, and I wonder how innocent I sound to her. "Not everyone thinks postpartum depression is a bad thing. Not even all brujas."

"*How?*" is all I can muster.

"Since it cuts off our magic, we can no longer go to Lunaris, which means we're able to stay behind to take care of our newborns. Without it, we'd have to leave them in the care of twelve-year-olds. There are manadas where mothers are forbidden from accessing Felifuego before their child turns two."

I recall the red-and-black Felifuego leaf that looks like it's singed. The one that protected me from the Sombra in my dreams. When I found it in Señora Lupe's class at El Laberinto, she said it's the only known cure for postpartum depression—and it's hard to spot, so brujas depend on the wolves' keen eyesight to hunt for it.

"Here," says Nuni, handing me what looks like a bottle of Septis, only smaller. And instead of blue, it's pink.

"What is it?"

"Protection. Take one before sex."

I feel my cheeks burning. "Oh, I don't—I mean, I'm not—"

"Don't be ashamed," she says, staring at me intently. "This is your only body. Take care of it."

After my heavy talk with Nuni, I follow Tiago's scent into the trees.

I find him shirtless, a sheen of sweat glazing his skin. His feet are planted as he grips an iron bar that's sticking out of a trunk. It must have been part of a gate once. Tiago tugs, his muscles growing taut, and when the metal slides out, he falls back a few paces from the force of his effort.

Then he looks at me.

"Hi." My gaze strays down the perfect ripples of his torso.

"Let's go," he says, and he spins around and disappears through the trees.

I race after him, pulling on my lobizona powers without shifting, until I'm running at full tilt, nearly as fast as I would as a wolf. I chase Tiago's scent, a wild beast on the hunt, until I reach the end of the trees.

The sky over us is gray, but in the distance the sun has ripened to red as it sets. We're on a rocky precipice where we can see the ocean extending endlessly into the horizon. Behind us is a different view altogether, and I understand why Tiago brought us through the trees instead of the settlement.

There's a knot of charred land that tells me this is probably the eruption point. And since it tilts down, the lava must have oozed right through the middle of the manada, destroying everything, setting off blasts, and stopping just shy of the patio de comidas.

"I'm not mad at you," says Tiago, and I force my gaze to stay above his neck as he takes my hand and presses it to his chest, right by his scar. "I'm *scared* for you."

His pulse is racing, and he takes my other hand too.

"We're going to be fine," I say. "Zaybet thinks we can get enough Septimus here before the full—"

"It's not just about this moon, Manu!" His voice cracks on my name, fingers tightening around mine. "It's *every* moon. Now that they know a hybrid exists, they'll never stop coming for you."

Something about the word *hybrid* hurts, even though it's what I am. "Well, I can't do anything about it," I say, my hands going limp in his. "I was born this way."

"That's not what I mean," he says with a sigh. "I'm sorry. I just don't want this for you—"

"And I do?"

"You're the one who chose to broadcast the truth to the world!"

"Before Yamila beat me to it! I was never going to stay hidden, and Cata's cover story wasn't going to hold for long. *In a pack species, there are no secrets*—you're the ones who taught me that."

"Funny how we're only a pack to you when it's convenient."

"What's that supposed to mean?"

"Why didn't you come to us first?"

"I already knew your opinions! And I'm more grateful than I can express to you guys for all you're risking—but you're not the ones facing *extermination*. If they're going to kill me, at least I'll die as myself."

My voice gets scratchy and my eyes burn, and I spin away to hide my tears.

I've been trying so hard not to fall apart, but *nothing* is mine. That's why I didn't decorate my room at the Coven or unpack my clothes at the academy. I'm not safe anywhere on this planet.

"You're right." Tiago comes closer but doesn't touch me. "I'm sorry. Please forgive me."

When I turn, his blue orbs look so lost that I couldn't stay angry if I tried. I let him take my hands again, and as he crushes me to his bare chest, he murmurs, *"The fool doth think he is wise, but the wise man knows himself to be a fool."*

I smirk into his warm skin, and when we pull apart, I say, "*I had rather have a fool to make me merry than experience to make me sad.*"

His mouth hitches up on one side, and I ask, "Why are you so triggered by all the attention you get in Kerana? I mean, if you wanted to lay low after the whole lobo invencible thing, why be the star player of a championship-winning Septibol team?"

"Because one reputation was earned, the other was not."

"You don't think surviving an encounter with a Lunaris demon as a thirteen-year-old merits admiration?"

"Admiration?" His voice fades on the word. "All I did was split away from the pack, then I got lost after nightfall. It was my first visit, and I broke the only rule of Lunaris."

He blows out a hard breath. "I didn't see the demon before it attacked me. It's pure *luck* I'm not dead. I just managed to evade it long enough that by the time its claws sliced into my chest, day was dawning, and it ran away. I was literally saved by the light."

"But you *survived*." I press my palm to his cheek.

His eyes sear into mine, and he says, "Manu . . . there's something I've been wanting to tell you."

I wonder if he's finally going to share whatever it is that's been weighing on his mind, and I drop my hand.

I think he's still struggling with the words, then I realize his gaze is locked on something beyond me.

I twist my neck and spy a creature surfacing in the ocean. It's large and dark, like a whale coming up for air. Only where the blowhole should be, a hatch is opening, and a head pops out.

The Septima's auburn hair blows in the wind as she scours the island, and my heart plummets to the ground.

Yamila found me.

24

We race back to the camp, where the Encendedoras are starting a new fire. "Don't!" calls Tiago.

"They found us!" I say, out of breath. "The Cazadores—"

"Just one ship," he cuts in. "It's possible they're just scouting and don't know we're here."

"But Yamila is with them."

At the name, a chill blows through the group.

"*La Espiral*—" I start.

"Is hidden," says Zaybet.

I look at Laura wildly, thinking of the last time I saw the ship on the surface. "It spiraled underground," she assures me. "They won't find it."

"*You're* the one we can't let them find," says Zaybet to me. "Same goes for you three, since Yamila knows you're together."

"Is there enough invisibility potion for four of us?" I ask Nuni.

She shakes her head. "Just one."

"What about us?" asks Tinta. "We can't be found with Manu either, remember?" He holds up his wrist like he's showing Zaybet his watch, but all we see is brown skin. "The whole Coven will be at risk if the Cazadores learn who we are and discover our horarios."

The horarios can't be removed outside el Mar Oscuro, but I'm sure that doesn't mean a talented Jardinera couldn't sense their presence and try tracing the Coven's location—and the whereabouts of every Covener.

I think about how the resistance has stayed hidden all this time, and I realize the sacrifices Septimus must have had to make. The *us* versus *me* mentality required for the Coven to still exist. I can't let the whole movement come crumbling down because of me.

"Let's not just stand here!" says Fideo. "We need to hide—"

"Where?" demands Ezequiel.

"There's too many of us! They'll sense our presence."

"Then let's *leave*—"

"You don't think they'd notice all of us charging down the hill? Or a fleet of ships taking off?"

"A fleet," I repeat, quieting everyone down. "But not *one* ship."

I look to Zaybet and Laura. "What if the seven of us leave, and the Cazadores find everyone else here? What would they do?" I turn to Tinta y Fideo. "They can't prove I was with you. Would they even suspect you?"

"They'd ask to see their Huellas," says Zaybet, frowning as she turns it over in her head.

"They could link us to the Coven—"

"How?" I ask Tinta. "I thought most Septimus don't even think it's real. You could just claim to be part of some weirdo lunar worshipping cult or something."

The brothers sport twin bemused stares, but Cata understands. "You're here for a retreat," she says to them, cottoning on to my idea. "You're lunáticos."

"What's that?" I ask.

"Septimus who think there's a special lunar energy the night before the full moon that they can tap into—basically, what you wanted," she says with a wave of her hand.

"Tinta y Fideo's presence will brand this as a quirky, rich, young Septimus fad," says Zaybet, nodding along. "But you need to sell it. We can't lose this place. We won't find another discreet location like this one to open a portal, not in time anyway."

Tinta y Fideo nod in unison.

"Looked like they were docking by *La Espiral*," says Tiago. "We can't risk them hearing the slightest sound in the woods, so our safest bet is to cut across the volcano to the other side of the island, then climb down from there."

"But we'll need to cut back across on the ground to get to the ship," complains Zaybet. "Where we're most exposed."

"Not if I bring the ship around to you," says Laura.

"*No.*" Zaybet shakes her head.

"They would hear all of us moving through the woods, but not *one* of us. Alone, I won't be noticed. I'll be stealthy. Besides, I control *fire*—trust me, if this island goes, I'll be the last one left standing."

"I'll be her eyes and ears," says Enzo, and he looks at Laura to see how she'll react. Instead of telling him off for his chivalry, she nods, and his chest puffs out with the charge. "I'd only slow you down anyway, since you're covering twice the ground," he tells Zaybet. "Laura and I will have to move carefully, and that's better. I can listen closely."

Zaybet looks like she wants to argue. Instead, she says, "You'll come pick us up on the other side of the island."

"Here's where you can meet us," says Tiago. While he confers with them to explain, I approach Nuni.

"Do you want to come with us?"

She shakes her head. "My presence will lend this gathering more credibility as a *quirky, rich, young Septimus fad*. Plus, I've got the right potions to bribe the Cazadores if it comes to that."

"Once they're gone, we'll send word through el Hongo so you can return," says Fideo.

"We're still a few Septimus short—"

"Let's worry about that problem *after* we solve this one," he says to Zaybet in exasperation. "Now hurry! And be quiet—we shouldn't risk talking anymore."

We nod and turn to go, but suddenly Tinta whispers, "Wait!"

My heart freezes, and I expect to see the Cazadores ambushing us. Instead, he strides up to Zaybet, grabs her face, and gives her the kind of kiss I've only seen in movies.

When they pull apart, she looks like she's going to speak, but he presses his finger to her mouth, a reminder of his brother's instruction.

Laura has to tug on Zaybet's arm to get her moving.

The seven of us dart into the dead settlement, across the barren crater and onto the sea of dried magma stone with wavy designs. I hear our friends making noise at the campsite to draw the Cazadores to them, buying us an escape window.

The marching of footsteps grows more pronounced, like the Cazadores just picked up their location. They probably would've smelled them out anyway. At least this way it will seem like the "lunáticos" have nothing to hide.

Laura and Enzo signal that they're going to enter the woods, and Zaybet pulls each of them in for a hug. An aura of white steam haloes the brujas as they embrace, and when they pull apart, their eyes shine bright with their power. Fire and ice.

Then the five of us run across the flat stone, our steps muffled by the dirt.

We're heading to the precipice where Tiago and I spotted the Cazadores, only this time we're picking our way through the devastated manada. As we step over whorls of lava stone, it feels like we're racing across the back of a fiery monster that could awaken any moment.

The ground grows more knotted, and the air starts to feel balmier. Red flickers in the fringe of my vision, like embers caught beneath the earth, but each time I focus on a spot, the stone is as dark as ash. Without Laura, we don't have a fire conduit to control the element if it gets out of hand.

As the night grows darker, our eyes start to glow like colorful stars.

Cata slows down, and I link my elbow with hers to pull her along. At last I spy the twisted formation I saw with Tiago earlier. The precipice is just on the other side.

When we reach it, Tiago and I can look down to keep an eye out for *La Espiral.* Once Laura signals us it's safe, we'll come down.

"We're almost to the lookout point," I say in a soft voice to encourage them as we round the corner. "Right over—"

"What'd I tell you?"

The husky voice is like a paralyzing agent for my bones, and I stop speaking, moving, breathing, as I come upon an Encendedora flanked by a pair of lobizones.

"These four are always a step ahead," says Yamila, oxygen burning from her stare. *"Were,"* she corrects herself, bloodred eyes aflame.

"Nicely done," says her brother.

He stares at Saysa in a way that makes me want to stand between them, and Tiago edges closer to his sister, hands curled into fists.

"Looks like the student just beat the master, Tío," says Nacho, reaching around Yamila to punch another lobizón on the arm.

My father blinks his coral-colored eyes and finally looks away from me.

He strides up to Cata, his supposed only relation here, and hugs her. "¿Cómo estás?" he asks, and jealousy pumps in my chest, even though I know he can't hug me without giving himself away.

"Looks like you've picked up a fifth," says Yamila, sizing up Zaybet. They're the same height. "Who are you?"

"A journalist. By law, reporters are neutral bystanders who can't be prosecuted for observing without interfering."

"This is kind of an extreme situation, don't you think?" Yamila cocks her head, her voice a purr. She's enjoying this. It's probably the best day of her fucking life.

"Law still applies."

"Going to need to see those credentials."

"I left everything back home when I went on the run."

Zaybet may be a resourceful arguer, but Yamila won't play with her food for long. We need a plan—a way *out*.

I look at my father, who's still next to Cata. He's watching me, his expression hollow. There are purple bags under his eyes, and his whites are webbed with red, like he hasn't been sleeping. He looks like he's running on fumes. Between protecting Ma and keeping his cover with the Cazadores—plus worrying for me—he doesn't seem to be coping well.

"How'd you find us?" I ask Yamila to buy us time to think.

Her gaze goes to Saysa, whose eyes widen with recognition. "I'm actually surprised you came here, considering Saysa's source."

"This place was *my* idea," says Zaybet.

"Remember that day?" Yamila asks Saysa, ignoring Zaybet.

"We'd been drinking the flowers in Lunaris, and I was listing off all the abandoned places I wanted to explore when I became a Cazadora. You were too young, couldn't handle your drink, and you passed out somewhere in the middle. Wasn't sure you'd remember this island since most Septimus don't like to look on scorched earth. They think what's burned is dead. They forget fire renews."

Nacho pulls out what looks like a piece of rope from his pocket. "So, Tío? You thought they'd be somewhere sketchy like Kukú, trying to pay for special passage to Lunaris, but Yamila was right."

"Leave Tío alone," she says. "Even when he disagreed, he never abandoned us."

I don't understand why they keep referring to Gael as their uncle. Cata would have told me if we were related to this pair.

My father puts an arm around Yamila, and either he's the world's best actor, or he really does care for her. "I would never abandon you."

I can hardly breathe. "Y-you know each other?"

"He's the reason I applied to the academy in El Laberinto," says Yamila, relishing the effect her words are having. "He and my dad served as Cazadores together. Your teacher is my *family*."

As I stare at her and Nacho, I remember the news story from el Hongo. A pair of kids clutched their mom's skirt at their father's funeral. He had been a young Cazador, with auburn hair and kind eyes.

Their father is the officer who died in the Fierro uprisings.

"Shocked to see your teacher betraying you?" Nacho taunts me. "Imagine how you'd feel if your sister's friend tried to kill you."

The four of us edge closer to Saysa. Gael's brow sets in a hard line, and I worry he's about to blow his cover.

"I was hoping I'd find you alone," says Yamila to me. "Tío Gael has been preaching mercy, but I gotta be honest, I don't know that I have it in me."

She's close enough that I can feel the heat rolling off her skin—the mound of magma we're standing on is a power source for Yamila. She isn't afraid of losing this time because we aren't any match for her here.

When she's close enough to breathe on, her voice melts into something intimate. "I wonder what would happen if I torched you in front of them."

We're both thinking of when we last came up against each other in Lunaris.

"Would you burn?"

Her eyes light up like wildfires in the night, and before she can expose me, I leap back and transform. My body screams in pain as my skeleton reconfigures, and I hear the guys around me start to shift too.

"Sorry, ladies," says Yamila, as I lift my fanged face to a wall of flames, blocking off Saysa, Cata, and Zaybet. "Looks like you're still sidelined."

The fire illuminates the dark air, and Nacho and Gael stare down Tiago and me. Nacho's wolf form is almost as large as Javier and seven times more menacing.

"You're under arrest," says Yamila. "You can fight us if you want"—the blaze in her eyes brightens—"but I wouldn't recommend it."

We need to run!

Gael's voice breaks into my head. His desperate tone is at odds with his glower, as he and Nacho take threatening steps forward. He's holding a rope like Nacho's, and his coral gaze is cold. The only sign of his turmoil is the sweat beading on his forehead.

We'll get your mom and keep going.

Tiago jabs his elbow into Nacho's chest right as the Cazador reaches out to bind his wrists, and they start swinging punches. To keep Yamila from registering Gael's delay, I swipe at him, and he only dodges at the last instant.

I don't want to live my life that way, I say as we spar.

Doesn't matter—you can't stay! Gael lunges for me, and I twist away.

"Don't be such a Gaucho, Tío, and get her already!" shouts Yamila, as Tiago and Nacho crash to the floor, wrestling.

I'll arrest you, then tonight we'll break out, says Gael.

What about my friends?

They'll be fine. They're all promising Septimus who got carried away—the tribunal won't punish them.

Nacho howls in pain as Tiago stabs his arm with his claws, and now it looks like we're winning, since Gael hasn't engaged.

The wall of fire goes out, and the brujas are back in view. Then Saysa screams and drops to her knees as flames ignite in her hands.

Zaybet's eyes flash, and ice forms around Saysa's skin, snuffing out the fire. Tiago howls for his sister, his voice rife with pain, and as he turns toward her, Nacho digs his claws into Tiago's side.

When Tiago cries out, I feel a fury like I've never known before. Without thinking, I leap onto Nacho's back and sink my fangs into his neck.

I'm repulsed by the hot, salty taste of his hairy skin, but it's worth it to hear his yelp. Then Gael is pulling me off Nacho, and Tiago is on his feet again, and Yamila's eyes are explosive.

I want her to direct her fury at me, but now she knows where she can inflict the most damage.

Her magic is instantaneous.

There's no way Tiago or I could reach Saysa in time.

Cata's pink eyes flash, and I just barely spy the silver outline of a force field—it forms so suddenly around Saysa that Yamila's blast of heat bounces off the barrier and detonates on the ground like a bomb.

A splash of scorching lava bursts into the blackening air, and Zaybet freezes it before it lands on the ground.

There's a strange foghorn sound coming from somewhere beneath us, and then the earth begins to tremble. I look at Saysa, but her eyes aren't alight. The tremor isn't magical.

It's the volcano.

Terror constricts my chest as the quivering intensifies into a quaking. Gaps in the whorls of stone beneath us light up red, like the monster inside this island is awakening.

"Do something, unless you want to kill us all!" Cata demands of Yamila, but the latter's eyes are already glowing, like she's trying.

"I can't control it!"

Yamila sounds frightened for the first time.

The four of us wolves transform back to human-sized, our other form consuming too much energy. Magma starts seeping up to the surface, and we're all jumping to avoid contact.

Zaybet tries freezing the ground, but the lava keeps burning through her ice.

"We have to run!" shouts Saysa, and we charge at the trees. Nacho takes his sister's hand, and Gael holds mine in a viselike grip.

Tiago is pulling Saysa and Cata forward, while Zaybet runs alongside us, protecting everyone by keeping watch for volleys of fire. Her metallic eyes flare each time lava approaches us, frosting it over.

The forest is in view, puffing black smoke, like trees are burning.

Tiago is in the lead with Cata and Saysa when the ground begins to break apart.

Ice spreads through the fissures as Zaybet seals each crevice, trying to keep the island from cracking open. But she's pulling on too much magic.

"Let me try!" Yamila's eyes are as aglow as the lava, and blood begins to trickle down her nose. But instead of stabilizing, the fracture lines only deepen.

"You're making it worse!" Zaybet's voice is so weak that I pull away from Gael.

"Channel my energy!" I call out, running to her—

A massive explosion rocks this whole side of the island. A wave of lava geysers from the volcano's opening, and I scream when I see where it's going to land.

Tiago only has time to shove Cata and Saysa to the ground and throw his body on top of them as a shield before the killer wave crashes down—

Zaybet freezes the lava inches above Tiago's body.

None of us moves for an eternal moment. In the midst of the chaos, we stare in disbelief at the red tidal wave.

It looks like it's been crystalized by the moonlight.

"That's twice now," says Saysa with a nervous laugh, once she's on her feet.

The Congeladora flashes her feral grin. "Remember that next—"

The ground Zaybet's standing on cracks, and her eyes illuminate as it ices over. But the frost melts almost the instant she freezes it. The volcano is becoming too powerful for a single water witch to control.

A fracture line between Zaybet and us begins to expand, and Tiago and Gael sprint toward her. I leap forward too.

Zaybet runs ahead, but she's losing steam. She nearly falls

into the widening fissure, but a strong wind from Cata blows her back.

"Hold on!" calls Tiago. He's about to leap across to Zaybet's side when she lets out a bloodcurdling scream.

The ground beneath her feet has burned completely to lava—

And she's swallowed by the magma monster below.

25

Time hangs suspended, and even breathing is excruciating. Then a silver light flashes from where Zaybet fell—

The ground cracks beneath us, like we're all about to be consumed along with her. But instead of burning to ashes, we're blasted by icy water and swept off the cliffside.

I scream, my entire body stinging as I plunge into the ocean. When my head breaks the surface, I cough and gasp for air as I look up at La Boca. There's smoke, but the lava isn't visible from here. It's only a matter of moments before it flows into the sea. I hope the Coveners got out okay.

I'm bobbing in the water, and in the distance, Tiago is holding onto Saysa and Cata, both of them retching and panting.

I don't see Gael or Yamila or Nacho.

Or Zaybet.

My breath catches—

A rumbling sound makes me spin around. A large craft

emerges from the watery depths, and as it spirals, revealing an entrance, we swim into *La Espiral*.

Enzo meets us by the opening.

"Where's Zaybet?" he asks the moment we're inside.

Sadness chokes me, and I fight against giving in to my grief yet. None of us answers him as we step into the shell-ship's core, where Laura is at the helm. She looks from one face to the next and demands, "Where's Z?"

Like me, my friends can't seem to find the words. We just stand in silence, our clothes dry and our hair dripping water onto the floor.

Laura and Enzo didn't see the eruption. They have no idea all is lost—in every way.

"Just tell us," says Enzo, running a shaky hand through his curls. "Was she captured?"

How do we tell them that Zaybet, our heart, is gone?

When he can't get an answer from us, Enzo turns to Laura, who looks livid. "Why didn't they arrest *you*?" she demands, glaring at me. "Let me guess, Z created a diversion so you all could run? Well, guess what? We're not leaving this island without her, even if we have to trade you all to get her back—"

"She wasn't arrested," says Cata, her voice dull. "The volcano activated and she . . . she fell."

The horror of Cata's words hangs in the air, and Saysa's sob breaks the stillness. Cata holds her close as she cries, and the two of them fold to the floor. I feel the tears rolling down my face too, but Laura and Enzo just stare at us in confusion.

"We need to get out of here before the Cazadores see us," says Tiago, his mournful voice a dirge.

"But Zaybet," says Laura.

"She's gone," says Enzo, something between a statement and a question.

They both seem to be in a trancelike state as they turn to the helm, and Laura places her hands against the charred prints while Enzo keeps a lookout. They don't say another word.

I have no idea where we're going. I'm not sure they do either. Laura just sails us through the ocean, her gaze never pulling away from the panoramic view.

"What happened back there?" I ask as Tiago and I join Cata and Saysa on the floor.

"When a bruja dies, she unleashes elemental magic," says Cata. "It's our inheritance, I guess. We can only perform one spell, and a lot of times it addresses the need of the manada—like setting off a tormenta that enchants the land and helps grow better ingredients for potions."

Saysa is still crying, and Tiago takes her hand. I don't need them to explain that Zaybet used her last spell to send us to safety. She sent the wave that washed the four of us out to sea.

There's a cracking noise at the back of my throat, and Tiago pulls me into his chest as the sobs crash over me. After what feels like a long time but might only be minutes, I hear Saysa whisper, "I-I can't believe she's gone."

"She was the most natural leader I've ever known."

I'm not the only one looking at Tiago when he says that. There's something so vulnerable about his velvet voice, and tears begin to roll down his cheeks.

Enzo darts over, faster than a heartbeat, and hooks his fingers around the neckline of Tiago's shirt. His green eyes are bugging out of his face, like he's just shattered his shock.

"*Where is she?*" he roars in demand.

Tiago doesn't resist, but his lack of reaction says enough. Enzo backs away, like he's changed his mind and doesn't want to know.

Laura narrows her gaze at us in suspicion. The news hasn't registered for her either. They're in denial.

"After you left, Yamila found us." Cata strokes Saysa's hair while she recounts how the Cazadora struck at Saysa with her magic, right as Cata's force field formed, and the blast of energy activated the volcano. "Zaybet saved us from the lava, but that volcano was too much for one Congeladora. Once the ground opened beneath her—she was gone."

Laura buries her face in her hands. Enzo cradles her when the weeping starts, and his own tears drip onto her curls. At last they believe us, probably because it sounds like something Zaybet would do.

She was a hero in life, so why not in death?

"I should've been there," Laura whispers to Enzo, clinging to him. "This is my fault."

"We both left," he murmurs into her hair.

"You came to protect me. But I didn't protect her. She needed her Encendedora." Laura chokes on her cries, and Enzo starts stroking her back and coaxing her to breathe.

It feels so invasive to sit here, listening to them grieve, when Zaybet died for us. If she hadn't frozen that red tidal wave, I would be mourning Tiago, Saysa, and Cata's deaths.

We didn't stand a chance at saving her. It was like stepping on a mushroom—she was there one moment and gone the next. The volcano consumed her.

There's no body to bury. No proof of her passing. Who will tell her family? And *Tinta*? I think of their cinematic parting kiss, and this whole thing feels unreal again. It's like a story that stepped away from its outline. This can't possibly be the final draft.

"You need to leave."

Laura stands over us. She and Enzo have stopped crying, and now they're holding hands, staring down at the four of us.

"I won't turn you in because her death would be in vain," she says, her chin trembling, "but you can't stay on this ship. So tell me where to drop you."

Saysa looks to her brother.

"Home."

Laura doesn't see us out. She only hugs Saysa and Cata. I trail behind the others as Enzo leads us down the tongue-like passage, and I feel a poke of heat in the middle of my spine.

When I turn, Laura is holding something in her open hand.

I'm at her side so fast, she blinks.

"Zaybet was making this for you. It's not finished. She gave it to me to burn some effects into the gold, but I didn't get to."

I take the round locket she hands me, its thin chain hanging off my fingers. The center of the gold case is riddled with tiny openings that form a star-like pattern, and there's a fine outline of a sun's corona around the star, which looks like a sketch for some effect that never got done. It kind of looks like my eye.

There's a glimmering through the tiny holes that makes them twinkle like real stars, and I pop open the lid.

Instead of a picture, inside is a ball of ice. As I'm watching, it evaporates into a pair of misty sevens that come together to form my *M* symbol. Then it hardens back into ice.

"Thank you," I say, my voice shaky.

Laura nods and turns away from me, like my presence is triggering. So I clasp the locket around my neck and slip it under my cloak as I hurry down the passage. By the time I make it to the door, the others have disembarked, and it's just Enzo waiting for me.

Enzo, whose parents see him as broken and who's lived so

long at the Coven that it's like he was born there. Now he's homeless and best friend–less because of me.

"I'm sorry," I start to say, but he just shakes his head like he can't hear it and pulls me into a hug.

"You have to hate me," I whisper as we separate. "I cost you Zaybet and the Coven and your horario—"

"That's not what happened," he says in his raspy voice, his green gaze steadfast on mine. "We risked our lives because your life matters. That's how a pack species should treat everyone. It's what my parents should have done for me."

He reminds me of when ICE separated the mom from her baby at Doña Rosa, and I became enraged that man-made borders matter more than people. "I wish everyone thought like you," I say.

"I was just a shadow when Zaybet joined the Coven," he confides, his voice rough. "She taught me to like myself. And I've never known her to believe in anyone the way she believed in you. So promise me something."

I nod because the tears make it impossible to speak.

"When you can't fight for yourself anymore . . . fight for her."

It's the dead of night when we stand on the banks of an island, carrying no bags and veiled in our wintry cloaks from Marina. We're in the shadow of a harbor where dozens of ships are docked. I sneak a glance behind us as we make for the trees, but *La Espiral* is already gone.

The woods must be shallow because there's light flickering ahead. On the other side of the trees is a moat surrounding an opalescent construction ten times larger than the Colosseum.

Rívoli is a manada built into the sky.

The city is enclosed in glowing white stone that makes me

think of the opal doorknob of the Citadel. It refracts the light into bands of icy blue, creating a prism effect that looks otherworldly. I stare up at an ascending series of tiered gardens—seven stories in all—each balcony bursting with foliage and waterfalls.

Perla once showed me a postcard of a painting she loves. An artist's rendering of the Hanging Gardens of Babylon. It's the only one of the ancient Seven Wonders that doesn't have an exact location because no one can confirm it existed. There's no archeological evidence.

Maybe this is it.

"Piedra de la luna," says Saysa as I ogle the view. "*Moonstone.* It's the scarcest stone in Lunaris and believed to hold special protective properties, also making it the most valuable."

"Your manada—it's—"

"*Loaded,*" supplies Cata, whose eyes are as wide as mine. "It's one of the top two wealthiest places in Kerana."

There are a handful of crystal bridges frozen along the water's surface, but presumably in a place this fancy they'll be checking Huellas. "How do we get in?"

"Follow me."

Saysa steps back into the woods' embrace, and the rest of us follow. "First thing a Jardinera does when she comes into her powers is plant a secret door in her room."

She wends through the trunks like she's searching for one in particular, and I'm reminded of the morning she led me through the Everglades to visit Perla.

"We live in el Barrio Norte, which is on the highest level—"

Saysa face-plants to the ground.

Her fall is so sudden that neither Tiago nor I catch her. The upraised root she tripped on wasn't there a moment ago.

"Missed you too, Catatree," says Saysa, sitting up and brushing dirt off her indigos.

I'm pretty sure I didn't catch that last word right.

"*Catatree?*" echoes Tiago as he pulls Saysa to her feet.

She grows very interested in a speck of nonexistent dust on her sleeve as she answers. "I, um, started working more on my English after meeting Cata in Lunaris. I used to sit under Catatree, and she'd shift her limbs to shade me from the sun and toss me a surprise fruit whenever I hadn't eaten in a while. I wanted to name her, and I don't know why that stuck."

Cata kisses Saysa's cheek. "Sounds like you two have some talking to do."

Saysa faces her tree-friend. "Look, I already explained when I left that I would be in school for a few years, so I don't know why you're—"

The root that tripped her begins to bury itself into the soil, like a giant worm burrowing.

"Wait, I'm sorry!" says Saysa. "You're right. I should have visited more."

The root stays still for so long that it starts to feel impossible it ever moved. Then I leap back as it shoots into the air, forming an archway. We follow Saysa through, and then we're inside a brown passage.

"Thanks," says Saysa, laying both palms flat against Catatree. Her eyes light up with magic, and the three of us wait for them to finish communing. "We'll only be another minute," says Saysa, turning to us with her eyes alight. "Cata, she wants to meet you."

"Oh," says Cata, sounding pleased. She presses her hands to the wall, and her pink eyes flash on.

Tiago and I look at each other.

It feels like the first time our eyes have met since La Boca. If he was afraid for me then, it's nothing to the way he watches me now. Like I'm already lost to him.

"Let's go," says Saysa, and we walk down the dim passage

until light spills out, and we step inside a bedroom. Behind us, the wall has already hardened into solid bark.

The space we're in is large but crowded with plants of every size and variety. A thatchwork curtain covers one wall, like the ones Saysa and Cata made in La Boca. The ground is uneven, the ceiling arched and odd-shaped, and small sprigs of green break through the crevices.

Saysa slides open the curtains, revealing a floor-to-ceiling view of the stars and ocean. The sky looks less black now, like day is breaking through. She caresses her plants on the way out the door, and we pad down a hallway into a spectacular home.

The tree house isn't exactly split-level; it's more meandering-level, and it seems to branch off into various alcoves and arteries. When we reach a wide space with wooden tables and comfortable-looking couches and chairs, we find Tiago and Saysa's parents on an olive couch by a floor-to-ceiling window, watching a large pantaguas.

My gaze locks on the image onscreen.

Zaybet.

"¡Los chicos!" says Miguel, and Penelope springs up and cries out in relief. Their parents clutch Tiago and Saysa to their chests, and I'm stunned when they hug me too.

"They said on the news you were with this poor Congeladora who died," says Penelope, panning her gaze across us. "How did you get away?"

"Zaybet used her magia muerta to get us to safety."

A somber silence follows Saysa's words, then Miguel says, "You must be starving."

I don't know if they're speaking English for my sake, or if it's their custom, but they sound fluent. They must have spent time at a manada abroad.

They usher us to the long table, and as soon as we sit, they ply us with sandwiches de miga, reheated empanadas, and what looks like vanilla yogurt with slices of fruit. We pick at the food, but none of us seems able to stomach much.

"What was the plan at La Boca?" asks Penelope. I feel both parents' eyes on me as I sift through the yogurt for a sliver of strawberry.

"We had enough Septimus to open a portal to Lunaris," says Tiago.

"What about long-term?" asks Miguel.

"Obviously we didn't get that far."

"How are you, Manu?" asks Penelope, and at last I meet her sapphire stare, so like her son's.

"I'm okay." I look from her to Miguel. "Look, I know I'm a fugitive, and you're worried for your kids. If you don't want me in your house, I'll—"

Tiago's hand shoots out for mine so fast that everyone notices.

"You're welcome here," says his mom, her eyes lingering on our locked fingers.

"The mother of our species—*Kerana*—was human," says Miguel, flashing the dimples Saysa inherited. "So we're all half human as far as I'm concerned."

Penelope doesn't agree or disagree. When she looks at me, I don't see Jazmín's disdain or Yamila's judgment. In fact, it's not me she's interested in at all.

"What about the full moon?" asks Tiago. "It's in two nights."

"We'll figure it out, hijo."

Penelope holds her hand out, and he laces his fingers with hers. She looks at him with sadness in her gaze. It's the same emotion I couldn't identify in Diego and Zaybet's eyes.

Penelope wanted an easier life for her son. She wished for him to be happy.

"Zaybet's duelo starts in a few hours," says Miguel. "We haven't had someone this young die in a long time, and to honor her, all manadas are officially in mourning. Your mother and I will feel things out and see what we can come up with. Until we get back, *stay here and do* not *be seen.*"

"I recommend sleep," says Penelope. Saysa was quick to stifle a yawn, but her mom was quicker in noticing. "It's almost morning."

Miguel hugs his kids again, while Penelope escorts Cata and me down a passage that leads to another wing of the house.

"Pick whichever room you'd like. There's a library at the end of the hall, and you already saw where the kitchen is when you get hungry."

"Thanks," I say, and she kisses our cheeks before parting. When we're alone, Cata and I explore the rest of the area, scoping out every guest room. There's five in all. Cata picks the largest one, and I opt for the room with the skylight.

"How long before they're sneaking in?" she asks me with a grin. But I spy the ends of her smile falling as she turns away, and I think I know why.

"They accepted *me*," I say softly, as she's slipping into her room.

"It's different," she says. "You can give them grandchildren."

And as her door shuts, I consider her words.

Can I?

As far as I know, two werewolves have never reproduced. What if it's not possible?

The thought of not being able to bear children is a jolt to my whole system. I don't think I knew how certain I was about wanting kids until this moment. What if I'd never realized I was a lobizona, and I married a human? Would we have been able to reproduce?

I've been in bed staring at the stars and considering my fertility for almost an hour when I hear him.

"What are you doing here?" asks Tiago.

"The better question is," says Miguel, "what are *you* doing?"

Tiago pauses, then—"Getting a book."

"At this hour?"

"I can't sleep?" It sounds like a question.

"How about I read to you? Worked wonders when you were little."

"Forget it, Dad."

"No, it'll be fun! We still have your baby books . . ."

I chuckle into my sheets as their low arguing fades away, and I desperately hope they can't hear me.

As I relax into the mattress, I feel a kind of relief I haven't felt in too long. It takes me a while to identify why—but once I do, sleep settles over me at last.

Tonight is my first time in a Septimus *home*.

A few hours later, my friends and I meet in the kitchen within a few minutes of each other—donning bedclothes and bed hair—thanks to the clanging of bells. They mark the start of Zaybet's duelo.

Penelope and Miguel have already left, but we perk up at the sight of the plump arrollado de dulce de leche next to the calabaza gourd. The roll cake is dusted with powdered sugar, and there's a message written in the snow: STAY HOME.

After we've devoured every last crumb, Saysa says, "I don't want to miss Zaybet's duelo."

"You can't go," says Cata. "This is your home manada. You'll be recognized. Tiago, tell her."

"Cata's right," he says. "Except that we're masters of disguise."

"*Yes!*"

Tiago smirks as Saysa leaps to her feet and sprints away, while

Cata and I exchange confused looks. She comes back dragging a suitcase. When she pops the lid, a variety of flashy colors spill out. I spot wigs, hats, gloves, cloaks, dresses, heels, and more.

"What is all this?" asks Cata, pulling out a crystal tiara.

"When we were kids, Tiago and I used to put on shows for our parents. We roped in our friends and our productions got big enough that we started accumulating costumes and set pieces—here," she says, handing me a wig of long blond hair.

I arch my brow. "No."

"She's already the tallest bruja around, and now you want to give her blond hair?" Cata wrenches the wig from Saysa. "Why not just draw an arrow?"

"Don't help me," I beg Cata.

"Try this one," says Tiago, holding out a wig of short black hair. His fingers make my scalp tingle as they corral my strands and squeeze them under a cap. Then he spins me around to slide the wig on, his face inches from mine as he inspects my hairline and adjusts the bangs across my forehead.

His lips are so tempting, I start to lean forward.

"There."

He stands back, admiring his work, and Saysa and Cata look up from the suitcase.

"Perfect."

"Passable."

I look in the mirror. The black bob accentuates the sharpness of my features, and the color contrast only makes the yellow of my eyes stand out more.

"For the final touch," murmurs Tiago, coming up behind me.

I watch in my reflection as he slides a pair of black sunglasses on my face.

"A duelo is the only time we're allowed to hide our eyes."

26

It seems strange that my eyes are comforted by the presence of their cage. Must be an ocular brand of Stockholm Syndrome.

When we leave the front door, we're in a cul-de-sac of tree houses. There are seven massive branches, with openings into different homes, and they all meet in a central knot. Each limb is decked out in a different style. One has a stone walkway lined with sculptures, another boasts a frozen slide, and Tiago's family's is ridged, like a staircase, and fringed by a railing of ivy twined with blue flowers that glow like the ocean.

We rush down the steps toward the central knot before any of the neighbors see us. There's an entrance into the trunk, and as soon as we head in, the bark closes around us. Then it feels like we're descending.

"Elevator," says Tiago. He's wearing what looks like a blue fabric polo helmet. It scoops low along the back, with a long brim in front. Saysa is wearing the blond wig.

"I don't know how either of you deal with long hair," she complains, tossing the strands behind her shoulder. It's hard to reconcile her doll-like look with the real Saysa.

We step out onto a vast park boxed in a high hedge, where thousands of Septimus are clustered on blankets. We're in the shadow of the monstrous moonstone structure, with its seven stories rising so high that the tree crowns where we just were seem as unreachable as the clouds.

Everyone is spread out picnic-style on the longest blankets I've ever seen. They'd need to be huge to accommodate all the extended family members gathered. Every blanket's got at least a couple dozen Septimus. Children are running everywhere, and their parents are visiting friends or standing around talking, so we don't catch many stares.

Tiago told me the first thing I should do is identify the Cazadores. They'll be looking for me at every duelo in Kerana.

We make for the park's outer perimeter and walk in the shadow of the high hedge, searching the crowd like we're looking for our families. I spot a pair of lobizones threading through the blankets, scanning everyone's faces, and I nudge Tiago. They look like cops.

We pick up our pace, until we've put plenty of ground between us and them, and then as we're walking, Saysa takes a sidestep and disappears into the hedge.

An instant later, a hole opens up beside us, and Cata slips through.

When the next opening appears, I slide in.

On the other side of the green wall is an empty Septibol stadium. We're still moving to keep pace with Tiago, and Saysa runs ahead a few steps, then her eyes glow and a slit opens in the foliage. Tiago steps through.

None of us speaks since the wolves picnicking closest to the hedge would hear us. As would any Cazadores patrolling past. We line up against the hedge, but even with my enhanced vision, all I see are green leaves.

Saysa's eyes illuminate, and small peepholes appear in the foliage, just large enough to see through. I pull off the sunglasses for a better view.

There's a hot spring at the center of the park, steam rolling off its surface. Brujas in red and black are filing toward it, and after greeting one another, the Encendedoras form a circle around the water. Within moments, hundreds of them have gathered, and when they hold hands, I feel the static of magic on my skin.

There's an explosive *boom,* and a blast of heat smacks my face as the spring water geysers up—and dissipates into a smoky red mist that filters the sky in a twilit tint. Then a familiar voice whispers through the darkness.

"Yo fui Zaybet." *I was Zaybet.*

Cata told me brujas of each element would be offering their own magical tribute, but I wasn't expecting to hear Zaybet again. And I can't help noting how in life she was defined by her magic and gender, but in death she's free to be just a name. It takes a long time for her voice to fade from my ears.

While the Encendedoras return to their families, the brujas in browns and greens begin to gather, and I survey the blankets overfilling with parents, aunts, uncles, grandparents, great-grandparents . . . As I watch their raucous reunions, more than anything, I want to find Tiago's family's blanket.

I picture one day introducing Ma to Penelope, Miguel, Cata, Saysa, and most of all, Tiago—and it strikes me that I'm not fantasizing about some abstract notion. *This* is the future I want.

A rumbling starts underground. The Jardineras at the hot springs are holding hands, and the earth shakes more and more, until the geyser blows again. Millions of leaves flurry into the air and rain over the park, each one heart-shaped. A few of them scatter over the hedge, and I catch one. It's a beautiful olive shade of brown. Almost the color of Zaybet's skin.

No, not almost.

Exactly.

I inhale the leaf's earthy aroma, and Saysa lets out a muffled cry. As she weeps into Cata's chest, leaf in her hand, Tiago squeezes her shoulder and I take her other hand. Tears roll down my face too.

We're not alone in our mourning. Many in the crowd are also consoling one another, even though they didn't know Zaybet.

I've never experienced a loved one's death—aside from believing my father to be dead for most of my life—but living among humans has made me numb to it as a concept. There are so many casualties being constantly touted on the news that it would be overwhelming to grieve for every single one.

Yet the Septimus seem to value every life. Their telenovelas may be just as violent and melodramatic as human ones, but their media feels more like an escape from their world, not a reflection of it. I've never heard of any species in the animal kingdom that feels the loss of a random individual this deeply.

And it fills me with hope.

If the Septimus take death this seriously, then maybe the tribunal will be looking for a reason to let me live. I just have to give them one.

While the Invocadoras gather round, I count the Septimus on the blanket closest to us. Fifty-nine, since their eight wind witches have just walked away. The Jardineras have tears in their eyes as they return to their family, and the other brujas enfold them in hugs. They're all crying.

A chill infects the air, and I look at the hot spring right as a cloud geysers up, and a strong wind whooshes forth and blows across the park. The breeze carries notes of the briny sea, and I breathe in Zaybet's scent.

It feels like she's right here, and I turn around, expecting to see her approaching, like in La Boca.

"Damn—"

The spell sends Tiago's hat sailing through a patch in the hedge. Before Cata can blow it back over, a pair of boots steps up to it.

The Cazadores I saw earlier.

We keep still as they look around, searching for where the hat came from. The shorter one looks into the hedge, like either he sees something, or it's just occurred to him that someone could be hiding here.

He steps closer.

"Ay, gracias," says a Septima with a deep voice, stepping between the hedge and the officers. Her black hair is pulled into a tight bun.

"An Invocadora losing her hat to the wind—what a sight I must make!" she says in Spanish with a musical laugh.

When the Cazadores walk away, she turns her steely gaze to the hedge, like she knows we're here. And I recognize Marilén, Tiago and Saysa's great-grandmother.

Saysa parts the foliage, and Tiago yanks Marilén through so fast that she closes her eyes, and he has to steady her a moment. "Perdón," he apologizes in a low murmur that's barely audible.

She straightens, and her gaze lights up as the air ripples around us into a force field. "We can speak freely," she says, pulling her grandkids into a tight embrace.

She hugs Cata and me next, and again Tiago and Saysa's family surprises me with their acceptance. "When did you get back?" she asks.

"Last night," answers Saysa. "Mami y Papi are figuring out a plan for Manu for tomorrow night."

Marilén's gaze focuses on me, and I brace myself for resentment for putting her family in danger. Instead, she smiles and pans across all our faces, lingering on Tiago and Saysa.

"I'm proud of you."

It's the last thing any of us were expecting, and we exchange round-eyed looks.

"I'm going to tell you something no one else knows, not even your parents or grandparents."

Saysa and Tiago edge closer, eager to hear a family secret.

"The love of my life wasn't your great-grandfather," she says, her voice deepening with feeling. "She was my tango teacher."

Cata gasps, and Saysa steps forward to take her great-grandmother's hand.

"In our younger days, my husband and I were professional dance partners," Marilén explains to Cata and me. "Claribel trained us." She looks down at Saysa's hand and sandwiches it with her other one. "Your great-grandfather discovered our affair, I'll never know how, and gave me an ultimatum. It was my children or her."

When she looks up, her eyes are wet.

"So I made the only choice I could." She turns to Tiago, then Saysa. "Don't take this the wrong way—but I've always regretted it."

The admission is so brutal, it eclipses the beauty of this duelo. It isn't some flowery trick or dazzling revelation. It's stark truth, and it's realer than any tribute offered to Zaybet.

"I'm proud of you," says Marilén again, taking Cata's hand and joining it with Saysa's. "For doing what I couldn't."

Something electric passes through them. I see it in the flashing of Cata's and Saysa's eyes.

What seemed impossible just a moment ago has come true. A family member knows about them *and approves.*

"It's almost over. You need to hurry home."

Before his great-grandmother deactivates the force field, Tiago touches her arm. "How'd you know we were here?"

She gives him an indulgent smile. "Who do you think gave your parents all those wigs and costumes when you asked for them?"

The force field vanishes, and Saysa opens the hedge so Marilén can slip out.

We peer through to see if it's safe for us to go, and now the Congeladoras are gathered around the hot spring. But instead of doing their magic, the other brujas are approaching them and paying their respects. Zaybet was one of theirs.

Penelope must be up there.

As I survey the blankets of families, some of the longing to join them I felt earlier has abated. Like a once-great fire that's dying, the first bite of cool air coming through.

Now as I imagine my future with Tiago, I wonder where Saysa and Cata fit on the blanket. After Marilén's admission, all I see around me are children born without choice. Because no adult dares to stand up for them.

Water geysers into the sky, like the blowhole of a whale, and millions of droplets freeze in the air, forming a familiar metallic gaze.

Zaybet's Congeladora eyes shine in the sky for one brilliant moment, the sun's gleam making them look alight with magic. And as I bask in her revolutionary vision for the last time, I know what I'm going to do.

Zaybet's final spell has been cast.

27

We're home before Penelope and Miguel return from the duelo. They find us sitting at the table, dressed in bedclothes, like we haven't left the house.

They hug Saysa and Tiago for a long moment. I don't blame them, since they just attended the duelo of a young bruja whose final act was to save their children's lives.

"We have good news," says Penelope, while Miguel ducks to inspect something on his shoe. I think I see him wipe his eyes.

"What is it?" asks Tiago.

"We've been able to get Anestesia."

Penelope pulls out a syringe from a pocket of her deep blue dress and sets it on the table.

"*How?*" he asks.

"I said I wanted it for you. In case one of you came home and I needed to keep you safe during the full moon. Everyone's been so worried for us since they saw you on the news that they were eager to help."

Anestesia puts a Septimus in a magi-medi coma, and it's only used by healers or law enforcement. Which means they just broke the law for me. "Thank you so much, but I can't accept this. I don't want to put you in any legal trouble."

"Manu—"

"Tiago, you said so yourself. Now that the tribunal knows there's a hybrid, they're never going to stop coming for me. What do you think happens to those who get caught helping me?"

I look to Penelope and Miguel, the desperation thick in my voice. "It's one thing for us to be here in secret, we won't tell anyone, but if you involve others, they could turn you in—"

"No one in our manada is going to betray us," says Miguel, authority laced into his voice. "The law is important, but our community comes first. Protecting one's neighbor takes precedence over following orders."

I appreciate the distinction, but I know Yamila. She's not going to stop coming for me. And just like a Lunaris demon, if she gets bored chasing me, she's going to go after easier prey. Like the Septimus I care about most.

"Thank you for your concern, Manu," says Penelope, her eyes soft, "but please let us help. We don't want the Cazadores' rash actions to cost us more girls' lives. Let us get you through this full moon, and once we're back, we can come up with a real solution."

Tiago's eyes are practically bulging from his head, and I ask, "What about Tiago? The Cazadores know he's with me—and Saysa and Cata have been exposed too."

"We'll say Zaybet's death scared them, and as soon as they came to their senses, they left you and came home."

"*What?*" snaps Saysa.

"No way!" says Tiago.

But I nod my assent. "Then I'll do it."

Tiago opens his mouth to argue, and Cata says, "Manu agreed. Let it go."

"Wise words," says Miguel, reverting to better spirits. "Now, who's ready for some food?"

The mood lightens, and even Cata cracks a smile.

As we pass around cuts of meat and bowls of salads, a protective aura seems to settle over the table. It feels like my friends have dropped their armor because there are parents in charge now, so everything will be fine.

But it's hard to find the magic in bubbles when you've seen how easily they pop.

The full moon is coming.

I can feel it in my uterus.

I've been staring at the stars through the skylight for a couple of hours when I finally feel like I've waited long enough that it's safe to get out of bed. I comb through the clothes in the guest closet until I find the white dress I glimpsed this morning. The instant I saw it, I pictured wearing it on a date with Tiago.

It's the kind of dreamy thing a girl in a movie would wear to walk along the beach at night—thin straps, soft V neckline, fine fabric that's form-fitting but not tight. I tame my hair down as best I can, and I even dab on some red lipstick I find in the bathroom drawer.

I stare at Zaybet's locket, and I consider taking it off. But that feels wrong somehow. So instead, I slip it under my neckline, so that only the fine gold chain is visible.

When I look at myself in the mirror, I wonder if I'm really this girl. I'm not a bruja or a human, after all. I'm a *werewolf*. Maybe I should just put on jeans and a T-shirt.

Yet when I go to pull off the dress, my gut twists in protest, so I leave it on.

I keep my steps soft as I pad past the kitchen, and I take the passage I saw Tiago disappear down earlier. There's a flash of light ahead, and I topple into someone's hard chest.

His dad?

Shit—

I exhale in relief when I sniff hints of cedarwood and thyme and that intoxicating third ingredient. "I was just coming to see you," says Tiago, his gaze widening as he takes me in. "But now I feel underdressed."

His bedroom is more rustic than the rest of the house. The walls aren't buffed, so they look like actual bark, and there's a gaping crater in the ceiling. The hole is about the size of Tiago's massive bed—which is perfectly lined up with it.

My skylight has nothing on this view. He can see the whole night sky.

There's a protruding knot of roots on the ground, right by an opening in the wall that seems to lead to a deeper alcove. I start gravitating toward it, but I glance over my shoulder just in case. "Is this okay?"

Tiago flashes me a smile. "Snoop away."

I climb over the roots and enter what is definitely the best part of the room. It's a round balcony enclosed by so many narrow tree limbs that it looks like a cage. Through the gaps, I can see the ocean and the skyline. Lining the perimeter is a circular cushion, and as Tiago flops down, I picture him spending his childhood here reading.

I'm about to join him when I spy something resting between two boughs. It looks like a guitar, but with double the number of strings.

"You play?" I ask, picking it up. I've never held a guitar before. It's much lighter than I expected.

"A little," he says with a shrug. He doesn't meet my gaze, and I remember what Saysa said, about how he makes having a talent seem like a burden.

I hold it out to him. "Can you play for me?"

He looks up from the guitar, wearing the expression I'd wear if he asked to read my journals. "I'm not great," he warns as he takes the instrument in his hands.

I step back and watch him perch at the edge of the seat, holding the guitar like he hasn't held it in a while and has felt its absence. Gentle with his touch, he tunes the different knobs, like he's refamiliarizing himself with a landscape he knows intimately well. His brow furrows in concentration, and when he strums, it's a different sound than I expected.

Richer, deeper, more a cross between a guitar and a piano.

When he's finished tuning, he begins to play a song so sweeping and haunting and heartbreakingly beautiful that it's hard to believe it's coming from a single device. It's like a one-instrument orchestra. The melody feels complete on its own, like it doesn't need anything else—

"She lights up the night,
like a lost drop of day,
a sunbeam gone astray."

Tiago's sensual voice unspools me.

Somehow, my feet deposit me on the cushion next to him, my movements minimal, unwilling to break his incantation. The infusion of his vocals is so perfect that I can't believe I ever liked the song without them.

*"She rearranges the stars,
paves new paths with her feet.
She makes my heart beat."*

He looks up at me on the last lyric, and my own pulse stalls.

*"Ojos de oro,
Sos lo que adoro.
Te quiero en mis brazos,
Mi querida Solazos—"*

The music cuts off abruptly. Like a cord got yanked out. Tiago sets the guitar aside and mutters, "It's rough. I'm still working on it."

His speaking voice sounds a-melodic now. English or Spanish aside, *music* is Tiago's true language.

My pulse is racing too rapidly to speak.

"I started writing it the night we met." He searches my face for a reaction. "I borrowed one of the school's guitars and practiced in my room. Pablo wasn't thrilled."

"I-I love it," I say, my throat dry.

The tension in Tiago's expression eases. "I hadn't played since Argentina. Music was something I thought I'd lost in the move, but meeting you brought it back. You helped me find my voice again." He takes my hands in his. "I'll do whatever I can to help you find yours."

I feel the emotions stinging my eyes, so I push in and press my lips to his.

He kisses me back and slides my body onto his lap, his hand running down my spine. "There's so much I want to show you," he murmurs into my neck.

"Show me, then."

I get to my feet, and he blinks. "*Now?* Why not wait until we're back?"

"Because I got dressed up."

I hook a hand on my hip, and a devilish smile curls his lips. "It *would* be a shame to waste that dress."

"So you like me like this?" Now I sound less sure.

"I do." He stands and takes me in again, only his gaze travels extra slowly.

"Do you wish I dressed more like a bruja?"

His eyes snap to mine, the blue no longer soft like the sea, but hard like a sapphire. "I can write you a better song."

"What?"

"If I haven't made myself clear." He takes my chin in his hand. "I like you *every* way, Solazos."

His arms close around me, and our mouths crash together. My heart races as a tingling sensation spreads across my skin—

"Carried away," he says, breathless.

His eyes are aglow, and there's a light stubble on his face. "Let's get going."

Now I would rather stay and finish what we started, but there's no point in saying so because he's already by the door.

I follow Tiago out of the house, and then I start to climb down the steps to the elevator, but he takes my hand and shakes his head. Instead, he transforms.

As his body breaks free of its form, I feel the tug in my uterus, and I rip out of my skin too. When the agony ends, he reaches for a low-lying branch and climbs up to a higher bough. He holds out his hand for mine, but I don't take it.

I start backing away, then I break into a sprint and leap for the branch. When I catch it, I pull myself up the way he did.

We keep climbing, limb by limb, through the tree's crown. I feel the bark digging into my skin and the leaves scratching my face, but none of it bothers me. This body was built to move this way, and the more momentum I get, the more confident I feel. I go from trusting my muscles to carry me, to feeling that I can take on anyone who comes at me.

In this body, I feel like I can do anything.

We break through the crown and pull ourselves onto a narrow wooden platform that extends across the treetops. Above us, the sky is infested with stars, surrounding an engorged moon that's nearly round.

The platform we're on is lined with colorful hot-air balloons. I look at Tiago, and even though he's in wolf form, there's something precocious about his expression. A sparkle in his gemstone eyes reminds me of the night we met, when we survived the lunarcán.

Jump!

He leaps off the wooden plank into the sea of treetops.

Tiago! I cover my mouth with my clawed hand in horror—

But he doesn't fall.

He's latched onto some kind of invisible netting, and he starts to climb up, like he's trying to reach the sky. By now I've seen enough of the Septimus world to know that if I jump, something will catch me. So I take the leap.

I sail through the air, until fine, silky threads kiss my skin, and my fingers and shoes hook into webbing. Up close, it glints in the starlight.

Telarañas, says Tiago, and I look up to meet his face a few feet above me.

Spiderwebs.

Try to keep up. Then he's off like a shot.

I reach up and try to move my arms and legs like he does, but I can't get his speed. *We're not all Spider-Man!*

He looks over his shoulder and doubles back. *We don't have eight limbs, so our power is in our hips.* He thrusts his from side to side in an exaggerated motion.

I bark out a laugh, but I do what he says, and I swing my hips. As soon as I shift my weight to my middle, my arms and legs move more easily, and I pick up speed until I close much of the distance between us.

We keep climbing and climbing, and I make the mistake of looking down—we're so high up that Rívoli is a forest enclosed in glowing walls.

When I look up again, Tiago's gone.

Tiago?

I climb a few more feet, and a tingly barrier washes over me, as solid ground manifests beneath my feet. I'm in a landscape of silver grass that looks like Lunaris at nightfall.

Tiago is next to me, already back to human form. My own body caves in as I shrink.

"I-is this a pocket world?" I ask, catching my breath and looking around in awe at the glowing plant life surrounding us.

"Sort of. It's a midnight garden," he explains, and as I watch, a ray of moonlight hits a purple flower, and it blossoms open on the spot. "But it's not exactly ours."

"I don't understand," I say, falling into step with him as we follow a narrow trail between long-stemmed plants.

"Lunaris likes to keep her realms separate. Septimus interact very little with insects and animals. We're omnivores, so the whole predator and prey thing still applies, but we each have our own domains."

We arrive at a wider area, where rivulets knot together and roll through the silver grass, and I admire the glimmering foliage of this garden. Just one of the many secrets the moon keeps from the sun.

"There's a theory that Lunaris does this so the killing doesn't get out of hand." At my expression, Tiago clarifies, "Like brujas using pesticide potions to keep bugs away from their plants, or wolves being tempted to hunt animals for fame or fur or fun."

We go down a shadowy path that winds through a patch of reedy trees. "But are we even allowed here, then?" I murmur. I start to feel whispers of webs on my skin, and I run my hand over my face.

"If we respect one another, we can coexist. Don't you think?"

I answer him with another question. "Do you think that about Septimus and humans too?"

"I don't know." He takes a moment to consider it. "The closest we get to the human experience is childhood, before we have our powers. But part of the fun is knowing we'll inherit them one day. To grow up surrounded by magic and know you'll never have it . . . That's different. I can see many humans not being gracious or understanding."

I think of how I felt when I first arrived at the academy without any abilities, and I know he's right.

We step into a colorful meadow surrounded by copper-trunked trees with cotton candy crowns. Their shedding has coated the field in a quilt of puffy pastel clouds. I look at Tiago in awe, and he laughs at my expression.

I break into a sprint across the cottony ground, remembering the crystal marketplace of El Laberinto where Tiago and I shared our first kiss. Only instead of ice-hard, this field is so plushy that my feet sink down, and I feel like I'm bouncing along the cloud tops.

After a while, I look for Tiago, but he's vanished.

"Tiago?"

My voice hangs in the air, but there's not a stir of movement.

"Cut it out."

The silence grows thicker the longer it holds.

"Seriously, don't—"

A flash of sapphire and teeth vaults from behind yellow and aqua clouds, and I shriek and spin away.

But Tiago is faster, and he takes me down in a burst of pink and lavender.

"Never run from a predator," he growls, pinning me beneath him, his lips grazing mine. "You only tempt us with the chase."

I roll my eyes. "You're losing it."

"*Blame the moon,*" he says in a low voice, as his mouth softly, slowly, traces my jawline. "*She comes more near the earth than she was wont, and makes men mad.*"

"Well, you know what they say about that," I murmur, my breath snagging as his lips brush my collarbone. "*Madness in great ones must not unwatched go.*"

Tiago pulls away, and I wish he wouldn't each time I think we're about to get started. He did ask me to be his girlfriend after all.

"What's this?" he asks, tugging on the thin gold chain around my neck until the locket is in his fingers. I'd buried it in my cleavage, but it spilled out.

"A gift from Zaybet," I say as he inspects the sun and star etched into the gold. "Open it."

When he does, he stares for a long moment at the ice as it keeps altering its form and displaying my symbol.

"I never knew how powerful my sister was," he says, like he's talking to the locket. "That's why Saysa was acting out. She knew I couldn't see her as a Septimus in her own right. She was just my little sister to me. But Zaybet saw her. She saved her life—more than once."

He looks otherworldly with his dark skin haloed in moonlight. "If Zaybet had been born a wolf, she would have had the world at her feet. It's fucking wrong."

His blue gaze grows blustery, and I circle my arms around

him, until our breathing is in sync. When Tiago tips back to meet my eyes, I know from the gravity of his expression that he's finally going to say whatever it is he's been trying to tell me.

"In Lunaris, wolves can only track their own bloodline."

I'm confused. Then I remember—

"You never said how you found me in the stone mountain."

"There's one exception to the family rule."

His accent resurfaces slightly, making his voice more musical. From the way he's looking at me, I'm struck with the certainty that this is about to become a core memory. A moment that will bloom within me forever.

"I'm in love with you, Solazos."

Tiago's eyes hold mine in their beam, and when I reach for an inhale, there's no air to suck in.

Then his mouth captures mine, and like his song says, we light up the night.

A tingling sensation extends through my veins, like I'm plugged into el Hongo. I feel as rooted to the earth as these cotton candy trees.

I exist.

I am seen.

I am loved.

"Estoy enamoradísima de vos," I say, my voice trembling. *I'm so in love with you.*

Tiago's breathtaking smile raises the tempo of my pulse, and I know now, more than I've ever known anything, *this is what I want.*

Saysa and Zaybet would be disappointed, but my heart isn't in their revolution—it's in Tiago's hands. I want to read novels with him every night, and maybe even attempt to write one someday. I want to visit Lunaris every full moon and explore that world the same way I once longed to explore outer space.

I want a life among the Septimus, with a family and a manada and a purpose—and I want my parents safe and by my side.

If I can just convince the tribunal I'm not a threat, maybe they'll allow me this much—just the right to live a quiet life with Tiago, nothing more. I'll never claim the spotlight again or violate any more of their laws.

"How did things work out for that guy in *The Chocolate War*?" I ask, thinking of *Cien Años de Soledad* and how lately I don't seem to finish any book I pick up. "Was disturbing the universe worth it?"

Tiago hesitates, and I already know.

Nothing changes.

"Solazos, you're crying," says Tiago, taking my face in his hands.

"I'll miss you," I whisper.

"It's just three nights. I'm the one who'll be miserable without you. You won't even notice—you'll be Sleeping Beauty, and I'll wake you up with a kiss."

Tiago's fairy tale ending is tempting, but late. I don't believe anyone else can secure another's *happily ever after* anymore. Not a prince, not a parent, not a pack. I have to slay this dragon myself.

"Tiago, I don't want to lie to you anymore, so when I say what I'm about to say, I need you to listen and respect my wishes. Okay?"

I can feel his entire body tense. "What is it?"

"I'm going to turn myself in."

His eyes fill his whole face, and I can practically see the explosions going on in his mind, the battle between supporting and protecting me that's constantly taking place within him. The alpha mentality that's ingrained in him facing off with his gentler nature.

"That's a *death sentence*," he says at last.

"I'm dead either way."

From the blank way he's looking at me, I know he's never had to wonder about his own life's worth, or if there's a place for him in the world. How can he hope to understand how it feels not to be given any choices, when all he's ever had is an abundance of them?

"Everything we've done." He sounds like he's out of breath and each word taxes him. "What was it for if you give up?"

"I'm not giving up. Running away would be giving up. The Septimus system needs to change. You said so yourself. We can't keep waiting for someone else to come along and make the sacrifices we aren't willing to make."

I hear Saysa and Zaybet in my voice, and I realize my desire for a humble existence with Tiago isn't entirely true. That's not all I want. I also want to force the system to see my friends and me and make real changes.

I want both a family and a revolution.

"I'm not trying to control you, Manu, but if the roles were reversed, you wouldn't want me going on a suicide mission either!"

"You're right," I say, trying to guide us in a more productive direction. "But some risks are worth taking. I mean, you walked away from your life to go on the run with me. Some would qualify that as a suicide mission."

"I ran with you because when I fell in love with you, I saw a future for myself for the first time. I know everyone thinks I have all these doors open to me, but what good are a million choices when none of them are what you want?"

"Then you understand what I feel," I say softly, "because none of the options open to me are what I want either."

His face falls, and I know this will hurt for him to hear, but it's the only way I can explain myself. "Do you know that while we were at the duelo today, all I wanted was to sit on your family's blanket? But when I picture that blanket, it's not just us I see on it. I also see my parents. And Saysa and Cata and all our friends.

If you and I were to have children, I would want to bring them into a world where they can grow up to be whoever they want. That's why the options open to us aren't enough. I want more."

Tiago looks so forlorn as he exhales, and tonight feels like it's slipping through my grasp. This isn't how I wanted it to go. I need this last night with him.

"You're going to Lunaris soon. Let's not spend tonight sulking." When he doesn't say anything, I try something else. "Why don't you show me how you were planning to awaken me from the Anestesia?"

I lie back on the soft ground and shut my eyes, arms limp at my sides.

My senses sharpen as I await Tiago's touch, his quiet stealth alerting me to every millimeter of my body. And when his mouth brushes mine, I inhale sharply.

The air is perfumed with Tiago's tantalizing musk. His tongue parts my lips, and I arch into the kiss as his arm slides around the small of my back.

I hook my fingers around the hem of his shirt, and I tug until I've freed him of it. Tiago's eyes are soft as he strips off my dress's straps. With my period almost here, my cups are fuller than usual, and he reaches back to unhook my bra—

But something flickers in his dreamy gaze, like rational thought trying to break through. And before he can pull away to do what he probably deems the "right" thing, I yank my bra off myself.

Tiago's eyes widen as he looks down, all logic gone from his gaze. I hear a hurried echoing sound that I think are footsteps, but then I recognize his heartbeat. *Racing.*

I take his hand and place it on my knee, then I slide it up my thigh, shocking myself with my own assertiveness. I don't feel insecure. If anything, I feel . . . *empowered.*

Tiago's fingers are warm on my skin, and I let go as he takes over, tracing higher and higher, until I gasp and press against his chest, pulling him in for a kiss. The moment our tongues touch again, I feel a rumbling in my blood.

The shift is coming.

"Solazos," murmurs Tiago as his fangs file down and his stubble grows in. "Are you—"

Claws curve from my fingers as I pin him down and clamp my mouth on his. Pain and pleasure battle inside me as we make out while the transformation takes hold, until neither of us can speak out loud again.

We should slow down, he says into my head as our mouths clash. *Once we give ourselves over, we won't be able to stop—*

I don't want to stop.

Are you sure? He pulls back just enough so I'll meet his gaze.

Yes, I insist, shutting him up with the force of my kiss. My fangs cut into his lips, drawing blood. The metallic taste coats our mouths, subduing the last vestiges of our humanity. Tiago rips my dress off, and I can hardly think after that.

I'm not interested in holding back.

I want to know what happens when I let go.

I took Nuni's pink pill tonight.

28

The sky is gray by the time we return to Tiago's room, sunrise just a couple of hours away. I should go to my bed before his parents wake up, but Tiago insists I stay with him. He promises to take all the blame if we're discovered.

I curl into his chest, like we used to do in our room at the Coven. I wait until his breathing deepens, and within a few minutes, he's asleep. I watch him dream, trying to commit to memory the sculpted features of his face, the strong curves of his arms, the warm weight of his skin.

I love him so much that I might never leave.

I only force myself to get up by thinking of how much more Zaybet sacrificed. I'm careful not to wake him as I sneak out, and I pad to the back wing where the guest rooms are. But instead of opening my door, I open Cata's.

She's passed out on the bed, golden-brown strands strewn

across her face, and Saysa's head rests at her side. I nudge Cata's shoulder hard enough to rouse her.

Her eyes fly open, and I press a finger to my lips so she knows not to make a sound. *Get dressed,* I mouth.

I don't wait around. I head to my room, shower at lobizona speed, and change into indigos and a shirt, tucking my locket under it. Then I make the bed and tidy up the room, stuffing the only thing I'm taking with me in my pocket. I wait for Cata in the hall.

"What is it?" She crosses her arms the instant she sees me, primed to argue.

I pull her farther away, into the library, and say, "I need you to turn me in."

"Go back to bed—"

"We both know Yamila's out for blood, and now that we've involved Saysa and Tiago's family, they're going to be in her line of fire."

"This is a *powerful* manada. They can protect you."

"At what cost? Look at Zaybet."

Cata grows agitated and starts pacing in front of the shelves. "That was extreme—there's no reason to think anyone else will die. We've been making decisions on our own, and they haven't panned out. I think we should trust Penelope and Miguel—"

"I do trust them; it's the tribunal I don't trust!"

I grab her arms and force her to stop moving and look at me. "We both know Yamila will find me. Our own families have suffered enough by our parents' bad choices—let's spare Penelope and Miguel. They've done too much for us already. They don't deserve this."

From the way she bites her lip, I know I'm right. "What exactly is your plan?"

"I want you to reach out to your mom to arrange a private meeting for you and Yamila, with Jazmín as witness. If Yamila comes alone and agrees to your terms, you'll turn me over."

"And what are those terms?"

"Immunity for you, Saysa, Tiago, and your families."

"And what about *you*, Manu?" She sounds exasperated.

"This is my choice, Cata."

She shakes her head and stares at me like none of this makes any sense. "Why are you making me do this?"

I hate myself as I say, "You're the only one strong enough to do what needs to be done to keep us safe."

My compliment doesn't go over as well as I'd hoped because she looks like she's swallowed something sour. "Tiago—"

"Knows."

I think she hears the catch in my voice because she stares at me but doesn't argue anymore. Now she understands.

Tiago can't do this for me.

Nor Saysa.

It's only Cata.

After using Tiago's parents' caracola to reach her mom and arrange the details, Cata makes us stop by the kitchen so I can eat something. But I can't stomach even the thought.

"At least have mate," she says. "You'll need your strength."

I swallow the hot drink, and right as I'm setting down the calabaza gourd, I see him.

Tiago is shirtless, the whites of his eyes lined with red, bed hair pointing in every direction.

I stay completely still, like an animal caught in a predator's gaze.

Cata takes my arm and tries to move me, but I don't budge. I want to kiss him one last time, but I know what will happen if I do.

He's stoic, but I understand. If he moves a muscle, he might stop me.

I have no idea how I make it out of the house, but when the door shuts behind us, I drop to the ground and take deep breaths.

I hear something break in the distance.

Like a sob.

Cata steadies me, and without a word, she leads me to the elevator. We take it up instead of down. "How'd you know this was here?" I ask when we step out onto the wooden platform with the hot-air balloons.

"You weren't the only one out on a rendezvous last night."

She picks a nondescript gray balloon speckled with subtle stars, something that won't draw eyes in the predawn light. As soon as I've climbed in, we shoot straight up in the air.

It's a good thing I didn't eat, or I would have regurgitated by now.

I look down as we climb higher, squinting to spy a trace of the spiderwebs or the midnight garden, but I can't see any of it. The ground is just a tapestry of green enclosed in a sea of blue, and soon we're flying through the clouds.

"How do you know where you're going?"

Her pink eyes bright, Cata says, "I'm calling on the wind to lead us to Belgrano." Her face is pallid, and it's not from the flight. "Why are you doing this?"

From the sound of her heart racing, I know her emotions are at the wheel. So I try to make her understand, both for her sake and the sake of our flight.

"Do you know my eyes don't change in the human world?"

From her lack of surprise, she does.

"Saysa told you?"

She nods.

"My whole life, I wore sunglasses. I understood all the reasons why, but that logic didn't shield me from the shame. I felt ugly and wrong and *abnormal*."

I see the word written in Ma's writing on the back of the photograph Yamila burned.

"It wasn't other people who made me feel bad about myself. It was the hiding."

The flight smoothens out as Cata's pulse slows.

"You and Saysa knew Tiago was trying to tell me he loved me, but I didn't have a clue. Not just because he's the first boy I've ever even talked to, but because growing up, I could never imagine anyone loving me."

I feel my eyes welling with water. "And if I keep hiding now, I'm not just saying I'm unworthy. I'm saying everyone like me is too."

"You're not the only one who feels unlovable," says Cata, and the balloon shakes with the quiver in her voice.

I frown. "Saysa is head over heels in—"

"She wants what I can't give her."

I stare at Cata and see a young Marilén forced to make an unconscionable choice. Saysa or society. Cata is the true Lily Bart.

"What about what Marilén said?"

"It's easy to long for the life you didn't live, Manu. It can never disappoint you." Sometimes Cata seems older than the world.

"Every day," she murmurs into the wind, "I grow more and more like her. It's my curse. To become my mother."

"Cata, you're not—" I go to take her hand, but she slides out of my reach.

"*I am.* I'm turning you in. I'm betraying our pack. Saysa will *never* forgive me." Her voice is thick with emotion.

"I'm sorry," I say, her agony a dagger twisting in my gut. "I didn't think it would be good to bring her to meet Yamila right now. I was worried she wouldn't take it well."

Cata's eyes look almost watery, and I panic that I've just broken them up. "You make the hard decisions, but Saysa knows you don't make them on your own. Tiago will back you that this was my choice. You obviously wouldn't turn me in without my consent—and you've had plenty of chances and lots of good reasons! You told me I was your mom's redemption with the Cazadores. No one would have blamed you if you'd turned me in at the start, when you didn't even know me. But you didn't."

"I—"

She looks like she's going to say something but changes her mind. Then her shoulders droop in defeat. "I came so close, Manu," she admits. "I knew how much my mom wanted it, and I was so desperate to impress her. If you'd never transformed, I-I don't know what I would have done."

The last words blow out like a dying wind, a dark admission of the soul.

I'm not sure what Cata is truly capable of either. What I do know is she needs someone in her corner as much as I do.

"Choice reveals character—not *what-ifs*," I say, staring into her pink eyes. "I'm sure you wouldn't have betrayed me."

And yet, part of me wonders if Cata is right that every bloodline has its curse.

I think of Ma's favorite book, *Como agua para chocolate*. It's a mother-daughter tale about Tita, a girl who longs to be with the man she loves, and Mama Elena, who stands in her way. Tita's overpowering emotions infect the meals she prepares, affecting everyone around her in ways that spiral beyond her control.

The book ends with Tita's great-niece—also nicknamed Tita—inheriting her recipes, implying that this story will go on repeating itself. Ma loves that twist, but I remember being overcome with a crushing sense of doom when I read it.

Maybe there are some chains we can never break.

Sunlight cracks the cloud covering, and the sky clears to a cool blue dawn. Then a city of purple trees comes into view.

"As Tiago's best friend," I say, "you agree I'm doing what's best for him in the long run, right?"

Cata slows the balloon down as we get closer to the manada. "In all five years I've known him, Tiago has never made a choice of any consequence. Brujas have always courted him, and opportunities have always found him. Coach was the one who asked him to try out for the team. Tiago never pursued anything for himself. Until you."

Her words lift me up as much as they knock me down, and I'm no longer sure I made the right call.

She crosses her arms. "So no, as his best friend, I don't agree. I know for a fact you just walked away from the best thing that's ever happened to you. And knowing that you could do it . . ."

She doesn't finish the thought, but I understand.

If I can do it, she can too.

Bald branches pierce the air, their ends flattened into landing pads, most of them packed with parked balloons. Ma told me Argentines are anything but early risers, and from the lack of air traffic, this seems to extend to their supernatural brethren too.

Last time we were here, I saw this manada from the ground up, but this view tells a different story. Every treetop is its own scene. One looks like an amphitheater, another is a skating rink, and we descend over a third that's an idyllic green park. Cata lands us with a jolt on the outskirts of the greenery, alongside a couple of other balloons, and I reach into my pocket and pull out the bottle I brought with me.

It's a balmy, breezeless morning, and it seems we're the first visitors of the day. I take in the foliage, inhaling a medley of sunbaked dirt and sweet flowers. But Cata's eyes are trained on the invisibility potion in my hand.

"Any idea how it works?" I venture as I scan our surroundings for a sign of Yamila. There are bushes of palm fronds that are as tall as small trees, so it's hard to be completely sure.

"I've read each variety affects everyone differently," says Cata. "Depends on your magical constitution."

"How long will it last?"

"Few hours, but you can end it sooner if you want. Every spell is anchored to an element—you'll know what it is as soon as you taste it. When you're done, just break the spell."

I pause my lookout to stare at her. "What?"

"It's hard to explain. If it's plant-based, you might feel a tightness somewhere, like a sense of vines constricting your veins. To break it, you just need to move that limb and shake off the paralysis. Make sense?"

"Nope," I say, and since Yamila could show up any moment, I tip back the potion in one gulp.

I feel a strange watery sensation in my throat, like I swallowed ten times the amount of liquid. The water level keeps rising, drowning my organs and vocal cords, until I can't speak or breathe.

I widen my eyes at Cata, and she looks on in matching horror as I choke—

"Manu?"

I'm trying to say *help me,* but the words won't come. Water just keeps filling every crevice, until I'm sure it will start leaking from my ears and nose.

"Where are you?"

I blink as the water settles.

Even though I'm not breathing, I'm still alive.

I'm here, Cata! I try to speak the words, but no sound comes out. It's like being underwater.

"Manu! Talk to me!"

Cata sounds panicked as she spins in a circle, squinting. I reach for her hand and squeeze it to let her know I'm okay.

She lets out a piercing shriek, jumping a few feet into the air, undoubtedly rousing every Cazador in the city.

"Calmate."

The low, commanding voice telling Cata to calm down makes my spine stiffen.

Yamila is approaching from behind a thicket of palm fronds, wearing tight red pants and a black sweater. Her eyes are ablaze like her magic is locked and loaded. "You're the one who asked for this meeting, so no hysterics."

Cata's cheeks grow as pink as her gaze, and she climbs out of the basket to meet Yamila on the grass. I'm not sure how much energy I'll have without breath, so I take a test step. When I don't hear any noise or feel any dizziness, I leap down from the balloon as lightly as possible, standing astride Cata.

I brush her arm *softly* to let her know I'm here. *Please don't let her scream again.*

"Let's get this over with," says Cata, her fingers itching the spot where I touched her. "Call my mom."

"Aww." Yamila's bloodred gaze dims down. "It's so inspiring how close you two are."

"I was going to say that about you and your brother—only I mixed up *inspiring* with *incestuous.*"

I brush Cata's arm again, more firmly this time. I don't need her pissing off Yamila. I'm trying to keep her and the others out of trouble, so if she risks her own chances of getting a deal, none of this was worth it.

Yamila stares at Cata in silent evaluation, and I notice something's changed about her. She seems less . . . *smug*.

Maybe Zaybet's death humbled her. Or maybe she's not taking this meeting seriously.

"If you're wasting my time, I will arrest you," she says.

Cata rolls her eyes. "Why would I risk everything by coming here just to waste your time?"

"Why would you risk everything for an outlaw you barely know?" Yamila's throaty voice seems to sharpen the edges of her words.

"You know, I never got what Saysa saw in you," muses Cata, adopting the Encendedora's sultry low register. "She thought you were this trailblazer because you were the youngest Cazadora, and you won a bunch of distinctions for upholding the law . . . but all I see is the wolves' good little lapdog."

Yamila's eyes smolder like a dragon ready to strike.

I feel my transformation trying to break through the potion's power, as the Encendedora steps up to my cousin, just inches from my face.

"I guess that's why your mom prefers me." Yamila's voice is now a purr. "If my daughter was a deviant, I would be just as disgusted."

The temperature drops as Cata's eyes swirl with light, and I feel my body trembling, caught between the shift and the potion—then Yamila reveals a handheld pantaguas that was tucked into the back of her pants.

"Down, witch. Mommy's watching."

Jazmín's watery image ripples onto the waterscreen. As soon as her amethyst gaze settles on her daughter, her stern expression cracks with concern. "¿Cómo estás?"

"*I'm fine.* Let's just get this over with."

"I've written up an affidavit that I shared with Señora Jazmín," says Yamila, her demeanor now dispassionate and completely different from before. "In it, you swear that you and your friends were confused and swept up in youthful idealism, and what happened in La Boca snapped you out of the lobizona's spell. This document ensures that you and all your families will be immune from prosecution."

Cata looks at her mom, awaiting confirmation. "It checks out," she says, bags under her eyes. "I woke up the school's lawyer to review it. As long as your information leads to Manuela's capture, no one else will be in any trouble."

"Okay," says Cata, sounding less confident now. "If you're sure then. That this is the right thing."

She's not talking to them.

"It is, mi amor," says her mom, and Cata cringes.

"So where is she?" Yamila sounds suspicious.

"How do I know you're not just going to arrest me as soon as I tell you?" challenges Cata. She's buying me time.

"*What?*" snaps Yamila.

"Catalina, she's not going to do that," says Jazmín, her expression stern.

"She's not trustworthy!" says Cata, arms crossed.

"That's it. I'm arresting you."

"*Told you!*" blares Cata at her mom, as Yamila whips out a pair of braided bracelets.

"Yamila, don't—Catalina, please—" Jazmín sputters, while Cata's eyes light up with magic, and the Cazadora moves in with her handcuffs—

I open my mouth and suck in a breath of air.

Oxygen fills my lungs, and I feel a headrush as my body manifests. When I look around, all three of them stare back in shock.

Before I can say a word, Yamila slaps the bracelets on my wrists.

My body goes cold.

I can't feel my power. I can't transform. I can't access any kind of strength at all. It's a sickly sensation, a whole-bodied achiness, and I feel smaller than ever before.

"Manuela Azul," says Yamila, a warmth in her voice like she's relishing every word. "Per the laws of the tribunal, you are under arrest and subject to stand trial in Lunaris."

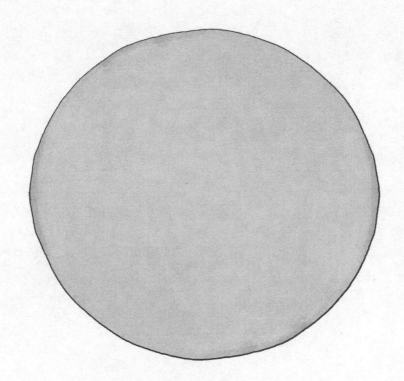

PHASE IV

29

The easiest way to describe it is a bronze key. Except it's disassembled into seven pieces, and Yamila clicks them all into place as though she could do it blindfolded. She looks like a soldier assembling her weapon.

As soon as she got me in custody, she told Cata to take off. When my cousin tried to hug me, Yamila burned her hand in warning.

"It's okay," I said before Cata could do anything stupid. "Go. I love you."

Her eyes widened in surprise, and I was taken aback too. I guess saying it to Tiago made it easier to say at all.

"I love you too." Her voice was hushed and thin, not like we were declaring our affection, but more like we were saying goodbye.

Then Yamila gripped my arm and led me across the grass. I

was so weak, I couldn't even shake her off. There's an elevator in the tree, like in Rívoli, and we descended to the ninth floor.

Yamila stabs the key-like bronze thing into the bark, and a doorway appears. She twists it open and shoves me inside.

The condo is small, like Perla's. We're in a living room with a kitchen attached, and lying on the gray couch is Yamila's brother.

Nacho snaps upright.

"Why is she *here*?"

"If I take her in, she's out of our custody."

He frowns. "Isn't that the point? Don't you want everyone to know you caught her? Isn't that what you're after—the credit, the glory, the ego stroke?"

"Shut up." She rolls her eyes, but Nacho is right. Why is she holding me here?

"Call him," she says.

He shrugs and pulls out a caracola. "Who are you calling?" I ask.

Yamila pushes down on my shoulder, and I collapse to the floor. I try getting back up, but it's like my muscles can't hold me.

"We got her," says Nacho. Then he drops the conch shell and activates the large pantaguas on the wall.

"I need a shower," says Yamila, leaving me on the floor as she walks deeper into the space. "Watch her."

Nacho pointedly raises the volume of the show on the screen, but his gaze falls on me. The look that crosses his features makes my muscles tauten with readiness. *Fight or flight.*

Leaving the volume high, he reaches down and lifts me in his arms. I try pushing against him, but it's like trying to move a wall. His hands are rough as he carries me into the nearest room and drops me on the bed. Then he shuts the door.

Everything in me goes cold as he perches beside me, the burl and bulk of his weaponlike body weighing down the mattress.

"I've worked it out," he says, casually resting a hand on my ribcage. "You must've crawled into my truck when I was staking you out. My sister is so damn secretive that I didn't know you existed. So you outplayed me."

He bares his teeth in a predatory smile, and his fingers dig in, like he's trying to hook them into the rungs of my ribs. "Problem is, if anyone finds out, I'm fucked. So what do we do?"

"Polish your resume?"

His smile widens, and I regret my remark. "I'm guessing that's a human joke. Still, I'm glad you have a sense of humor. You're going to need it."

I swallow.

"You're already facing the death penalty, but it'd be such a waste if others had to die with you. I'll make you a one-time offer that expires as soon as I stand up: Keep my name out of your mouth, and I won't kill the one person you left unguarded."

My mind explodes with faces. Ma is with Gael, and my friends can protect one another. "What do you—"

Person.

He didn't say Septimus.

My whole being seems to shrivel as his meaning settles on me.

"Took you a minute, but you got there," he growls, leaning in so that I can smell his rank breath. "El Retiro apartment 3E. I have her scent. I'll track her down wherever she goes. My sister already knocked her out by accident when she broke in to search for Fierro. Idiot should've trusted me to do it. What do you think would happen if your abuelita ran into a big bad wolf?"

I can't think through what he's saying. Or I'll have to face the fact that I haven't looked out for Perla or Julieta or any of the women from the clinic. I abandoned them.

"Do we understand each other?"

I just want his hand off my chest and his breath off my face. "Fine. But if you *ever*—"

"Save your threats. Just honor your word." His lips linger so close, they're almost on mine. "Don't know why you're shrinking from me. Not like anyone will ever touch you again."

Footsteps echo outside, and Nacho is through the door before my next heartbeat. I exhale and shut my eyes in relief.

"Where is she?"

Nacho didn't close the door, so even without access to my abilities, I can hear them. "Tossed her in the room so we wouldn't have to look at her."

"Why *that* room?"

"What's it matter?"

"*I* sleep there!"

I open my eyes and scan the space. It's small, with just a bed, closet, armchair, and a storage shelf. There's a framed image of a family—a pair of good-looking parents and two young kids, a boy and a girl. Yamila has wild auburn hair and fiery eyes. She can't be more than five or six.

Standing behind her with his hand on her shoulder is the fallen Cazador. They both look just as they did in the footage from el Hongo. A second picture sits adjacent to this one. It's two young Cazadores receiving an official award for something. It looks like they're partners.

One is Yamila's father.

The other is mine.

Current-day Yamila strides inside. As she shuts the door behind her, my skin feels scratchy with nerves.

I should be in the custody of the Cazadores by now, not in

hiding again. Why did she bring me here? Does she want to wait until Lunaris so reporters can capture her carting me through the Citadel like a trophy kill?

She settles into the armchair. "Your mom is missing," she says, watching me closely for a reaction.

I try my best to keep my face impassive as I hold up my cuffed wrists. "Why haven't you taken me in yet?"

"Because I'm not after you," she says, and I let my hands fall.

"What do you mean?"

"I want your father. *Fierro*."

I stare at her, trying and failing to remain aloof. "Well, I can't help you."

But even as I say the words, there's a triumph in her eyes, like she's reading my lies. I wish I was as quick as Cata at spinning a yarn, but all I feel right now is tongue-tied.

"Tell me who he is."

A fiery hunger burns through her guard, making Yamila look younger. Like the little girl in the picture. Just another casualty from one of the many families my father ruined.

This is why she's been coming after me so hard. She wants to avenge her dad's death. It's not me she's obsessed with—*it's Fierro*.

A voice greets Nacho, and Yamila springs to her feet.

Despite all she's done, there's something almost innocent about her expectant expression as she stares at the door. When it swings open, a pair of coral eyes meets mine.

My father stares at me in bewilderment, a sweaty sheen laminating his light skin.

"Speechless, huh?" says Nacho.

"What's going on?" asks Gael, turning to Yamila.

Whatever her expectation, Gael's reaction falls short. "*I did it,* Tío. I caught her."

"But—how?"

"Your niece panicked. Because of what I—what happened." No matter how much bravado she puts on, Yamila's slipup betrays the remorse she feels over Zaybet's death.

Given what I now know about her father, I can understand. He was killed in the line of duty, and instead of avenging him, she caused another innocent's death.

"That wasn't your fault."

The care in Gael's voice is impossible to miss. Or fake.

I stare as he edges closer to Yamila and rests a hand on her shoulder, tipping his head down to look at her. "I failed her too. We all did. You don't carry this guilt alone."

Now I understand what Cata feels when Jazmín praises Yamila. I'm so jealous that if these cuffs weren't on me, I would be ripping out of my skin.

"I thought you'd be proud I captured her."

"I am." He lets his hand fall, like he's just remembered I'm here. "But why is she *here*? Why haven't you brought her in?"

"You're going to like this," says Yamila with a growing grin. Nacho moves in to listen, as if she hasn't clued him in either. "We're going to use her to find Fierro."

"*How?*" asks Gael.

"Either she tells us where he is," says Yamila, her voice growing colder, "or we dangle her as bait."

Gael and I lock eyes, and I have to look away because a ball of panic is rising up my throat.

"If she knew where he was or how to reach him, she would be with him," Gael points out.

"He can't do that," says Yamila, like she's anticipated this argument. "I think he's protecting her mom."

Gael's poker face is impenetrable. "How will you bait him without alerting the Cazadores that she's in custody?"

"I already sent an anonymous tip to the media. *Sources say the hybrid is in custody in Belgrano and will be tried under the full moon.* He'll know it's true when he can't reach her the usual way. Then we'll wait for him to attempt a rescue. I have a brigade of Cazadores waiting to jump him when he shows."

"Assuming he's even still around," mumbles Nacho. "Or that this is even his kid."

"I'm telling you he rescued her mom," she says, rounding on him. "There's no one else who could have pulled that off."

Gael stuffs his hands in his pockets. "Sounds like you've been very thorough. Not sure how I can help."

"Everything I've learned is from you. I thought you would . . ." She seems at a loss for words. "I thought you'd be excited. We're close to catching the wolf responsible for ruining our lives and destroying our families! Look what he's done to you—you never married or moved on. *He broke you.* And I understand, Tío," she says, gentler than I thought she could be, "because he broke me too."

Gael's gaze is lined with guilt, so much that it's brimming over the coral and threatening to spill out of him. How he's been able to swallow it for so many years of looking out for Yamila and her brother, I have no idea.

He presses his lips together and nods. "You're right, Yami."

He doesn't seem able to say more, and Yamila takes his arm. "Let's eat something. You look a little pale."

But he's staring at me, unwilling to move. "Have you fed her?"

"Do I have to?"

Gael casts Yamila a stern-but-indulgent look and pats her arm as they leave the room. "Why don't I do it, while you update the troops?"

The door swings almost shut, leaving a sliver of space for their voices to float through. "Don't forget your training," says Gael.

"That door should stay shut at all times, and we only speak in whispers."

"What can she possibly do at this point?"

"*Any* information in a prisoner's hands—"

"Can be used against you," says Yamila, finishing Gael's sentence like she's heard it a million times before. Then the door clicks closed.

Moments later, it opens again. Gael walks through with a plate of empanadas, shutting the door behind him. His expression is so drawn now that I'm startled by the effort it must have taken him to act normal in front of the others.

He sets the food on the bed next to me and takes my hands in his. *Are you okay?* he mouths, unable to give voice to the words because Nacho would hear.

Mom? I mouth back.

Just left her. She's safe. He starts rubbing my wrists, where the cuffs are binding me, and I feel a warm energy course through me. *Did Cata really—*

I shake my head and mouth, *I asked her.*

His fingers freeze, and the edges of his face fall. He looks like a portrait of heartbreak.

Tears burn my eyes as I answer his unasked question.

I can't live like this.

Everyone else in my life would demand a longer explanation. But not Fierro.

Run away with your mother and me.

I throw my arms in the air and emphatically mouth, *The full moon is in a few* hours—

I have Anestesia. He's so excited that he almost whispers the word. *Two injections. Your mom can administer them.*

It's still so tempting to run away with my parents. To be far from any government's reach. To live with my family.

But that road doesn't lead to a future with Tiago and Cata and Saysa and a family of my own. It leads back to El Retiro, and a life I've lived before.

What if they rule against you? he urges, reading the answer on my face.

What if they don't?

His hands clasp mine as panic explodes in his expression, and he's half-mouthing, half-whispering, *"Cariño, your mom told me you're a big reader, but this isn't one of your storybooks. The tribunal is merciless. Please. We were kept from each other your whole life. We only just met. I can't—I won't lose you, Manu."*

Tears bullet down his face, and his voice breaks through. "Please. Give me a chance to be your dad—"

"Shhh." I shake my head so he'll stop because now I'm crying too. *Nacho threatened Perla,* I mouth, needing to change the subject as urgently as I need to pass on this warning. *She needs protection.*

Gael nods in assent, but his eyes look explosive. "I won't let anything happen to you," he breathes, and the way he says it sounds like there's something else hiding behind the promise.

A secret.

"Sos mi vida," he murmurs, his thumbs wiping away my tears. *You're my life.* "I love you."

Then he cradles me to his chest, like I've never been held before. I feel his lips on my head as he presses a hard kiss onto my hair, and my muscles unclench, a lifelong knot in me loosening, like I've found the safe harbor I used to daydream about with every Miami sunrise. We stay together for a timeless moment, and it feels like both the longest and shortest embrace of my life.

When he pulls away, he nudges the plate of empanadas toward me. Then he snaps to his feet, drying his face on his sleeve, and takes a few breaths until the shininess in his eyes dullens.

Before he walks out, my father is gone.

The pain in my uterus tells me the full moon is imminent. Still, Yamila stations us in a corner of the street, in the shadow of a purple tree, with Cazadores hidden all over.

She's so eager that the air tastes singed.

Of course, no suspect shows up, since Fierro is embedded in her own party. However, hundreds of other Septimus come out to witness my perp walk to the portal.

It's soon so packed on the streets of Belgrano that Yamila's hidden Cazadores have to come forward to form a protective perimeter. Gael and Nacho flank me, and after the emotional moment we shared back at the safe space, my father has barely acknowledged me.

I know it's just an act, but even if some small part of him is really pulling away, I couldn't blame him. It's not like we've known each other long. And I saw it in his eyes—he doesn't hold any hope for me in the legal route.

I can hardly stand to think about what happens to him and Tiago and Saysa and Cata and above all *Ma* if—

But I can't go there.

My uterus gives another painful twist, and I notice a spasm in Gael's neck and a shiver in Nacho's leg.

"He's not coming, Yami," says Nacho for the seventh time. "I told you you're chasing a ghost. He's gone!"

"But then who broke out—"

"*Her mother?* I don't know, but you're reading too much into it. Just because you got one conspiracy right doesn't mean every far-fetched idea you have is true! Right, Tío? Tell her!"

Yamila looks at Gael, and he studies her like a parent putting off bad news. Her shoulders fall before his words do.

"I think whatever you do, your father would be proud."

Her eyes sparkle, and even Nacho looks speechless. Yamila straightens her spine and steps forward.

"Let's go."

We march onto the nearest mushroom patch, and we're sucked underground. Only this time, el Hongo's white webbed walls lead us down a passage.

So we walk until the tunnel ends . . .

Aboveground, facing the ivy-covered wall of the Citadel.

30

It's not day or night in Lunaris.

Time is suspended somewhere in between.

The horizon is a gradient of pinks, ranging from ballet slipper to hot magenta. Puffy green clouds float through the air, like they're packed with chlorophyll instead of water, and golden stars twinkle through the atmosphere, like sun droplets. Yet all of this is just a backdrop for the moon.

Its pale glow has an almost yellow tinge, like a light bulb, and there's a shadow falling across it that looks like a wolf's profile.

La lobi-luna.

It's a moon that arises only when blood might be spilt.

I don't know how I know that. It must be what Saysa meant about information traveling through the air in Lunaris.

My skin crawls with dread as I turn to see not white mist behind me, but flanks of Cazadores. Hundreds of them, standing ramrod straight, staring from me to Yamila and back to me. Her complexion is a shade smugger as she steps ahead of us, making it clear who's leading this pack.

I'm a head taller than her here, but Nacho and Gael are still bigger than me. I try reaching out to my father with my mind. *Can you hear me?*

I don't feel a connection, and I look down at the braided bracelets circling my wrists. My nails aren't capped with claws, nor do I feel fangs. They're still stifling my power.

Nacho shoves me forward as a path parts for us in the crowd. I feel the scrutinizing stares of the Cazadores I pass, but I keep my gaze level. My pulse is all over the place, my legs leaden, my throat clogged.

Since there's no white mist, the view ahead is clear, and I can see where we're going. It looks like an elaborate tree stump that's the size of a massive stadium, with steps carved into the bark and openings throughout. As I get closer, I think of *The Giving Tree*, one of the first English stories Perla ever read to me.

Ma is my giving tree.

She gave and gave and gave, until she had nothing left for herself. Even now, I'm being selfish. If I die, it will kill her.

Nacho's claws dig into my skin as his hand closes around my arm, and we cross through an archway in the bark.

All the oxygen leaves my body. The tree stump is hollow inside, and above us are mushroom shelves jutting from the walls, spiraling all the way up to the pink Lunaris sky. Every single shelf is packed with Septimus.

The entire population is here. I can't make out individual faces, but I know Tiago, Cata, Saysa, my teammates, the Coveners— every Septimus I've ever met must be watching.

By now, Nacho and Gael are practically dragging me across the earth, to the center of the stump, where there are seven towering stone thrones set atop an elevated dais. Sitting in the seats are seven cloaked Septimus, their black robes concealing everything about their identities.

"Sus señorías," says Yamila, and the entire place starts to quiet down. "Les presento a la prisionera Manuela Azul." *Your honors, I present to you the prisoner Manuela Azul.*

Yamila's voice reverberates through the stump, her words floating up to the lobi-luna. Sheets of water glimmer into existence along the walls, reflecting my petrified face in closeup to everyone watching.

The judge in the middle nods, and Yamila spins to face me. She snips my cuffs.

I suck in a deep breath, waiting for my Lunaris-granted power to flare inside me, but I still feel too weak.

The freedom lasts only a moment.

Thick, ropey vines punch through the ground and coil around my arms and legs, binding me chain-style to the earth, holding me in place. Yamila and Nacho turn away, but there's an explosive force in Gael's stare again, and I'm almost relieved when Nacho says, "Tío, come on."

Even though all I want is for my father to hold me again, so I can feel like everything will be all right.

"Sus señorías," says a recognizable voice, and I turn to see Cata's father. *My uncle.*

Bernardo is in black robes, but his hood is pulled back, exposing his eyes and salt-and-pepper hair. While he speaks, a Septimo comes to stand beside me. He wears his hair in a ponytail and has a ring on every finger.

"Me duele tener que decirlo, pero hemos sufrido un golpe muy fuerte con la muerte de Zaybet Marina." Bernardo's grim voice expands through the air like smoke. "Deberíamos pasar esta luna honrando su memoria y no perdiendo el tiempo con este juicio. La ley está muy clara en estas circunstancias."

It hurts me to say it, but we've suffered a strong blow with the death of Zaybet Marina, and we owe it to her to spend this moon honoring her memory and not wasting time with this case. We already know what the law says in these circumstances.

"Sus señorías," says the wolf beside me, an oiliness in his tone like he's used to greasing tough situations.

"My client no doubt knows the predicament she's in, and she's not looking to inflict more pain," he goes on in Spanish. "We will stipulate that her existence is problematic, but we would ask this tribunal to reconsider the usual sentence for this crime." His voice rises and falls through the chamber like an orchestra. "If we kill her, we miss our chance to study a specimen unique to all of history!"

I blink.

This is my attorney, and *that's* his defense? That I need to be studied? He hasn't even met with me yet—how can he defend my right to live without knowing who I am?

"We can't take that risk," argues Bernardo. "She's too dangerous." He twists his neck to look at me, and as he advocates for my execution, I see no humanity in his cold stare. He doesn't know I'm his family, but I doubt he'd be acting differently if he did.

"As far as we know, she's the first of her kind to survive birth. She's evaded us for seventeen years. We don't know what she's capable of—"

"Precisely why we shouldn't execute her yet," says my lawyer. "We need to examine her limits. Don't tell me you're actually afraid of this *niña*—"

"Why not?" asks Bernardo somberly. "She's already cost us a promising young Congeladora."

The silence that follows falls over me like a shroud.

My own attorney isn't arguing for my innocence or freedom. Just my scientific worth. This isn't a mistake . . . It's a *travesty*.

"I want to speak."

My voice breaks the tomblike quiet.

The middle judge bangs a gavel so hard my teeth chatter.

"The accused may only speak to her lawyer," says Bernardo, his jaw tight. This time, his voice doesn't carry to the spectators. Then he steps away from my lawyer and me, as if to give us privacy, even though his wolf ears can pick up every word.

I look up at my attorney, but before I can open my mouth, he says, "No tenés elementos para ganar un caso." *You don't have a case.* "Plead guilty, and I'll get you clemency in your sentencing."

His private demeanor lacks the passion of his public performance, and as his gaze drifts to the nearest screen, his ringed fingers tuck back a strand of hair.

"Trust me, niña, this is your only chance."

My heart stirs in my ribcage, like an animal trying to break free. It's a different power coursing through me now. I didn't come all this way just to be silenced.

"I think I'll represent myself," I say. Then I peek at Bernardo, who's standing against the far wall. My words must have carried to him, but he doesn't react.

"You need a lawyer because you don't know the law." The attorney's bushy brow furrows in indignation. "And I'm the best there—"

"Can I hire someone else?"

"*Hire?* With what semillas? I've taken you on out of the goodness of my—"

"Ego, I know."

His face grows so contorted, I think he's going to transform. "I want a different attorney," I insist, waving Bernardo over. Confusion fogs his gaze as he approaches us, but movement by the judges catches my eye.

The head judge tilts their neck a little.

"What's going on?" Bernardo looks from me to my lawyer.

"Couldn't you hear us?" I ask.

My former lawyer lets out a harsh laugh. "For our safety, magic is suspended in a capital punishment case. Only the judges can access their powers. You don't know anything about the law, and you want to represent yourself—?"

"What are you talking about?" asks Bernardo, rounding on me.

"I want a new lawyer," I say, forcing my chin to stay level.

"And who do you think is going to represent you for zero semillas?" asks my uncle.

"Diego . . . I don't know his manada name. He's a student at El Laberinto."

This time, five of the judges shift in their seats. Only two of them don't react. Those must be brujas.

"You're not serious," says Bernardo.

"I am."

We stare at each other for a long moment, then he turns to the tribunal and says, "Sus señorías, we ask for a recess."

I raise my shoulders to my ears as the head judge bangs his gavel again, and the images on the screen are replaced by a countdown from 5,000.

Every second, the number ticks down.

Then the ivy tightens around me, and I'm yanked belowground.

When the spinning in my head stops, I'm alone in some kind of burrow, with only dirt surrounding me. I feel the walls for an opening, but there's no way in or out.

"Hello?"

No one answers me, and I can't hear any sounds. Are they just going to let me suffocate down here?

"What the fuck's going—on," I finish lamely as a wolf-shadow lopes along the wall, coming closer.

Then at last, a flesh-and-bone being steps out.

"Diego!"

I throw my arms around him, and he gives me a tight squeeze. "Are you okay?" he asks, his periwinkle eyes shiny as they search mine. He looks shaken to his core.

"I need you to defend me."

"*Me?* I'm nowhere near qualified! I'm just a student—"

"*Please.*" My voice cracks. "I just—I want a chance."

Diego exhales, and I'm sure he can see that I'm one breath away from falling apart.

"Manu, I give you my word I will do everything I can to get you out of this, but I think you should reconsider." When I only cross my arms, he says, "Fine. Then I need you to be brutally honest with me, and we don't have a lot of time."

"What I say to you is protected by attorney-client privilege, right?" I ask, proud that I watched so many legal procedurals growing up.

"No, that's human stuff. In our legal code, the individual is always dwarfed by the common good. So, say you were to tell me about an organization you came into contact with that according to the tribunal presents a clear and present danger to our commonwealth, then I would be honor bound to report it, and you would be obligated to testify to what you know."

He obviously pieced stuff together at the Septibol match. He must have realized the Septimus in the audience weren't members of the press. I take a moment to think, then I share as honest an account as I can about my life, including everything that happened since I arrived at El Laberinto, without mentioning the Coven or naming any individuals who helped me.

When I finish, he says, "This is great, Manu. We're almost out of time, so is there anything that Yamila or Jazmín might have on you that you think could hurt you?"

What comes to mind is how I dodged Yamila's magic. Yet

the fact that Tiago never brought up what he saw me do when the piratas attacked makes me feel like he's sending me a message without sending it. If he's hiding the knowledge even from himself, and Diego just told me that as my lawyer he still has to prioritize the greater good over me, I decide against it.

"Just everything I told you. So will this be like a human court? With witnesses and a jury and everything?"

"Yes and no. Bernardo is the prosecutor, and I'm your defense attorney—but the tribunal is both judge and jury. They stay silent throughout the proceedings, ruling on motions only through the gavel, until they're ready to deliberate. Then they'll speak."

"Why are they hooded?"

"There are more judges on the tribunal, and they protect their identities in capital punishment cases so they don't suffer reprisals. They can choose to reveal themselves at sentencing."

"Do they force witnesses to take truth potion?" I ask, thinking of what Jazmín did to me. Diego's jaw dropped when I got to that part of my tale.

"No. Lunaris has her own way of determining trustworthiness. You'll see."

I blow out a hard breath.

"Why?" he probes. "What other secrets do you have?"

I swallow. "Well—*Fierro*. Aren't you honor bound to report that too?"

"Guess it's a good thing I'm not honorable then," he says with a flash of teeth. "Now, we need the tribunal to see that you don't pose a threat. So we'll argue you're innocent because . . . *because you're not guilty*. You had no say in the circumstances of your birth. You may be part human, but you are also Septimus, and to execute you without a real crime sets a dangerous precedent."

"Sounds like we'd be shifting the blame to my parents."

"Technically—"

"I can't let the tribunal turn their attention to them." I shake my head vehemently. "I need to know they're safe, even if I have to use my life as a distraction."

Diego nods like I just said something smart. "Yes. We need to hold their attention. And to do that, you have to tell a good story."

He looks around us like he's seeing beyond the dirt walls. "The past couple of moons, you've lived out the kind of adventure they write books about. So we engage them with your tale, and we force them to see you as not just a biological specimen, but a living being. We'll call character witnesses so the judges get to know you through your friends' eyes. We're going to make the case that regardless of birthplace and birth parents, you're one of us."

"Bernardo will just twist everyone's testimonies to make it sound like I've manipulated them. Like *la ladrona*."

"Manu, you can't lose hope now," says Diego, grimacing. "Whatever fight led you to this, you need to channel it because this is the moment you're going to need it. Your trial hasn't even started yet."

I nod and ball my hands into fists. "What happens next?"

"Defense goes first. I can call up to three witnesses, then it's the prosecution's turn. If the judges still need to hear more after that, we each get to go another round. Then they'll deliberate."

My gut knots up, and nausea churns in my belly. "I don't know why I thought I could do this," I say, my eyes burning again. "Cata tried to talk me down, but I wouldn't listen."

"That's because you were listening to yourself." He takes my hand. "We don't discuss it, but there aren't a lot of students that look like me at El Laberinto."

I nod because I saw that there weren't many Black students at the school.

"I get what it's like to want to make the system see you," he goes on. "Colorism isn't just limited to humans."

"I'm sorry," I say, thinking of the Coveners, each one ostracized in their own way by a social narrative.

Diego's fingers squeeze mine, and as my gaze refocuses on his, he says, "There are as many reasons to think you're la ladrona as there are to think you're the long-lost turtle Manuelita from the lullaby we ironically stole from humans. *It's all a matter of perspective.*"

He infuses his voice with warmth. "Bernardo will use scare tactics to make you out to be a monster . . . but we're going to open the judges' hearts and show them you're really Manuelita come home."

31

When I'm back in the courtroom, everything is as it was before, except the screen is no longer counting down. It shows me with Diego by my side.

"Now that the accused has settled on counsel, she's shown us just how *seriously* she's taking the situation," says Bernardo in Spanish, emphasizing the word like he sees Diego as a joke. "We submit she comes from a tainted lineage and presents an existential threat, therefore we charge her with treason and recommend her execution."

I feel the blood drain from my face. Conversations break out, but I can't hear the words.

"The defendant, Manu"—a hush falls as Diego speaks—"pleads not guilty."

Now everyone's talking louder, and the head judge has to bang his gavel.

"How do you figure?" Bernardo demands.

"Easy," says Diego. "She's done nothing wrong."

"For *starters,* she ran from the law."

"So did her friends, but you're not asking for their heads."

"Her antics caused the death of a promising young bruja!"

"From what I understand, that was a botched Cazadores operation."

Bernardo bristles. "All of which is ancillary to the fact that she's *illegal.*"

"Something over which she has no control and can therefore not be found guilty of—"

"She's not one of us!"

Diego's expression clears, like at last Bernardo has spoken the right words, and he says, *"Prove it."*

"She confessed in her broadcast that she's half-human—"

"You're quoting her out of context. She also said she'd been in hiding, her strength repressed, until she found us and made friends for the first time and discovered her power. She belongs in our world."

"That is not for her to decide."

"Exactly," says Diego. "It's up to this tribunal." He turns to face them. "As you don't know Manu yet, I doubt you'd take her words very seriously right now. Instead, I'd like to call forth witnesses whose testimonies will paint a picture of her *ordinariness.* Yes, she's a lobizona and a hybrid, but in every other regard, she's no different from you or me. She deserves a chance."

My heart pumps extra hard as he echoes my plea. "Among humans, she was a seed planted in the wrong garden, a bud that wouldn't bloom." A crescent moon dimples Diego's cheek. "But in Lunaris's soil, she's blossomed."

"So goes the tale of la ladrona," says Bernardo.

Diego chuckles. "Nice try, but a bedtime story won't sway

this tribunal, especially when it's obvious you have a political agenda."

Bernardo's eyes narrow. "Meaning what?"

"You want to believe she's la ladrona because if her existence is normalized, then you have to accept she's the next evolutionary stage of our species. There are as many reasons to believe she's one as the other. Yet to embrace that would reinforce the opposition party's view that in-species procreation is not enough to grow our numbers and the only true path is to make inroads among the humans and open our borders to some of them. You're using her to further your politics—"

"That's preposterous! You better watch yourself." He strides up to Diego, who to his credit holds his ground. "You're still a schoolboy, so let me enlighten you. We don't bring our personal politics into this sacred chamber."

Diego doesn't back down. "Then admit it's equally possible that Manu is proof that cohabitation with humans could be a path to the future."

"*Prove it.*"

"Prove she's la ladrona."

The gavel comes down, like the gauntlet has been thrown, and Diego looks at me with alarmed excitement in his eyes. "Both sides have arrived at their arguments," he explains. "Defense goes first."

Stepping up to the tribunal, he says in an amplified voice, "I call Saysa Rívoli to the stand."

A moment later, Saysa strides in. Her eyes are red and puffy, and they trace the vines binding me with such intensity that if she had her magic, they would probably spring open.

Diego rests a hand on Saysa's shoulder and steers her to the empty space between us and the tribunal. "Please state your name and schooling," he says, standing across from her.

I can only see the back of her head from here, but I watch her face on the largest screen.

"S-Saysa Rívoli," she says, her voice shaking. "I'm a third year at El Laberinto."

As she speaks, a white aura begins to glow around her small frame, like she's a ghost.

"You first met Manu two moons ago, on the first night back from Lunaris," says Diego. "Is that correct?"

She nods.

"I need a verbal answer."

"Yes." Her aura brightens.

"Good." Diego gives her an encouraging nod, but that only makes her expression tauten, until she looks constipated. "Please describe those circumstances to the court."

"She—Manu—was my best friend's roommate." *Best friend* comes out rushed, and as she says it, something shifts in her aura. The white glow grows a light gray tint.

"Jazmín—Señora Jazmín—said she was a new transfer when she brought her to Cata's room. That's her daughter. My best friend—"

"Thank you," says Diego, cutting her off as her aura darkens to a deeper shade of gray. It's not a lie detector, exactly . . . more like a *secret* detector.

"Saysa, I'd like you to close your eyes for me. Can you do that?" I see the back of her head nod, and the screens on the walls show her eyelids flickering with nerves. "What were your first impressions of Manu?"

"When I first met Manu . . ." Her features start to relax, until the only lines on her face are the comma-shaped creases on her cheeks left behind by her dimples. "I thought she looked lost."

As she speaks, her voice regains its natural cadence. "There was an innocence about her that made her seem brand new.

Like a blank page. I think I was drawn to the mystery, but it also made me feel this instinctive need to protect her. Even though she doesn't need anyone's rescuing." Her aura has lightened to a soft silver.

"How can you explain that instant connection you felt?" Diego prods.

"It was like meeting a member of my pack."

He nods like it's the answer he wanted. "Every single one of us knows that feeling," he says, panning his gaze across the mushroom shelves. "When we meet one of our own, and a new piece of our puzzle clicks into place. It's the way we know that even when we're lonely, we're not alone. It's the strongest of binding agents, and the only magic that can tell us where we belong—*friendship*."

As I watch Saysa, and I think of all she's done for me, I know Diego is right.

"Do you have any reason to believe Manu means the Septimus any harm, or has any secret powers we don't know about?" he presses her.

"Not at all," answers Saysa, regaining her warm complexion. "In fact, she saved my life on the Septibol field."

"Tell us about that."

"It was the day Manu's lobizona powers manifested. We were playing against El Laberinto's pro team, when the ball was shot at my neck, too quickly for anyone to react—except Manu. She practically flew." Her eyes widen with horror. "I didn't mean that literally—she can't actually fly, I just mean she's a powerful—"

"Go on," says Diego.

"If Manu hadn't sprung into action, I might not be here right now. Her wolf instincts kicked in on the spot. She's a natural."

Diego seems to think this is a powerful closing point because he lets her words linger in silence for a beat, then he says, "No further questions. Thank you, Saysa."

Diego winks at me as he returns to my side, projecting confidence, and Saysa squares her shoulders as Bernardo takes his place.

"Hello, Saysa," says her girlfriend's father.

"Hi," she says to Bernardo, her shrinking voice betraying her nerves.

"Do you think there could be another reason, beyond chemistry, why you were attracted to the accused so quickly?"

"I—" Saysa's face reddens, and her aura grows grayer. I'm sure I know where her mind's gone: Does Bernardo know the truth about her and Cata?

"I just thought she could use a friend."

"A friend like *you*?"

"I don't know what you mean." Her aura is as thick as smoke now, and even though her secrets are her own, just by exposing their existence, Bernardo is casting shade on me by extension.

"What I mean is you're not exactly a model citizen either, are you?"

"¡Objeción!" shouts Diego over my hammering heart. "This whole line of questioning is out of bounds. Saysa isn't the one on trial."

I don't know if Bernardo is aware of Saysa's involvement in the illegal distribution of Septis, or if he's hinting at her sexuality, or if he's learned of her attacks on Nacho and Sergio—so I'm relieved when Diego puts an end to it.

Bernardo gives him a lazy shrug. "It goes to the accused's character if her character witness has questionable character. We are a pack species, after all."

"Fine," says Diego, but instead of backing down, he says, "If your issue is with this witness, we won't waste any more of the court's time. It's a good thing we have such a deep bench to pull from."

He nods at Saysa. "Thank you. You're excused."

Her smoky aura dissipates to nothing, but in her eyes, a different storm is gathering. Her eyebrows furrow like she's ready to fight, and Diego grips her arm and guides her out before she can speak.

"One martyr at a time, please," he whispers to her as they pass me.

I try to meet Saysa's gaze before she goes, but Diego's body blocks us, and then she's gone.

"I don't think you'll have any objections to our next witness," says Diego, returning to my side. "She's top of her class, a model student, and comes from a fine family, as I'm sure you can attest to. Defense calls *Catalina del Laberinto*."

Bernardo must have anticipated his daughter would be called to the stand, but his eyes shutter on hearing her name.

The day is beginning to set when she walks in, the air taking on a red tinge that deepens the pink of her gaze. Cata looks straight ahead as she approaches, without letting her view stray in one direction or the other.

"Please state your name and schooling for the court."

"I'm Catalina del Laberinto, and I'm a fifth year at the academy." Her voice is cool, clear, and crisp. Like her heart is on mute.

"Good," says Diego, as a white aura manifests around her. "And just so everything is in the open, please state who your parents are."

"My mom is the headmistress of the school, and my dad . . ." She swallows, her composure faltering for a breath. "Is prosecuting this case."

There's a rush of reactions as the information spreads to those who either didn't know or didn't make the connection.

Diego waits for the murmurs to subside, extending Bernardo's discomfort as long as he can. "So you were Manu's roommate for a whole moon. Tell us about her. What's she like?"

Cata crosses her arms. "*Hairy.* I'd find hairballs all over the bathroom."

Heat scorches my cheeks. Chuckles break out in the mushroom shelves, not like they're laughing at me, but with me. As if it's a common issue with werewolves.

"Also, she's a little *too* neat. She'd put things away the instant she finished using them, make her bed every morning, that sort of thing. Oh, and she whimper-snores."

By now my face is aflame, and all I can think about is Tiago having to listen to that at the Coven. The Septimus in the shelves are chuckling again, and it feels like they're starting to find me a bit too funny.

"She wasn't a loud sleeper at first," Cata goes on, arms no longer crossed, like she's enjoying her control of the crowd, "but once she tapped into her inner wolf, it was like ripping off a muzzle!"

Diego grins along with the spectators. "She sounds like a werewolf, all right. So why do you think your mom bunked her with you?"

"She wanted me to spy on Manu. She sensed something was off about her, and she asked me to report back what I found."

"And did you?"

"No." Her aura flickers.

"Your mom must've been pressuring you. I'm sure your life would've been so much easier if you'd just done what she asked. After all, you didn't know Manu, nor did you owe her anything. So why didn't you?"

"It's like Saysa said. I felt a connection. *Manu is family.*"

Since that's literally true, her aura doesn't darken with secrets.

"Is that why you went on the run with her last moon?"

Cata nods. "It didn't seem like anyone was willing to give her a chance and hear her side of things."

"Do you have any reason to believe her biological makeup makes her a threat or presents a difference between her and other Septimus, aside from being a lobizona?"

"I think she's just as powerful and flawed as the rest of us."

"Thank you." Diego returns to my side, and from his half-dimpled smile, he clearly thinks we did well.

The air grows charged as Bernardo takes his place. As father and daughter stare at each other, I flash to seeing them together last Lunaris, when she ran into his arms. This must be crushing her.

"I'm proud of you," says Bernardo, and Cata blinks in surprise. "Yamila says a big reason she caught Manu was *you*. That you turned on your friends to feed her intel. So now that the worst is over, and no one can hurt you, tell us, hija—what do you know about the accused that you're afraid to say?"

The chamber is the quietest it's been, and as I watch Cata's face on the screen, by now I know the signs of her quick thinking. She sucks in deep breaths like she's trying to gain control of her emotions, but from the way her eyes move to every corner of the courtroom, I know it's just a distraction while she lines up her words.

"Zaybet's death scared me," she says in a halting tone. "I didn't want to see any more of my friends hurt, *including* Manu. So I decided to place my trust in you and hope you'd do the right thing."

"But I didn't, did I?"

Cata frowns, and even Diego looks confused.

"Instead of coming to El Laberinto with you and your mom, I stayed in Kerana and indulged my ambition. I abandoned you."

If my throat stings from lack of breath, it's nothing to the shock Cata must be feeling. I watch her eyes go blank on the screen, like for once her powerful brain has overloaded.

"I'm sorry, Catalina," he says softly. "I'm sorry for what your mother and I put you through. It wasn't fair. But I know you're a good girl at heart, and I don't blame you for acting out. Your mother and I got so distracted by our disagreements, we stopped seeing you."

Cata's mask holds in place, keeping her expression frozen, but her aura is growing dustier, cloudier, and her hands ball into fists.

"You didn't get to grow up like the other kids," her father goes on. "With siblings and two parents. So it's understandable if you felt an affinity for humans and their broken homes. I don't blame you for protecting the accused, or rebelling against me. I don't even blame you for changing your name—"

"Well, that's a relief!"

Cata's anger erupts in a volcanic shout.

"I don't remember a home before El Laberinto," she says to her father, her face red and splotchy. "I wasn't even *two* when I left Argentina with Ma and Gael. I only remember having a father when I turned thirteen and became a bruja. I would look forward to the full moon every month, not because of Lunaris, but because I would get to be your daughter. And you would parade me past all those important politicians so they could pat you on the back for the pretty doll you had a hand in making. And I ate it up because I wanted you to love me. I wanted to impress you enough to make you consider spending a month in El Laberinto getting to know me. Or maybe even invite me to come stay with you."

Tears dive off her lashes.

"But you didn't. *Not once.*"

Her voice breaks on the word.

Bernardo doesn't speak, his eyes locked into the pink beam of her gaze, and it's unclear if his plan worked or backfired. If he wanted to make it look like Cata has deep-seated issues with her parents, he succeeded—but I don't think he expected his shot to rebound.

Once it becomes clear that neither Bernardo nor Cata are going to end their staring contest, Diego intervenes. He places a hand on Cata's arm and guides her out. It looks like Bernardo might try to say something, but Diego glares at him so hard, I'm afraid he's going to sink his fangs into Bernardo's neck.

Cata's watery eyes look my way as she passes, and I give her a small nod because I don't remember how to smile.

It's nighttime now, and the moon is so low in the sky that it takes up the whole view, bathing the proceedings in white light.

"For our final witness," says Diego, "defense calls Santiago Rívoli, *el lobo invencible.*"

I hold my breath until he enters.

It hurts to see him.

It's only been a few hours, but the time feels like decades. We stare at each other as he approaches, and even after he's passed me, he twists his neck to keep looking. He only faces forward when Diego speaks.

"Please state your name and schooling."

"Tiago Rívoli, fifth year at El Laberinto."

"You're also the top scorer in the junior Septibol league, and the first Septimus in recorded history to survive an encounter with one of the six remaining demons of Lunaris."

Tiago doesn't respond since Diego didn't pose a question.

He's just establishing Tiago's credibility. Reminding everyone who he is, as if that's necessary.

"You could marry anyone you wanted."

Again, Tiago stays silent.

"Yet you're in love with Manu."

Sound explodes in my head, and I realize that talking has broken out in the shelves. My stomach knots, and I catch the head judge's chin dip a notch, the first time any of them has moved in a long while.

Once the room has quieted down, Diego asks, *"Why?"*

Tiago's answer is instant. "I know who I am when I'm with her. I feel a stillness, and my turmoil ceases."

His voice is a ballad, and there's a velvety silence as his aura brightens. But his words feel familiar. They tug at my bookish brain.

"Every piece of Manu—her courage, her sunny eyes, her terrible poker face, her love of books, the wolfish thrill she tries to stifle at the onset of adventure—*is inwoven with my deepest life.*"

I can hardly breathe.

He's quoting *The House of Mirth*. I remember thinking of that quote last moon, when I realized I loved Tiago. And the fact that he gets this about me makes me love him all the more. Makes me want to break free of these vines and run into his arms. Makes me—

I feel the ivy in my right wrist slacken a little.

The rest of the vines tighten on my other joints, but the plant on my right wrist stays slightly loose. I didn't command it like a Jardinera . . .

I *numbed* it.

"That's beautiful," says Diego, and my attention snaps back to Tiago as applause breaks out in the stands. The clapping echoes through the chamber, overwhelming us with sound on the ground, and the head judge has to bang his gavel twice.

I might lose my hearing after this.

"I was hoping for a clearer explanation, but your words are the epitome of a schoolboy in love," says Diego, and there's soft, mollified laughter from the crowd. "However, you must have considered the legal issues you'd face. Septimus law states a wolf may not marry another wolf."

Everything down to the blood in my veins freezes.

Tiago's aura flickers, and I scowl at Diego. Why the fuck would he bring this up now? Does he want to add to my charges and get Tiago arrested too?

"How do you feel about that?" Diego prods Tiago.

"I think Manu's existence invalidates labels. The system defines most of us by one identity—bruja or lobizón—but Manu defies classification. She can't be caged by a category." His aura begins to brighten again, his skin glowing like a real guardian angel. "She's a flower that's never finished blooming."

I hardly notice when Diego's finished his questioning and returned to my side. I only snap out of the bask of Tiago's words when I hear Bernardo's voice.

"You're quite the Romeo, Tiago," he says with a knowing smirk. "He too was fickle in his love. Why should we believe your feelings now, when for years you've been mooning over my daughter?"

There are enough gasps in the crowd that we can hear them from down here. I feel like I'm living in a telenovela as everyone reacts to this gossipy twist of events.

Tiago's expression remains calm, his aura clear. "My wolf found hers in Lunaris."

His answer settles Bernardo's challenge because shocked

reactions spread through the crowd, and instead of banging his gavel, the head judge turns to confer with the others.

Once the room settles, Bernardo says, "You claim the accused defies classification. That means she contains multiple identities. Could one of those be la ladrona?"

My stomach clenches. Tiago saw me deflect that pirata's magic. I stare at his aura and try not to think of the loose vine on my right wrist and what it could mean.

"No."

His aura is as clear as his voice. Tiago truly believes I'm not la ladrona.

Bernardo is practically growling when he says, "No further questions."

The head judge bangs his gavel, and the screen starts to count down again. Then I'm sucked belowground.

Only this time, I'm not alone.

A Cazadora is waiting for me.

32

"Where's your daddy?" asks Yamila, her sultry voice making the question sound wrong on so many levels.

"You still think Fierro is alive?" I ask with as much bravado as I can muster.

"I know he got your mom out." She steps toward me, and I root myself to the spot, refusing to give ground. "There's no other way she could have pulled that off."

"Then I guess you overestimated his concern for me because he's obviously not here." My voice is barely above a whisper, her nose inches from mine.

"Or he's biding his time until the verdict." Her gaze narrows in a way that makes me feel like she's reading all my secrets. "Maybe he thinks they'll actually let you off . . . since he doesn't know what I know."

There it is.

The thing I've been dreading.

"And what do you think you know?"

A slow smile spreads across her face. "You deflected my magic . . . *ladrona.*"

I attempt a shrug, but I'm too tense, and the move comes off as a jerk.

"Or maybe you're just not all that powerful," I taunt. "It's what the other Cazadores will think if you testify to that."

A wave of heat presses, but I don't let Yamila's dragon breath intimidate me.

"You think you can manipulate me?" she asks, and I don't know if my words have affected her or not, but I can't let her do this.

I'm desperate.

"Help me get out of this," I hear myself say, "and I'll help you find Fierro."

Before she can answer, Diego strides in through the wall.

"Okay, I just checked, and the first witness he's calling is—" He stiffens on seeing Yamila. "You shouldn't be here."

"I was just making sure the prisoner wasn't left unguarded," she says, her bloodred eyes locked onto mine. "We don't know what secret powers she might be hiding."

Once she's gone, Diego turns to me. "What did she want?"

I swallow. I can't tell him. He could refuse to represent me. "Nothing. She was just trying to intimidate me."

After all, maybe my plan worked.

If Yamila doesn't testify, no one can connect me to la ladrona.

Back in the courtroom, the sky is pink again. I guess this is the new version of daytime for now. The vines bind securely around me, and I wonder if I can loosen them again, only this time I don't dare attempt it.

Bernardo calls his first witness.

His wife.

"Jazmín del Laberinto." She drags out her name, like she's enjoying the effect it has on him, and an aura glows around her. "Headmistress of the academy."

Hers is a smokier halo than any of my friends'—as if her baseline of secrets is higher. I wonder if it's a common thing with age, and the accumulation of experiences, or if Jazmín is just particularly adept at lying.

Could be both.

"Yamila caught the accused, but you were the one who first discovered her, is that right?"

"I was suspicious of her from the start," says my aunt, her sharp amethyst eyes staring back at me from the screen. By the intensity of her gaze, it's like she knows I'm watching and is looking straight at me.

"That's why I placed her in my daughter's room. To keep an eye on her."

My daughter.

"So you handed over the entire investigation to our child? Or did you also reach out to the Cazadores, per protocol?"

Our child.

Under any other circumstances, I would be relishing the expression on Jazmín's face. What little color she has drains from her cheeks, and she looks like she just got a sopapo—a smack across the face.

"I contacted the Cazadores right away," she says, biting off every word, "and I had them come in and inspect all the students' Huellas. They decided everyone checked out."

"What happened next?" he says quickly, like he's uneager to cast any shade on the Cazadores, no matter how peripheral.

"Her performance in class was all over the place, and her

instructor Lupe and I couldn't figure out what she was hiding. Until she revealed herself to be a lobizona."

Maybe I'm imagining it, but there's a difference in her voice when she says that last word. Almost like she's switching into a different accent.

"And at that point I assume you called the Cazadores again?"

"No," she says, frowning. "My brother, Gael, knew right away that something was wrong, but he urged me to keep it quiet until Lunaris. It was his idea I turn Manu—*the accused*—over to Yamila then."

"So Gael took the law into his own hands," says Bernardo, and I hear the hatred he holds for my father soaking his tongue. "Seems old habits die hard."

"That's not what happened. My brother was being smart about it." Her voice is deathly low, and for the first time, I pick up on how much she loves Gael. However much they disagree, however extreme their behavior, their bond is the unbreakable kind.

"Gael knew the Cazadores didn't find anything the first time, so he assumed the accused must have secret powers we didn't know about. Otherwise, how could she have fooled such highly trained officers?" It's clear Jazmín is well-versed in her husband's weak spots. "We decided to let her think she was safe, while we coordinated with the Cazadores behind the scenes."

"Yet Lunaris did not go as you planned," Bernardo reminds her, probably because of her dig at his officers. "What happened?"

"She eluded the Cazadores for a second time, I presume."

"And what does this tell you?" Bernardo growls through gritted teeth.

"It tells me she's dangerous and a threat to our law enforcement."

At last they seem to have arrived at the point he was leading her toward. "What about your students' loyalty to her, as expressed to us moments ago? How do you explain her influence on them?"

"It shows me she's manipulative and a threat to our children."

"And what of the death of young Zaybet?"

Jazmín manages to make the iciness of her gaze look like moisture. "It proves the accused is a curse on our species and a threat to our very existence."

"¡Objeción!" shouts Diego. "This witness is not qualified to make any of these assertions!"

"Withdrawn," says Bernardo with a shrug like he's not bothered either way. He's already made his case. "No more questions."

Diego takes a deep breath before stepping up to face the head of his school. "Señora Jazmín," he says with a nod.

"Diego, you're doing a wonderful job." The smile looks out of place on her face. "You're one of the most impressive students to have graced our halls. You and Yamila are now two of our biggest success stories. I'm proud of you."

"Thank you," he says, bowing his head in acknowledgment. "Then I hope you understand it's now my duty to question you rigorously."

Jazmín's smile wilts at the edges. "Of course."

"Let's go back to how you followed all the proper protocols. You admitted Manu to the academy even though she wasn't registered—isn't that a violation?"

"As headmistress, I can take certain liberties. I believed it better to keep her under my watch while I contacted the authorities."

"Only that's not what happened," he says, knitting his brow. "You contacted the Cazadores for a general check of the school. You didn't tell them anything about *Manu.*"

"I was worried I might not be operating from a place of pure objectivity, and the best way to be sure was by asking an impartial party. I knew if I told the officers my suspicions, I would be biasing them, so I decided to recuse myself."

Diego frowns. "Why would you have a bias against my client?"

"I'm embarrassed to admit it," she says, feigning a fragility she doesn't feel.

"Take your time, Señora Jazmín," says Diego kindly.

"Well, it has to do with my daughter. I was worried."

"But you're the one who roomed them together—"

"No, it's not that. I didn't fear for her life, I feared for her heart." Her gaze cracks on the screens. "I knew my daughter and Tiago were unsuccessfully trying to hide their feelings for each other from me, and the truth is, I approved, wholeheartedly."

I stare at her aura as it churns, but since it's already a charged storm, it's impossible to tell when she's being forthcoming from when she's holding back. But I know by her own admission that Jazmín was aware her daughter loves Saysa.

She wrings her fingers like she's embarrassed, and I want to hand her the Academy Award.

"The night I met Manu, what I didn't mention, is I didn't come across her alone. She was with Tiago. I could tell she had already bewitched him. He's the first one who found her, alone in the woods, and brought her into the school, thinking her a lost lamb. Not realizing she was a wolf in sheepskin."

Her words have an effect. I can feel the atmosphere tensing.

"Just so I understand," says Diego, "you feared you were acting out of a protective parental instinct and not pure logic?"

"Exactly. But as Señora Lupe fed me more and more troubling reports of the accused's class performance, I decided to keep a close eye—and then, of course, her powers revealed themselves, and she joined the Septibol team, and you know the rest because you were there. It's *you* she replaced on the field, right? Goalkeeper?"

"Yes, and she's sublime," says Diego with a warm smile that makes all of Jazmín's attempts look as fake as they are. "Just one last question. Why didn't you simply ask to see Manu's Huella for yourself and contact her manada to get the real story?"

"I knew she didn't have a Huella," she says, squaring her shoulders.

"How?"

On the screen I'm watching, Jazmín stares straight ahead in that way where it feels like she's addressing me again. "My daughter told me."

Her words are a stab to the heart.

But I refuse to believe them.

"What are you talking about?" demands Diego. "When?"

"That first night, she went through the accused's things. The next day, she reported back that she couldn't find a Huella anywhere. So I called the Cazadores, and when the accused managed to outmaneuver them, I realized how dangerous she truly was. I decided the best thing I could do for all of us was try to earn her trust and gather information."

I'm not looking at Jazmín anymore, I'm focused on her aura. For all its grayness, it doesn't darken when she talks of Cata's betrayal. And somehow, I know it's what Cata was trying to tell me.

She did betray me.

But only for a minute. And she's more than made up for it since.

Now I know why she looked at me like that on the balloon ride to Belgrano. And why she was so eager to get me a forged Huella in Lunaris, to make up for what she did. I won't let Jazmín drive a wedge between us because that's what she's trying to do.

"And in the name of *gathering information*," says Diego, "did you break any laws?"

Jazmín stiffens. "None that I can recall."

Her aura tells a different story. There are more dark spots in the grayness.

"You don't recall administering truth potion to a minor without parental consent?"

Jazmín's jaw clenches, and at last the feigned tenderness fades from her face. "I gave her a minuscule dose, it only lasted moments—"

"What was it your husband said about you and your brother having a history of taking the law into your hands?" asks Diego.

"I had no idea what I was dealing with, and I had the lives of all my students to consider!"

"You know, I think you're right, Señora Jazmín. You *are* biased against Manu. But it's not to protect your daughter's heart. It's to secure your own ambitions."

He steps closer, his voice lower but still amplified across the chamber. "Perhaps you're ready to move on from the name *del Laberinto* after all."

"¡Objeción!"

Bernardo steps forward, beside his wife, but Diego doesn't back down. "What's your husband offering you and your brother in exchange for your testimony?"

Bernardo looks to the judges. "Sus señorías, *¡objeción!*"

"Are you hoping the tribunal will lift your sentences—?"

The head judge bangs his gavel, and Diego falls silent. Jazmín and Bernardo glare at him as he returns to my side, his chest heaving.

Bernardo exchanges a calculating look with his wife, and it's unclear who won this round. Then he nods at her and says, "You are excused."

As Jazmín walks past, her purple eyes cut to mine. I don't see fury or hate, like I was expecting.

I see fear.

Only I'm not deluded enough to think it's for me. Which means she's worried about Cata or Gael. My friends all have their immunity deals, but my father is on his own, embedded in the enemy camp. Is Jazmín afraid his identity has been compromised? Or is she as terrified as I am about what he might do to protect me?

"I call Yamila Belgrano," announces Bernardo.

The Encendedora marches in with her back arched and chin high, like some kind of hailing conqueror. "Yamila Belgrano, Cazadora," she says in her low voice when she takes the stand.

Her aura is red. Like the smoke I used to see in her wake in the human world.

"I want to congratulate you on your excellent hunting," says Bernardo, his eyes filling with a pride he didn't show for his daughter. "You are an inspiration to all brujas."

Not Septimus. Not Cazadores. Just brujas.

"Thank you, señor."

"Are you familiar with the legend of la ladrona?"

"I am."

"What has been prophesied about her?"

"She will be born of a Septimus and a human, and though she may look like us, her eyes will give her away. She's predicted to be stealthy and manipulative, and she will use those traits to sneak into Lunaris and embed herself among us. She'll steal the wolves' power and match the witches' magic. She will be the world's undoing."

Bernardo nods along with her. "The defense has painted a picture of the accused as a good kid who just wants a chance, and he's painted my wife as an unstable and self-interested witch. Yet you are an officer of the law and the only Septimus who has squared off with the accused physically—and she's managed to best you each time."

Anger ripples across Yamila's expression, but she forces a nod. "Sí, señor."

"More than anyone else, you have been exposed to her abilities from up close. Based on the criteria you cited, and everything we know about her, we can agree she checks off all the traits of la ladrona—save one."

My stomach tautens.

"So, tell us," he goes on, his words wringing my insides, "can she match the witches' magic?"

I stare into Yamila's bloodred eyes on the nearest screen, inwardly begging her. The red aura flickers on and off, like signal interference. Maybe my pleas are getting through.

She said it wasn't me she wanted. If Fierro is who she's after, and I've offered to deliver him, there's no reason to sell me out now.

After this is over, if I survive, I'll worry about a strategy. For now, I just need her to say—

"Yes."

The air leaves my lungs, and the room. The chamber grows so stale, I don't think anyone is breathing.

Then Yamila takes her killshot:

"The accused dodged my fire."

33

The gavel comes down three times, but it's no use. No one will shut up, and some Septimus are scrambling, filing out of the chamber like I might incinerate the place.

Next thing I know, I'm sucked underground.

This sudden silence is worse than the cacophony of noise, and I wait minutes that feel like hours until Diego walks through the wall.

"What the fuck, Manu?"

"I-I'm sorry—"

"What part of *tell me everything* did you not understand?"

"The part where you abandon me when you learn I'm a *monster!*" I choke on the word, and then I grip Diego's wrists, digging my fingers into his skin like they're claws.

"Please, please, please don't walk out on me. I'm not what she says, I swear, Diego, I would never hurt any of you—"

"I know!" The anger in his face melts into frustration. "You think I believe in that superstition?"

When my grip doesn't ease up, he says, "You're unprecedented, so of course your abilities are unpredictable—*but that doesn't mean you're wrong.* Only I can't make anyone believe that if you won't."

He raises his hands with mine still attached and cups my cheeks in his warm palms. "If you can't be honest in here, and show me the complete you, then you will always be in hiding. It's called shame. And if you show shame on that stand, it will spread like flames to everyone watching. So leave it here. What are you ashamed of?"

I drop my gaze to the ground, feeling supported by his hands on my cheeks, and I whisper, "I think—I think maybe I am her. *La ladrona.* I did what Yamila said, I deflected her magic. And the other day, I cracked an Invocadora's force field. I'm pretty sure Tiago knows, but he hasn't brought it up."

When I look at him, Diego is nodding like he understands. "He wanted to protect you in case the Cazadores interrogated him under duress."

Sort of what I figured.

"And now"—I breathe—"in the courtroom, I-I loosened a vine on my wrist."

I see the flash of shock in the depths of Diego's periwinkle gaze, but it burns out quickly, like a shooting star.

"There's something wrong with me, isn't there? I saw your reaction. Do you think I'm la ladrona now?"

Diego drops his fingers from my face and blows out a hard breath. "I'm not interested in labeling you, and that's not how you should be thinking either. Forget la ladrona lore. It's *their* narrative, not yours."

"You don't get it," I say, shaking my head. "If I'm la ladrona,

I'm not *me*. I'm a footnote in their story, a mistake that never should have been. Then they've really taken everything from me."

"Manu, you're not—"

"How do you know? I spread darkness wherever I go! Look what I got Cata and Tiago and Saysa and their families into! My mom, Perla, *Zaybet*—I'm a plague, I curse everyone I touch—"

"Or, you could look at it as you're just that easy to love."

"What?"

Diego squeezes my shoulder. "You inspire intense loyalty in others because life has been so spectacularly unfair to you, yet your spirit doesn't dampen. That's not darkness, Manu. What we're drawn to is your light."

I let him pull me into a hug, and I lay my head against his shoulder, not sure what I would do if I didn't have Diego by my side. "Thank you for everything you did up there," I whisper, unable to say more without breaking down. "What happens now?"

"You're going to be put through the trials."

I leap away from him. *"What trials?"*

His expression falls, and seeing him deflate makes my pulse speed up. "Truthfully, I don't know. That's as far as I got in my ladrona studies. There was a time when Septimus put brujas accused of being la ladrona on the stand, sort of like the humans' Salem witch trials. We didn't kill anyone—but we tortured them."

I can't summon my voice to speak.

"But that was in the past," he adds quickly. "In this century, there have only been a couple of accusations. As soon as we get back up there, the trials will begin. You'll be transported without leaving the courtroom. It's hard to explain. Whatever happens, however strange, just go with it."

"And do *what*? I have no idea how to pass—"

"You do," he says calmly. "You know what to do because you did it before. At your Septibol tryouts."

Before I can ask what he means, vines close around me, and I'm yanked up to the courtroom, where everyone is already gathered and waiting.

Diego is at my side a moment later. But as soon as he appears, Bernardo says, "Your services are no longer needed."

"I'm defense counsel—"

"The trials must be faced alone. Surely as *counsel* you knew that?"

A couple of Cazadores step forward, and it's clear if Diego doesn't go on his own, they'll be happy to escort him. My friend looks at me in resignation, and if not for the vines holding me in place, I would shatter.

He rests a hand on my shoulder and says, "You're *Manu*."

And as he walks away, it occurs to me that this whole time, Bernardo has referred to me as the accused, but not Diego. He's been repeating my name, reminding me that's my identity. None of those other labels are mine.

I don't have to claim them.

Bernardo exits after Diego, and then I'm alone facing the judges, bound in chains of ivy, my face magnified on the screens overhead, with almost a million Septimus watching. The head judge bangs his gavel, and my binds disappear—along with everything else.

I'm not in the courtroom anymore.

I'm on the golden grass of Lunaris, staring at the black Citadel wall in the distance. Before me is a misty barrier, veiling what lies ahead. The sky above is pastel yellow, pink, and blue, and I stretch my limbs, rejoicing in my liberty.

Something dark catches my eye, and a grin overtakes my face as my wolf-shadow bounds toward me.

It runs in circles like a playful puppy, and I hear myself giggle. The sound is so foreign, it doesn't seem mine. My shadow leads me along at a quick trot, and I'm warmed by its companionship.

Hurry.

I don't so much hear the word as *feel* it. There's a timer on this freedom.

I've no interest in going back to the Citadel, so I rush through the mist, and then I'm standing before a wall of colorful crystal colonnades. There's a black space ahead that looks like a gap between teeth.

As I enter the pass, there's something somber and sad about the location, like it's a mausoleum or a cemetery. My wolf-shadow lopes ahead, and the wall beside me darkens, like a second shadow is taking form.

Something massive is pressing into the crystal, in slow, watery detail, and at last I see a face. A severe-looking Septimo with fine eyebrows and thin lips.

As I keep walking, another portrait manifests, of a Septima with a head of red ringlets. More faces begin to fill the walls as I break into a sprint, and soon portraits cram every square foot of the cave, unveiling at the speed of my feet.

I relish the run as much as seeing each new frame. There must be hundreds of thousands of them.

When at last I see light ahead, I slow down. The portraits begin to slow too, like the artist has grown tired. I reach the end of the passage, and right as I'm leaving, a final face presses into the last patch of wall space.

She has brown skin and thick hair and yellow eyes.

I look into my reflection for a long time. And when I step out into the light, I feel *seen* by Lunaris.

My existence has been documented. No matter what this tribunal rules, this is proof I belong. *I count.*

My shadow and I run toward the mist ahead, but a bang booms out, shaking the land. Like the judge's gavel, only more ominous.

My wolf drops to the ground, ears pinned back, and I turn to see a single face forming across the crystal colonnades. She has metallic eyes and white-tipped black hair.

Something Pablo said comes back to me. He told me the Septimus know when one of their population passes because their face is gone from the Caves of Candor.

And as Zaybet fades into the ghost of a memory, it feels like she's disappearing for good.

Sadness pierces me like a blade. I bend forward from the pain, and my wolf-shadow tips its snout back and howls a long mournful note.

I feel something building inside me, like I'm going to throw up. I fall to my knees, as the monstrous thing claws its way up my throat, and then I tip my neck back, and—

Owooooo!

When at last my shadow and I step through the mist, the day has given way to the pinks, reds, and purples of dusk. I'm on the golden field staring at the Citadel.

It's over? I don't get it. That was the whole trial?

I step forward, and all at once the sky begins to bruise and swirl. An electric, pungent aroma hangs in the air, and my hair flies around me as a storm blows in.

I break into a run.

The wind howls in my ears, pressing against my chest, trying to slow me down. Remembering Tiago's training, I let go of all my thoughts and give myself over to my body. Until I'm cutting through the bands of air, breaking free of my chains.

I run at the speed of a lobizona, whatever the fuck that is.

They want to know if I can keep up with the wolves? Let them wonder if the wolves can keep up with me.

The Citadel's black wall grows larger, and I feel a thrill racing down my spine as thunder rumbles. Tiago was right—I relish the rush of adventure. Same way I used to count down to lunaritis.

It's funny how I didn't think I kept any secrets from Ma, and yet I never told her about my monthly dreams. Even if Perla hadn't been attacked, I'm not sure how much longer I could have waited before I went hunting for answers.

Ma doesn't understand why I snuck into Nacho's truck that night, after she gave up everything to keep me alive. I gambled her sacrifice in one seemingly rash decision. But it was a decision I'd been building to my whole life. It was a part of me I felt compelled to hide from her—and myself—because I was afraid Ma would think I had too much of my father in me.

Golden lightning webs across the charged clouds at my exact moment of understanding, and I scream as the bolt strikes in front of me, singeing the grass. The blast of heat blows me back, and there's a chill at the base of my skull, like silver frost is infecting the air.

The gales are growing so powerful that soon they'll be hurricane strength. I curve against the wind, barely vertical anymore, my shadow leaping and yapping to encourage me. But it's too much.

The weather is fueled by our emotions.

I hear Tiago's musical voice like he's here, speaking into my thoughts.

Lunaris can manifest our feelings.

It's a memory. Tiago told me this last moon. If I can't quell the elements with magic, maybe I can settle myself. Be an anchor through the storm, instead of collateral damage.

I stop running and try to hold on to the ground, digging my claws in as deep as I can. Then I shut my eyes and focus inward to settle my heart and calm this swell. But it's Perla's voice I hear in my head.

Tranquila, Ojazos. Hasta el sol se cansa de brillar. Cerrá los ojos y respirá ondo. Relax, Ojazos. Even the sun gets tired of shining. Close your eyes and breathe deep.

I focus on my breaths, until the oxygen I inhale brings Perla closer and closer, and my exhales push the tribunal and this trial farther and farther. My hair stops whipping my face as the winds settle, and when at last I open my eyes, the storm is gone—but the sky is purple.

A wave of silver is aging the grass, and I spring forward, my wolf-shadow at my side, as I race toward the moonstone doorknob.

I'm not sure what any of this just proved, but I hope it's at least clear that I didn't use any special abilities—

My shadow lunges right as a spear vaults for my head, and I roll out of the way in time to see a green vine.

While my wolf snaps and claws at the ivy that attacked me, another vine rears up, and I'm weaving between their strikes.

I wonder if the tribunal wants to see how I gained access to the Citadel in the first place. It's a private rite of passage, but nothing in my life is mine. I guess that's why those who love me try to keep me hidden. I can only belong to them in secret.

I dodge another spike, and then I grip the ivy as it rears, the thorns digging into my skin, and I swing myself forward, landing in front of the door. I feel a paralyzing chill as all the light in the sky vanishes, and my fingers close around the cool white stone.

I twist, and at last I'm in the Citadel.

It's nighttime, and the sky is littered with stars. Only I'm still not safe. Four Septimus box me in, hooded robes concealing their faces.

They're all wearing black, but since there's four of them, I get the sense they must be brujas of each element. I just don't know which is which.

I turn in a circle from one to the next. They don't move or make any sound, which only makes my pulse pound harder.

The first trial proved I'm a descendant of Lunaris, and the second one showed I accessed the Citadel with my wolf strength, not bruja magic or some secret ladrona ability. So this trial—

I scream as fire scorches my leg, and I drop to the ground.

The earth beneath me starts shaking, and I try to leap up using my good leg, but a blast of air blows me onto my back.

The ground pummels at my spine, and I spring up just as a frozen finger stirs my thoughts, or that's how it feels when the brain freeze torments my mind.

I try rushing at one of the brujas, but a force field shoves me back.

I bend my head down and charge at another, but a wall of flames lights up, and my face feels like it's been scorched. I screech and taste blood in my mouth as I fall to the quaking ground, patting my cheeks, expecting my skin to peel off. But it doesn't. The pain is all internal.

These aren't brujas.

They're *gods*.

I've never seen anyone command magic like this. I charge the hooded figure in front of me, then at the last instant I spin to attack the bruja next to her. An ivy vine uncoils and swipes at my arms, and I slice it with my claws.

The plant retreats to nurse its wound, and there's a hissing sound behind me. That must be the Jardinera.

My feet start to burn, and I jump from one leg to the other, the ground like hot coals. I've never moved so fast in my life. I'm jumping off each foot like I'm trying to generate energy.

Something hard and sharp knocks into my head, and my whole skull burns from the pain. I get pelted again and again, and I see that chunks of ice are falling from the sky, directly over my head. Wherever I try to run, a force field pushes back, like padded walls. It's maddening.

The pain is making me nauseous. I think I throw up. I can't tell. I'm about to pass out.

My body is in searing agony. There's water blurring my sight and blood clogging my throat, and I don't understand how any *one* Septimus—bruja or wolf—could survive this. It's impossible.

I see something snakelike shoot at me, and as I reach for the vine, I suddenly feel the magical connection linking it to the Jardinera controlling its attack. Somehow, I sense that I can sever that control, loosening its hold and freeing the vine from the spell.

I concentrate, casting around for the feel of the magic—

Then I remember what Diego said. He told me to do what I did at my Septibol tryouts.

I'm not supposed to pass this trial.

If I defeat the brujas, I'm la ladrona. It's what they fear, why I pose a threat—my *power*. So to pass, I have to fail. I have to be powerless.

I let the vine swipe my shoulder with its shark-sharp thorns. Branches and stones and other debris fly at me, and I lift my arms to defend myself, until they're too bruised to hold up anymore. And the last thought that crosses my mind as I crash to the ground is how strange it is that it's this hard to be yourself in life.

I'm not getting back up.

The pain is delirium, and part of me wants to say fuck it all and dig deep into my true well of power. To defy their magic and their rules. But it's too late—they've broken me.

My bones, my mind, my heart. I can't tell if I'm hot or cold, if I'm moving or still, if I'm screaming or silent. The torture isn't even torture. It's nothing. It's numbness. I can't feel.

But I endure, for Ma, for my friends, and for myself. Because I deserve a real chance. Like Diego said, there's no shame in wanting to fit in. To belong.

The shame is that I have to pretend to be less than I am to be accepted.

The courtroom comes back into focus, and I'm not sure what's going on. I'm standing upright, the vines holding me in place again, as though nothing happened.

I can't feel any of my injuries, but the memory still stings my mind, phantom pains I can't erase. They will leave their own scars.

I'm standing before the tribunal. No Bernardo, no Diego. The whole population is in the mushroom shelves, watching the screens. I don't know how much of what just happened they've seen. All I know is they're remarkably quiet.

My shoulders slump forward.

I'm tired.

"We are ready to deliberate on your legal status," says a voice in Spanish.

I look up in shock as the head judge pulls back his hood. He has a bushy gray beard so thick it looks like fur, and he speaks in such a low voice that he makes the million-strong chamber feel small and intimate.

"Is there anything you would like to say in your defense before we begin?"

My mouth opens, but no words come out.

Diego was worried Bernardo would call me to the stand because my aura could expose all the secrets I'm still keeping. Not their contents, but their existence—Ma's location, Gael's identity, Cata and Saysa's relationship, my ladrona abilities . . . And my cloudy halo would only make me seem less trustworthy.

And maybe I'm not trustworthy.

After all, I've been a secret my whole life. I've never known any other way.

"If there's nothing, we will proceed—"

"Wait."

There are gasps above me, and I hurry to add, "*Sus señorías*. I would like to say something."

34

Day breaks through the dark covering overhead as the head judge nods for me to go on.

"I'm Manu." My eyes flick to the screens to see in what color my aura glows. But nothing happens.

I don't have a halo like the others.

Something about it makes me feel empty, and I realize I should have stayed silent. This must be a sign I'm not one of them—

"You are not on the witness stand," says the head judge, still speaking softly, though with a bite of impatience. "That is why you do not have an aura. The trial is over. Your words carry no official weight. All I am offering you is a simple courtesy."

My stomach clenches, and the emotional appeal I was about to make crumbles to dust. I can cry about my unjust lot in life all I want, but they don't care. I'm not part of their pack.

"This is *all* just a simple courtesy, though, isn't it?" I ask, my throat like sandpaper. I feel a violent impulse in my hands, like I want to flex my fingers. I want to break something.

"Go on," he says.

"The trials are inconclusive. They prove nothing, which I'm sure you know, since you intend to spin this any way you want. You can claim my face showed up in the Caves of Candor because I forged it with my dark magic, or that I accessed the Citadel like a wolf because I stole your power, or that I got my ass kicked by the brujas on purpose. You weren't going to give me or Lunaris control over my narrative anyway. You were always going to decide what you wanted."

He doesn't interrupt me, so I take it as my cue to keep going.

"You think I'm different. That I don't fit in anywhere. I thought that too. But over the past month—*moon*—I learned I'm not all that unique. As Diego put it, I'm not alone in my loneliness. There are so many of you who are caged in your bodies, same as me, only you have slightly better disguises. But you're still just as unhappy and afraid and in danger. You can't live the life you choose or love the one you want or be who you truly are. It's to you I speak now."

There's a rumbling in the audience, and I look up from the tribunal to the mushroom shelves. Some Septimus are no longer looking down at me, but around at one another.

I remember what Zaybet said before my first demonstration, how the point was to show those who are on the fence that there's a different way. They have options. Life is never hopeless.

"I want you to know Yamila didn't capture me," I say, and rather than quieting down, the murmuring reaches a new pitch. "Catalina didn't turn on me either. I asked them to bring me in. Others may not understand my reasons, but I know some of you do. You know there are many shades of dead. Your heart can stop beating in so many ways beyond the literal."

If curiosity is something that must be ignited, I just set off a wildfire. While talking breaks out, I think of Perla, who gave up on herself when her husband was assassinated. I think of Gael, living alone in El Laberinto all this time. I think of Ma's life and mine in El Retiro. I want to say so much about that life, but I can't risk circling too close to the topic of my parents. I'm actually shocked they haven't come up yet.

I also don't want to get too close to Nacho and how I hitched my ride to El Laberinto. So I keep a wide berth of those details.

"All I've ever wanted is to be accepted for being me," I say at last, once the conversations quiet a little. "To know where I belong. When I stumbled into your world, I thought I finally found the answer, only the reality is so much worse. I didn't just cross a border into a new land—I stepped into a role you've written for me. I've been labeled a villain for the crime of being born.

"Whatever you decide, I am a child of Lunaris as much as the rest of you. Can you honestly say you've seen evidence in this case that proves I mean you harm? Am I truly the ladrona you've been waiting for?"

The head judge leans in. "We are not interested in factualizing some old fiction. This tribunal is built on laws, not legends. Our sole interest here is in discovering whether you are an existential threat to our species, and that is something only we can answer, not you, not Bernardo, not your many colorful character witnesses. All any of you can do is provide us with your truths, and the seven of us will determine their design."

He bangs his gavel, and a timer goes up on the screen, only I don't disappear belowground.

The judges gather round to deliberate, and since none of us have our powers, we can't hope to hear them.

We're just going to sit here this whole time? I look up to see what the other Septimus are doing. Most are talking in clusters.

Some are getting up to stretch their legs. Others are staring intently at me.

Whatever happens next, they can't unhear everything I said. Even if the tribunal and Cazadores clamp down, there are always more soldiers on the ground than generals. And the Septimus are finally waking up.

I watch a bruja hand her kid a purple apple. A group of older teens are huddled together talking excitedly. A collection of dads engage in debate, while their wives wave to witches they recognize in neighboring shelves. And I wonder again, *what if I am la ladrona?*

What if they're right to fear me?

The tribunal, like Diego, doesn't believe in la ladrona. In my old life, I would have sided with them. Magical realism, superstition, telenovelas—the border between fantasy and reality was always clear, and I had the line down. But what defines reality when it comes to a race of witches and werewolves?

Who determines what's real?

We are the narratives we tell ourselves. But do we shape language, or does language shape us? Do we define words, or do words define us? If everyone keeps insisting I'm this monster, how soon before I become her?

The timer vanishes from the screens before it's reached zero, and there's a rustling in the crowd as the tribunal disbands. The judges return to their rightful places, and there's no need to bang the gavel because the courtroom is on mute.

My heart races as the head judge stares at me, and the other judges pull back their hoods. The two Septimas are an Encendedora and a Jardinera. I think of what Diego said about colorism being a problem even among Septimus, and I note that only one of the judges is Black.

"This tribunal has come to a decision," says the head judge.

"We have reviewed precedent for cases of known hybrids and found that all such beings have been categorically found guilty and sentenced to death."

The word sends an icy chill down my spine. I've been in mortal danger before, facing imminent destruction, and yet I never felt my death more keenly than I do right now. The calculation and anticipation makes it torturous. I would rather my life end out there, in the fields of Lunaris, facing the elements, than in here, by this tribunal's cold hand.

"Yet this tribunal takes a more modern approach."

I blink. What does that mean?

"The accused, while in violation of our laws, is not at fault for her condition. We are uneasy with the prospect of sending someone to death who has not committed a crime, but rather is the result of one."

My chest inflates with oxygen, and I can hardly believe Diego's argument worked. I'm not going to die.

"However, we cannot allow history to repeat itself. And while there is no evidence of Yamila's claim that the accused has special powers beyond the usual, we cannot dismiss the circumstances of her birth."

Now the head judge stares directly at me. "We cannot allow your lineage to infect our bloodstream. Nor can we allow others to feel emboldened to sire their own hybrid offspring. So while we spare your life, you are sentenced to live it out alone. You will stand apart from the general population, ostracized and isolated, as a warning to anyone who thinks to try this. All future hybrids will not receive this mercy."

I'm alone.

I'm an exception.

It's everything I never wanted.

"As there can be no guilt or innocence in this, you will bear a different burden. A label to dissuade anyone who would pluck a human. Not lobizona or ladrona. Henceforth, you are *Manuela la ilegal*."

I'm illegal.

Literally.

Permanently.

I'm a head on a pole in ancient times.

"You have run from us before, which shows you can never be fully trusted. Therefore, you will be placed under constant supervision. You will not interact with others or keep in touch with old acquaintances."

I barely hear him.

My heart is slowing down in despair. He might as well have killed me. This is worse. To watch the world but never be part of it. To never speak to anyone I love again. To be forever a spare.

I'm so far from the moment that I don't immediately realize the head judge has stopped speaking. Everyone above me looks as confused as I feel, but the judges seem to be in deep concentration.

They're listening to someone.

I furrow my brow and use all my focus to try summoning my power to hear the speaker. A pain flares in my temples, but I push past it until I pick up on a whisper. I think I hear the word *arma*. Weapon.

The head judge turns to confer with the others. What just happened? Someone made an interjection, and now they seem to be reconsidering something. Their ruling?

Is the death sentence back on the table—?

I stare at the head judge's bushy gray beard as he faces me again. "As we were saying, given that you will require constant attention, and you cannot form any attachments, the most pragmatic approach is for you to work in the employ of the Cazadores."

"*What?*"

I can't hold back my reaction. It didn't sound like that's where my sentence was headed before. What would make them change their minds?

But my question is drowned out by an unintelligible shriek, and everyone looks around for the Septima who made the sound.

I already know who it was. I just dealt Yamila a fatal blow without lifting a finger. Only I'm too numb to celebrate.

"As your counsel so eloquently argued, you have not committed a crime," the judge continues. "Unless—or *until*—you break the law, we would rather not lock you up preemptively. Though we can, if that's what you prefer."

I shake my head.

"All Septimus must contribute in some way to the wider community. You will use your *unique* skill set to assist our agents in whatever capacity is required. You will be surrounded by law enforcement, so no more disappearing acts. Prove yourself to be trustworthy, and you will live out a comfortable life of service, with real purpose. So what will it be—Cazadora or prisionera?"

I swallow, hard. My family. Friends. Tiago. Our future. Gone.

I can hardly breathe. I feel more corpse than alive.

But I *am* alive.

That's the point.

I've been given an exception no other hybrid has or will experience. And if I give in to despair, I'll have wasted my chance to make a difference.

I promised Enzo that even when I stop fighting for myself, I'll fight for Zaybet. Just because I didn't get the verdict I wanted today doesn't mean I stop here. I have to prove to them that I belong just as much as they do.

Among law enforcement, I can help others who need it. After all, Fierro himself was—*is*—a Cazador.

"I'll join the Cazadores," I say, and my stomach flips as I announce it because despite all their rules, I'll still be part of something. A fraternity. It may take me a while to endear myself, but I managed it with Cata, so what's a few thousand officers?

"You will report to Bernardo," says the judge, and I deflate a little. "You will be provided lodgings, food, and other provisions, but you will not receive any semillas for your work. You may only speak when spoken to, and you are not to forge any sort of bond with anyone beyond the professional. You will be escorted by a Cazador or Cazadora at all times. Are these conditions clear?"

"Yes," I say, the feeling of slow death back.

"Then this case is adjourned. You are hereby remanded into the custody of the Cazadores."

He raises his gavel, but before bringing it down, he adds, "Your first assignment is to bring in your parents for their judgment."

35

With a bang, I'm whisked through an exit behind the tribunal by a pair of burly officers.

Outside, the day is starting to dim for the third time. Once it goes fully dark, we'll have to catch a portal back to Earth. My trial lasted our entire visit.

I'm still processing the last words the judge spoke to me as I'm marched into white mist. On the other side are the sand dune dwellings where Tiago and I first got together last moon, and I'm led into a cave that's glowing gold like it's occupied.

Bernardo is inside.

"Stand guard by the entrance," he says to the Cazadores flanking me. "Don't let in anyone without a badge."

I'm not cuffed, so I have full access to my powers. Yet for all his grandstanding at trial, Bernardo doesn't seem afraid to be alone with me.

"When we return to Kerana tonight, you will be brought to headquarters. You will do exactly as you're told. Understood?"

I nod, then I say, "Yes."

"To gain access, you will need this badge on you at all times. And for this badge, you will need to swear an oath of loyalty here, in Lunaris. This realm will hold you to your word."

I feel a chill inside me, like Lunaris is listening.

"Repeat after me. *I, Manuela la ilegal, hereby swear to honor Lunaris, to serve the Cazadores, and to defend and protect the Septimus from all threats*—including humans."

It sounds like he added that last part just for me.

My throat feels dry as I gather myself to utter my new name. "I, Manuela la-la *ilegal*"—tears burn my eyes—"hereby swear to honor Lunaris, to serve the Cazadores, and to defend and protect the Septimus from all threats. Including h-humans."

He tosses something silver at me. When I catch it, the blade slices my palm.

"*Ow!*" Blood drips from my hand, down the silver blade.

"Now stick the dagger in the sand," he instructs me, and I do as he says, stabbing it into the ground. The cut in my hand heals, and the blood on my fingers and the handle vanishes.

"Blood has sealed your oath," says Bernardo, and as a warmth buzzes in me, I register that I just chose sides between my two halves. Not that it matters, since there's no war between Septimus and humanity that I know about.

"You are now ready to receive this." He takes out a bronze badge that's heptagonal and looks somewhat familiar. "You'll have to learn how to assemble and disassemble it, but for now just keep it with you at all times."

This is the bronze key Yamila had. I take the warm metal in my hand and pocket it. It's heavier than I expected.

"Won't I need some kind of paperwork?" I ask. "Like a Huella?"

Bernardo stares at me like I just spoke a different language.

"Your identity was ruled *illegal*. That means you remain *un*documented. You only continue to breathe thanks to the mercy of the tribunal, but you do not belong. Is that distinction clear?"

I can't nod.

I can't accept it.

Just then, three Cazadores spill inside.

At the sight of Gael, I grow simultaneously calmer and more anxious. His face is so drawn, his features so pale, that I worry about what he'll say.

"This is a fucking joke!"

Thankfully, Yamila's theatrics keep Bernardo from looking too closely at Gael. "She can't actually join us—"

"Calm down," says Bernardo. "You're making this personal."

Are you okay? My father's voice speaks into my mind.

No! I'm not okay! I shout back. *I messed up, Dad. I should've never turned myself in.*

His eyes soften, and I don't know what I said that eased him.

It'll be okay, he says, his voice so tender, it doesn't sound like him. *I won't let anything happen to you, hija.*

When he calls me *daughter,* I realize I referred to him as *Dad.*

"Keep her hidden until the portals open," says Bernardo, instructing the three of them. "Just in case her friends get any ideas."

"I'm telling you she's got other powers!" snaps Yamila. "We have to go back in there and tell the tribunal to change their ruling—"

"You need to calm down," says Bernardo.

They told me I have to turn you and Ma in, I say into Gael's thoughts in a panic.

Believe it or not, he says calmly, *I have experience creating false trails and evading the Cazadores from the inside.*

"You need to *wake up!*" Yamila is shouting. "She's our greatest danger, and now we're just going to reward her with our highest honor? Some of us trained our asses off to get here! She's barely got one moon of schooling done!"

Nacho nods, like he's also annoyed I'm skipping the line.

"I'm not saying you're wrong," says Bernardo, "but this is out of our hands. Even I can't do anything—"

"Of course you can! Go back in there and—"

"That's enough."

Bernardo's voice is so icy, he sounds like Jazmín. From the stunned look on Yamila's face, I doubt she disappoints him often.

"First, you suspected there was a lobizona, and you didn't say anything," he says to her. "Then you revealed you knew she was a hybrid all along. And worst of all, you waited until the trial to tell me she *dodged your magic!*"

By now he's shouting, and he turns to Gael, his anger taking new aim.

"You're acting just like your mentor here! He too was on top of the world once. His ego got so fat, he forgot he was part of a pack and decided he'd capture Fierro alone."

My uncle looks at his brother-in-law with open dislike. I don't see any trace of Cata in her father. His voice seething with restrained rage, he tells Gael, "Just because the tribunal saw fit to reinstate you doesn't change anything between us."

"You're damn right," says my dad.

Their eyes are so fiery, I worry they're going to transform.

"Since you were *instrumental* in discovering her," Bernardo tells him, "I'm assigning you to babysit the lobizona."

My heart inflates with so much hope that I feel my muscles relaxing for the first time. My jaw hurts, like it's been clenched for a while. Even Dad's face lightens, and we stare at each other.

"Yamila and Nacho will supervise you."

Now my heart is weighted down with a ballast, and it plunges.

"Who better than you to show Yamila the error of your ways?" Bernardo asks Gael. "See that she doesn't go down your misguided path."

Yamila points to me accusingly. "There is no way I'm working with that fucking *freak*—"

"Leave. Now."

Bernardo doesn't raise his voice, but there's a lethal edge to his words. He looks at Nacho. "You'll be my liaison for now, since you're the only one who's shown any good sense."

Nacho's gaze drifts to me, and I know it's a warning to keep my mouth shut. He wouldn't want Bernardo to know it was he who brought me into their world unawares.

"Make sure they keep their distance until we're back in Kerana," he tells Nacho. "I can't deal with more hysterics today."

Nacho turns to his sister, and her eyes light up like she's daring him to touch her. Then she spares me a nasty glare before leaving, Nacho marching after her. I'm going to have to keep an eye on him and make sure he's not a threat to Perla.

When it's just the three of us, the cave feels like it's gotten smaller. Bernardo is looking between my dad and me like he's deciding who he dislikes more when a new contender enters the ring.

His wife.

"What are you doing here?" he asks her in greeting. "I told them to let in Cazadores *only*—"

"I'm your *wife*. Or have you forgotten?"

"I'm not the one who changed my name," he says with a low growl. "Or our daughter's."

"That was Catalina's choice," says Jazmín with chilly disdain. "I didn't make it for her."

"What do you want? Or let me guess, it's your brother you came to see."

"Actually, I'm not here for either of you. I've come on behalf of your daughter. She wants something."

Jazmín's amethyst gaze slides to me, her haughty expression souring, and Bernardo shakes his head. *"No."*

"Just a few minutes."

"Absolutely not."

"Bernardo." Jazmín's iciness could set off a winter storm. "Your daughter, whom you barely know and just cross-examined like a common criminal in front of the entire population, wants a few minutes. Am I clear?"

Whatever she has on him, it must be good. Because he nods, once, curt. "Fine."

His voice is low, but the wolves standing guard at the entrance still hear him. An instant later, Cata steps in—followed by Saysa and Tiago.

"No, I didn't say her friends—"

"Let it go," says Jazmín to her husband. "And let's give them a moment alone."

I can hardly believe what she's doing for us. She must be desperate to win her daughter's affections back.

Bernardo looks like he's reaching for some semblance of authority, so he points to Gael. *"You* stay."

On his way out, he crosses paths with his daughter. Cata looks strangely small with both her parents here.

"Everything you said," he breathes. "You were right."

Then he marches out, no apology, no kiss, no looking back. He's not going to see his daughter for another month, and it doesn't even seem to register.

When I look at Cata, I worry she's going to be crestfallen.

Instead, her head is a notch higher. I don't even know if she wants his love anymore. What she wanted was his respect.

Once it's just the five of us, Tiago pulls me into his arms, and I inhale his musk like it's the last breath I'll ever take. Cata and Saysa come over too, and the four of us hug for a long time.

"I hate this," says Saysa.

"Me too," says Cata.

I'm so sorry, Manu, Tiago says into my mind.

No, I'm sorry, I say into his.

Don't be. It was unfair of me to expect you to prioritize us over your life.

Sounds like he's been talking to Cata and Saysa. *But you're part of my life. One might even say you're* inwoven *with my deepest life,* I add, quoting Edith Wharton.

Do what you need, he murmurs. *I'm not going anywhere.*

When we pull away, Tiago hangs onto my hand, and as I look into his eyes, I see what I've only ever seen in Ma.

Love without conditions.

Cata's pink eyes flare with light, and I feel a tension in the air around us. A force field. "I can hold it up for a few minutes so the wolves outside can't hear us," she says. Then she pins me with her stare and says, "That was quite a speech."

"It wasn't a speech. I just thought I deserved a voice in my own judgment."

"Well, you did it." Saysa's eyes are clearer than they've been in a while. "You should have heard what they were saying out there. In one moon, you did what the Coveners couldn't do in ages. You shook shit up for real."

In her gaze, I see a glimmer of Zaybet's zeal.

"What about you?" I ask my friends, preferring not to think of my own fate. "What happens next? None of you are in trouble, right?"

"Thanks to you," says Cata. "Tiago and I are going to accept the Cazadores' recruitment."

"What?" I stare between them, my eyes wide.

"Nothing matters more than this fight," says Tiago, squeezing my fingers. "And like Fierro taught us, what better way than infiltrating from the inside?"

He smirks at Gael, who now edges closer to join our conversation.

Even though I'm forbidden from interacting with them, the fact that Tiago and Cata will at least be nearby fills me with hope. "What will you do?" I ask Saysa, who is holding up better than I expected.

"I'm going to take time off from school."

I pick up on something slightly different between her and Cata. Not a coldness, exactly, just some extra space.

"Are you guys okay?" I ask, my pulse panic-pounding in my ears.

"Yeah," says Saysa with a shrug. "I mean, I'm still pissed at *both* of you. But there's a lot I haven't explored about my magic, and I think this is a good time to study it."

Cata takes her hand, and Saysa leans into her. I lean into Tiago too. I can't believe it's only been one moon since Gael sent us on a mission to plant a new garden and form a new pack.

"So, the Coven," says my dad, panning his coral gaze across us. *"How was it?"*

"Unbelievable," says Saysa, longing in her voice like she already misses it.

"Were you a member?" Cata asks him.

"I only went a couple of times. Just enough to know what they needed. I couldn't risk getting involved. What'd you think of el Mar Oscuro?"

"Unreal," says Tiago, shaking his head.

"We were boarded by piratas!" says Saysa.

"*¿Piratas?*" echoes my father. "Can you believe in all my life I never ran into any? What happened?"

While Saysa and Cata speak over each other, I whisper into Tiago's mind. *I know we said a lot of things, but I'm not holding you to any of it. I want you to move on and be happy. I'll always be grateful for everything you've done for me—*

"No," he says out loud, and Cata cuts off her description of the dormilona potion.

Tiago pulls me into him, and this kiss is everything. Maybe even my last.

I breathe in his lips, inhaling his light to every part of my body, even the corners drowning in darkness over my destiny. So I don't forget how good he feels. And when we pull apart, he speaks to me in the only love language we understand.

"I would not wish any companion in the world but you."

When the Cazadores make my friends leave, it's just my dad and me in the cave.

I don't know how to do this, I think, and I can't tell if I'm sending the thought telepathically, or if it's just my inner monologue. *I don't want to be alone all my life. I can't.* I feel sobs building in my chest. *I'll die of loneliness—*

Manu. My dad steps forward and steadies me with his arm, his voice gentle but firm. *Two moons ago, there were no lobizonas and all hybrids were subject to execution. Look how much of our world you've already changed. Maybe next year Diego will introduce amendments to the law. Maybe in a few years, you, your mom, and I will be reunited—and all of this will just be a bad memory.*

I don't know how he does it, but he makes life feel survivable. Just like Zaybet used to do.

Until then, protect your hope. Gael's gaze is unblinking. *Don't let them know where you keep it. Do you understand me?*

I shake my head, and he says, *Don't let them see what matters to you, and they won't know where to strike.*

The words make me ask, *What did you offer them?*

He frowns at me like he doesn't understand the question, but I know he offered the tribunal something in the last moment of my sentencing. He's the only one in that room who cared enough, the only one who probably has the right leverage. *Why did they give me the chance to be a Cazadora?*

He shrugs. *I said I would come back to work for them.*

That's all it took?

I agreed to build them something they've wanted from me for a long time. A defensive device, should humans ever discover us. Let's leave it there.

I'm sorry.

Don't be. Gael's coral eyes shine overly bright. *It was the least I could do for you, and it wasn't nearly enough.*

Will they suspect anything since you spoke up for me?

They think I'm soft on you because you were my student.

What about Ma? My heart breaks at the thought of when I'll be able to see her again.

She's in Buenos Aires. I'll fill her in as soon as we're back.

Tell her I'm sorry for letting her down. I just needed to do things my own way.

You haven't let anyone down, least of all your mom and me. We're proud of you. What you did, that's braver than anything I ever did as Fierro. You inspire me.

And in his gaze, I don't see Fierro or Gael. I see my dad.

I lean forward, and I'm glad when he holds me like he did in Belgrano. Despite everything I've lost, I found him. We pull apart at the sound of footsteps, and a Cazadora steps in.

"Give me your hands," she says, and I hold them out. Her green eyes glow with light.

I feel a pulling on my bones, a tugging on my life strings, like when Saysa touched me in La Cancha. When it's over, I'm tired and my muscles are worn. The ends of my hair look gray, and my skin is wrinkly. It seems like I've aged fifty years.

"This will only last until you're back in Kerana."

"That's long enough," says Gael.

We head out and cross white mist into the transportation hub that looks like the surface of the moon. There's a big commotion, and I see a line of Cazadores holding back a crowd of Septimus who are clamoring for the chance to talk to me.

At the very front are Saysa and Cata, along with Diego, Pablo, and Javier. Just beyond them, I spot Nico, Gus, and Bibi—I wonder if they're back together—Enzo, Laura, and Tinta y Fideo. The younger brother's eyes are red and puffy, and his is the worst pain of all, because he lost both Zaybet and his future with her.

Cata and Diego are rounding on Bernardo.

"Manu deserves to have friends!" shouts Cata.

"That's not up to you."

"Fuck the tribunal!" growls Pablo, his eyes swirling like liquid ink as his fangs come down. Javier has to physically restrain him from going after the Septimus prosecutor.

"Let us at least say bye to her," says Diego.

"You heard the ruling, *counselor*—"

"High court rulings only take effect when we set foot on Earth!"

"Just to say bye, what's the harm?" It's Miguel asking. Penelope is beside him.

I see Tiago last.

From his grieving expression, I realize something has to die tonight.

Us.

At least for now.

Dad told me to hide my hope, so I will. I'll bury my love for Tiago deep inside, where it can fuel me. I'm not giving up. I'm going to fight for us. Which reminds me—I still owe him a line of Shakespeare.

I reach for the channel into his mind, and I send a classic.

The course of true love never did run smooth.

Tiago's blue blaze flashes. He's scanning every face in the crowd. Of course, he won't recognize this one.

Gael and I are almost to the portal, and then my connection to Tiago will sever. But right as I'm about to step through, his eyes lock with mine.

I don't break our gaze, until it feels like he's seeing through my disguise. And his musical voice fills my head as the tunnel's darkness swallows me.

The only way I can help you is by loving you.

Hearing Edith Wharton's words, I think even Shakespeare would approve. After all, it wasn't the Septimus' magic or might that saved me.

There is no label—in any language—with the power to liberate.

The only truth we can offer one another is love.

EPILOGUE

CATA

Everything and nothing has changed.

We're in Flora's crown, breakfasting with our teammates like any other morning. Yet everything is different, and nothing can be the same.

I sense a cold front blowing in, and I look toward Flora. Ma is standing with Señora Lupe, and I wonder how long she's been watching me. Then I feel the ends of my mouth curve up as I realize something else.

I don't care.

In a twist even I couldn't predict, the trial that cost Manu her freedom liberated me. It was like a shot of Olvido: Once I left that courtroom, I couldn't remember why I used to find my self-worth in my parents' validation.

My grin only grows at the outrage rounding Ma's eyes, and I

keep staring until she glides into the trunk. I feel the stirrings of a storm in the air, and the hairs on my arms tingle with magic that I long to unleash.

Tiago sits closer to me than usual, our hands almost touching as he sets the mate down. His expression chastens mine. He's spent every night in my room, tangled in the sheets of Manu's cot.

After the trial, Tiago, Saysa, and I faced no consequences. This whole time, I was terrified of what would happen if we got caught, but Manu was right. Every choice belonged to her alone because the consequences were always hers to bear.

It takes me too long to register our friends' silence.

I glance up at Tiago, but his gaze is distant. I brush my arm against his, and he doesn't react. I press harder, and still nothing. So I jab my elbow into his side.

Pain zaps down the length of my arm, and I suck in my breath as my eyes burn. Tiago glances over with a slight frown, like he can't decide if he felt something. Cradling my elbow, I give him a pointed nod.

Say something! I want to shout at his broken face.

My skin is going to bruise. If Saysa were here, she'd take away my pain with a caress . . . but she didn't come back. She stayed home with her parents. She's decided to transfer to Los Andes to study her healing magic.

We're—we're on a break.

But it's temporary. This is just the first part of my plan. On the balloon ride to meet Yamila, I told Manu I can't give Saysa what she wants. Only after the trial, I realized I can't give my parents what they want either. I have no interest in becoming Yamila.

The truth is, I want what Saysa wants. And I don't see any point in denying it anymore.

"*Tiago.*"

My voice comes out sharper than I'd intended.

He blinks, like he's trying to see past Manu's absence. I survey our friends, who watch us with expectant expressions. Pablo's arms are crossed. Javier hasn't touched his food. Nico has barely spoken. Gus and Bibi aren't arguing for once, and Diego hasn't even brought a book with him.

They all look worried. Except Pablo, who just seems suspicious. I feel the breeze before it ruffles his hair, and again my magic stirs, itching to burn off some emotion.

Tiago wanted me to make our announcement. We both know I would do a better job. But so long as it's a wolf's world, a witch's words will carry less weight.

"Cata and I have something to tell you."

At last Tiago finds his voice. It sounds like an instrument that's out of tune.

My mouth is suddenly parched, but to take a drink now would feel too dramatic, so I wait for him to finish.

"We—we accepted the Cazadores' recruitment."

Javier's cheer goes off like a bomb, and when sound filters back in, I register that Nico, Bibi, and Gus are also celebrating. Beyond our circle, I watch other wolves whispering the news to the brujas in their vicinity.

Pablo and Diego have yet to react. They're too observant to surprise. From the intensity of their stares, they know there's more.

Tiago is looking to me, and I nod for him to keep going. But he grits his jaw, like he was hoping I'd stop him.

I almost hate him for it. Like this choice isn't gutting me too. But we agreed on a plan last night, and now we need to be willing to make the sacrifices it requires.

"There's something else," says Tiago.

I can't remember the air ever standing this still.

"Cata and I are engaged."

The quiet expands, until it grows so loud that it feels less like a pause and more like a vacuum of sound. Everyone heard Tiago's testimony at Manu's trial. And our friends heard me declare my love for Saysa in Lunaris two moons ago. Yet this is our first test.

If we fail now, our whole plan is foiled.

"In seven moons," I say, taking Tiago's hand to sell it, "we're getting married."

The Cazadores aren't going to let Tiago anywhere near Manu if they think he's in love with her. And my mom will probably do anything to keep me away from Saysa. This is our only loophole.

We just need to convince everyone that Manu was a fleeting distraction for Tiago, like all the other girls have been, from his constant love for . . . *me*.

If we can sell our classmates on the story my parents spun in court, we stand a chance at gaining the Cazadores' trust. Then we can get close to Manu.

And like Tiago said last night—*We'll start a new Coven*.

"I knew it!"

Bibi is the first to snap out of her shock. She wrenches me into a celebratory hug, but when she pulls away to meet my gaze, she's not smiling. She knows what it's like to be in love, so she understands our sacrifice.

Javier lifts me off my feet, but his boyish grin doesn't extend to his eyes. Our friends won't be fooled, but Tiago and I aren't putting on this performance for them. It's for the rest of the school.

Diego and Pablo are last to react. More than anything, they look sad. While Tiago and Pablo hug, Diego wraps me in his arms.

A gust rattles the boughs above us, and I call to it with my power, my vision brightening to the point where I can see the bands of air. I fashion the current into a force field that hovers around our joined heads. "No one can hear us," I say as we pull apart.

From the warning in his periwinkle gaze, I prepare for a lecture. "I'm in," he says instead.

The air bubble bursts in my shock. Diego has been preparing his whole life to serve on the tribunal. He's always upheld the law.

My gaze crosses with Pablo's next, and he nods at me like he's also in. I look to Tiago. Now his eyes seem fully present, and when he reaches for my hand, there's no hesitation in his grip.

Manu showed us what we couldn't see: We're all invisible until we step out of hiding.

She took on our system and fought for us.

Now we fight for her.

As I follow the brujas out of El Jardín to La Catedral for our classes, I sense a new ease in my steps, like I'm adopting Ma's glide-like walk. But it's not confidence so much as caution.

I feel like I'm racing through El Laberinto with a lit candle and trying desperately to keep its small flame alive.

For the first time in my life, I know what real hope feels like.

And already, it's everything.

ACKNOWLEDGMENTS

My personal acknowledgments are included in *Lobizona,* so for *Cazadora* I want to acknowledge the people for whom I wrote this series:

For all the families at the border that were dismantled and destroyed over paperwork.

For all the parents wondering if their children will ever heal from the trauma.

For all the women abused in detention centers and forcibly sterilized.

For all the lost children who will never know their own stories.

And for the reckoning that is to come.

LUNARIS